To Bob –

Old Wives Tales

By

Electa Kane Tritsch

with huge admiration
for everything you've
made clear to me.

Electa

ISBN: 1-4033-4314-4 (e-book)
ISBN: 1-4033-4315-2 (Paperback)
ISBN: 1-4033-4316-0 (Dustjacket)

Library of Congress Control Number: 2002108006

This book is printed on acid free paper.

Printed in the United States of America
Bloomington, IN

1stBooks – rev. 09/20/02

ACKNOWLEDGMENTS

Anything that takes six years to produce, by necessity involves more people than can be appropriately acknowledged. Some are long-standing influences. The mental seed-planters: the real Mr. Caton; Paul Mitchell who taught me to think; David Hall who taught me to think rationally; Bob Campbell, the man who made archeology happen and whose presence is sadly missed. The exemplars: Elizabeth Chapman Kane, my mother; Sarah White Kane, my grandmother; Margareth Arnold Chamberlain, my godmother. Women strong in different ways, and loving.

Old Wives Tales has benefited from many people's expertise and encouragement: Victor Peskett of Metfield, the English connection; my favorite critical historian Bob Hanson; Jim Kaufmann who studies Dedham Pottery and Barbara Nashawaty who makes it; Ed Bell and Kathy Wheeler, archeologists *par excellence*; Barbara Leighton and her lifetime of Medfield stories. Colleagues and friends from the Radcliffe Institute Writing Seminars and from the Newton Writers Group, together with Pam Kunkemueller and Phyllis Goodman Tritsch, showed me the way from fact to fiction through a lot of 'tough love.' Geoff, my husband, wasn't tough at all, bearing with me through it all, infinitely patient and confident. He and John and Ben make being an old wife worthwhile.

The Chapmans of Mill Farm

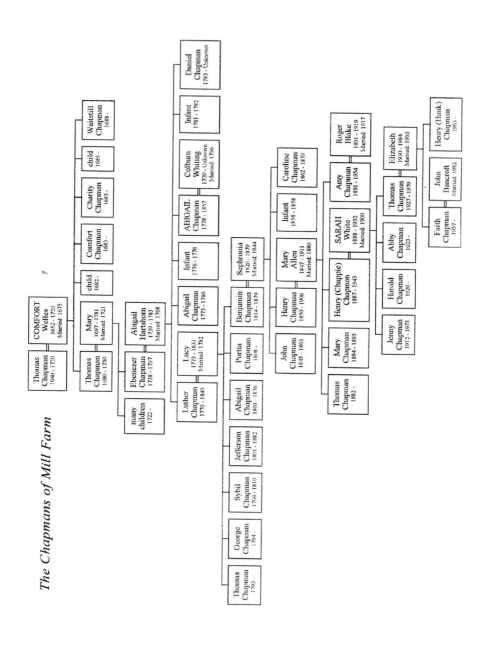

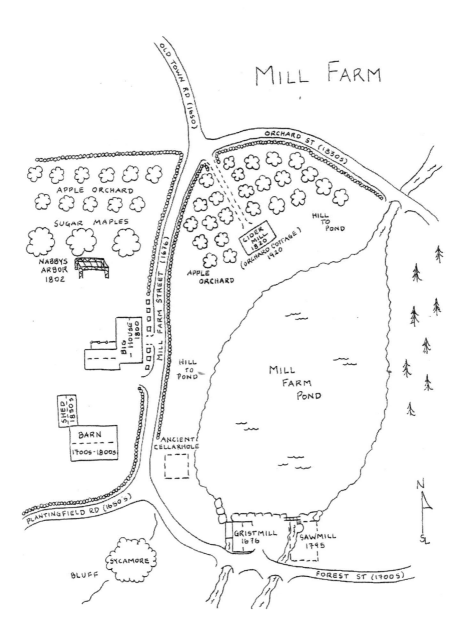

MILL FARM

LAYER I: SURFACE COLLECTING

*Surface collecting is the first time you come in
contact with artifacts in an archeological excavation.
You wander around the test pit you've staked out and
you really look at it.*
    — *Dr. Nora Tunney, **An Archeologist's Handbook***

June 1995

    The knoll overlooked a New England mill pond where two
Canada geese nudged their goslings toward shore. Wisps of breeze
still cooled a shady patch of lilacs on the rise but the day would be hot
soon.
    A metallic clunk in the silence had the gander craning his neck.
Then a girl appeared on the knoll, blonde, wearing brief white shorts
and sturdy hiking boots. She was talking earnestly to the young man
who followed, his tee shirt an explosion of fluorescent color. The two
carried rakes and long-handled tree loppers that glinted in the sun.
Muttered honking began on the pond as the geese drifted farther off.
    "I'm still not sure how Dr. Tunney knows this hill is a site."
    The girl's voice was low, as if she didn't want her doubts
broadcast. A small crease showed between her delicately plucked
brows. Sound carried, though, in the morning quiet and the woman
who next appeared was already grinning.

"Instinct, Pam. Instinct." Nora Tunney's eyes squinted when she smiled, despite the baseball cap shading her forehead. "Archeology is half instinct, half hard labor."

She swung a bulging backpack to the ground. "The Commission didn't warn you of that when they signed you on?"

Pam flushed. Her stammered reply was cut short.

"We certainly did not, Nora." This from a white-haired man working his way upslope with wood-framed mesh screens tucked under both arms.

"The Medfield Mill Commission wasn't about to risk losing strong young backs by the threat of hard labor," he went on, with an expression that managed to tease and encourage at the same time. Pam's blush faded and she reached to help Mr. Whiting with his screens.

Nora knelt to tighten a work boot lace as the crew arrived and deposited equipment around the knoll's perimeter. She surreptitiously scanned the half-dozen people as she got up, deciding they were what her father would call a motley bunch. Eighty-year-old Peg Wentworth, five feet tall, whose work pants were tied at the ankle. Ralph Whiting, professor emeritus, wearing half-glasses that defined the end of his nose. Tall and earnest Jane Ogden, flowered garden gloves already in place as she clutched a bucket of brand new trowels. Dewy-eyed Pam, a sophomore from Chickering Junior College and her companion, Andrew who, judged by build alone, should be playing football instead of trowelling. Serious Doug Avery, an honest-to-goodness anthropology major from U. Mass. The Levalliere brothers, senior and junior, were there at their parents' urging. They needed a constructive high school summer. Levalliere Senior had cameras draped around his neck and an ancient fedora shading his eyes.

The group collected to stare at the pond and an old grist mill at its far end. Tall and short, old and young, their excitement was palpable and their comments rushed over each other. It was too much for the geese who, muttering still, glided away.

Not your normal field crew. Nora looked them over. *But then, this is not your normal job either. Thank God.* She was nodding to herself when she realized attention had shifted to her. She grinned self-consciously, pushed her cap back and took charge.

2

"Well! I think we'd better tackle Pam's question before we start getting dirty. It's a good question," she added quickly. Pam was already turning pink again. "Obviously there's more to defining a site than instinct, but I wasn't entirely joking when I said that. Intuition, experience, previous research – they all went into laying out this grid."

Her hand swept over the small hilltop where numbered wooden stakes and white string lines defined a broad rectangle. The string ran above a sketchy row of stones on one side. It threaded through the lilac stand where they had gathered.

"You've heard Peg Wentworth talk about this site before now. She's been working on Chapman's Mill and the whole Medfield-Chapman history for years. That's the 'previous research'."

In a silent footnote, Nora thought what a shame it was that Hank Chapman couldn't be more interested in researching his own family's history.

"I guess I'm here as the 'experience' part of the formula." Ten years and three or four dozen field contracts documented that record. "A lot of my experience and training has been at New England archeological sites. So I have an idea of what to look for and how to go about finding it."

Ralph Whiting, Peg and Jane Ogden nodded. That was, after all, why the Commission had hired her. She had an excellent reputation. Nora hesitated and pursed her lips in concentration.

"The 'intuition' part is the hardest to explain, obviously. I know. It verges on touchy-feely. But I'm convinced that an archeologist has to listen to intuition – professional instinct, if you prefer. Has to use that instinct, as well as all the evidence and standard procedures, to pinpoint sites that have something to say beyond what written history can tell us."

Nora gave a definitive nod, then wondered if she was trying to convince the crew or herself.

Pam looked convinced. She was listening with apparently rapt attention, though Nora guessed from the way her eyes moved, she was also running a quick comparison check between herself and the boss lady. Nora could live with that. After all, she'd been born with a decent body, did hard labor for a living, had a head of hair that made her mother jealous, and even tanned with relatively few freckles. A number of past boyfriends had found her quite acceptable. Her field uniform might not be quite up to undergrad standards. Army pants and broken-in tee shirts couldn't compete with minimal shorts and bare midriff but Nora guessed that the trade-off in briar scratches and mosquito bites would level the field in a couple of days. If only the other challenges would prove to be as simple.

Nora caught herself. This was the start of a new dig, and no time to be having doubts. Research, experience, instinct all pointed to this one as a winner. It had to be. She'd pledged her career on the outcome.

The doubts had gotten really bad last spring. She'd been working a contract job in Dover, Massachusetts. She'd had doubts before, of course, but April was worse than usual. After months of poring over maps and tromping through briar-covered, boulder-strewn terrain in freezing weather, the job for Boston Edison had run out and she hadn't located a single site. Edison would be delighted: no need to pay for further work or, more expensive yet, to reroute part of a power line. She was less thrilled. In the survey world, coming up totally empty-handed was almost unheard of. An archeologist expected to find stone chips from prehistoric tools, or traces of a long-dead hearth. Even a fifty year old dump site. This time, though, Edison apparently had picked a route so inhospitable even the locals had avoided it. At first Nora thought it was ironic, that in an area occupied for 8,000 years, the only hint of human presence was a stray scrap of charcoal and a broken booze bottle. But such a complete lack of finds in such a big area gnawed at her.

On the last day of fieldwork, the day of soft breeze and sunshine they'd looked for all spring, Nora packed off the crew back to the city to begin the final, ritual beerfest. They'd flop down in their grubby clothes, drink cheap beer, trade war stories and laugh a lot. Later she'd join them. It was one of the perks of working hard in hard conditions, as a team. But first she had some thinking to do.

Making excuses about checking a map reading, Nora turned back up a steep path to the top of Noanet Peak. She stretched out on the granite bedrock and tried to understand an empty landscape. Sun soaked into her chest, and a breeze tickled the back of her hand. Chickadees and a passing crow punctuated the silence.

They had to have been here. Short and sinewy, maybe, holding a flint-pointed spear and listening for sounds of game in the woods below. Right here, standing on these rocks, gazing out at the distance. She pictured an ironworker, in collarless shirt and tweed trousers, from the mill nearby. He'd break off the burnt end of a clay pipe stem and drop it. Maybe seeing smoke, or faint buildings over there toward Boston. Maybe a woman in hiking boots and voluminous walking skirt. She'd reach for field glasses and her daypack buckle would break. Invisible history. New England is crowded with it.

A pebble dug into Nora's back. She squirmed in search of comfort. *So is the lack of artifacts my fault? Evidence overlooked? More test sites? Wrong test sites?*

Wrong person?

Nora pushed herself upright and scowled at hazy skyscrapers on the horizon. A conviction separated itself from the unanswered questions. She had no doubt people had been here, with or without artifacts. They had lived flesh and blood lives and it was her job to keep looking for the evidence. She'd find it, she'd interpret it – if not for Edison, then for the next client. And the one after that. That's what archeologists did. She nodded emphatically and strode back down the trail. But despite her resolve, the drive back to town was still full of doubts.

A number of beers and war stories later, Nora trudged up the last grubby stairs to her apartment. Artie was meowing inside the door as she pulled a letter out of her mailbox. *Medfield Mill Commission* the envelope read. Medfield, she thought. Right near Dover and Westwood. Letting herself in, she tore the flap open but loud protests and fuzzy head-butting at her calf interrupted. An immediate crisis to deal with first. After a plate of tuna bits silenced Artie, Nora went back to the letter. More Edison projects? She needed the money. But please, something other than catbriar and boulders. She sat down and stared at a mill wheel logo on the envelope, torn between anticipation and dread that this would be more of the same. Finally she pulled out the letter.

> *Dear Ms. Tunney:*
>
> *I am writing on behalf of the Medfield Mill Commission to solicit your bid for intensive archaeological investigation of the Thomas Chapman Mill Farm in Medfield. This property was recently donated to the town by Mr. Henry Chapman. We are quite proud of the site, dating to 1670, when Thomas Chapman became the second miller of Medfield.*
>
> *The state Historical Commission recommended that we engage a professional archaeologist to survey and excavate before we begin restoration or other improvements, and your name was one of those given to us. We anticipate that this project will extend over the next one or two summers.*

Nora scanned the rest of the letter: the usual disclaimer about limited funding but great enthusiasm. Quite a bit of organizing already; a crew of volunteers, involvement with a nearby junior college, and the whole project ready to start in June.

The letter was signed *Ralph Whiting, for the Commission.*

It sounded a bit quirky, as surveys went. An all-volunteer crew? Impressive organizing from volunteers, though. Of course, they probably expected to come up with absolute proof of the Chapman/seventeenth century connection. Past experience told Nora that clients who thought they knew the answers beforehand could be difficult. And what did "restoration or other improvements" mean? Still, it sounded like the site had huge potential. An old mill, a First Period house, three centuries of land use.

She stood up restlessly and leaned an arm against the kitchen window frame. Next door, the Carreras' pipe arbor was black against the glare of their security light. The grape vines were leafing out, she noticed. They'd cut the glare soon. She thought about the letter again. The Medfield Mill Commission would certainly be an enthusiastic client. The timing was great. A gust of wind set the leaves shimmering as flickers of excitement lit the gloom that had trailed her from Dover to Somerville. Maybe this was the project she'd been waiting for, the one she'd almost given up on in a career of bottom-line survey work. Nora grinned to herself. Probably not even much catbriar. The flickers grew to a glow. Mill Farm just might pan out. This could be a big one. Tunney intuition said so.

She didn't lose any time writing back. Four long days later, Ralph Whiting called to suggest she come for an interview, "just so you have a chance to see who we are," he said with what Nora decided was diplomatic inversion. In fact, the interview turned out to be remarkably laid back. Apparently this small-town board could make decisions with a lot less fuss than corporate bigwigs. Whiting and an octogenarian Miss Wentworth ("Call me Peg. Everyone does.") made up two-thirds of an ad hoc hiring committee. The interview felt more like an enthusiastic chat. Had Dr. Tunney run across other sites with both cellarholes and old buildings? (Yes. A tanyard north of Boston included the owner's house. It also reeked to high heaven.) Speaking of smells, Peg remembered, the old pig farm in Medfield had a fascinating history. Peg elaborated. Ralph Whiting thought of a similar site. Nora found herself swapping anecdotes with them.

Along the way, a third and probably significant Commission member, Hank Chapman, stopped by. Chapman, of the Chapman's Mill family, was catching a flight to Montana. He stayed just long enough to offer a charmingly apologetic grin and say he trusted Ralph and Peg to ask the right questions. Nora suspected that, lineage or not, he might be the committee lightweight. If so, he was at least a decorative one. A tall frame and casual shock of brown hair managed to carry off the L.L. Bean look he affected, and his voice was engaging.

"Your resume's impressive, Dr. Tunney. That Chicopee mill project especially sounds intriguing." He reached for the door knob. "I'll look forward to hearing more."

Nodding to the others, he was gone while Nora's mouth was still forming a coherent reply.

She was surprised he'd digested her resume so thoroughly. Of course, he might have picked a random project from the page. She sat back down with Ralph and Peg and forced her shoulders to relax. Lightweight or not, Hank Chapman had gotten her attention. On the one hand his manner was abrupt to the point of rudeness. On the other, he had a smile and a handshake that were intensely – but unconsciously, somehow – personal. At best, a distracting mix on the job.

Before the evening ended Ralph and Peg surprised Nora, excusing themselves for a brief conference in the next room. They returned with job offer in hand. The pay was low, but there was free housing across from the site if she would consider it, for two digging seasons and the winter in between. Nora silently weighed the luxury of living in a single place and working on a single site for more than a year, versus a few fat paychecks.

She tried to sift through the pros and cons before she leapt to say yes. The over-eager advance planning, the working with volunteers. Was there some hidden agenda the board would spring on her after she'd signed on? Then she reminded herself of the Edison winter and a quiet vow she'd recently made. The vow that if she couldn't accomplish something substantial, she'd quit archeology. Start again at something she'd do well. Become a baker maybe – cream puffs and cheesecake and no catbriars. But Mill Farm had potential. She'd actually live where she worked and work with people who actually wanted to find something. There was the small catch that her landlord would be Hank Chapman. Would that be a hassle? If so, she'd dealt with hassles before.

Intuition, she reminded herself. *Listen to what's inside.* She glanced across the table at Ralph's and Peg's encouraging faces. *Intuition says this is going to be right.* This was not a tough decision.

"When do I start?" Nora asked.

*   *   *   *   *

"So, everyone up for a little hard work?"

Nora's question brought the crew back from their study of the knoll and the pond below.

"Work up here won't be the whole survey, but I want you all to learn some technique before we start testing the rest of Mill Farm. We'll start with some surface clearing where I've laid out the grid, but somebody needs to cut back these lilacs."

"Oh no!" Jane Ogden's evident shock was emphasized by a flower-gloved hand to her heart. "Can't we just leave them alone?"

"Unfortunately Mrs. Ogden, if you notice, the excavation grid runs right through the clump."

Peg Wentworth shook her head. "They have been here a long time. As long as I remember. I don't suppose we could just shift the grid line?"

Nora began to realize she was going to have to move a lot more slowly with this group than the normal crew she directed.

"The string parallels what I suspect is a wall line, Peg. I laid out the grid based on my understanding that the Commission wanted to define the Chapman house before we moved on to anything else. Am I right on that?"

"Oh yes!" Mrs. Ogden tended to speak in exclamations.

Peg was reluctantly nodding but Ralph Whiting was slower to answer.

"There are so many things we want to do, Nora, as you know. Certainly the house is a big one." He drew out the last word, indicating there was more to come. Nora had a terrible suspicion he might take this moment to spell out the Commission's plans. It would not be a short explanation, she knew, and the crew was already fidgeting. Besides, Nora thought, despite all the organized preparations, the Board still seemed to have some unfinished business. Peg's occasional raised eyebrows and Ralph's head-shaking from time to time the past month made her suspect some major disagreement still had to be resolved.

Andrew rescued the moment by clearing his throat in the silence.

"Um, Ms. Tunney? Last summer I worked landscaping and sometimes we just dug out bushes, roots and all. You know, balled them up and stuck 'em in someplace else. Couldn't we do that?"

Nora nodded, impressed that the big quiet kid was willing to speak up. But then she almost immediately shook her head.

"You'd disturb too much information, Andrew. Think about this for a minute: what if a lilac had rooted in the nice rich ash of a cooking hearth? You pull it out of the ground and the hearth is destroyed. Gone. All you have is a few bits of charcoal and some pot shards."

"Sounds like a pretty good find to me," he muttered apologetically. There were some nods around the circle.

"But a 'pretty good find' is all you'll ever get that way. If the Commission wants the most thorough data recovery possible, pretty good isn't going to be good enough."

Nora kept her voice calm and let the idea hang in the air for Whiting and Peg and Jane Ogden to consider. A caution flag was waving in her brain. Their response was important. This might not be a Commission meeting but they were still three-fifths of the board, and if they chose to make this a board decision, it would undermine her management of the project. It would also determine whether she could do the research she'd been trained for, the work that would accomplish what she could not, on her last job. The slow, methodical work needed to locate Chapmans and all those other silent people whose broken possessions lay underground.

Everyone was eyeing her warily, and suddenly she found herself wanting to find a compromise they all could live with.

"But Miss Wentworth made a good point. In tree-terms, these lilacs are artifacts in themselves, aren't they? I certainly think Mill Farm needs to rescue at least one for posterity. Call it a 'cultural landscape feature.' What does anyone think about that option?"

It wasn't clear whether Nora's suggestion or her handy professional jargon brought responsive smiles, but the brief and unexpected set-to was over. Commission members nodded. The crew began debating which clump could best be saved, and the early-morning tension drained away, quickly replaced by enthusiasm for a fresh start. Nora wondered how often she would have to negotiate instead of excavate on this project. The thought made her tired.

Once Andrew showed off his skill by removing the chosen lilac — Nora noted with relief that no features appeared in the process — the crew started site clearing. The site had been laid out as a checkerboard of one-by-one meter squares, and Nora assigned teams to work on alternating squares. The grid was aligned with a single definite row of stones sticking up through leaves and brush near the pond edge of the knoll. Conceivably, she said, this might be a foundation line but it was too early to tell. What if local legend were wrong? They might be looking at nothing more than a natural depression and some rocks, not an Ancient Cellarhole at all. Determining that was their first assignment.

To the novice crew, finding almost anything was an adventure, so excitement began as soon as last year's leaves were removed. As they surface collected, they laughed at the idea that bits of styrofoam cups and brittle plastic would be catalogued as "artifacts." They were thrilled to discover an exotic peach pit, even when it turned out to be a butternut from a nearby tree. Doug Avery, the anthropology major, immediately suggested radiocarbon testing some black, crumbly chunks. Nora gently let him down as she identified decaying bark, not charcoal. Everything was cause for speculation and discussion, even if it did all post-date 1900. It was just as well the finds were recent, Nora thought, for crew members disintegrated more than one rusty can, and dug some enthusiastic holes in the process of refining their digging techniques.

"Keep it level," Nora kept repeating. She laid a cautionary hand on Andrew's overeager trowel.

"Never dig deeper in one spot than another," she warned the Levalliere brothers. They would remember until something interesting surfaced.

"Remember: the key to dating deposits is associating objects *all on one level*."

Nora repeated herself a lot. Using only the side of a trowel blade to scrape away dirt was definitely a learned behavior.

Technical glitches aside, there was always a special lift in starting a new project, with everything still to discover and no dead-ends yet in sight. The mood would catch Nora up and carry her along like an amiable tornado, only to dump her eventually, like Dorothy, in a spot she barely recognized. One evening as the crew-in-training left, Nora wandered out of the makeshift field lab in Mill Farm's barn and looked for a quiet spot to sit. Just to let the newness settle. She hadn't had much time to sit since she'd packed up her gear and left Somerville behind. Artie strolled along with her, distracted by the occasional need to pounce on a bug, but otherwise sticking close, not yet sure of his territory.

Mill Farm Street ran past the dig to the lower end of the pond where it split, half continuing left over the pond's outlet and the other half, known as Plantingfield Road, curving back toward town. Straight ahead at the turn, the mottled bark of a massive sycamore gleamed softly. Nora headed for the tree, thinking she would prop herself against it and watch the dark come down. But just a bit further she spotted a better seat. The knoll that edged the pond's west side ended as a miniature bluff, and the view from the top took in the whole site.

She settled herself cross-legged and watched the young family of geese glide across the pond. Crickets chirring in the underbrush enchanted Artie, who crouched at the ready, ears scanning like radar dishes. Nora began to unwind and the warmth of the rock where she sat recalled that other day, at the top of Noanet Peak. Was it really three months since she'd lain there, feeling her life as an archeologist coming to an end? Then the Mill Farm project had magically appeared, offering everything she'd been missing. Nora had very little sense of engineering this good fortune – of controlling it at all – and that thought would be enough to make her uncomfortable if she let it. But this particular evening she was determined not to think too much. She had just come to relax and surface collect.

As Nora became still a truck started up near the head of the pond, deep throated and slightly putt-putting, getting louder and more annoying as it moved down Mill Farm Street. She winced. It could use a good muffler. But it would go away momentarily and the stillness return. The low roar slowed at the corner and idled briefly. Then unexpectedly it stopped. Nora glanced over her shoulder in irritation and did a double take. A World War II ambulance was pulled up under the sycamore, red cross bright against the olive drab.

For a moment she imagined the truck disgorging stretchers, but only Hank Chapman appeared, tall and thin, dressed in chambray shirt and slightly baggy khakis, brown hair combed to one side over a high forehead. He had a strong jaw, Nora noticed, and a long face. As he walked toward her Nora wondered how he managed to look both inquisitive and disarming at the same time.

"I thought that might be you, Dr. Tunney," he said. "Great evening to be out, isn't it?"

"It is." Nora searched for conversation. "That's quite a truck. I don't imagine there are many of those around?"

"The only one in Medfield. It was my uncle's."

Curiosity got the better of reserve. "Did he use it here? As an ambulance?"

"Nothing so interesting, I'm afraid. He collected classic 'machines', as he called them, and didn't much care what make or function they had. This is actually among his more useful ones."

She nodded, searching again. "You know, Mr. Chapman, your…father, I guess it is? has done a wonderful thing deeding this site to the town. It's an invaluable gift of history."

Hank looked at her with eyebrows raised in question. Then his face lightened.

"Aah! No, I'm afraid it's me you're talking about. My dad's been dead quite a while. But thanks. It seemed as if the town would get more out of the spot than I do. Besides," he added, "Half the folks here think it's theirs anyway. Fishing, skating. A few late night skinny dippers …" His voice invited comment but Nora didn't notice. She was stuck at his announcement.

"All of this is your property?"

If square acreage was any indicator, this guy had to be worth more than the whole Tunney clan put together. Not that that made any real difference, of course, but it certainly rarified the situation.

She'd checked out the place when she first came, making notes on landscapes to survey and features to test. The three acres Hank had deeded to the town was only a small corner of the family's eighty-acre spread but, like the site, the whole farm focussed on the mill pond. The narrow rectangle of water was bounded on the east by a brooding pine-topped ridge; on the west, by more level ground where Mill Farm Street ran. Toward the downstream end was the lilac-covered knoll which, even on first inspection, seemed a likely spot for old foundation remains hidden among the gnarled old roots.

Nora had walked across the dam that stretched from the knoll eastward toward the pine ridge. A shingle-sided grist mill still stood by the outlet, handsome even in decay, and a patch of boulder-strewn ground next to the mill hinted at another building long gone. The grist mill had been boarded up, tight enough that Nora could see little inside except bits of machine parts and stray boards.

From the dam there was also a teasing glimpse of roofline at the pond's upper end. Green lawn, a canoe upended near the water. The building was hidden by apple trees though, and clearly lay beyond the town's three acres. So did seventy-seven other acres, she reminded herself, looking at the orchard and the pine grove, at maples in the distance and imagined fields beyond that. How hard was it going to be, she had wondered, to talk the Commission – the family, for that matter – into surveying all eighty acres? That was where the real story of Mill Farm lay, after all, not just in a few building remains. She had shrugged at the time. That was a Wait-and-See, not to be resolved by wishing.

A third clump of buildings, standing at the midpoint of the pond's west side, was clearly the main Mill Farm complex. It was set off from the road by a fieldstone wall. A two-story house, stark white, faced squarely on the pond. Nora thought the house looked awkward, skinny almost, but she had taken an immediate liking to the faded red barn beside it. Layers of sheds and outbuildings in varying stages of disrepair attested to the barn's long working life. One single-story wing reached like an arm from the barn toward the house. This had turned out to be the Shed, actually a railroad apartment with bedroom tucked under the eaves; kitchen, living room and study nudged into line on the first floor.

Hank's voice brought Nora back to the ownership question she'd just asked.

"It's a nice place to live," he said.

"Understatement must be one of your talents."

He shrugged and turned the conversation.

"How are you making out in the Shed? Quarters are a bit cramped, I'm afraid."

Nora had to laugh. She thought of the green view from her bedroom window and the dozen steps it took to get from work to sofa after a long day. "Believe me, Mr. Chapman, when a third-floor walk-up is your basis for comparison, these quarters are fantastic."

"I don't know about that, but I guess the commute's better. And a swimming pool in your front yard."

He was trying to be friendly, she thought, watching him gesture toward the pond, and perhaps just a bit disingenuous. The combined effect reminded her of some basic differences between them. Difference of location. Difference of perspective. Of course Hank Chapman didn't 'know about that.' He'd grown up here, surrounded by all this green space. Different experience from the Preston Street backyard in Lawrence where she'd grown up, where size was measured in square feet and her little brother spent half his time clambering over the chain-link fence to retrieve the balls he'd hit into Mrs. Dracott's roses.

She tried to connect the pond in front of them with Red Cross swimming lessons at the Y, but a fleeting image of late-night skinny-dipping was destroyed by Artie suddenly pouncing at a frog who had piped up nearby. The attack set off a series of splashes along the bank as tadpoles and parents escaped to deeper water. She wondered uneasily how many other forms of wildlife lurked in slimy mud at the bottom.

"I may not be quite ready for the swimming, but I'm really grateful you're letting me live here."

"Well," he said, "the Shed has always been used by special people, and I can't bring myself to rent it like the Big House. I'm glad you like it."

Nora was suddenly reminded of her first impression of Hank Chapman as a dangerous mix. Here it was again. Was he intimating something by "special people"? Some expectation maybe? A potential glitch in her perfect situation?

"In my grandmother's day a couple named Hub and Duddy lived there." Hank went on talking in Nora's silence. "By the time I was growing up, though, it was Aunt Jenny's."

"Favorite aunt?"

"She had time for a little kid."

A flash of recognition had Nora mentally kicking herself for unjust thoughts.

"I know just what you mean. My Gramma was like that. I'd sit across from her chair and we'd play Go Fish on her lap board. She had time to listen."

Hank nodded and they shared a companionable silence of memories before he spoke again.

"Listen, I didn't mean to ruin your peaceful evening. I've got to go anyhow. Early start tomorrow. I just wanted to check on how you're settling in."

Nora discovered she was less eager for solitude than she had been when the evening started.

"I'm doing fine, thanks. But by the way, while you're here, I've been meaning to ask you about Chapman family papers."

"Papers?"

"Yes. Could we talk sometime about any documents you might have from your family? They could be a lot of help with property research."

Hank's expression was noncommittal and Nora elaborated, assuming he needed further explanation.

"You know, a family bible perhaps, old deeds, maybe a photo album that shows the farm or the people who lived here?"

"Maybe." His tone was suddenly cool. "There isn't much you'd want to bother with. Odds and ends in the attic ..."

He stared off toward the darkening pond. Nora wondered if she'd overstepped some unmarked personal boundary. Then Hank suddenly gave Nora one of his easy grins.

"I'll look around sometime. But right now I've got to head out. Leave you and the cat and the frogs alone. That is your cat?"

"Yes, Artie."

"Named for someone?"

Nora had the grace to blush. "Actually his name is Artie Fact. My father thought it was a charming name for an archeologist's pet and it unfortunately stuck."

"Well, Artie and Nora, it's been nice talking. I'll look forward to next week's Board meeting."

"Oh, that's right, the Commission. You're going to be there?"

"Plan to."

"I haven't met Mr. Majors yet."

"He's an experience."

Hank's briefly raised eyebrows left Nora wondering how to take that comment, but he offered nothing further except a quick goodnight. Nora watched as the ambulance started with a cough and rumbled off into the dusk. She waved away a swarm of mosquitoes bent on distracting her from sorting out mixed impressions. Hank Chapman certainly didn't come across as the self-important family heir she had originally imagined. And he seemed too polite to make a convincingly lecherous landlord. Surprising he wasn't more interested in his own family's papers. What was that all about? But then, she reminded herself, some people just weren't into research. Maybe he was a hands-on type. Certainly pleasant company. Unmarried even, if lack of a ring meant anything. Not that that was particularly relevant.

Nora took a last swipe at the mosquitoes and stood up. Enough. She had a job that was secure, an amiable landlord, and the satisfaction of knowing the survey was bound to be interesting. No need to belabor that. It was time to start work on another project she had been putting off.

Back inside, she arranged a box fan in the window of her tiny study as the laptop warmed up. When the screen glowed green she perched forward on her desk chair and scowled resolutely at the blank page until the words came. Then her fingers moved fast, as if the words had been written long before in her brain.

AN ARCHEOLOGIST'S HANDBOOK
Part One: Surface Collecting

Surface collecting is the first time you come in contact with artifacts in an archeological excavation. You wander around the test pit you've staked out and you really look at it. You notice the oyster shell and the bent nail, the foil and the glass shard tucked in among the leaves and roots and you pick them up, carefully tucking them away. They don't mean much yet: stray bits of trash pointing to what? But you hope when you dig deeper you'll find more to add to these first bits. And you hope if you dig deep enough, with enough care, all these bits of human history will fit together like some complex jigsaw puzzle, and you'll see the big picture that has lain hidden underground.

*   *   *   *   *

By the end of the first week the novice crew had pretty well mastered the scraping and dumping and sifting and searching that made up archeological routine. Ralph Whiting left for a family wedding, vowing to be back the moment it was over, fretting at all he would miss in the week to come. The crew stripped the site of its overburden and leveled off their assigned squares, finding interesting surprises along the way.

Some of the first interesting lumps and bumps to appear were old cat burials. The Chapmans had been a cat-loving family, and their pets were laid to rest at the edge of the lilac grove. All that was left were stray bits of satin blanket binding from the winding sheets, and small collections of bones. The crew marveled at the tiny size of animals without their fur, and gently transferred them to a mass grave beneath the sycamore across the road.

Pam was horrified when one of the Dead Bodies turned up in her own square. She begged to move as far as possible from the burial she'd uncovered, so Nora set her to work two squares farther north, in the heart of the lilacs. The grove had been much too thick there to provide burial room. Nora was surprised, therefore, when Pam, nervously clearing the loam away from a gnarled stump in the middle of her new square, came across more interesting finds. First there was a doll's teacup, broken but complete, with a bit of gold rim and a shadow band of pink flowers that had survived years of frost and wear. The cup was enough to engage the rest of the crew who alternated work and monitoring Pam for the rest of the day.

Their vigil was rewarded by another treasure, tightly trapped in the roots, which Pam discovered at quitting time. She had swept away enough soil for everyone to make out blue-decorated pottery in a very strange shape. Whatever it was, they all agreed it was certainly not a basic dish. Nora watched Pam working, tired, impatient, with fingers obviously itching to pull the shard out. After all Nora's *keep it level* lectures, that wasn't going to happen the first time something really interesting turned up. She called a halt for the day, stopping a chorus of groans by assigning Doug and Andy to help Pam the next morning.

"Come on, guys. With three of you working, we'll do it right; cut back the stump and roots, record it all, see what the bush has been hiding all this time."

They silently resisted.

"Remember, I never said archeology was a quick process." She kept her tone light, hoping it didn't betray her concern over a potential revolt. The director of a volunteer crew could only direct if they agreed to it.

But Peg came to her rescue, admitting her knees had had enough for one day, and Levalliere Senior became an unexpected ally, pronouncing the light too low for the photography he took so seriously. Reluctantly, others agreed and began the nightly collection of tools. Pam brushed at her find one last time and shrugged. The first palace revolt was at an end, but Nora had to put up with loud, if only half serious, complaints all the way back to the storage closet in the barn.

Next morning began with great anticipation. Here was mystery, suspense, treasure — all the things that made up for the drudgery of digging. Pam and her new partners were fresh enough to be patient, but they worked fast and everyone else hovered as the iron-hard roots were chopped, clipped and finally lifted out of the way. If nothing else, Nora mused, the crew had already learned that lilacs were stubborn. And that that was why lilacs made such good markers for old house sites.

There wasn't much hiding under the stump besides the blue and white piece. Another broken bit of doll china, acorns forgotten by an industrious squirrel. But the blue-and-white made up for the rest. Pam gently dusted off the loosened dirt. Doug Avery measured and noted location on the plot plan. Levalliere Senior carefully composed the requisite pre-removal photos. Nora crouched beside the square and made sure they followed all the rules but her fingers, like the others', itched to lift the object out. Everyone was guessing.

"Looks like Dedham to me," Miss Wentworth said.

"Is it broken? It doesn't look broken."

"What is it?"

"Some kind of statue or something."

"Maybe it's a cat statue in a cat graveyard."

"Wow! It's in great condition!"

The fussing was finally done and Pam won the right to remove the artifact from its dirt bed. She cradled it nervously in the palm of her hand and wiped it off with her thumb.

"It's a bunny!"

"It's so cute!"

"Way to go, Pam!"

Pam glowed with the pride of a new mother as the crew oohed and aahed over a ceramic rabbit. He was sitting upright, ears stiffly alert, features picked out with blue brushstrokes. Only the tip of one ear was missing. The whole figure wasn't more than three inches high.

The bunny passed carefully from hand to hand around the circle. Peg Wentworth took it by its head and turned it over. Sure enough, when she brushed off the base, an indented rabbit outline appeared.

"Yes indeed! Here's the bunny stamp. This is Dedham Pottery."

Those who knew, crowed, as the others looked confused.

"Arts and Crafts style," Nora began explaining to the younger members of the crew. "Actually made down the road in Dedham. About when, Peg?"

"Well, early twentieth century, anyway. Crackleware, they call this. I must admit it's never done much for me. Dedham made some really nice art pottery though – one-of-a-kind vases and such. But I seem to remember the war did them in, sometime back in the 40's."

"Surely a cute little bunny like this is one of a kind." Jane Ogden's words were a statement rather than a question. She was cradling the piece in both hands.

"My understanding is that crackleware dishes were the Dedham Pottery production line, Mrs. Ogden," Nora was careful with her words. "I don't believe they were very valuable while they were being produced, but of course a lot of it has broken over time so this bunny probably is pretty rare by now." She retrieved the rabbit and held it up, glancing around the circle.

"I'll tell you what I think makes this little guy a real rarity. It's probably the last thing I'd expect to find on a site around here. Artifacts are people's *trash*, right? Broken and discarded stuff. An occasional lost item mixed in. I mean, think about it. Turning up an intact figurine is about as likely as finding a gold coin."

That was an invitation to fantasy for most of the group, who had the site transformed into an Old World tomb filled with jewels and precious metals by the time lunch break was over. Eventually the bunny was bagged and labeled, and the crew went back to work, each one secretly hoping to be the next to find treasure. Nora wandered from square to square, ostensibly supervising, occasionally dropping an expected reminder. The rabbit was bothering her, though, an inexplicably *whole* fragment of the past. When she came to the square where Peg was patiently scraping away, she crouched down and asked a purely theoretical question.

"How do you suppose that bunny got here, anyway?"

Peg carefully set her trowel down and considered.

"I don't imagine we'll ever know, do you?"
Nora grimaced. The thought was surprisingly upsetting.
"So much for surface collecting," she murmured.

THE BLUE BUNNY

July 1917

The thud of the heavy knocker was inordinately loud in the early morning quiet. It startled a gray cat out of his doze in the parlor wing chair. It sent a six-year-old galloping toward the kitchen.

"Mama, Mama! Somebody's at the front door! Can I get it?"

It almost made Sarah lose her hold on a soapy lamp chimney, and she raised her eyebrows in surprise.

"Give me a moment, Jenny. We'll answer it together."

Who could be calling so early in the day? Hub was a back door man when he came in for his coffee before chores. Besides, he had come and gone an hour ago. Duddy, his wife, came in the front way sometimes, but she'd no more think of using the knocker than Sarah herself. Mr. Sims, the mailman, would not be by until close to noon, if then. There was precious little mail to fill the six-month void in the Chapman household.

Sarah carefully set the lamp glass down on the cloth-covered drainboard and wiped wet hands on her apron. Then, Jenny stepping on her heels in excitement, she headed out front. She quickly caught back a stray bit of dark hair with one of her combs and swung the door open to an extraordinary sight. The white-haired woman standing just beyond the granite doorstep was so nearly dwarflike she made Sarah feel tall. She was dressed in an old-fashioned cape coat – a man's garment but for its perfect tailoring to her size and its delicate lavender tweed. Sarah noticed serviceable gloves and cap; sturdy, well-worn walking shoes, and a canvas bag hanging at her side. There was no conveyance in sight, no horse or motor car, and Sarah entertained the brief notion that this apparition had appeared by magic, out of nowhere.

"Good morning." The apparition's voice was cheerful. "I'm Isobel Arnold. My husband and I just bought the stone camp up by Rocky Woods and I walked down this way to see if your 'Fresh Eggs' sign has been put out of business by the War Board?"

Sarah recovered her manners and extended her hand. "How do you do? I'm Sarah Chapman. And this over-eager little girl is my daughter, Jenny."

Jenny was intent on pushing herself as far into the doorway as possible, the better to stare at this magical old lady. Sarah firmly moved her to the side, but there was amusement in her face as she did so.

"Please come in. I can certainly get you some eggs. It's one of the few benefits of farm life in wartime."

The woman grasped the doorframe for support and hiked herself over the high threshold into the front hall. Her halo of wispy white hair came to Sarah's chin.

"If you'll just step through here," Sarah gestured into the parlor. "We put a fresh batch in the pantry this morning."

They walked past the gray cat's chair and a table crowded with photos in wood or silver frames. A laughing little girl seated on a porch rocker, the stiffly posed matriarch presiding over a family picnic, a wedding scene of handsome groom and bride swirled round with satin. Largest among them stood a plain-framed portrait of a solemn man in army uniform.

"You have a man in uniform, I see?" Mrs. Arnold probed.

Sarah paused on her way to the kitchen, studying the portrait as she answered.

"My husband, Henry. He's been in France with Mr. Hoover's Food Commission since March."

"Ah, yes. Surely they've been recalled, with America in the war and all?"

"Not exactly. He only went for three months, we thought, to work with the relief effort. But by the end of that time we were in the war and he was asked to stay on. Something to do with setting up supply lines, I believe. Seems he was too good at what he did. But God willing, he'll be home the end of August."

"Hmm. "The older woman's sound was sympathetic. "Must be very difficult to manage the farm without him."

"It is."

Sarah drew a breath as if to say more, then clamped her mouth shut and turned toward the kitchen, abruptly changing the subject. "You're down from Rocky Woods? That must be quite a walk for you, isn't it?"

The older woman lifted her chin a bit higher. "Goodness no! I've been 'walking,' as you put it, since I was a girl. Why, I'm a charter member of the Sierra Club. I've walked over mountains that don't even have names yet, carrying a full pack." She chuckled and shook her head. "The day I can't make it the mile or two from the Woods to here, I might just as well give up and die."

Sarah felt herself blushing. "Oh, dear, I am sorry, Mrs. Arnold. I'm afraid I've spent too much time recently judging ability from the perspective of a six-year-old." She reached to stroke Jenny's hair but the little girl, spotting an overall-clad man in the barnyard outside, ducked away, her fascination with their visitor replaced by more familiar pleasure.

"Uncle Hub! Can I have a ride?"

The women watched as Hub effortlessly tossed Jenny up to the seat of a towering hay wagon.

"Send her back by lunchtime, Hub," Sarah called.

The weathered face nodded acknowledgement as he settled next to Jenny and coaxed a slow-paced horse out of the yard.

"What a fine, bright spot to work in," Mrs. Arnold commented, moving the conversation beyond Sarah's embarrassment.

Sarah glanced around the kitchen she knew so well, taking in the sunlight that stole under south-facing awnings and glanced off the lamp chimneys drying by the sink. She smiled fondly.

"It is, isn't it? Even in the depths of winter the sun gets in here. Some days we hardly use the rest of the house, this room is so warm. We're thinking it will come in handy this year, what with the coal shortage they're predicting."

Mrs. Arnold nodded emphatically. "That's one of the reasons George and I took the stone camp. It's a nice little summer place, of

24

course, but it comes with its own woodlot, too. I guess, if things got any worse, we could always winter here, as well. The fireplace in that house is big enough to heat a barn!"

"The wood will surely come in handy. But don't you think, now that we're in the war, the Germans will have to give way soon? I'm hoping we'll be well on our way back to normal before winter gets too far along."

There was little conviction in the response. "Well, let's hope so. Though it seems the world has seen less and less of what one might call 'normal' these past three years."

Mrs. Arnold set her bag on a ladderback chair by the kitchen table. The action interrupted Sarah's thoughts and she moved to pull out a second chair.

"Where are my manners! Please, do sit down while I get your eggs. Will a dozen do? I'd normally have twice that to offer, but the heat this past week has put the hens off laying."

Reassured that a dozen would be fine, Sarah opened the pantry door at the end of the kitchen and Mrs. Arnold caught a glimpse of stacked dishes and glassware. Beneath these was a broad, waist-height shelf where pitchers and cake tins crowded beside a breadbox and covered bowls. Closed cupboards hid their contents underneath. Sarah returned with a bowlful of eggs and the two women transferred them to the waiting canvas sack, wrapping each one in the toweling brought for the purpose. The shared task led to further conversation, of chickens and local fish, sugar and its wartime alternatives. Sarah eased the last egg into place and made a decision.

"Mrs. Arnold, could I offer you a glass of lemonade before you go? The day is coming on quite warm and you must be thirsty after your walk."

"Why don't you call me Isobel. Everyone does. But I don't want to keep you," Isobel demurred, getting up. "I can see you're right in the middle of things."

"Mrs. Arnold – Isobel, I am always right in the middle of things. It comes with children and housework anyway, but since Chappie's …" she caught herself. "Since my husband's been gone, I seem to need to be two people at once. Not that I don't have help," she rushed on. "Hub, whom you just saw, and his wife have been here a long time. But it's harder and harder to get day labor; first with the War

Effort, and now the draft. I should be out there now, helping Hub with the haying." A flash of guilt crossed her face, and she pressed her lips together to contain it. "But I confess, it's such a pleasure to see a new face and chat about something other than crops and food, if only for a minute. Please stay for a bit."

Sarah's earnest request met with a twinkling smile, and Isobel sat back down.

"Lemonade sounds delightful," she said.

As Sarah started for the icebox Isobel shrugged off her coat and arranged her hands together on the table.

"Perhaps, if you wish to avoid discussing crops, you'd be willing to tell me about your farm? There is a venerable look to it, from what I've seen."

"Venerable enough that I'm sure you don't want to hear the whole story." Sarah was smiling as she set down two glasses. "It has been in my husband's family since time immemorial. And there's a mill too, down at the foot of the pond. Mill Farm, it's called. Dates back to the 1600s, they say. There's an old cellarhole you can just see from here, where that clump of lilacs is. I wish Chappie were here to tell you about it. He's the only one who can keep the Chapmans straight – which ones ran the mill and which ones built the farm. Which ones we brag about and which we tend to pass over."

Sarah's voice remained light as she joked about the long Chapman genealogy, but she found it hard to keep the smile in place as her husband's absence became almost a presence in the room. Isobel looked at her appraisingly.

"Your husband is much on your mind, is he not?"

"No more than for most wives, I'm sure," she answered quickly. "I keep reminding myself he's not in combat. And he has assured me the government is sending a replacement any day. But ..." Sarah paused, trying to put words to thoughts she had not spoken before, "... his face pops into my mind unexpectedly. Just now, for instance, when I couldn't answer your question. When I need to decide the planting schedule without him. Or Jenny needs reassurance and I am at a loss... ." She shook her head silently and wrapped both hands around her glass.

"Well!" Isobel's voice was brisk. "Sometimes I pry too much. How about some more lemonade?"

Without waiting for an answer, she leaned forward and tipped the pitcher toward Sarah's glass. She served herself another splash and brightly went on.

"You know, I'm looking forward to exploring around here while the weather's fine. George and I never came out this way much, before we thought of buying a camp. I think the closest I'd come was Will Robertson's place in East Dedham. And that's not exactly country!"

Sarah was glad to change the subject. "Robertson's? I'm not familiar with the name."

"Well, let me think of the real name. A pottery... Makes delightful cottage wares. But Will's real talent is in making some of the most beautiful glazes this side of China. Despite everything he's had going against him," she added to herself.

"There is a firm near the mills called the Dedham Pottery," Sarah offered. "I don't suppose they're connected?"

"Oh, yes, of course! Dedham Pottery. They used to be in Chelsea, you know. The Chelsea Keramic Art Works. Will and his father Hugh, and a brother who went off to California. Moved out of the city and changed their name. Actually I was just in there the other day getting some plates for the camp. They're really quite ..." Isobel searched for a word. "Whimsical. Bands of little creatures chasing each other around the rim. I bought one of each – for variety, don't you know? Bunnies and turtles, ducks, a truly silly-looking owl, butterflies. Quite delightful."

"They sound it." Sarah had an inspiration. "And they might be just the thing for Amy's wedding present. My sister-in-law," she explained. "Amy's determined to marry her young man before he's posted overseas. She's quite adamant about it."

"Just as long as the date's not too soon," Isobel cautioned. "Will's been having a terrible time filling orders since the war started."

"Ah! What you meant about things going against him. I can imagine a pottery must be facing a lot of shortages – it's not exactly war material."

Isobel hesitated, then answered cryptically, "That's certainly one of his problems."

She stood and picked up her sack. "But do go. George and I have known the Robertsons for years, since Will was just a boy. He does do a fine job with special orders, even if they're a bit slow. And besides," she gave a knowing nod of her head, "you could use a change of scene, you know. Why not set aside a morning for a nice trot to Dedham; do your errands, take care of your sister-in-law. A body doesn't shoulder responsibility well if she can't see the road beyond the wall, so to speak."

Isobel gave Sarah a sharp nod that added weight to her advice. Sarah smiled as she walked her visitor to the door.

"I might just take you up on your advice, Mrs. Arnold. Just as soon as haying's done." She laughed suddenly, surprising herself with the unfamiliar sound. "You see, I cannot seem to escape from 'as soon as' even now, but I promise I will, and I'll let you know what I find for Amy and Roger."

She swung the door back and Isobel held the frame as she eased herself back down to the granite stoop.

"A good decision, Mrs. Chapman. And be sure to give my best to Will when you go."

With a final wave and thanks for the eggs, Isobel hitched her bag over her shoulder and strode off. Sarah lingered for a moment in the shaded doorway, listening to cicadas tuning up along the roadside and watching the dwarflike woman disappear.

By evening, the midsummer sun had left the house hot and airless. Sarah took pen and writing paper from the slant-top desk in the bedroom and carried it down to the kitchen table, where a small westerly breeze was almost enough to counteract the heat from the kerosene lamp. People and animals were fed, everything was washed, chores were done until first light when they would start all over. Hub and Duddy had retired for the night and Jennie was in bed, fast asleep with Raggedy Ann.

This was Sarah's time to be with Chappie. As she always did, she closed her eyes and recited the advice to wives and mothers she had read months ago in the *Dedham Transcript*:

> *When writing to your loved ones, ever strive for a cheerful tone. Remember, whatever the difficulties we at home may encounter, they are as nothing compared to the challenges faced each day by our brave menfolk overseas. Do not burden them with petty worries and disappointments. Rather let your words be encouraging, expressing your pride in their courage and determination and the constancy with which you share their patriotic duty.*

Then she summoned up an image of her husband: tall, thin, Yankee to the bone, bending near a dim lamp to read each word she wrote.

Dearest Chappie,

It is hard to believe a week has gone by since I last wrote! Your presence was often felt in that time, you may be sure. Life has been busy and the summer churns on. Hub sprayed the apple trees – both orchards are done – and has been scything the grass around them. If this weather keeps up, he says we'll have to mow again before the summer's over, though how we will manage without more help, I can't imagine.

She reread the last sentence and frowned, then carefully edited.

...he says we will mow again this summer, so there'll be extra hay for sale this year.

Duddy has been up to her elbows in preserves, as usual. She and Jenny and I spent a delightful morning on Noon Hill picking blueberries. Jennie's pail never did get very full (though her face was certainly purple enough!) but we managed to gather a bit more than six quarts. Not a bad haul, you'll agree. Your Mr. Hoover would be proud of us.

The garden is doing fine. I found a bit of shade for the salad greens this year, so we'll still have them a bit longer, despite the heat. Lots of beans coming, and the brussels sprouts look promising. Potatoes have been hilled, and look like long mounded green stripes at the end of the garden – very pretty, if I do say so and much more practical than the zinnias I used to plant. Of course I can hear you snorting at the notion of "pretty" potatoes – though perhaps you would not, come to think of it. I suspect potatoes would look more than pretty right now in the places you have been. How desolate poor France must look this summer – and for summers to come, I fear. I study the photos in the Post and can see nothing but ruin everywhere. How will those poor people survive when there is not even a tree for shade? Much less a field of potatoes or a grazing cow!

She paused again, rereading, then crossed out everything she had written after *come to think of it.* Crossing out was easier than coming up with a replacement, but focussing thought on her husband alone made words of encouragement easier.

I trust the charge you have accepted is progressing well. Certainly Mr. Hoover chose a worthy man to get the job done. I have no doubt that as soon as our boys engage the enemy this wretched war will end, and you will have made it possible for them by laying the groundwork. I am vastly proud of knowing a man who can do so much for so many!

But I had better stop writing in this vein or you will end up with a swelled head. Let me tell you instead of your daughter's latest accomplishment. She and the Whiting children down the street have been spending hours playing in the pond this summer. Hub built them a little float near shore. Jenny bravely paddles out with the others, who are very protective of her, because much as she loves being on the float, she has always had to slide herself back into the pond, holding on tightly all the way. Somehow all her bravery in the water has not extended to getting her head wet. Then just yesterday, I think Roy Whiting had teased her once too often, for without as much as a by-your-leave, Jenny leapt up, and launched herself right off the raft! My heart stopped altogether. Before I could even think about moving, though, her head popped out of the water and after a surprised gasp, she began to laugh! She positively crowed with delight, and paddled back over to the raft, and tried it again, and again. She must have jumped in twenty times before Joe Whiting came by to collect his brood for supper. When you come home you'll find we have a little otter on our hands instead of a little girl. I can see it won't be long before you'll teach her to dive off the dam. Then I'll <u>really</u> have something to fuss about!

Last Thursday I finally came up with an inspiration for Amy and Roger's wedding gift. (No date yet. I think Amy's hoping you'll be home in time to walk her down the aisle.) Anyway, you know the lovebirds won't have two nickels to scrape together when Roger comes back from overseas, so they will be needing much more practical items than Limoges serving pieces. I heard there is a pottery over in Dedham that makes informal tablewares and it occurred to me that we might present them with a barrel of china for their newlywed's table. Doesn't that seem like a good idea? I think I'll hitch up Ebenezer and take a ride over that way when the last of the hay is in, to see if the notion will fly or not.

I confess, a chance for me to "just set" (as Duddy would say) in a little peace and quiet is very attractive. I shall improve my time on the journey daydreaming of you. So, my love, on the first clear day after you receive this letter, imagine yourself riding next to me in the trap. Just soak up the feel of summer as we amble down High Street. Smell the roses along the Blanchards' fence and the new-mown hay on that stretch by Tubbs' foundry. That way we'll be side by side again, if only for a moment.

Foolish fancy, I know. But times like these remind me you'll be coming home in a few short weeks and let me feel the ties of love that bind us together, half a world apart. Be safe. Know that you are always in my prayers and my heart.

She sat very still, her hands resting on the written sheet, as the words echoed in her head and Chappie felt close again. Finally she sighed and, giving a small smile, picked up her pen again.

> *Until next week, ever your devoted wife,*
> *Sarah*

An afternoon away, at last. Humming in Sarah's head distracted her as she gave Jenny a fleeting kiss. Caught up in the hum were glimpses of the stops she'd make, the papers she needed, the list of items to see to in a day of shopping. Sarah brought her thoughts up short and turned her full attention to her daughter. One thorough hug restored the connection and Sarah admonished the eager little girl to mind Duddy until she came home. Then she hiked up the hem of her skirt and climbed onto the buggy seat, settling her straw hat more firmly toward the front of her head. She clucked at Ebenezer and waved goodbye. Hooves and wheels stirred up a wave of dust as the trap jerked into motion and the journey to Dedham began.

Sarah sighed deeply and the humming began to recede. No more tasks to crowd into the morning hours at home. Nothing to do at all, in fact, until the slow-trotting horse pulled into Dedham village. Sarah spread out the ample gores of her twill driving skirt, and lifted a wisp of red-brown hair back into place at the nape of her neck. She was grateful for the moving air, despite its burden of dust, for the day promised to be humid and still again, even though there was no sun in sight. Was this the second, or third hot spell of the summer? Perhaps it was all just one, interminable, like the days of worrying and war. The potato blossoms might never set if the nights didn't cool down soon.

Nothing to be done about it right now, though. She would not let this day be spoiled by worry about what she could not change. So, back straightened and shoulders set, she turned her mind to the task at hand. How many errands could she accomplish and still be back before supper? There was the surveyor's of course, for Chappie's plan. Duddy was running short of canning jars. And cloth for the bedroom curtains she'd vowed to make before Chappie came home. Once at the mill outlet, the pottery building was just across the way, so she should be able to fit it all in if she didn't dawdle.

The buggy rolled under an arched roof of maples along the ancient Hartford Turnpike, and stiffness began to ease out of Sarah's back. The flat layer of gray cloud seemed less drab than usual, a backdrop to set off dust-coated leaves and pallid blossoms along the roadside. The road climbed gently through Westwood while creaking buggy and chirring crickets soothed the tension that seemed to occupy so much of Sarah's mind. Sounds and sights of the rural turnpike seeped in. Fisher's blacksmith shop was doing a booming business in repairs, thanks to wartime shortages. The Willard Gay estate was getting a paint job. Clean white picked out classic trim on the century-old house. A massive catalpa shaded another yard, fat white blossoms forming nosegays above its green leaves. Daylilies everywhere, and masses of sweet pink roses tumbled over Blanchard's fence. Bouquets of daisies lined Mr. Dean's fields. Sarah remembered bidding Chappie to come on this ride with her, and his invisible presence kept her company. Ebenezer's hooves clopped quietly through the dust.

She swayed with the creaking buggy seat beneath her and gazed, half-seeing, at the road ahead.

Too soon, it seemed, two hours were gone and the iron wheels rumbled onto macadam at the Dedham common. With a sigh, Sarah brought herself back from reverie. At the watering trough in Memorial Square she stopped to let the horse drink, thanking her lucky stars again that he was old, and imperturbable enough to ignore the sputtering engines and wailing horns of passing motorcars and trucks. She had no great desire for the auto Chappie swore he'd buy when the war was over. But it was becoming troublesome to drive the trap in built-up areas. The motor vehicles caused such a ruckus there was barely a day when some poor horse didn't shy, or its owner lose control.

Sarah turned the buggy toward Mr. Pilling's office and hitched the reins to a post outside while she saw to the survey Chappie wanted. Before the war, Chappie had taken to buying up land upstream from the mills. Farmer or not, he was always looking for ways to make the mills more productive; working at improving the draw, trying to increase the power coming off the wheel. *Maybe we can't compete in size,* he'd say to anyone who'd listen, *but Chapman's Mills could be the most efficient operation in Norfolk County. Why, there's enough water upstream to run these mills practically all year.* Then he'd mutter, *Have to control the flow, though. And control the flow means own the flow — or at least the land around it.* Then he would start into his views on the pros and cons of turbines for seasonal waterways. And his brows would knit over piercing green eyes as he leaned toward his listener in the intensity of his opinions. Sarah loved him for his intensity, for his decisiveness of action when he had made up his mind about something. As if his decisions activated him and spurred him on, to bring alive the things that he envisioned.

Of course his decisiveness had brought on the situation they were in now, she reminded herself. When Herbert Hoover had recruited men to manage the massive food relief effort in Europe, he'd sent a personal invitation to Chappie to join them. Because of his reputation, Mr. Hoover said, and his knowledge of both agricultural production and food processing. Chappie was moved to do his part and no argument Sarah could make about family or farm exemption would penetrate the commitment in those green eyes. So he had gone abroad, attached to the armed forces but not a soldier, for a limited stay that didn't seem to end.

Eventually Sarah, not Chappie, engaged Earl Pilling to survey the new additions to Mill Farm, and now it was she who studied the meticulous plan of land stretching long and narrow on both sides of Mill Brook. She wondered how many months would go by before Chappie could see it himself, before he could get back to work on his vision of their own private future. Mr. Pilling was eager to discuss her husband's ideas for improvements, and ready to expound on a number of theories of his own. Sarah felt the fragile peace of her ride to Dedham slipping away, and excused herself as quickly as possible. Mr. Chapman should be home soon after the end of August, she assured the surveyor. Mr. Pilling would be better served to share his thoughts with him, she said politely. And, she added silently, not try to engage *her* in a discussion she did not understand, that only served to remind her how ineffectual she was in Chappie's place.

By the time she left Pilling's, Connors Store and canning jars appeared to be a treat. She understood canning jars and what went into them. Beans and peaches were safely part of the here-and-now, and she knew what to do with them. There was comfortable familiarity in snapping the beans and blanching, or peeling the peaches and feeling the juice between her fingers. And when the canning jars were filled and processed, they would be safely stored away right where they were supposed to be, ranged on long dark shelves in the cold cellar, ready and waiting for sale or Sunday supper. She and Duddy would spend a lot of time with canning jars this year, more than usual perhaps, but at least she knew what she was doing.

An hour later, the trap turned down the road by Mill No. 2. Sarah pulled off to the side under a tired maple tree. Dusty leaves stirred limply in a faint breeze, and she sat for a moment, letting the air cool the back of her neck. The buggy stood in a vacant lot, a small pocket of stillness. From one side came the rhythmic thud of heavy looms weaving cotton yardage. Across the lot, a broad-shouldered carter and a sandy-haired youth rolled wooden barrels across a loading dock. They shouted to each other as, with surprising care, they maneuvered the heavy barrels onto a waiting truck. Behind the building where they worked, a chimney blew steady streams of light smoke into the sky. The brick smokestack, one of two, dominated the landscape beneath, its conical shape proclaiming as well as any sign, that this was a pottery.

Sarah decided that taking care of Amy's present first might leave her time to spare, which she would happily spend in the fabric showroom. So she climbed a set of dusty stairs to the pottery's second floor entrance. A sign was nailed up next to the doorway. White background, blue border, the word DEDHAM centered over POTTERY, with a bunny in profile beneath them.

She stepped through the open door and was stopped in her tracks by the heat. The humid stillness outdoors was twice as oppressive inside. Tall windows standing wide open along one wall had no effect. She looked around the long, high-ceilinged room filled with rough wooden tables and row on row of shelving along one wall, wondering if she could bear the heat long enough to examine all the contents. Every surface was covered with dishes and pots, vases and figures of glazed earthenware.

No one was in the room to wait on her. Sarah finally decided a quick look around would be enough at least to tell whether she was willing to suffer the heat as long as it took to place an order. She began to stroll past the first table, stacked high with dinner plates, each pile similar in its crackled white glaze, but varied by an array of blue-painted borders. Someone, with childlike simplicity, had outlined a parade of baby chicks pecking its way through blue grass. In another stack fantastical sea dolphins gamboled around the rim. Further along, blue iris bowed in oriental grace and white birds sat atop potted orange trees.

Another table was all cups and mugs, creamers and sugars, the same blue borders circling their rims. Cereal bowls and serving pieces rose in lopsided towers next to pitchers molded with morning and nighttime scenes on opposing sides. Sarah smiled at the tableful of eager bunny-shaped salts and peppers, and hump-backed turtles whose pierced shells served as flower arrangers. Isobel's enthusiasm had not been misplaced. The dishes were charming, a perfect choice for a newlyweds' cottage.

By the time she reached the far end of the showroom there was still no clerk in sight. Guessing an open doorway led to the workrooms of the pottery, she decided to take matters into her own hands. Someone must be back there.

"Hello?" Sarah peered through, stopped by a 'No Entrance' placard. There was no sign of life.

"Is anyone there?"

Again no answer. Sarah turned back toward the display room and wondered what to do next. She was not going to stand about indefinitely in such insufferable heat. Perhaps she should speak to the carters she'd seen on her way in?

Suddenly an impatient voice growled, inches behind her, "What'll it be then?"

Sarah gasped and swung around. Her handbag knocked against his arm, he stood so close. She wondered how anyone as massive as this man could possibly have appeared so silently. At the same time she found her hackles rising at the workman's execrable manners. Wartime, she reminded herself. Those not engaged in military production must put up with such help as they could get, unfortunately.

"Goodness! You startled me." She stepped back and raised her head a bit higher.

"Couldn't hear the bell out back." He lifted a rag to his forehead and wiped at the sweat, though there was nothing to be done about the damp patches that darkened his collarless shirt. Sarah noticed — or tried not to notice – a stiffly flattened finger sticking out almost straight and another, scarred and angry-looking, on his right hand as it clutched the rag.

"I regret having to disturb you. I'm wondering if someone might help me with an order?"

A brief frown creased his forehead at the question.

"Guess I can do it. Rest of the crew's tied up out back. Can't stop everything whenever somebody wanders in."

Sarah's annoyance rose. She was, after all, a paying customer, or would be if he didn't talk himself out of a sale, but this was no way to convince her to buy Dedham pottery. She put on her chilliest expression and explained her presence meticulously.

"I am Mrs. Henry Chapman. I've driven here from Medfield at the suggestion of Mrs. Isobel Arnold, to look into ordering a set of dinnerware for a wedding gift. I understand that *Mr. Robertson...*"

she couldn't resist putting a certain emphasis on the connection, "...is acquainted with Mr. and Mrs. Arnold and I've been told to ask for him."

Sarah's brisk tone faltered as she watched a broad, slightly lopsided smile replace the sullenness on his face.

"Isobel! You should have said so in the first place."

She raised an eyebrow.

"Allow me to introduce myself, ma'am. William A. Robertson, all appearances to the contrary, at your service. How are Isobel and George, anyway? Now that you mention it, I do remember their saying something about a place out in Medfield. They've moved in, have they? They're a swell couple, if I do say so. Known them for as long as I can remember. And you, Mrs...Chapman is it? You been acquainted long?"

Robertson's flood of words came so quickly that Sarah had trouble knowing what question to answer first.

"No. No, actually I just recently made Mrs. Arnold's acquaintance. She seemed quite charming, though. And spoke highly of you, Mr. Robertson."

He chuckled as he vainly swiped at some more sweat.

"I'm afraid she might think twice if she saw me like this. Sorry for the appearance. It's next to impossible to keep the spit and polish going in the middle of a kiln firing. Especially in this danged heat!"

"I do apologize, Mr. Robertson, for taking you away from your work. Perhaps there might be a more convenient time? Or should I telephone? I am quite aware of the heat."

Sarah felt the short poplin jacket sticking to her back and half hoped he would send her away. Even the dusty, lazy-moving air of the vacant lot seemed pleasant by comparison with the showroom's oppressiveness.

"No, no. You're here now." Robertson tucked his well-used rag in a pocket and added, "Besides, you're a friend of Isobel's, and she's seldom wrong when she picks people."

"I really don't know her all that well," Sarah protested, "To be considered 'picked', that is. She came by our farm to buy eggs, that's all, and we ended having quite a long visit before she left."

Robertson grinned again through his thick moustache.

37

"She'll do that, all right. Get her talking and it's hard to slow the lady down. I will say she tells good stories, though. But how about you, now. You say you're on a farm?"

"Mill Farm, in Medfield. My husband's family's property."

Sarah was surprised at Robertson's inquisitiveness. It was not impolite, precisely, but few people she knew would allow their interest in another's business to be so apparent, especially at first meeting. Undoubtedly, direct questions were preferable to his earlier taciturnity. Still, it seemed appropriate to cut the discussion short. Besides, the afternoon was moving on and the trip home still lay ahead.

"But Mr. Robertson, I don't wish to take too much of your time," she went on. "It is clear you are shorthanded, and I must be getting back soon, as well. I was hoping I might place an order before I go?"

Robertson was not yet ready to abandon a favorite topic.

"Mill Farm, hmm? Boy, farming! That's the place to be in this man's war. Fresh air, steady work, good return. Why, with the Aggie Department calling for more of everything, and the Food Administration sending all our crops overseas, it's the farmers who count now. Just look at how beef has gone sky-high. And even a basket of apples will run us poor city folk a dollar or more. Your man must be resting easy on what he's making these days!"

Robertson shook his head and made one more pronouncement. "Not like us fools who're scrabbling just to hold things together. When all the time we're losing workers to the munitions plants and the War Board holds back our coal."

Sarah had held quite still during Robertson's polemic, at first surprised by his naïve idea of wartime farming, then increasingly incensed by his ridiculous comparison of his position with her own. Finally she'd had enough of this garrulous man's opinions.

"Mr. Robertson, my husband is not 'resting easy'. He is in France," she snapped. "He has been there for almost six months, through calving and plowing and planting a double-sized garden. He has been there while the gypsy moths ate the leaves off all those trees supposed to produce expensive apples, and while haying has had to be done. I have run the farm with the help of one hired man and his wife. We feed the cows. We hoe the corn. We can't get day-labor because they, too, have gone into the war effort. Half our fields are fallow, and the mill has had no business since last March. My daughter only remembers her father from a photograph. You may believe me when I say that none of us is resting easy, and I do not take kindly your suggestion that we are!"

She stopped to catch her breath, and pursed her lips tight. She had thoroughly lost control.

"Now, Mr. Robertson, could we please talk dishes!"

Robertson was studying her, a bemused expression on his face.

"Well, Mrs. Henry Chapman, seems I owe you an apology. My tongue tends to run off with my brain, those rare times I have an audience." He politely gestured her toward the front counter.

His immediate apology only served to make Sarah feel worse. Not only had she lost her temper, she had lost it at a person whom she barely knew. And her abominable behavior had brought to the fore all the worries she had thought to put aside for just this one day. Seven miles to Dedham was not far enough, apparently, to escape the facts that had changed her life. And Mr. Robertson's apology was too late to undo the damage. Sarah collected herself with a small sigh, and followed him to the front.

"I apologize as well, Mr. Robertson, for speaking so shortly. Your comment certainly did not warrant such a tirade."

"It's nothing," he replied. A wry smile lifted the edge of his moustache. "I've heard much worse."

The subject was closed. Both of them proceeded to discussion of patterns and quantities that would make up Amy and Roger's set. Robertson proved to be more of a salesman than he first appeared, ferreting out samples of unusual borders, convincing Sarah to include covered servers with the dinnerware. The tension between them lessened as he regaled her with stories of the designs' inventors, and the high jinks of the Davenports, brother and sister, who worked for him. Clearly, Sarah thought, Robertson loved to talk. She appreciated that he was doing so to put her at ease after their unfortunate introduction.

As Robertson wrote up Sarah's order he glanced over at her.

"So, you like this line of wares we've got, hmm?"

"They are delightful, Mr. Robertson. I can't help thinking what a contrast they are to the china my husband and I received at our wedding. Ours was lovely. Gold-trimmed, very formal. But the dishes

you make are so … so friendly, I guess, for lack of a better word."
She hesitated, searching for a better explanation. "It's as if you don't
have to dress for dinner when you use these plates, and that's suitable,
I think, in this present day and age."

He nodded in satisfaction.

"Good. I thought of doing these a while ago. 'Will Robertson,' I
said, 'you'll have to find something besides this art stuff.'" He
gestured broadly at the wall lined with shelves of vases and
ornamental pieces. "They may be my pride and joy, but they're too
danged pricey for regular folks to buy." He turned back to Sarah and
shook his head. "Can't pay the help and buy the stock with pride and
joy, can you?"

Sarah contemplated the question more seriously than he had
intended. She had found herself enjoying the world his words
described, where art and imagination ruled, tempered only by the
sometimes strange whims of the buying public.

"Perhaps not, Mr. Robertson, but if you let the joy go missing,
then all the rest is just so much drudgery. And there's certainly more
than enough of that, these days."

He studied her soberly. "Very true, Mrs. Chapman."

There was an awkward silence.

"Well! Before you go, perhaps there's something here for that
little daughter of yours who's missing her dad."

"For Jenny?" Sarah was surprised he remembered. Robertson
headed to one of the tables, continuing to talk over his shoulder.

"A sweet name, if I ever heard one. And you're lucky indeed
having a child by your side. My son, now, he's all grown up already.
Thinks he's something big at the shipyard downtown. Rumor has it,
he's making me proud."

Muttering to himself, he added, "No thanks to his mother, that's
for sure."

Then he turned around to Sarah and held out his left, uninjured
hand. Sitting up in the broad palm was a small crackleware bunny,
ears upright, blue eyes alert.

"Maybe this'll suit Jenny's fancy. Cheer her up a bit?"

Sarah started to protest, even as she smiled at the rabbit's silly
perkiness.

"And perhaps you'd consider it amends for my earlier manners?" Robertson went on. "I promise you, I do not make a habit of growling at customers."

Why not accept? Sarah thought. A gift freely given should be freely received. And Mr. Robertson was undoubtedly right that Jenny would adore the little figure. Certainly a more exciting memento from shopping than the drawing pad Sarah had found at Connors'.

"You are very thoughtful, Mr. Robertson," she began.

"Will Robertson, ma'am. 'Mr.' never set quite right."

She hesitated at the familiarity. Then she reached to take the proffered gift.

"You are very thoughtful, *Will* Robertson. My daughter will be delighted. And again, I apologize. I do not make a habit of snapping at total strangers. But I had better be on my way. You'll let me know when the order is done?"

"As soon as it's packed," Will nodded. "Mrs. Chapman, it's been a pleasure."

He bowed her through the doorway of the pottery. Sarah crossed the yard to Ebenezer, dozing in the shade, and climbed into the trap. As she gathered the reins to go, she was surprised to see Will still watching at the door. She bowed her head towards him as she pulled away and Will returned a loose salute in her direction. Sarah gave a quiet sigh and gave herself up to the rhythm of going home.

The robins were scolding their young to sleep and dusk was coming on as Sarah turned up the kitchen lamp. She wished she could just go out to the porch and sit for a spell, quietly rocking until the nighttime breeze picked up and began moving through the house. But it was Sunday, and time for letter writing. She composed herself and repeated her ritual incantation. *When writing to your loved ones ever strive for a cheerful tone.* It conjured up a lean, tan face carved with smile lines, and deep green loving eyes above.

Dearest Chappie,

It's hard to believe just a week has gone since I wrote you last. The time seems stretched somehow, perhaps from the heat. Is it anywhere near as hot there as the 90+ degrees we've had? I think we've all turned to soft rubber, and are stretching like the time,

41

oozing along from one patch of shade to the next. Even the geese on the pond have all but abandoned their squabbling and just drift lazily about, only emerging long enough for a snack in the orchard, then back they go for another dip.

Jen is in the water three or four times a day and I confess, I've spent more time there than usual as well. There is something infinitely luxurious about peeling off shoes and hose after a hot morning's work, and easing toes and ankles into water that still runs surprisingly cool. I dabble my feet and watch the ripples spread.

But enough of toes. The farm is holding itself together. The hot spells have made the tomatoes very happy. First squash are in and the beans are going great guns. We have a regular market stand set out along the wall: baskets and boxes of produce from all the extra we planted this season. Folks help themselves and leave money for what they take, on the honor system, mostly. I assigned Jen the task of checking the cash box two or three times a day, and she takes her responsibility very seriously, as you may imagine. It's not a get-rich-quick scheme, but we make better than pin money, and if food shortages become worse I believe we could sell everything we grow.

Sarah frowned and crossed out her reference to food shortages. She guessed Chappie must be eating poorly enough that reading about the farm's plenty would be as much as he wanted to hear.

Haying is finally done. I'm sure I never fully appreciated what a scratchy business that was, when all I saw of it was tidy hay mows and you with some straw in your hair. Now that the straw is in <u>my</u> hair, I find myself selfishly grateful for the limited rain we've had this year. Hub thinks we may not be haying a second time after all. There's plenty to get the livestock through the winter, don't worry, but we may not put much up for sale. The extra corn we planted last spring will just have to make up the difference. I believe it will, too. We've had lots of compliments on how sweet and tender it is.

What else to tell? She found it hard to get her thoughts beyond rows of vegetables and swathes of hay, cleaning the henhouse and keeping her own house halfway respectable. But a husband in France, whose waking hours were spent either in frustrating bureaucracy or horrifying scenes of war, did not want to read about scrubbing bathtubs. Sometimes letter writing was a challenge.

"Tsk!" Sarah shook her head at her own absentmindedness. She had forgotten curtain material in Dedham the other day. Not that she'd had a minute since to work on the curtains, she reminded herself. But there was a topic that might entertain Chappie.

I had quite a time in Dedham a few days ago. You remember I was thinking of taking a day to run errands?

Sarah went on to recount what she had seen and done. She described the surveyor's eagerness to talk to Chappie. She detailed her success finding dishes for Amy and Roger.

I confess I almost left the pottery empty-handed, though. First there was no one about to take an order; then the man who appeared was so unkempt, and so unpleasant that I was tempted to just walk away. Who should he turn out to be but the owner himself! Mr. William Robertson bears a remarkable resemblance to a large brown bear. I will say that his manner improved considerably before our business was done, and he even went so far as to send a little ceramic bunny home to Jen. I think he has a great fondness for children. Surely he must have had them in mind when he began making the charming borders on his dishes.

She laid down her pen and looked over what she had written. Four pages of close-written words to bring a semblance of home life to Chappie. Sarah tried to imagine where he would be as he read the letter, but found it impossible to do so. Any place in France, a grand room in a chateau or a corner in a noisy bistro, was equally beyond her imagining. Equally foreign, distant, hardly conceivable. A small, sharp pain suddenly gripped inside, under her breastbone. It wasn't physical, she knew. It was something between fear and anger at the gap she could not bridge between them.

Goodness! Look at my rambling. It's a good thing you'll be home in a month or two, or I'd turn incoherent. I will stop now, and save what other news there is till next week. Hub and Duddy send their best. I'm enclosing Jenny's latest work of art — a "portrait" of her Dedham bunny. All my love ever,

Sarah

* * * * *

43

August 14, 1917
Mrs. Sarah Chapman
Mill Farm Street
Medfield, Massachusetts

Dear Mrs. Chapman,
    Your order of dinnerware has been made up and is being packed this afternoon. We will ship it at your request, or you may collect it here at your convenience.
    Should you choose to come this way, I would be happy to offer you a short tour of the workings, or not, as you prefer.

> *I remain,*
> *W A Robertson*

*   *   *   *   *

A fresh breeze swept up Pottery Lane as Sarah turned the trap off the main road. The night's showers had washed away some of the dust, she noticed, but fluttering leaves in the vacant lot still drooped from lack of moisture. Across the lot, the brick pottery building rose three stories from the street, although its siting on a hillside reduced the back side to two floors. From the back, a long low ell stretched perpendicular to the main building, its roof pierced by two conical smokestacks that identified the kiln shed.

Sarah drove over by the loading dock and left Ebenezer in the only piece of available shade, next to the building. Then she headed for the entrance by the blue rabbit sign. As the door swung open, a clear-toned ringing startled her. Glancing back, she spotted a small brass bell still bouncing up and down on a metal strap behind the door. She was smiling at her jumpiness when Robertson's bass voice overrode the bell.

"Mrs. Chapman. You're not one to waste any time responding to messages. It's a pleasure to see you on this fine day."

Sarah turned around, startled again by the man's silent movements.

"Oh. Good morning, Mr. Robertson. I certainly appreciated the promptness with which you filled my order. You led me to believe it might take much longer than a month."

He was much better turned out than the last time she had seen him. Jacket and vest were in order, a clean white handkerchief showing in his breast pocket. His bow tie was somewhat askew, but it was tied and his hair was slicked down. More important still, there was a spark of good humor in his eyes that suggested this meeting would be significantly less stressful than their last encounter.

"Dame Fortune smiled at last this month," he explained. "We burned a full kiln and didn't lose more than a quarter. Even as we speak, there's a full shipment on its way to San Francisco and we've nearly enough wares ready to stock another kiln. So long's I don't lose another mold man to munitions work, we may even meet our orders this year."

Robertson's voice was warm with satisfaction at his success. His whole presence radiated an optimism Sarah hadn't imagined he possessed. She smiled at his pleasure and asked after her own order.

"I figured you'd probably want to inspect before you hauled it all away," Robertson replied. "Had Charlie leave the top off the barrel so we could dig some out. If you're willing to get sawdust on those skirts, I'll take you back to the packing room to see."

Sarah assured him sawdust was a good deal better than what she contended with at Mill Farm, and Robertson led the way toward the 'No Entrance' door where she had stopped on her first visit. This time, she stepped through to a dim hallway that held an open-cage elevator and a well-worn staircase. Sarah glimpsed a sunny room on the other side of the building before she followed Robertson into the packing room. A long table stretched down the center, with miscellaneous dishes left on it from the last shipment. The sawdust bin stood in one corner, next to ranks of strong wooden barrels. Sawdust and wood shavings carpeted the floor.

It was the smell of shavings Sarah noticed first, warm and fresh. She followed Robertson toward an open barrel by the table and saw a stack of saucers surrounded by cups, all resting in a pillow of sawdust. Stylized borders formed an intricate blue and white pattern against the tan shavings.

"Charlie left this for last. Wanted you to take a look and praise him on it, I suspect." Will held out a squat round teapot, belted with a band of clover leaves. On the lid, a leaping rabbit formed the knob as it raced toward its blue clover breakfast.

Sarah laughed in pleasure. "Oh, yes! It's wonderful!"

Will pulled out a covered sugar and creamer, and salt and pepper shakers. He burrowed under the saucers and brought up a shallow serving dish. Soon the table was mounded with blue and white as Sarah exclaimed over each new piece that appeared.

"There's a lot more, down underneath." He shook his head. "Probably should have left it out, after all. You interested in seeing the rest?"

"Interested, certainly, Mr. Robertson. But don't go unpacking any more on my account. These are perfect. I'll just be sure to be there when Amy and Roger unpack the rest. I can hear Amy carrying on now, she'll be so delighted." She stopped to survey the mess they had made. "But shouldn't I help you put this all back together?"

"Nah. I'll just track Charlie down and get him to deal with it. The boy needs exercise anyway, sitting on his keester all day. Hmm. Beg your pardon." Robertson was nonplussed for a moment. "Anyway, I'll go roust him out. Unless you want to come along?" he asked awkwardly.

"If it gives me a chance to meet the artist who painted all this, it would be an honor."

Will twitched his moustache in amusement and gestured her to the door. Sarah wondered if she should bring up the offer in Robertson's note to 'tour the workings,' but held her peace. She might be here at a bad time. A pottery owner was undoubtedly a busy man. Perhaps some workman could show her around though, just for a minute, before she went back to Mill Farm.

As they headed for the dim stairway Robertson turned to her and raised an eyebrow.

"Are you interested in seeing where the famous artist got his training?"

"Oh, yes! If you have time."

He smiled and called out, "Hey, Maudie. We've got visitors. You receiving?"

A soft murmur of response met them as they turned the corner and entered the sunny room Sarah had noticed earlier.

"Mrs. Chapman, this is Maude Davenport. Maudie, Mrs. Sarah Chapman has come to inspect the works."

The woman seated facing one of the long windows was completely still. Only the hand holding a long delicate brush moved over the surface of a tall vase. Her head was in profile, bowed toward her work, thick hair pulled back at the nape of her neck. High forehead, straight nose, lips curved in a ghost of smile. A white kitchen apron covering her dark patterned shirtwaist showed smudges of earlier work. Silent concentration, like a halo, surrounded her.

Will stopped where he was and waited. Maude finished the figure she was painting. A small sigh broke the spell, and she dropped her brush into the jar of cleaner beside her. When she turned to greet them, Sarah was struck by the aura of self-containment Maude Davenport possessed. Maude's gentle smile of welcome extended to her heavy-lidded eyes, but there was in them, as well, a quiet observation which studied, and learned, and stored away for future thought. Sarah could not imagine a more dramatic contrast than that between Maude and Will Robertson, with his ready opinions and open face, his vibrant energy and volatile temper.

Mirroring Sarah's thoughts, Will commented, "You might not think to look at her, but Maudie's the one who keeps us all in line around here. Not only is she our star painter, but she puts her hand to the books and she's a whiz at smoothing ruffled feathers. Especially mine," he added, and grinned at Maude. Sarah found herself wondering how long these two had known each other.

"If I were paid for feathers instead of pots, I'd be a rich woman by now." Maude's voice was gently teasing. There was definitely a familiarity between them, Sarah decided.

"If wishes were horses, Maudie..." Will turned back to Sarah. "Maude, here, is our chief decorator. Most of those magnolias and ducks and such are her doing. Special pieces as well — presentation trays and coats of arms and such."

Sarah nodded and turned to Maude. "I gather from Mr. Robertson that you are also responsible for training the rest of the decorating staff?"

Will guffawed and Sarah wondered what was so funny.

Maude smiled more gently and replied, "Our staff is perhaps a bit smaller than you expect, Mrs. Chapman. My brother Charlie is the only other decorator here right now, although he spends a good part of his time down at the potting wheel. I did have a hand in training him, back when he first started in '14, but there's little more I could teach him at this point."

She spoke ungrudgingly, clearly proud of her brother's talents. Sarah tried to reorganize her thoughts of how the Dedham Pottery worked as Will nodded in agreement.

"Aye, he has the makings of a real artist, that one. Give him a picture and he can whip it out before you can blink. Ships, houses — anything that comes to mind. And he's got the knack for the wheel. Throws a vase that'd make my father proud, and _he_ was a potter!"

Will glanced down at his maimed right hand and an expression of disgust crossed his face.

"Good thing, too. I sure as bejeesus can't do much in that line anymore."

Maude began to say something soothing but he cut her off and shook his head dismissively.

"No matter. Listen, Mrs. C., you want to visit here a bit while I roust out Charlie to repack the barrel? Won't take but a minute and then I can give you a quick look at what else goes on, if you're still interested?"

"Oh! Certainly. Whatever you suggest. I don't want to be a bother..."

"Not a bit." Robertson's voice was cheerful again. "Be back in a minute."

Sarah turned from watching Robertson leave to find Maude observing her with slightly surprised interest. The woman's calm study was somewhat unnerving and Sarah searched for a subject to draw attention away from herself.

"Do I gather Mr. Robertson was trained as a potter, then?"
Maude nodded.

"In the Robertson family everyone learned everything about potteries. 'Soaked up clay with mother's milk', is the way Will tells it. His Uncle Alexander trained him on the wheel and then, when Alexander went west, Will took over his work. Will was looking to be very good at what he did."

48

She paused, and stared out the open window.

"There was an accident of some sort?" Sarah probed.

"The kiln," Maude continued, her words quiet as if she were telling herself a regrettably familiar story. "It happened before I worked here but, as I heard it, someone sold them a terrible batch of coal. They used it to fire a kiln of greenware. First it wouldn't burn at all, so Will added more to raise the temperature. Then it swung the other way, out of control. He knew the whole kilnload could be ruined if they didn't damp it down again but it was too late. Something happened. Maybe some of the ware exploded from the heat, I don't know."

Maude's eyes swung back to Sarah and searched her face as the story ended. "Will was right by the kiln when a piece of it blew out. It was a miracle that only his hand was damaged."

Even as Sarah grasped the tragedy of what she heard, she could not escape the feeling of being quietly examined.

"Thank God he survived," she murmured. "But how horrible! To be a potter with a crippled hand."

There was a flash of approval in Maude's face, that Sarah appreciated the significance of a craftsman denied his craft. Then her attention was caught by a movement behind Sarah, and her slow smile returned.

"Eavesdropping again, Will?"

Sarah spun around in embarrassment, wondering how much Robertson had heard of their gossiping. He seemed more disconcerted than upset.

"I'm surprised at you, Maudie. Gossiping's never been your forte. But I'm sure you just saved me as bunch of awkward explanations." Robertson looked at the pained expression on Sarah's face. "Besides, I came out all right, I guess, didn't I? Nothing wrong that a shot of whiskey and a hot soak won't fix. Never win any exposition medals for my pots now, though."

Maude immediately protested in her quiet voice.

"Pots, no, Will, but glazes – you've never lost that." She turned to Sarah. "Will's a color wizard. He holds all the secret formulas that made this pottery famous and he's always dabbling with others." She lowered her voice conspiratorially. "Charlie swears that some days he can smell brimstone through the door of Will's mixing room. You're dealing with a magician of high order. Don't take him lightly."

Sarah smiled and took Maude's words as a way of changing to a less painful subject. "I wouldn't think of it. But I'm also beginning to realize just how much I don't know about what goes into making a pot."

"That's why I'm going to show you around," Will said cheerfully.

"Oh! Well, then, Mr. Robertson, I'd be delighted."

He stood aside to let her out the door, then led the way toward the stairs. Sarah turned back for a moment to thank Maude for her time, and found her with the same surprised interest on her face as when they'd first met.

"I never remember Will agreeing to give a tour before. It's been very nice to meet you, Mrs. Chapman."

"Thank you, and you too, Miss Davenport."

Sarah followed Will downstairs to a long room at the end of the building. A wide shelf ran around three sides, its surface laden with gray-coated tools and turntables, odd pots filled with unidentified substances and abandoned rags. Will wandered over to one of the turntables and lifted a cloth off an irregular lump of damp clay.

"Looks like Charlie ran out of clay again."

"Ran out?" Sarah asked.

"The boy's got all sorts of grand ideas for Chinese vases, only he gets so entranced by what he's potting, he runs out of clay before he gets to the rim. I've watched him flatten a dozen pots in a row before he'll listen to my advice."

His left hand reached out unconsciously, smoothing a lump out of the abandoned clay.

"These clay bats are all cut to size for certain vase shapes. But Charlie gets distracted and his hands start working on something bigger." Will glanced up at Sarah. "Gotta have enough material to finish what you start, I keep telling him, else it's all a wasted effort."

He gently spread the cloth back over the bat, his right hand awkwardly trying to copy what his left did easily.

"No good dreaming great dreams if you can't make 'em work," he continued to himself.

Sarah hastened to change the subject.

"I gather not all of Mr. Davenport's work has been wasted, if those are his?"

She gestured toward rows of shelving between two windows, crowded with pale gray vases of all shapes and sizes. Tall cylinders and squat globular bowls, long-necked bulbous bud jars, classical shapes from the west and from the orient. One short shelf held dozens of miniature forms, like dishes for large dollhouses, or for very small flowers.

"Depends who's defining waste, I guess. Those are Charlie's, all right. I tell him he's my right hand man now, taking over the wheel work. But then, along with the crackleware he's supposed to be making, he whips up all these and leaves them for me to glaze." Robertson scowled in a fashion that was not completely dissatisfied. "As if there's much call for art pottery with a war going on. Sometimes I think Charlie just makes them because Maudie puts him up to it. If I'm busy glazing, she insists, then I can't spend time worrying the accounts."

Sarah raised her eyebrows knowingly.

"I am discovering there is always time to worry accounts, Mr. Robertson, don't you agree? It is one of the chores I've been managing for Mr. Chapman, that I find more distressing than I care to say."

They nodded at each other in knowing sympathy.

"Then don't say it, Mrs. C. Let's take a gander at the rest of the works instead, and leave sums and figures for another time, when they can't be avoided."

Robertson led they way back out and continued their tour in the casting room, where two men were at work. One, pouring thick clay slurry into two-part molds, was making pitchers, Will explained. The other worker stood at a potting wheel like Charlie's, but the clay on the wheel formed a low dome over a circular form. The jigger, as he was called, operated a thin, shaped metal arm, which was pulled down over the clay and used to smooth it thin and flat. Eventually, after the clay dried, the piece would be lifted off its form and turned upright, when it became recognizable as a dinner plate, molded top and bottom in one quick operation.

Will and Sarah followed a boy carefully wheeling a cart of partially dried plates into the next room. They left him unloading pieces onto racks as they wandered up and down between banks of drying wares. Sarah spotted a row of bunnies like the one given to Jenny. Will pointed out the range of sizes of serving platters. Across a wide center aisle, Sarah exclaimed over row after row of ghostlike patterns. The cobalt, Will explained, would not come up bright blue until it was fired. Then he pushed aside a heavy rolling door. Beyond, were two bulbous brick structures. Sarah recognized the kilns whose chimneys she had noticed sticking through the roof.

"And here's where the pudding's proofed," Robertson announced with a dramatic gesture. "Every piece of ware we make has to go through both those kilns before it's done. It is one of God's greater miracles when the greater part of a batch survives."

"You lose many pieces when they're fired?"

"Oh lady, we're lucky if half comes out to sell. It's all in the temperature, you know, and the regulation of it. If the coal is bad, if the weather changes – sometimes if one pot decides to explode from air trapped or whatever – we can lose everything we've worked on for months. It happened this summer. Why, you'll remember – when you dropped in the first time, I'd been up, nursemaiding a glost firing all night. Very finicky. Sets the glaze. Temperature has to be just right or all sorts of bad things happen."

"You had trouble with that one?"

"So to speak. You remember that hot spell we'd been having? How it finally broke, the end of that day?"

"Oh, yes. It was wonderful! The skies opened up and poured down rain. Jenny and I went wading in the puddles before the rain even stopped."

Sarah caught herself and blushed at telling such a story to someone she hardly knew. For a moment Will just looked at her, then shook his head.

"The skies opened up all right. And maybe half the rain in Dedham funneled down the chimney of that kiln."

Sarah frowned at the half-understood implications.

"Temperature must have dropped five hundred degrees inside, in about half an hour. By the time that rain stopped there wasn't a single piece of pottery left whole in the kiln. We took it out with coal shovels."

"Oh, I'm sorry! How much did you lose?"

"That whole San Francisco shipment we just finally got out this week. Ten or twelve dozen pieces. There was even a saggar or two of stuff I'd been working on. Had great hopes for some of the glaze trials I'd done..."

His voice trailed off at the memory. Then he seemed to recover his equanimity. "That's why Charlie's been messing around with the vases. I think he thinks he's taking care of me, making sure I get some more pieces done."

Sarah gaped at him, clearly appalled.

"I cannot imagine how you all must have felt," she began, shaking her head. "You, the Davenports – why, everyone who works here. You put so much work into the pottery. And it can be ruined so quickly. Charlie destroying all those half-made vases. Or Maude getting one stroke wrong. You even describe the glazes as 'experiments'. And then this business with the kilns. Why doesn't it drive you mad?" Her voice had risen with the incomprehensibility of what she imagined. "How can you work, never knowing if anything will come of it?"

Will pondered her questions for a minute.

"Maybe it's what you learn to expect," he said slowly. "Not so different from farming, I would guess. You don't expect too much to go right in this life. But sometimes, you know, it surprises you. You open up a kiln and things are whole." He warmed to his subject and his voice lost its hesitancy. "A crack here, a broken saggar there, but all in all, the firing's good. First there's the relief, that you didn't do all wrong. As you unload, and see what you've got, you get feeling pretty good about making a product that looks good, that stands up. You have enough to make ends meet. The stacks pile up around you and your whole crew feels good."

Caught up in the telling, Will unconsciously reached out his hands as if to draw another container out of the kiln. "Then you pull out that one saggar you've been waiting for, and you lift off the top, cursing and praying at the same time that there'll be something worth the wait." His hands curved themselves around an invisible shape and lifted it to eye level. "And there's a ruby just the way you want it. Or a flow like molten lava down the side. A celadon to make a Chinaman cry."

He turned to Sarah with his invisible vase, his expression intent. "Not very many. Maybe half a dozen in the whole batch. But they're work to be proud of. They remind me what I'm in this business for. They bring a heart joy."

Suddenly self-conscious, he chuckled. "Besides, you sell one of those and you've enough to buy gold for the next batch. That's what makes the dragon's blood glaze, you know. Pure gold. And that, as they say, don't grow on trees."

Sarah stood spellbound by an extraordinary man's invisible dreams. The dreams and their intensity were not so different from Chappie's imaginings about the future, she recognized. It occurred to her that the two men shared the same drive. But Robertson was without Chappie's restraint, the self-control born of an old family and tempered by years of public life. Did Will choose not to hide his enthusiasms? Or was he constitutionally incapable of doing so? The ease with which he shared private thoughts was as foreign to Sarah as making pottery. She decided she liked his intensity. Enjoyed the way his stories took her far away from life at Mill Farm. When his rumbling voice recreated the disasters and discoveries that seemed to characterize his existence, she forgot the tiredness that always dragged after her. She put aside her constant fear for Chappie. Fear and tiredness weren't gone, of course, but Will's voice had a magic that kept them at bay. It would be nice to have that voice go on.

Suddenly she realized Will's voice had actually stopped. She scrabbled through her brain to find a comment to make.

"Gold? Is red?" She berated herself for her inanity. Will didn't seem to notice.

"Aye, the Chinese way. My dad spent half his life studying the ancient glazes, running himself near bankrupt to keep a stock of gold. Funny, hmm? Most people spend their lives making things to get gold. But not Hugh Robertson. He got gold to make things." He tipped his head, smiling at her. "Kind of backwards, wouldn't you say?"

"No," she said slowly. "Gold is only precious for its rarity. And it seems to me that what your father made, and you are making with that gold is more rare. And therefore more precious."

"I'm glad you think that way, Sarah Chapman."

"It must be wonderful to take part in a kiln opening. What you describe sounds so..." She groped for the right words. "So suspenseful, so exciting. And how exhilarating to have a successful one!"

"It's a good feeling," he said comfortably. "Though it's probably not quite so enthralling as I may have let on. If you're really interested, I'll let you know when we do another one – later this fall sometime, I'd guess."

"Oh yes, Mr. Robertson, I truly am interested. We don't see anything like that on Mill Farm."

Will nodded and turned to lead the way out.

"You don't indeed, that's truth. And it's Will Robertson, remember. 'Misters' don't muck up their hands with clay and coal and such."

As she followed him through the doorway Sarah noted, "'Misters' have no qualms mucking about with gold, though, do they?"

Will chuckled and headed back to the showroom where Sarah was immediately drawn to the long wall of shelves filled with vases of every conceivable shape and color. She hadn't really looked at them before, being bent on putting together a set of dinnerware. Now she realized that the glass-front cases at the Boston Museum of Fine Arts did not hold pieces more elegant or rarer than some of these. Prominently displayed at the front of the shelves were a handful of dragon's blood vases.

Will stood back and watched as Sarah explored the shelves. His gaze moved back and forth from her face to the pieces she examined, as if he, too, was seeing them with new eyes. Finally he stepped forward and reached down a heavy dragon's blood pot from the shelf. Cradling it in one arm, he took it to the window to catch the light.

"Robertson's Blood, my dad used to call it. He was working on this as long as I remember, trying to perfect the color. This is one I'm rather partial to."

Will smoothed his broad hand over the deep even crimson, nearly flawless from rim to base. Sarah found herself watching his fingers, fascinated by the delicacy of his touch on the gleaming surface. She looked away to break the spell.

"Robertson's Blood is a worthy name for it. What a satisfaction it must be – to know you have the rare capacity to create such beauty."

"What's rare is a person thinking that way. It won't put bread on the table, and it won't get the business seen to."

"Just the same, it seems to me that creating something beautiful must be as valuable as bread and butter. Especially now. Lord! It seems the armies and their madness destroy more beauty in a single day than can ever be made up for. But *you* are one of the ones who can put it right, Will. Who can create this beauty and pass it to all the rest of us ordinary people, to be shared."

She stared at him intently, suddenly urgent that he understand the importance of his own talent, not knowing what other words to use to convince him. Will met her stare in silence, brows drawn together as he mulled over her words.

"You're a deep one, Sadie Chapman." He spoke into the heavy stillness.

Sarah shook her head in embarrassment.

"Well!" she exclaimed briskly. "I think I was a bit carried away. It seems I have difficulty putting the war aside." She smiled politely. "I'm very grateful for your tour, Mr. Robertson, and very impressed. I had no idea how much went into a vase full of flowers! But I think I have taken up too much of your time. Perhaps we could see if the barrel is ready?"

Will set his shoulders back and stood tall, as if he were returning to duty from some distant place. He replaced the pot on the shelf and moved to the sales counter, talking as he went about packing and sales receipts. The atmosphere between them slowly resumed an air of normalcy, politely formal, friendly at arm's length. Sarah was eager to leave, hurrying now to put an end to this strangely intense encounter. As she put away her receipt, Will looked up from the daybook where he'd been writing.

"I thank you, Mrs. Chapman. For your purchase and your patience." He hesitated. "It's been a long time since I've thought on what I do. It seems you make the dragon's blood glow a little brighter."

Nodding his head once in her direction, he turned away, leaving Sarah to make her own way out the door.

Dearest Chappie,

No! No – no – no - no! How dare they keep you any longer? You belong here. You are more important here than any place they say you need to be! Just tell them you __must__ come home.

Sarah shook her head and brought her clenched hand down on the scrawled words. Of course she would throw this away. Of course she could not write to Chappie half the indignation and tears she had gone through in — was it only just a week?

She had been so elated when Mr. Sims appeared with mail at the front door.

"Looks like a letter from your husband, ma'am," he'd said, with no pretense of subtlety.

Sarah could barely wait for him to leave before she opened it. It was the letter she'd been waiting for, the one where Chappie would tell them how soon he'd be home. No exact dates, she cautioned herself as she tore open the envelope. The censors wouldn't allow exact dates. To protect shipping, they said. But at least she'd know whether he'd be home for apple picking. Maybe even for her birthday if they sent him soon.

Instead, what she'd read on the page was almost incomprehensible. Something about troops arriving daily. The Expeditionary Forces needing more help. Strengthen supply lines. Plan for the winter in Europe and then he'd be through.

But the end of the story was unmistakable. *I've put in a request for replacement but there is little prospect for immediate action, as the situation requires more men each day, rather than fewer. I cannot say with any certainty how soon I might come home. Suffice to say a few pairs of warm socks would not be out of order.*

Sarah could not hold back a cry. Socks! Was that all Chappie could think about? Socks? When he had just written to say their lives were put on hold? She almost couldn't bring herself to read the rest although, as she admitted later, those were the words that got her through the days to follow.

My dearest Sarah, how I miss you and Jenny every single day. You can imagine what this news has done to me, especially when I think how hard it will be on all of you at home. I would give anything to be back with you right now. The one thing that perks me up a bit when I think of being away from Mill Farm, is knowing I've left it in the best hands possible. *I kiss your hands, my darling, new calluses and all, and only wish I were there to do it in person.*

Then there was a wonderful note to Jenny. He even remembered she was starting school. And words of advice to pass on to Hub. A special request that Duddy save him some crabapple jelly. And loving, closing words for her. But he wasn't coming home. For three months now she'd counted every day. Picked herself up when she was tired, cheered herself when she was glum, reassured their daughter if she worried. Reassured herself, truth be told, that every single day gone by was one day closer to safety and the end of their own small piece of war. Now, all of a sudden, there was no end in sight and she didn't know what to do.

She crumpled up her scribbled rantings and began again. *Dearest Chappie.* Sarah paused to study what she had written, as if it might contain some significant message. She thought carefully of how she would proceed, lifted her chin and sat straighter in her chair, her stance shaping the verbal tone.

All is well but, as you will gather from the date, the hectic time of fall is here! I am sorry, my dear, for missing my letter-writing last week. We received the oh-so-sad news about your extending and are still trying to adjust to its significance. Then, what with apples and grapes and Jenny's starting school, last Sunday got away from me completely. Sometimes, you are so thoroughly a part of everything I do, I lose track of time.

That wasn't entirely true, but time had certainly changed its meaning since Chappie had left for Europe. Sarah frowned at the little calendar standing at her elbow. How was it, two weeks could actually have passed, when each day took forever? She went back to the page.

Here's some news to put a smile on your face. Our daughter is now an official first-grader! I drove her down to the South School the first day, all gussied up in new dress and pinafore, a big red bow in her hair. Poor Jenny couldn't decide whether she was thrilled or terrified. She was greatly relieved to find three or four other children there whom she knew from church and such, and of course Polly Whiting is also in her class. The tears when I drove off were in my eyes, not Jenny's, and I've heard nothing but good reports since.

Now Jenny and Polly go together, and we take turns carting them down and back, on the rare day they don't walk. Mrs. Whiting has kindly offered to have Jen stop at their house for lunchtime, since it's a good bit closer to the school than ours. It does seem very silent at home, though, without Jennie all day.

Silent, but certainly not restful. Most days she lost track of time as she milked the cows and helped Hub at the cider press, harvested the last of the sweet corn or began digging the root crops they had planted in such optimistic quantity last spring. As often as not, it was Duddy who welcomed Jenny home from school, set milk and cake before her as she heard the first news of a six-year-old's day. Sarah would only know Jenny was home when she heard her call at the end of a field row. She would lay down her spade just in time to receive an effusive hug against her dirt-covered apron. After that was just a blur of things to get done before the day was over. It was hard to sort out anything to write, but she had to make the effort.

Our commercial operations are chugging along. Hub and I were just saying that the cider mill is at the point of collapse from exhaustion: it seems that half the town of Medfield has decided to have homemade cider this year. Folks are showing up with baskets of the sorriest little pippins you ever saw, from trees that can't have been tended for years. There's a general feeling that supplies are going to be significantly scarcer – and dearer – before this war is done. Anyway, our own cider is excellent this fall, though the apples are smaller because of last summer's drought. Hub says to tell you that he will rebuild the frame of the press this winter (if it manages to hold together in one piece that long). He has managed to chase out a number of bats who thought to take over one end of the building. Needless to say, they would not have improved the cider-making!

The cost of firewood is skyrocketing, what with so much of the coal going to the war effort. Hub, never one to miss a chance at a profit, has cajoled one of the Peters brothers into helping him timber the Rocky Woods lot. Jack Peters has been cutting and splitting billets small enough for coal stoves. Hub seems to think they will bring as much as regular cordwood, and I'm not one to say him nay, with the price of coal more than doubled from last year. Besides, I saw a woolly bear crawling across the road the other day wearing a stripe an inch wide! If the old wives' tales are right, we may be in for quite a winter. Wait and see...

What else to tell? It's hard to think of much, we've been so busy with the regular round of harvesting, apple-picking, canning and such. The water is finally back up in the mill pond, and the swamp land upstream is good and wet, so we shouldn't have any problem starting up the saw mill soon.

By the way, I picked up Amy and Roger's dinner service a while ago. I was right that it would be charming. Pretty: different borders, and the blue color is very rich-looking, which I gather is particularly difficult right now. I had a chance to look around the pottery works a bit. It was surprisingly small but quite interesting.

She paused again, not wishing to go on about the pottery, searching for a cheerful note to end on, knowing the raging she felt inside would never do to come out. Her eyes strayed again to the little calendar where Jenny had so happily crossed off the weeks through August, thinking Daddy would come home soon. Now September was half done and the page was still unmarked. Jenny had turned her back on the calendar as on a personal affront, refusing to be cajoled into keeping the routine, and nothing Sarah said had made a difference.

Sarah picked up her pen and drew a line through two long weeks, then turned to finish the letter.

Every time I write you, my dear, I know your return is that much closer, no matter how protracted the delay. It's one of the reasons I look forward to Sunday evening – that and the closeness I feel as I write. We will survive this struggle, Chappie, no matter how distant or lonely we may feel. There is nothing else to do but persevere, I think, and hold fast to the knowledge deep in our hearts that we love each other.

She pressed her lips together and nodded decisively. One learned from one's letters, sometimes. She just wished it wasn't so hard.

Another week crept by and Sarah ached all over. Apple picking was endless. If she closed her eyes, clusters of red apples loomed all around her, just beyond reach when she leaned out from the narrow ladder. Or they bumped her on the head as she climbed the rungs. She knocked into them and watched, helpless, as they fell overripe to the ground, there to be consigned to the cider press or sold at half their value as drops for the preserving kettle. The Chapman orchards were much bigger than she'd ever imagined, now that there were only a couple of young boys to help with the work.

The grapes wouldn't wait either. The vines on Nabby's arbor had flourished in the hot summer. Clusters to be snipped, picked over, washed. Then she and Duddy stirring and watching the big pots, bagging the mash, hanging it to drip in the cold cellar. Back at it again the next morning, juggling sugar and scalded glasses, pectin and hot paraffin.

This was all undoubtedly good, Sarah reminded herself. The cold cellar bins and shelves would be full this winter if they didn't run out of sugar. But right now even a warm bath and a clean nightgown couldn't take away the ache. It was inside, under the shoulder muscles and within the very spine itself.

Sarah resisted turning up the lamp over the kitchen table. The last light of an autumn evening was gentle, and she had no desire to illuminate the way she felt inside. Every week brought its own reminder of Chappie's absence. Just as she felt she was conquering one of his routines – new chores she'd never done, new concerns she'd never had to think about – something else came up to make her wish him home again. She stared out at long shadows stretching across the orchard and absently began to write.

You were often in my thoughts today. A beautiful day – the bright September sunshine you love so well, and air so warm I went without a sweater while Hub and I worked. The Concord grapes are thick this year: great full clusters to make the yellowjackets happy. I know you can smell them if you close your eyes. The heavy, sweet, musky smell we've savored in the past. Next year, my love, we'll cut them together again.

The apples, too, are ripening fast. Winesaps and Cortlands are ready now, with Romes coming soon. We're running out of time to pick them all, before they drop to earth of their own weight, and we have to share with the deer and the coons. "Our" tree is aging, alas. What apples there are, are still as juicy as ever, but there are fewer now than when we first made its acquaintance. One of its forks split off in the hurricane last month.

I stopped for a minute this afternoon, and sat under our tree, while Hub was off tending to other things. When I closed my eyes you were almost there, sitting with me against the trunk, the way we did that other afternoon. Was it so long ago? The light filtering down through leaves and fruit was the same. The softness, the warmth. That heavy sweet perfume of Nabby apples around us. When you touched me I felt every whiff of breeze ripple over my skin. You kissed me then and I closed my eyes, the better to see your lips against mine, to hear your breath in my ear so slow and sweet. I can feel the weight of you the length of me, feel the earth beneath and you above, holding me safe. Safe enough to dare loving you. Caressing the side of your face, the strength of your back, the heat of all of you. I am weak with wanting you. Feeling you lift me away from anything we had known. We loved each other long and well that day! September sun will always be that love for me. You and apples, food and fulfillment. You are with me when I hold to this. I cherish you and our memories together. I will not let go.

Sarah's fingers pressed down on the words, holding them tight on the page. She glanced out at the deepening shade and drew a shaky breath.

The light is fading and I must go to sleep if we are to finish this work. Come with me, dearest. Curl up beside me so I can sleep with my arms around you again. Truly I need you now. The days are getting short. Strange, isn't it? With a houseful of people around me I feel so achingly alone.

The writing blurred through unshed tears. Should she send a word of this to Chappie? How would he take it? A memory to cherish, maybe, but where was the 'cheerful tone'? Sometimes the ache inside just crept out, all unexpected. Sometimes an uncertain future was too hard to hold onto. Future and past. Memory and hope. They held her life together. But the present was some purgatory conceived by a Puritan god testing, every day testing, pushing, pressuring a woman – soul and body – beyond bearing.

She dragged her eyes back to the letter. It was too dark to write anything different. She wasn't sure she could think of anything different to write. Slowly, she folded the page, lingering over remembered closeness and pushing back the time she'd be alone again. But finally it was done and she slipped it in the envelope engraved with her name. *Mrs. Henry Chapman, Mill Farm, Medfield.*

"Oh Chappie," she whispered. "I don't know how long I can keep doing this without you."

62

Tears spilled over and she closed her eyes, frowning as she tried to will them away.

"That's not true," she whispered more vehemently. "I don't *want* to have to do this without you any more."

CHICKEN SOUP

June 20, 1995

At the end of the Whitings' long driveway, Nora pulled in between a Suburban and a Volvo. Her dusty pickup was looking a bit outclassed until Peg Wentworth drove up in a worn station wagon. Kind of evened things out. Nora tried to stack a notebook, a pile of hand-outs and the bubble-wrapped Dedham bunny in one arm and reach for her purse. Her feet already hurt in their respectable shoes. The bunny package was gently sliding off the edge of the notebook when Peg came to the rescue, catching the bunny in a free hand.

"Thanks a lot. I seem to be all thumbs tonight." She felt a flash of irritation. This was not a promising start to her first Mill Commission board meeting.

"Nonsense," Peg contradicted. "You'll be fine. And you look very spiffy."

Nora clutched the papers in one hand and tried to straighten the skirt of her just-pressed suit.

"I wasn't sure how formal a board meeting would be."

Peg looked comfortable in chinos and a plaid shirt, with a lumpy canvas bag hanging from one arm.

"You'll do fine." The older woman's shrug dismissed clothing as an issue and they started toward the front door. "You all settled in the Shed?"

Nora's mood instantly improved. "It's better than I ever imagined. I wake up to *birds* every day instead of traffic. I haven't smelled a diesel fume yet. Really, it's a wonderful place."

Peg nodded. "It should be. After all, the Chapmans have had three hundred years to get Mill Farm just right. Though it always amazes me, how much work an old place like that needs. Lately, Hank's been playing with the orchard, but he had quite a job on his hands fixing up the Big House a few years ago. I don't know why he didn't stay in his folks' house, come to think of it, after all the work he did."

"I've met the Downeys," said Nora. She had chatted across the barnyard with the mother of the young family who lived there now. She had also been rammed by Jason Downey in his orange and yellow Kozy Koupe. The dad was still a face and a nod from the car window as he left for work. "Did Mr. Chapman sell the Big House, then?"

"Oh no, he's just renting it. He took over Orchard Cottage for himself, up at the head of the pond."

Nora remembered the roofline among the trees, and an upended canoe on the far shore.

Peg shrugged. "Guess it's just more his style."

The Whitings' door chimes cut off further questions and Nora made a last quick tuck of hair behind an ear. Peg was right. She'd do fine. After all, she'd already been working with three-fifths of the Board for two weeks. Hank Chapman was innocuous. Mr. Majors was the only one she didn't know. Nora tried out the smile her gramma had always said was one of her best features. She hoped it still worked. She was feeling edgy and didn't want it to show.

"Nora! Come in! Peg, good of you to come."

Ralph Whiting held open the oak-paneled door and gestured them down a carpeted hallway to the dining room. Jane Ogden was placing neatly typed secretary's minutes around a long cherry table where a heavyset man in a golf shirt had already claimed the far seat. Mrs. Whiting came in with a tray of sugar cookies and iced tea. "Dr. Tunney, Medfield has needed an archeologist for a long time. I'm delighted you took the Commission up on their offer."

Her greeting softened Nora's edginess.

Jane Ogden was nodding eagerly. "I've been telling my husband all about you, Nora. Joe is a Selectman, you know, and he *strongly* supports anything having to do with Medfield's history. He says you'll be doing a great service to the town!"

Nora smiled politely and tried to ignore the permanent whine in Jane's voice.

"That's very kind. I only hope I can live up to everyone's expectations."

She turned to the man who had stepped forward and now shook her hand emphatically. *Chevy-Suburban*, Nora thought as he introduced himself. He had a no-nonsense voice that matched his build.

"George Majors. Glad you've started at last. All this government red tape about surveys and permits has held things up at the mill long enough. Hope you can get rid of it soon."

Nora was instantly sure he doubted her ability to do so, whatever *get rid of it* meant. His appraising look said that what he saw was a long-legged female in a nice green suit. Chances were, he considered Gramma's charming smile to be a sign of feminine weakness. She dropped the smile and groaned inwardly. Was this what Hank Chapman had meant about Majors being 'an experience'?

"I certainly will try, Mr. Majors."

Hank himself walked in before she needed to come up with another pithy comment. He greeted the others and sent a pleasant smile in her direction. Hank's arrival seemed to be an unspoken signal for everyone to arrange themselves around the table. Cookies and tea circulated. Hank sat near the door, chair pulled back so his long legs had room to stretch. Nora couldn't resist the thought that it also made it easier to quietly bow out whenever he chose. Ralph Whiting, seated next to Hank, cleared his throat and got down to business while Nora pushed aside a half-eaten cookie and wished she hadn't been too jumpy for dinner. It seemed ridiculous now, looking at this handful of familiar faces gently munching away. A meeting was nothing to get hyped up about. Must have been putting on a suit that had done it.

"Well, Dr. Tunney," Whiting began. "On behalf of the whole Medfield Mill Commission, I'd like to somewhat belatedly welcome you to town, and tell you how delighted we are that you are heading up the Mill Farm Project. Tonight we're starting a series of what I think of as 'work in progress' meetings, where you can keep us all up to date on the dig and that survey I gather you have planned and we

..." – he gestured at the members around the table – "can get your advice on what to do next."

He seemed to lean just slightly on '*your* advice'.

"Ralph?" Peg looked up from an amorphous piece of knitting that had emerged from her canvas bag. "Before we start on the dig, maybe Nora could fill us in a bit on her own background? Not the credentials, of course. We know she's qualified. But I was wondering what led you," she smiled at Nora, "to a group of well-meaning beginners?"

Ralph nodded agreeably and Hank looked up from the minutes with some sign of interest. Nora sent Peg a small nod of thanks for giving her an easy entree. She hadn't thought the edginess had been so obvious. Still, it was a really nice thing for Peg to do.

George Majors raised an eyebrow at the end of the table. "Give us some idea why any self-respecting professional would end up with a bunch of volunteers, you mean."

So much for being at ease.

Nora wondered how to be succinct and satisfy George Majors at the same time. She probably shouldn't start with seventh grade, when Mr. Caton danced on the desks. Nor was this the occasion to expound her triple-decker-sandwich theory of history. Her answer came out severely edited.

"I've been interested in history, in the past, since I was a kid. Some good teachers helped."

Jane Ogden nodded seriously.

What more to say? By the end of high school she'd had visions of spending her life uncovering lost civilizations beyond the next shifting dune. But Arabia was a long distance and a big bankroll away from Lawrence, Massachusetts, well beyond the reach of the Tunney family. She set her sights closer to home, and journeyed to the wilds of Amherst and the Berkshire Hills.

"I learned about New World archeology while I was at U. Mass., and decided I really wanted to work in New England."

"Good choice," Mr. Majors grumbled, surprising her by his agreeableness.

"After all," Nora added with a gramma smile, "Egypt may have royal tombs, but a lot of this area is still a mystery, archeologically. It's a fascinating challenge."

Maybe Majors wasn't going to be such a hard sell after all. She gave the board brief details of some of the more interesting projects she'd worked on, editing out of the narrative her postgraduate lesson in real life. She had left U.Mass. in 1985 with a Ph.D. and the absolute conviction that archeology was the single most satisfying occupation imaginable. At first, work had been simple delight. Very soon, however, she discovered that, while everyone was fascinated by archeology, almost no one wanted to spend money on it. Of course sometimes they didn't have a choice. Federal regulations and historic preservation laws required 'cultural resource surveys' for government projects and protected properties. So Nora found herself a paying niche as a contract archeologist, hiring out to developers and utility firms to survey areas about to be dug up or plowed under. The leisurely, thorough work of graduate school gave way to a hurried document check and a sparse pattern of shovel testing for signs of human occupation. A report produced under pressure, a detailed bill, then a move to some other town or region or period of history. And always, always the hope that the next contract would include the satisfaction just missing from the last.

"So I've spent much of the past ten years working in New England, with a lot of jobs right around this area, as you know. But the contract work I usually do, doesn't have half the potential of what you've started here at Mill Farm."

She had the Commission's full attention now, talking about their own project. She'd skip her personal evolution, during ten years of short-term contracts, to a nomadic existence that substituted unmapped bogs and overgrown pastures for the deserts she'd once imagined. Sometimes she worked with partners, sometimes with a transient crew of graduate students, always someplace different. If it's Tuesday it must be Chicopee. Or North Adams. Or Dover. The work was often challenging. Sometimes it was satisfying, if she made an unexpected find, or managed to save a small gem of a prehistoric site. But the satisfaction was declining as the answers she found were outpaced by questions. Besides, her social life was erratic at best. Even Artie had taken to caterwauling when they migrated to another job.

Nora looked around the table at the Commissioners who could not imagine what a plum they had presented her. It was time to wrap it up. But she had to convey to this well-meaning group that they were doing something special.

"As a contract archeologist, everything I've been doing is strictly to meet State regulations. Of course we'll do that at Mill Farm too, but I've got to tell you how wonderful, and how rare, your idea is, of parlaying requirements into a community education project. It's really exciting to be working with people again who are actually *interested* in the archeological process! And based on all the arrangements you've made, I'd say we all agree that spreading that interest – that concern – is just as important as what we discover about the Chapman family."

Nora looked for the nods of approval. Clearly the community was thoroughly involved. They had put together the summer field school through Chickering College. They'd fixed up laboratory space in Chapman's barn with big trestle tables and plenty of light, where artifacts could be cleaned and sorted. There was talk of lectures in the fall and local cable coverage of the dig. George Majors commented first, leaning over the table, hands pushing against the edge. His opening words caught her completely off-guard.

"Look, Ms. Tunney, obviously a lot of people around here think archeology is very interesting, just for its own sake. I spent my share of time as a boy, too, hunting for bottles behind stone walls. But some of us," – he leaned heavily on 'some' – "*some* of us think the one real reason you're here is to make sure the books are right about Thomas Chapman putting up a mill in 1670. We don't want to end up with a restored mill that's not authentic."

He pointedly looked in Hank's direction for support. A small wave of dread washed over Nora. So many things in Majors' little speech made her nervous. It wasn't that he didn't seem to care about education. He had a really naïve concept of archeology. She'd be very happy to pin an exact date on the mill but she knew how uncertain site dating could be. Worse than that, if the Board was firmly convinced they were sitting on a three-hundred-year-old site, Nora could be in big trouble if the underground evidence didn't agree with the history books.

Peg Wentworth stepped in, using her knitting needle like a baton for emphasis.

"Oh, come now, George, we all know you just want to start hammering away at that mill with Hank. But I think we still need to be clear on what comes first. We hired *Dr.* Tunney ..." – the emphasis was subtle, but unmistakable – "... to do work we don't know how to do ourselves. Whatever ends up happening to the mill, this is where our money goes for the moment."

Nora suspected Majors and Miss Wentworth did not often see eye-to-eye. And what was that about Hank? Jane Ogden's high-pitched voice interrupted.

"I *do* think it's especially important, though, that Dr. Tunney spend her time finding proof of the Chapmans in the 1600s, don't you?"

She looked around the table for confirmation. Nora was trying to decide how to explain the limitations of archeological testing when Ralph Whiting stepped in.

"I don't think we need to see this as an either/or situation. After all, Mill Farm has been here a long time, and the grist mill won't change much if it has to wait a bit longer to be fixed up. Don't you agree, Hank?"

Hank was being annoyingly silent over in his corner. He raised his eyebrows and nodded. Whiting turned back to Mrs. Ogden.

"And Jane, I'm sure we all agree with you that we'd love to have Dr. Tunney uncover a lot of seventeenth-century information."

"Of course," she said positively.

"I think for now it would be fair to say we simply need her to tell us what is underground at Mill Farm. How we deal with it later on will depend on what she finds, don't you think?"

Assorted nods and mutters indicated the Commission's agreement. Majors gave an impatient shrug. Whiting straightened his papers in a clear signal that this line of discussion was ending.

Wait! Wait! Nora's brain protested. *What's this about restoration?* It was almost unbelievable that in this day and age some of the Commission might really want to "restore" the Chapman grist mill. The specter of Historic Disneyland in the heart of Medfield made her shudder. Make-believe history at its worst. As she wavered between forcing the issue right away and being silent unless spoken to during her first meeting, Ralph Whiting called the question.

"I'd like to suggest we postpone further talk about results. After all, Dr. Tunney hasn't even had a chance to brief us on her plans yet. Perhaps another session next week might be useful. But right now let's take a few minutes to go over the work that lies ahead. If we may, Dr. Tunney?"

Nora had calmed down by reminding herself the Mill Commission would never have enough money to build a historical romance, whatever they were thinking. Besides, her real job for the evening was to present a broad research design. If she could just get the Commission to think beyond 1670 and restoration, they'd see for themselves how much more was involved than snatching one year out of history. *Sufficient unto the day...,* as Gramma used to say.

Nora gently began removing tape from the bunny packet, knowing the blue and white figure would do more than any words to refocus attention. The rabbit made its way around the table and she began her overview.

As she talked, she reflected on the rare luxury of spreading a survey over two whole seasons. Her unorthodox procedure of starting the novice crew with some trowel-and-dustpan experience was possible because of time. There would be time enough to map not just the town's three acres, but all of Mill Farm. Below-ground testing wouldn't be limited to a few widely-scattered test pits. The larger site survey could wait until next season, if the cellarhole turned out to be really interesting.

Much to her surprise, Nora walked the Commission through a two-year survey schedule with barely an interruption, and not a complaint to be heard. Ralph Whiting's diplomacy must have worked. On the other hand, maybe the Board was just waiting for her to dig herself in a little deeper before they attacked. By the end of the meeting, though, it really did seem that the members were impressed by Nora's planning. Even George Majors.

"Very thorough," he pronounced as he headed out.

Ralph ushered the others to the door as he complimented Nora on her 'breadth of vision.' Jane Ogden had Hank entwined in a lengthy description of the bunny discovery, to which he was listening with polite patience. Peg's help loading things back in the truck brought her earlier help to mind. Nora held out a hand in thanks and felt a reassuring familiarity about the other woman's callused palm. Peg smiled.

"Good job tonight. I think you weathered George Majors very well."

"Thanks. And thanks especially for keeping me from feeling completely on my own."

"The others aren't so bad. Jane and Ralph. Hank's a keeper, I've always thought, though he had surprisingly little to say for himself tonight."

"He's not always like that?"

"Oh, no. He can be positively voluble."

"I guess it's good, that he isn't voluble all the time."

"Not like some people," Peg agreed. "Only when he has something to say."

They wished each other good night and Peg headed for her station wagon. Jane Ogden, bunny saga finally done, waved gaily as her Volvo rolled down the drive.

Nora turned to find Hank across from her, his arms propped on the side rail of her truck.

"Your talk tonight was interesting. Can't wait to see what shows up on the rise."

This was the donor, Nora reminded herself, bound to be interested in the project even if his motives weren't clear.

"You're welcome to join us sometime," she said. "Every day except Wednesday during the week."

He was shaking his head.

"Saturday morning, too, if that's any help."

"Not right away, I'm afraid. This is our busy season."

She remembered the trip to Montana that had kept him out of the interview process.

"More cross-country business trips?"

"Just local this time." He remembered it too. "But I work in construction. We start at seven to beat the heat."

"Sounds like an archeologist's schedule. What are you working on?"

"Stabilizing an old house in Salem. The whole place is rotten, so we're propping it up before it all collapses."

Her eyebrows rose unconsciously. Big construction companies and Federal sea-captain's houses rarely went together.

"Are you doing a conversion of some sort?" Artsy condos, say, oldie-looking outside, state of the art kitchens and master suites within.

"No. Just repairs for a client who can afford it."

"I can imagine new sills don't come cheap," she said cautiously. "Do you do much work on old houses?"

"Old buildings of one sort or other. Somebody's always looking for a way to keep their landmark from falling down, you know."

"I'm sure." She tried to keep her tone inoffensive. "But some of that work is really quite specialized, isn't it?"

"Oh, yeah. I've worked with a mason who builds perfect dry-laid stone walls, but who insists we get someone else for seventeenth-century chimneys. We've had a wood carver who only does Arts and Crafts, and plasterers who stop at rococo. But it's always interesting, working on old buildings."

"I guess I didn't realize you did preservation work." She felt her way forward. "That's why you gave Chapman's Mill to the town, isn't it? To 'keep the landmark from falling down'?"

An idea was tingling in her brain. She hadn't defined it yet, but Hank Chapman's view of his mill was definitely involved.

When he finally answered her question, he spoke as if he were feeling his way around a thought that had been growing for a long time. "I've always thought Chapman's Mill was special because it used to be a *working* building. Just the kind of building most people think is ugly. I always liked it because of what it did. It provided the food people ate and the fodder for their animals. It's an important building and people need to understand that. That mill is just an incredible survival."

Hank stopped abruptly, but he looked hard at Nora, as if he were willing her to agree. She couldn't believe her luck.

"You know how rare it is to think that way, don't you, Mr. Chapman? Nine out of ten people I meet would rather tear down what's old and put up something new."

"Criminal waste," he spat out. He paused and in the silence Nora could almost hear his thoughts shifting. Eyebrows raised, he continued lightly. "But I guess we have something in common. We both like old stuff, hmm?"

"So it seems." A good time to push her advantage. "Speaking of old stuff, any luck finding family papers yet?"

"Papers. Yes, well, I haven't had much chance to look. Maybe when the rains come."

"Don't even think that. The rains come and we lose valuable work time."

"So do we. But if I'm not working I can look." Hank pushed himself away from the truck. "Anyway, I'll let you know. Congratulations again on tonight's performance."

A nod and a flash of easy grin as the ambulance rumbled to life, and he headed down the driveway. Nora pushed aside the irony of Hank's viewing her report as a performance, and concentrated on what she'd just learned. Maybe Hank Chapman wasn't such a lightweight after all. Whatever his big construction firm was, it seemed to have some sense of responsibility about old buildings. Seemed to understand what preservation was all about. It might not be into Historic Disneylands after all.

A slow smile spread across her face as she followed the little round ambulance taillights down the drive. Long ago, Gramma had cautioned her to be silent unless spoken to. And this was why. The idea that had tingled in her brain came clear. There was no need for her to make a big stink about restoration. The board had its own full-fledged preservationist. Hank Chapman would never go for restoring that mill. Fixing it up a bit, sure. But keeping all its layers of history intact. Not turning it into some kind of hokey museum. Of course he didn't seem to be much of a talker, she cautioned herself. She might have to prod him into speech when the big debate came. And it would come, eventually.

She hitched her skirt up far enough to make driving comfortable, and turned onto the short road home. For now it was enough to do what she was hired for, and know she had an ally on the Board.

The next day was Wednesday, Nora's weekday off, and her hands were coated with chicken grease when the door knocker clunked. Few things in the world were worse than stripping a chicken carcass –

something about all that fat made her think she'd never be clean again – but being interrupted in the middle of the job was high on her list.

"Just a minute," she yelled, frantically trying to run water hot enough to wash off some of the grease. "I'm coming!" By the time she could touch the doorknob, she was sure it would be too late, but a knock at her door was rare and she was curious.

The Shed's door led out of the storeroom-entry where Nora's refrigerator stood, too big to squeeze into her kitchen. Outside, a thick granite step welcomed visitors, but there was no roof overhead. In bad weather, she had already learned, you had to find your house key first, or risk getting wet.

Hank Chapman was very wet by the time she got the door open. Rain dripped off his long, straight nose and sheeted down his green slicker to form dark patches on the knees of his khakis. Nora was horrified.

"I'm so sorry to keep you waiting."

She stepped back to let him in but Hank continued to stand in a puddle on the step.

"I should have called first..."

Nora followed the direction of his look and decided her grease-spotted apron and baggy sweats might be discouraging. Come to think of it, they weren't exactly company clothes. But it was too late for that and he was soaked. She waved him in with a damp hand towel.

"No, no. It's fine. I'm taking apart a chicken, that's all, and couldn't touch anything. Come in. Take off your coat. What can I do for you?"

Hank ducked his head to make it under the lintel. Just inside, he opened his slicker and carefully eased a plastic-wrapped packet out from under his arm. He set it on a counter by the door, taking pains not to drip on it.

"I came across something you might want to look at when you have nothing better to do."

Nora was torn between Hank's packet and the chicken. His careful handling was intriguingly at odds with the offhand comment. Still, the chicken seemed more immediate. If she could finish the mess, she could get thoroughly clean. His next words made her decision simpler. Hank had done what she asked.

75

"I had to get into the attic the other day and remembered you were looking for memorabilia. Found this bunch on my way down."

"Really! Listen, could you take off your coat and come in? If you wouldn't mind waiting just a couple of minutes, I'll be done with the chicken and clean enough to touch whatever's in that."

She gestured toward the plastic with her chin.

Hank nodded agreeably and Nora left him to hang his dripping coat in the entry while she went back to work. It occurred to her that she was being very cavalier with a man about to give her research material. On the other hand, this *was* her day off. And clearly his construction job had been rained out, so he probably wasn't in any hurry. Sociability was all the occasion called for.

"Help yourself to a beer if you want," she called over her shoulder. "There's some in the refrigerator."

Hank came into the kitchen with a Boston Ale in one hand and his mysterious packet in the other. He settled comfortably on a stepstool as Nora finished picking the carcass clean.

"I just need to get this on the stove. It's the remains of Sunday dinner, and I'm hoping to eat it tonight."

"Looks promising. Do you spend a lot of rainy days in the kitchen?"

"Oh no!" Nora bristled. "I'm usually in the lab, or doing course preparation. I spent last week's rain at the State Archives. I have all the field notes to write up."

In fact, she loved being in the kitchen. It always conjured up her mother, who was forever cooking. An old-fashioned woman, Mom's idea of the proper venue for a heart-to-heart talk was across a cutting board covered with carrots and onions – or stripping a carcass for the pot. But the association seemed out of place here, and Nora felt awkward that her domestic, unprofessional side was showing.

"It's my day off, you know," she finished defensively.

"I don't want to interrupt anything. This stuff can wait."

"Don't be silly. I'll be done in a second. Tell me what you brought."

"Old letters."

"Letters? Great! Who are they from?"

"Sarah Chapman."

Hank took a drink of his beer and Nora waited for more information, but none came. She tried to draw him out.

"Am I right in thinking there's more than one Sarah in your family?"

"Could be. I haven't spent much time on genealogy. This was my grandmother, though."

"Well, tell me more. When were they written? Who are they to?"

Hank sighed as if the answers were hard to come by, but his tone warmed as he started talking.

"It's a bunch of letters all addressed to my granddad, Henry Chapman, in Europe during World War I. They were in Gram's trunk upstairs. Funny," he added in an aside, "I'd never looked in that trunk since I moved it over from the Big House. I really don't think they have anything to do with archeology, but maybe there's something you can use if you want to take a look."

"Of course I do! They sound fascinating. Have you read them yet?"

"Not really. I looked at one of the first ones... I knew my grandmother when I was a little kid. She was ancient. A hundred years old at least, I was convinced. Looking at that letter was really disconcerting, like meeting some brand new relation. She talks about running the farm, tells Granddad about 'little Jenny' – that's the dowager aunt who must have been in her seventies when I was growing up."

Hank hesitated, puzzling over what he had found. "And she draws Granddad close, somehow, almost as if she's chatting with a man right beside her, instead of writing to him across an ocean."

"It was really disconcerting." He repeated himself. "I felt like a peeping tom, opening somebody's love letters. A young woman writing to a young man whom she clearly loved very much. It was a view of my grandparents I'd never even considered."

Nora was struck by the flood of words from this usually terse man. Peg, she remembered, had commented about Hank's being *positively voluble when he had something to say*. These letters had certainly set him off.

"They sound impossibly romantic. Did she write for a long time, do you know? Are there any from him?" The last of the scraps went into the pot.

"Not really long. Maybe a year and a half, judging from the postmarks. They all seem to be in her handwriting, though. And there weren't any more in the trunk. I guess his are gone."

"That's a shame."

"Yeah. Those would be real history, wouldn't they? Can you imagine reading what he wrote about the Great War?"

"I don't know. It probably depends on what the censor left on the page. But I'd guess you've found a gold mine of turn-of-the-century Mill Farm information anyway. And frankly, that's what interests me the most."

"Really? Well, whatever you say. I'll just leave these here for you to go through when you feel like it. Maybe fill me in on any spectacular finds."

Hank sounded relieved as he started to deposit the package on the kitchen table. Suddenly it was important to Nora not to let him off so easily.

"I'd much rather have you take part in this, Hank. You'll know what Sarah Chapman is referring to when she describes something around here."

"Nah. You're the critical reader. I'd just take things for granted, about Mill Farm, and the family."

He was being awfully quick, making excuses. "Why don't you just call me if you have a question? You can always let me know if you find any details that could help with the dig – or the mill restoration."

"Restoration?" Nora feigned shock. "You mean preservation, I hope."

"Whatever," Hank replied easily. "I leave semantics to the politicians."

Nora assumed she should feel reassured by his casual agreement, but the political part of her wanted to make certain it was only semantics, not something more essential, that separated their points of view. She put the stew pot on the stove and added peppercorns as she considered how to proceed. She needed to get to know Hank Chapman better, to understand where he was coming from. He was giving very mixed signals about his family history. First seeming disinterested, then unearthing the letters; getting caught up in one, but holding back from reading more. It would be fun to look at Sarah

Chapman's letters. Maybe an hour or so of handling original documents, looking for clues, was just what was needed to put them on the same wavelength. Nora scrubbed her hands and gave Hank an ingenuous smile.

"Listen. I have a suggestion. What if we both read through just a few letters before you leave, so I can make sure I'm on the right track, and then I'll read the rest another time?"

Glimpses of the laundry pile in her bedroom, the notes she hadn't transcribed, the rest of the cooking she had planned, were shuffled over to a corner of her mind and she began looking forward to her own proposal. Her thoughts stopped short as she realized Hank wasn't answering.

"Of course if there's something else you need to do ...?"

Hank had paused by the table, scowling at the packet of letters. When he looked up again his expression was reluctant, but he nodded at Nora.

"I'll stay for a bit. It's my day off too, after all. Might as well spend it someplace dry and smelling of food."

She couldn't resist raising an eyebrow at his choice of reasons for staying, but kept her voice encouraging as she untied her apron.

"Then why don't we go on in the living room? The light's better and the seats are a lot more comfortable."

Hank led the way and commandeered the old corduroy chair. Artie, the cat, promptly curled up across the back, as if the two were old friends. Nora stifled brief thoughts on fickle male friendship and settled herself to do some work.

When Nora stood up to unkink her legs she realized their letter reading had lasted a lot longer than an hour. The drizzle was fading to dark gray outside the windows, and Artie had climbed down from Hank's chair, insisting it was time for supper. Hank glanced up with a vague smile, then returned to a closely-written page. While Nora opened new cat food she decided the afternoon's exercise had turned out better than she could have hoped.

They had found dozens of details in Sarah Chapman's letters that brought wartime Medfield, and Mill Farm, to life. Descriptions of plants and apples, tales of chickens and a barnyard character named Ebenezer. The saga of the hired man saving the old mill from washing downstream in a flood. All the things that Sarah found herself responsible for doing because her husband was half a world away. The carefully downplayed problems of a woman running a farm alone. It was clear even to Nora's urban eye that the work was endless. Why Chappie hadn't stayed home made no sense – he certainly must have qualified for an agricultural exemption. Had he decided to be a hero? She didn't want to hear Hank's opinion. He'd side with the man, whose sense of calling apparently came before his own wife. Nora had very little tolerance for Chappie's kind of altruism.

On a less contentious topic, they found out that Mill Farm Street was still a dirt road, and that the pond seemed to be a favorite hangout for local youth in hot weather. Nora was just thinking the letters put a fascinatingly personal spin on the study of landscape history, when Hank interrupted.

"Yes!"

He must have found another gem. Nora was surprised he'd become so engrossed in the reading. She had guessed he would bolt after a page or two, but that had been ages ago. He seemed to have gotten over his uneasiness, but it struck her how different it must be for him, reading words his own grandmother had written. In her case, Gramma Tunney had been alive not so long ago. Nora still heard echoes of her words. But Hank was hearing a literal voice from the grave. That had to be disconcerting.

"Yes, what?" she asked, putting fresh water down beside Artie's food. The cat didn't notice, his fuzzy white nose buried too deep in chopped veal to be distracted.

Hank came into the kitchen waving a page.

"I found my house! Listen." He scanned down to the words. *"Our commercial operations are chugging along. Hub and I were just saying that the cider mill is at the point of collapse... He says to tell you he will rebuild the press this winter.* Wait a minute..."

Hank flipped the page. "Here it is. *Hub has managed to chase out a family of bats who thought to take over one end of the building. Needless to say, we felt they would not improve the cider making."* Hank peered over the top of wire-rimmed spectacles with a grin so broad it made a dent in one cheek.

Nora was confused. "You're going to have to connect bats and cider and your house for me."

"Oh. That's not really obvious, is it? I'd always heard that Orchard Cottage used to be a cider mill, but I'd never found any real evidence. I figured it was just a storage shed in an orchard; that somebody had misinterpreted the cider press, the "mill", as a whole building. But here it is. Bats don't live in cider presses."

Nora was more struck by Hank's ability to interpret obscure information than by what he had found. It must be a side benefit of preservation work – this talent for understanding old building details.

"How did it turn into a cottage, do you know?"

"Sometime in the '20s my great-aunt, Amy, moved in. I think Granddad had it fixed up for her for some reason. He did a great job. Turned it into an English cottage with added perks like plumbing and a formal terrace. You'll have to see it sometime."

The flow of words was back. Nora remembered the tantalizing glimpse of roofline and green lawn that was all she could see of the Chapman cottage. It was what she thought of as a Long Driveway house and she was dying to see it.

"That would be nice," she said, carefully noncommittal. "Is there anything left of the cider-making operation?"

A twinkle came into his eyes. "The bats never left, for all Hub's efforts. There's still a family living between the attic and the lean-to. They twitter at me in the evening when I'm out on the terrace."

She looked at him with mild horror. "You haven't done anything to get rid of them?"

"Oh, no, we've got a good relationship. I provide them a quiet rafter to hang from; they keep the mosquitoes down. Not a small trade, since I'm next to the pond. I'd have to resort to screens, without the bats and swallows."

"Spoken like a true preservationist." Neither Lawrence nor Somerville had bred large numbers of mosquitoes, so Nora found little to recommend Hank's idea of natural pest control. "I'll take a dry backyard or a nice screen porch any day. Bats remind me of too many horror movies."

She led the way back to the living room and picked up the next letter in her stack as a way of changing the subject. The first thing she noticed was Sarah's mention of apples.

"Here's more about the cider making."

Hank peered over at her.

"It's dated September 20. Sarah writes, *The apples, too, are ripening fast. Winesaps and Cortlands are ready now, with Romes coming soon.*" She skimmed down the page looking for mention of other varieties, not paying much attention to the gist of what she was reading. "Mmm, sounds good. *That heavy sweet perfume of the Nabby apples around us. When you touched me I felt every whiff of breeze ripple over my skin. You kissed me then and I closed my eyes as I do now, to better see your lips...*"

Nora suddenly heard the words she was reading aloud and her cheeks got hot. This wasn't cider making. This was a love scene.

"Well, there's more. But not about apples. Maybe this is one you should read yourself."

Hank's expression was somewhat stunned as he read the rest of Sarah's letter. Afterwards they sat in silence and thought for a bit. Hank was the first to venture a comment.

"That's what I meant earlier, about feeling like a peeping tom."

Nora nodded. She agreed. The letter was embarrassing. So personal. So evocative. She found herself heaving a great sigh.

"Hmm?"

"I can't imagine what it must have been like – having a husband but not having one, with Chappie half a world away."

"Well, it wasn't as if she was all alone here."

Hank reacted to Nora's expression of disbelief by hurrying on.

"I mean, you're right of course. It must have been tough, but Hub and Duddy were here to help. Jenny to care for and play with. And Sarah was in a familiar place after all, not like her husband, getting shot at in some foreign country."

"That letter is not referring to helping out and child play," Nora reminded him.

She was going to go on, say something about Mill Farm not being such a familiar place if so much had been changed by Chappie's absence. But before she could, another thought silenced her. What did she know about marriage, or permanence, either one? Maybe being at Mill Farm *was* enough. The sense of belonging, the way she'd felt about their old house on Preston Street. Home base, where every room had associations, every chair had personality, and she could count on it never changing. Then the senior Tunneys had sold out and retired to a townhouse that, for all their trying, would never be home base.

"Do you feel that way about this place?" she asked, off on a tangent. "The familiarity, I mean...? Do you think all those generations of Chapmans living in the same place make a difference?"

"Probably, but I've got to say 'all those generations' can be a lot more nuisance than the bats you shudder at." There was a troubled look on Hank's face. Then he shrugged it away. "Other times, you may be right. I don't know about comfort extending beyond lifetimes but Mill Farm's a good place to be. Every time I go away, I know it feels good to come home."

A self-deprecating smile went with his final confession. "I can't really imagine living anywhere else."

What was there to say after that? A simple research exercise had turned into a half-day exploration; a letter had dug too deep, and both Nora and Hank found themselves confronted by thoughts too weighty for the occasion. As often happened when she found herself at a loss, Nora thought about cooking, and the smell of chicken broth offered a perfect change of subject. She jumped up and headed for the kitchen.

"The soup! I forgot all about it. Would you excuse me a minute?"

Hank's voice followed her from the other room.

"I should probably be going anyway. I'm sorry this took up your day off."

"No, no," she called back to him. "This has been fun. I just have to add some vegetables before it's too late. You want to stay for supper?"

She heard the carefully nonchalant voice she'd used earlier, when Hank half-invited her to see Orchard Cottage. She also reminded herself about the pitfalls of mixing business and pleasure.

"Hey, I'd love to." He sounded genuinely interested. "But I promised a client I'd drop by with some plans this evening. I'm guessing, from the smell, that that was a bad call. Any chance of a rain check?"

"No problem." A touch of disappointment, perhaps... "If you could hold on a few more minutes, though, I'll give you a batch to take home. There's enough here for the whole field crew."

That offer was enough to bring Hank to the doorway, grinning appreciatively.

"I never turn down home-cooked food. What can I do to make up for it?"

"You can go back and make sure we haven't skipped anything really important while I finish here. You know, glance through what's left. I'll go through them more thoroughly another time; I just want to make sure we haven't missed another cider mill or something."

Hank obeyed, and there was a comfortable silence as Nora added chopped parsley and herbs to the broth. A few minutes later he walked quietly back into the kitchen holding one of Sarah's letters and a piece of what looked like blank newsprint. He leaned against the doorframe and nodded in Nora's direction until she was thoroughly self-conscious.

"What?" The question came out sounding testy. "Did you find something?"

He continued to nod over his silly glasses. "I found something you won't believe. It's exactly the kind of thing you've been looking for."

"Are you going to tell me what it is, or just stand there nodding?"

"All right. Sit down."

Nora gave the pot a final stir and grabbed the stool, while Hank ponderously arranged himself on the other side of the kitchen. She thought he looked as if he were about to deliver a pronouncement.

"This is one of the early letters, that we set aside to read another time. Written during the summer before the cider-mill letter. Remember Great-aunt Amy of the Orchard Cottage? Well, apparently Sarah took it into her head to buy Amy's wedding present and guess where she went?"

Another suspense-building pause.

"The Dedham Pottery."

He stopped to let that sink in. A tiny suspicion of excitement began to warm Nora's middle. Had Hank actually found something significant?

"She talks about the china she picked...about the Pottery owner – he sounds like quite a character – and then she writes..." Hank had the grace to leave only the smallest pause before he started quoting.

"Mr. Robertson... even went so far as to send a little ceramic bunny home to Jen."

84

A small sound escaped Nora, but Hank held up a hand and said, "Wait, there's more. Down at the end she writes, *I'm enclosing Jenny's latest work of art - a "portrait" of her Dedham bunny.* And here it is."

With a flourish, he drew the newsprint sheet out from under the stationery page and held a child's drawing up for her to study. A blue-outlined bunny sat in great bursts of vivid grass, with a smiling sun-face overhead. His two ears stuck straight up. All that was missing, Nora thought, was a broken tip on one ear for it to match the rabbit Pam had found among the lilac roots. It was as close to corroboration as an archeologist could reasonably expect.

"*Terminus post quem*," she whispered.

"What?"

"The 'point after which' something becomes an artifact."

For the next few minutes Nora alternated between effusive exclamations and disjointed explanations of archeological time sequencing. Every minute or so she would stop to look at the drawing again, marveling that such an astonishing correlation had survived. Eventually, when she calmed down, she ladled quantities of hot soup into a plastic container and urged Hank to take more, despite his insistence there'd be none left for her.

Finally Hank headed for the door. He arranged to collect the letters the following weekend and admitted that reading them hadn't been as bad as he'd expected. They made a date for Hank to give Nora a proper tour of Mill Farm. She gave him an unselfconscious hug of thanks and waved him off, feeling a whole lot better than when she'd opened the door four hours earlier.

Nora was so elated that her own bowl of soup was almost gone before she remembered the discussion of mill preservation strategies she'd hoped to start with Hank. Nothing was lost, she thought comfortably. Sunday's tour would provide a perfect on-site opportunity to enlist support. She poured a cup of tea and went back to Sarah's letters.

DRAGON'S BLOOD

October 1917

The harvest rush was finally over. The brilliance of colored maples had mellowed to russet and burgundy oaks, as the season itself slowed down on the way to winter. There were still warm days. A spate of Indian summer had brought out all the yellowjackets desperate to survive and put the orchard, with its insect harvest of mushy drops, off limits to the children.

Mostly the weather was gray, though, as it was when Sarah set out for Dedham again. The sky was thinking about rain, but she guessed it might think about it most of the day without producing more than the gentle mist which softened the roadway now. She guided Ebenezer to the verge as a trolley went by. She could have taken the trolley, herself. Walk just up to Main Street and flag one as it came by. The line ran right into Dedham Square. But Sarah liked the quiet sounds of plodding hooves and iron wheels on the dirt roadway. Somehow time on the road was not lonely, like so many moments at home. This was time to mind-wander as the rumble and clop set rhythm to stray thoughts, or the flock of geese in the field nearby drew attention out of herself altogether. That was part of it, she was certain: on the road she lost consciousness of herself. Rather, she sat as silent observer, thoughts and sensations flowing through her as she filtered out a few for memory to work on later. It was very peaceful.

Only when she neared the Square did she recall the errands that brought her, and she mapped them out in her head as she turned

Ebenezer toward the Registry of Deeds. She was determined not to spend much time on errands. There would be time left, she promised herself, for an hour or two in the reading room of the historical society. She'd meant to stop in months before, to look for a Chapman genealogy, but somehow it had been put off for other things. Now, if the rain didn't come too soon, she would finally do it. A way of drawing closer to Chappie, maybe finding an interesting tidbit or two to share with him.

After the Registry, Sarah drove down to Mill No. 2, in search of cloth for Jenny's new snowsuit. A number of the shelves were empty, and she noticed that the woolen remnant bin was full of bolt ends in shades of khaki, olive drab and gray. Not what a little girl needed to chase away the winter cold. Finally, tucked in corner shelf, she spotted a royal blue. Dark enough to be serviceable, but a rich, warm color still. A color to set off Jenny's light hair and her cheeks that would glow with the cold. Black velvet for the chesterfield collar and trim. Buckles for pants straps; warm plaid flannel lining, and shiny black buttons for the coat. In a last look around the store, Sarah discovered a table of cotton remnants — prints and calicoes for quilts and aprons, table runners and shirtwaists. Out of them she chose a delicate blue and green print: nosegays of flowers on a white ground. She measured the cloth by arm's-lengths to be sure there was enough yardage for the bedroom curtains. There was, she thought, a bit left over. So she added a small roll of batting to her collection. Jenny would find a stuffed bunny rabbit under the Christmas tree.

Sarah watched the clerk wrap her purchases in brown paper, and she smiled at the notion of a bunny under the tree. Her mind put the calico bunny next to Jenny's Dedham Pottery rabbit, and it strayed from there to the table full of figures at the Pottery. Perhaps she should stop in there before she left? It was just across the way and, after her tour, she felt a certain proprietary interest in the place. Maybe Charlie had come up with a new design? She could look for a small thank-you gift for Isobel Arnold, to go with the dishes she had at Rocky Woods. Had Will been working on that shelf of vases? Found a new glaze? Had he opened a kiln yet, to find it full of success? Was he scowling at the world these days, or grinning at it with that twinkle in his eye?

A confusing man, indeed. Perhaps it might be best to avoid the pottery altogether.

Then Sarah remembered it was Maude who most often handled business. There would be no awkwardness dealing with Maude, and heaven only knew when she'd have another chance to find something for Isobel. Perhaps Hub and Duddy as well. A teapot, or thick-handled mugs for Duddy's hot cocoa. Yes, definitely a worthwhile stop.

Sarah tucked the yard goods under the buggy seat, covering the parcel with oilcloth to keep out the damp. Then she purposefully set off for the Pottery. Suddenly she was aware of her unbuttoned jacket, the lace cuffs that needed adjustment, the wisps of hair that always needed tucking back under her hat rim. Was she really so much more disheveled than usual? What did it matter, really, when Maude would likely greet her with an apron on. She frowned at her own fussiness, and opened the pottery door.

"Look who the east wind blew in! Good morning to you, Mrs. Sadie Chapman!"

Will's resounding voice greeted Sarah from the far end of the sales room, and put an end to her notion of a faceless errand.

"Mr. Robertson. I didn't expect to find you out here today."

Will brandished a fistful of papers at her. "Papers! Invoices! Packing lists! We've four orders to fill and Charlie swears we're short two barrels of goods. He's sent me out here on the off chance one of the hands piled the stuff on a sales table instead of a packing table." His eye scanned the room and spotted one table stacked high with dinner plates. "And sure enough! There they are." He shook his head in disbelief, "Though why, is anyone's guess. A body with half a brain would know we've done nothing for local sale in the past two months. Excuse me one minute."

Will stepped to the corridor doorway and yelled toward the packing room, "Hey, Charlie! Right again! There's a whole mess of 'em in here. Come and get 'em!"

He turned back and, unexpectedly, grinned wholeheartedly at Sarah. "Nothing like a little excitement to get the blood flowing, hmm? Now, tell me, what can we do for madam this fine morning?"

Sarah felt herself drawn to the good humor radiating from Will's smile. "I think madam would better do for you, by leaving you in peace as soon as possible. You seem to have more than enough to do today."

"Today, tomorrow. Small matter really. It's when there's *nothing* to do, a businessman gets worried. Actually, Charlie plays boss man at this point. He's the packer extraordinaire, and now that we've found this missing load, he'll be happy playing in the sawdust until the carter comes. Myself, I was thinking of a brief respite this afternoon, before we tackle the Stearns' Christmas order. Seems I've been working 'round the clock for as long as I remember, to get this lot shipped."

He paused and raised his left eyebrow inquisitively. "Tell me, Mrs. C., what would you recommend for an afternoon's entertainment? If you were I, and up for a respite?"

Caught up in Will's speculation, Sarah answered impulsively, "I'd hitch up Ebenezer and leave the farm behind. Do something positively without redeeming value or justification except for the sheer pleasure of doing it. I'd come here."

In the silence that followed, she suddenly realized her words might be misinterpreted.

"To Dedham, I mean. Of course, if I were you, I'd already be here, in Dedham, so perhaps that wouldn't suit as a respite at all." She hurried on, frowning slightly in concentration. "You might want to be out of doors. It's not exactly summer weather, but the air is mild, and the rain is holding off. There aren't many more days left of weather like this. Perhaps something sporting? Of course, I don't know what you enjoy doing." Her voice trailed off.

"Outdoors. Sporting? Fine idea! Though I must admit I'm not quite up to a fast game of football." He mulled the idea over and then exclaimed, "Wait! I've thought of a true gentleman's respite for an almost-summer day. How about boating on the Charles? Me in my boater and striped sack coat. Oh, and you with your gently twirling parasol. A canoe from the Dedham Canoe House, a leisurely paddle downstream – no, better make that upstream; it's a darn sight easier coming home – then a cold pint or a spot of tea to top it off." He bowed his head toward her. "Thank you, madam! I believe you've hit the nail on the head."

Sarah smiled at him, amused at the picture he painted of a Sunday outing that was all the rage. Of course this was a weekday, and a gray one at that, so the river would not be packed with pleasure boats. She couldn't imagine Will Robertson in a striped jacket, much less herself with a parasol...

"Oh!" Disconcerted, she realized she had been included in his fantasy. She discouraged it. "I'm sorry I won't be there to see you setting off on your expedition. I'm sure you would make quite a snapshot!"

Will spread out his hands, still holding the sheaf of forgotten papers.

"Why not? Be there, I mean. Surely, you could steal an hour or so for a quick paddle? It would all be quite proper, out in company and all. An end-of-season celebration. There aren't many more days left of weather like this, you know," he said, repeating her earlier words.

"Oh, no." Wishing the idea weren't so unconventional. "I'm afraid I couldn't. I've a number of other errands to see to."

"Now Mrs. C., I'm offering you a perfect jaunt with no redeeming value except for the pleasure of it. Just as you said you wanted." He paused, squinted at her in speculation. "You're not afraid of the water, are you?"

"Heavens, no! I live right next to a pond and ..."

"Good! I'll need someone to help me paddle the crate upstream against the flow, y'know. What do you say? Do you know how to bow paddle?" Will's tone was that of an unselfconscious, eager youth, caught up with enthusiasm for an adventure. His eyes asked the woman to take him seriously, though. Unsureness and challenge mixed in the bright black stare.

"I'm a rather good bow paddler, actually." Chappie had complimented her on it, the last time they went out. "It has been months since I've been on the river, though. Over a year...," she added wistfully. Will's stare was making her self-conscious, so she looked out the window at the soft grayness outside, and chose to respond to the lightness of his tone instead, the devil-may-care attitude which could put aside convention for a day, or part of a day, in order to simply enjoy life just as it came.

90

With more confidence than she was feeling, she quickly said, "If you can promise me safe return before the rain soaks us both, I'd be delighted to help you upstream."

"That's the ticket!" Will exclaimed. "A figurehead for the bow will chase the rain away!"

"Really! I did not know my looks would scare even the weather," Sarah retorted.

"Oh, no, you're to be the beauty at the bowsprit. To charm away the rain; to spur me on to greater feats of strength on the fearsome river." Will's face softened. "And beauty soothes the soul, remember. Seems to me you told me that, last time you came."

Sarah raised an eyebrow. She had not been the only one to remember that encounter. She suddenly wondered why on earth she'd just agreed to go boating with a near stranger in the middle of the week when it was about to rain. But before she could think it through, Charlie Davenport came in, pushing a cart before him.

"Charlie, my boy!" Will exclaimed, his tone once again boomingly self-confident. Sarah was relieved. "Looks like you're up for a temporary promotion."

The younger man looked askance over his wire-rimmed glasses, as he nodded hello to Sarah.

"Yes, indeed," Will went on. "I appoint you official big chief muckamuck for the next few hours, while I retire to a far, far better place."

"You're finally leaving town then?" Charlie asked mildly.

"Not on your life! The fair Mrs. C., here, has condescended to accompany me on a brief riverine excursion, to purge my soul of clay and cobalt. You'll see to the last of the shipment?"

Charlie agreed and the two men briefly discussed details of the work to be finished. Maude, too, was apparently off for a holiday on one of her beloved trips to the Museum of Fine Arts. There she would spend hours wandering through the galleries, sketchbook in hand. When Will was finished giving directions, he excused himself to Sarah, and went to fetch his hat and coat.

Sarah chatted with Charlie while she waited, finding reassurance in their simple conversation. She was determined not to dwell on the unconventional afternoon ahead. What it would be was a lark, that bore no further introspection. A chance in a thousand to be footloose

91

and fancy-free. God willing, she would not run into anyone she knew, to whom she would feel compelled to explain herself. Fancy-free was much sooner done than explained, if you were a respectable married woman in a country town.

Will returned wearing a Norfolk jacket and a proper starch-collared shirt, his hair slicked down and a shiny black bowler hat tucked under his arm. They said goodbye to Charlie, and Will ushered Sarah out the door.

"See?" he said, "No rain gear. I have confidence that your magic will fend off the rain." He hesitated. "I do have an umbrella, though. You think I should bring it?"

"Probably too late," Sarah laughed and shook her head. "But I'm impressed. You seem to have a whole wardrobe out back. Is this common practice at a pottery?"

A flush of color rose on Will's cheeks as he determinedly headed toward Ebenezer and the trap. Sarah hoped he understood she was only joking.

"I, ah, camp out there." Will's explanation was terse. "Kind of need to, you know, what with tending the kiln and all. Somebody's got to do night watch, look after the place, and all that."

"But surely you could find a place nearby? A rooming house when you need to be away from home?"

Will laughed, a bark with no humor in it. "Home! That went a long time ago. And most of my money with it. Damn the she-devil to hell." The last, muttered under his breath.

Sarah was shocked at the bitterness in his voice. She searched for something to say to show concern, without inflaming this unpredictable man further. At the same time she felt a tremor of doubt at the wisdom of setting off with a man who spoke of women with a curse.

"You…had a business reversal?" she asked timidly.

Will still didn't look at her, but his voice was not quite so vehement as he answered. "You could call it that, I guess. A 'business reversal.'" He savored the phrase for a moment. "More like the world turned upside down – or at least my corner of it." He lapsed into silence, reluctant to explain. As he helped Sarah up into the trap, she saw the scowl of memory on his face. Determining she needed to find out more before she let him drive off with her to parts unknown, she circled back to the subject as Will walked around Ebenezer to the other seat.

"Did it have to do with the kiln explosion?"

He swung himself up and leaned forward to unhitch the reins. There was silence as he paused, head bent in thought. When he looked up at Sarah, his face had lost the intimidating scowl. Instead, she saw an expression half-hurt, half-chagrinned as he nodded at her.

"You're bound to know, sooner or later. After the blast the doctors never did set my fingers back right. The useless things hurt like the devil for months on end. I wasn't too chipper about it either – kind of thought my life had just about finished. Anyway, what with me moping and doctoring myself with whiskey along the way, Mrs. Robertson up and decided I wasn't fit company any longer, for her or the boy either. Locked me out of the house and set out to track down all of my money that she and her shyster lawyer could get their conniving hands on. I would have given it to her if there'd been any! Everything I owned was tied up in the pottery and, when my dad died, there wasn't anything there either, not for a while.

"Anyhow, I guess I woke up one day and decided I was going to live after all, and this wasn't any way to do it. So I did all the right things. Cut out the drinking. Started to turn the business around. Even went back to Medusa, there, to see what we could work out. But I guess she'd gotten used to playing the witch. She decided she'd nail the lid on the coffin by refusing either to take me back or let me go, and told me I could rot in hell before I'd ever see the boy again."

Will's voice had gone flat as he finished his tale. He shook his head in bemusement at the inexplicable ironies of life and shrugged in resignation.

"So here I am, a married bachelor, father without child, penniless proprietor of a business known across the country. Not just what you had in mind for a respectable companion, I daresay."

Will looked at Sarah as if he expected her, too, to pack him off without further ado.

Many things had come clear to Sarah in the past few minutes. Will's fondness for children, his distrust of women, even his penchant for talking as if there'd be no tomorrow. She found his confession, rather than taking her aback, made her inexplicably more comfortable with him, certainly more sympathetic to his shifts of mood. The yearning she heard in his voice was familiar. It echoed the present emptiness of her own life. She had no difficulty making a decision.

"Fortunately Mr. Robertson, respectability is not like beauty – in the eyes of the beholder. I respect you for what you have tried to do with your life, against great odds, it would seem." She tipped her head to one side and raised her eyebrows in mock appraisal. "As to being a companion, if your feats of strength are as you touted earlier, and you know the river as well as you intimated, then you are precisely the companion I have in mind for this afternoon." Settling her hat firmly, she silently congratulated herself on Will's widening grin. "Shall we proceed?"

The boathouse was a long, low structure that hugged the riverbank. The street side was simple, its brown-stained shingles offset by yellow-painted wood trim. Over the big double door stretched a black sign proclaiming in gold: DEDHAM CANOE HOUSE.

"Now let's see if Pop is still awake," Will said, as he handed Sarah down from the trap. He led the way, turning right inside the cavernous entrance hall, toward a doorway marked *Boat Rentals. Daily and hourly rates*, the sign continued. *Two-man or larger canoes. Rowboats. For locker rental please inquire other side.* The boathouse was nearly empty. A pair of elderly gentlemen, fitted out with rubber waders and fishing gear, were sitting on one bench, comparing notes on the morning's catch. Three young men stood, laughing, by the French doors that lined the river side of the hall. There was an urgency to their joking, a brittle gaiety that marked them as soldiers, present or future, filling quiet spaces in their days with pleasure while there was still time.

As they entered the rental area, Sarah glimpsed a man and woman on the boat ramp outside, he with paddle, she with the requisite parasol which might end serving as umbrella this day. The shy look they exchanged as he gallantly helped her into a canoe spoke worlds of their feelings for each other. Sarah smiled reminiscently at the ritual of courtship she was witnessing.

Will's voice interrupted her reverie. "Mrs. Chapman, may I introduce you to Mr. Wilbur Fanning. Pop Fanning to those fortunate enough to know him well. Pop here is the soul of the Dedham Canoe

94

House, and knows more about the Charles River than the fish who swim in it. Isn't that right, Pop?"

The short, white-haired man behind the counter gave a toothy grin and nodded his head decisively in Sarah's direction.

"Darn right I do." His voice squeaked slightly, like an oarlock in need of greasing. "Ought to. Been up and down this river a whole lot longer than you've been walkin' on two feet, young man."

Sarah thought Pop Fanning was enjoying his role as old codger. Will grinned and said to her, in a confidential tone, "That's why I like coming here. I always end up feeling like a spring chicken, after Pop gets through comparing ages. 'Course he probably does it so I'll stay out longer, run up the bill a bit." He turned to the old man. "Isn't that right Pop?"

"Pah! Don't try to put that one on me. You git out there and take a nap, like as not. Never look tuckered out enough after, for you to have done any real work!"

"Now, Pop," Will retorted, good-naturedly, "There's got to be some benefit to slaving over a hot kiln all the time. Why, I get more upper body exercise than a lot of boxers I know! So, how about finding us a good canoe and a couple of paddles, so we can race the rain this afternoon? Not one nap, I promise."

Pop sized up Sarah in a quick glance, and shuffled off to the storeroom behind him. He returned with paddles which seemed made to order for them both, Will's long and heavy to suit his powerful frame; Sarah's shorter and lightweight, a woman's paddle for the bow. Leading them out to the boat ramp, Pop pointed toward a canoe tied at dockside.

"Might as well take that one," he instructed Will. Then, turning to Sarah, "It's good and dry – for the moment, at least – though how long it'll stay that way in this weather's anybody's guess." He shook his head in disapproval. "I don't know why Mr. Robertson couldn't pick a better day for an outing than this, anyway. Some folks don't have the sense God gave muskrats."

Will laid his hand on the man's narrow shoulder and replied, "Some folks don't have the choices God gave muskrats, Pop. We're just going to have to take our chances."

He flashed a mischievous grin at Sarah and knelt by the canoe to hold it steady.

95

"Madam? Your barge awaits."

Sarah gathered her skirt in one hand and stepped gingerly into the center of the canoe. Leaning forward she moved up to the bow seat and made to step over it, her foot tangling in the skirt hem as she did so. Will reached out to steady her as the unstable boat tipped wildly. Sarah felt herself flush with combined embarrassment at her ineptitude and consciousness of the strength of his grasp on her arm. She smiled uncertainly.

"I cannot be impressing you yet with my ability as a bow paddler."

Will laughed comfortably.

"Oh, it's way too early for that, Mrs. C. I have to show Pop here that I'm good for something anyway! Why don't you play the lady of leisure for a bit, prop that wicker seatback in the bottom, and recline in comfort before it gets too damp to sit down there?"

Part of her was miffed that he could so easily do without her help. But she was also grateful for his providing a quick solution to her awkward position. She took Will's other hand to steady herself and turned toward the stern, then eased herself down into the bottom of the canoe.

"I think it's safe now," she said with some chagrin. Canoeing was a great deal easier at home, when she was barefoot and wearing a shorter skirt. Her partnership in this adventure was not off to a great start.

Will stepped lightly into the canoe and settled himself in the stern. Sarah thought of the way he had silently appeared in the showroom, that first time they had met; how his step contradicted his size. She wondered if that might be true, as well, of the inside of him: a shyness of heart contradicted by the vibrant sureness of his speech. She stowed her paddle in the bow and adjusted the back support as the thoughts entered her mind, avoiding, for a moment, looking at the puzzling man who faced her. Meanwhile, Will pushed off from the dock and, raising his paddle in salute to Pop, who was muttering and shaking his head, he back-stroked out into the current.

For a minute the splash and swirl of the water was all the sound between them. Then Will got the rhythm of his stroke. The sound changed to a purling gurgle along the keel, as the boat glided upstream in the slow-moving river. He paddled contentedly for a few minutes and Sarah watched the tree-lined banks sliding backwards past her. She was startled out of her revery by the sudden rumble of Will's voice, singing deep and self-confident,

> *Up a lazy river by the old mill run*
> *The lazy, lazy river in the noonday sun*
> *Linger in the shade of a kind old tree,*

Sarah joined him, alto blending well with his bass.

> *Throw away your troubles;*
> *Dream a dream with me.*

This last, in some semblance of harmony: Sarah picking out a higher register as Will held a long and rumbling final note. They both laughed in simple delight at their success and fell to discussing other watery ditties they could try. By the time they had worked their way through "Down by the Old Mill Stream", "Shenandoah", and — through some stretch of the imagination – a number of sea chanteys, the earlier tension had eased. Conversation came easily as they compared stories of other songfests. Will regaled Sarah with the rousing times he had sung with a local German chorus before the war. There was the performance they had done for a group of fellow-countrymen in Lowell. Singing and eating had alternated all afternoon in a packed hall full of goodwill. They were finally seen off with packets of sandwiches and pickles at the train station. Even then, full of wurst and beer, they had harmonized the whole ride home.

Sarah remembered the evenings of singing at her parents' house, when the family would gather for Christmas. After the table was cleared and the women went to the kitchen to wash up, someone invariably began a carol as the dish water heated. By the time dishes were passed for wiping and stacking, three generations of women had joined in the song. Sarah and her sister singing descant, mother and aunt holding the tune, and gramma, up to her elbows in soap suds, humming along. More often than not, the men came in too, leaned against a doorframe or perched on the kitchen stool, joining the song.

"I'm sure there must have been countless dishes to wash on holidays," Sarah smiled reminiscently, "but I remember those times as the best part of Christmas. The sound, and the sharing... It was so loving!"

"You talk as if this is all past?"

"Oh, yes. Both my parents have died. Now we have Christmas at Mill Farm, but somehow it's not the same with just the five of us. Chappie's brother is down in Texas, much too far for them to come. And this year ... well, there may only be four if Chappie's still in France."

A tired sadness had crept into Sarah's voice as she spoke. Will turned the subject quickly, not wanting to hear the sadness, to let it spoil their day. "There are four at home you say? Who besides you and little Jenny in the family?"

"Not family, exactly. Hub and Duddy Branch. The Branches have been old friends of the Chapmans forever. Hub and Duddy actually grew up in Maine, but Chappie invited them down here when he took over the farm. He needed help and, truth to tell, I don't think Hub was doing so well down east at the time. They've been a godsend to us, especially with Chappie being gone. I don't know how I'd have managed without them. So they are pretty much family, actually." Sarah paused, and her eyes suddenly twinkled. "Besides, Duddy's bread baking has mine beat any day!"

Will chuckled and nodded his head.

"Family that's not family is sometimes better than what is." His voice was unresentful when he spoke. "I guess Maude and Charlie'd be that for me. Many's the time they've fed and entertained me at their folks' place, and of course I'd go under in a minute without them at the pottery."

"The Davenports must be very pleasant people to work with."

"Aye. Maude's a gentle one. The little sister I never had. Charlie's a killer, though. Days you'd think he'd nothing on his mind but frolic." Will grinned reminiscently. "He's led us a wild chase from time to time. Once, down at their cottage on the Cape, he had us out crabbing. Got so involved with the foolish crab races we almost didn't make it past the tide coming in. Maudie and I got good and wet around the ankles wading in half-freezing water!"

"But not Charlie?"

"Nah. His crab had so far outdistanced ours he'd reached the other side of the gut by the time the first waves rolled in."

"Come to think of it," Will frowned, "he was the only one to eat crab that evening after all. Our stupid creatures ran right into the water and disappeared."

"They don't sound so stupid to me."

Will raised his brows and stared at Sarah quizzically. Then he guffawed. "No. No, I guess they don't. Sometimes it's hard to tell smart creatures from dumb humans, isn't it?"

Sarah looked at Will in his ridiculous bowler hat, the brim edged with drops of mist. She glanced down at the beads of wet clinging to the rough wool of her jacket. Surely they were a sorry lot to be seen by anyone on the bank. She was surprised to find it didn't bother her overmuch.

"I think we may come close to the 'dumb human' category, Mr. Robertson, if we don't head back soon. There's a big black cloud behind you that doesn't look content to simply mist."

Will stopped in mid-stroke and glanced over his shoulder at the lowering sky. "Well, Mrs. Chapman, you remember I said it wasn't your turn yet, back there? I think your turn has come. If you can finagle yourself onto that bow seat without tipping us both into the drink, we could use your strong right arm to get us home."

Sarah raised her brows in question, then shrugged as if to absolve herself of blame for what was about to occur. Slowly she turned onto her knees, facing forward, then grasped the gunwales and, keeping her weight low, stepped over the seat. The canoe teetered a bit but her toe stayed out of her hem. Will had a brief view of her bottom raised to the sky, then Sarah eased onto the wicker seat and drew the paddle out from under. She shot a triumphant glance over her shoulder and settled her hat more firmly on her head.

"Call the stroke, Captain!"

Together, they drove their paddles into the river and picked up speed. The sound of water rushing past the bow accompanied a driving, deep-voiced chantey Will invented with each stroke.

The combination of cold air rushing past and increasingly heavy mist had Sarah shivering before they were halfway back. She shook her head at the foolishness of the whim that had brought them to such a ridiculous pass, then grinned to herself at the delight of acting crazy. At the same time her shoulders were tensing against the chill, she felt elated by the challenge. Here they were, she and Will, having gotten themselves into a ridiculous situation, being chased by storm clouds and well on the way to being drenched. There was nothing for it but to keep going. They couldn't just leave the boat and walk away. So whether they got drenched or not, didn't really matter. But they *could* paddle their hardest and weather be damned. The blood thrumming in her ears kept time with the strokes of her paddle and in the stern she heard Will's stroke in rhythm with her own. He must be matching his to what she did; surely he could set a quicker pace if he were on his own. When her shoulder protested the unaccustomed action and she shifted her paddle to the other side, the plinking sound of drips across the gunwale behind her told her Will was mirroring her move. Occasionally a snatch of low-voiced humming would float forward from the stern. Sarah could picture Will, eyes sharp on the currents ahead, a half-frown of concentration offset by half-grin delighting in adventure.

He only asked once after her welfare, when a gust of wind caught them from the back, and a great shiver ran through her.

"You doing all right up there, Sadie Chapman?"

"I'm fine," she replied, wondering why on earth she really meant it. "Just shaking off the damp a bit."

"Not long now," he reassured her.

The next bend in the winding river brought them in sight of the boathouse, and minutes more brought them alongside the dock. A few diehards still fishing off the ramp looked askance at the foolish pair out pleasure-boating in the rain, then turned their attention back to the more serious concern of trawling for catfish near the bank. Will grabbed the dock and stepped out, steadying the canoe for Sarah to do the same. She waited while he secured the boat to its mooring, conscious of the ache across her shoulders and the waves of shivers she could not suppress. Will straightened up to find Sarah watching him, her hands gripped on the handle of her paddle, which she leaned on like a walking stick.

He came close to where she stood frozen in place.

"You look like something from a comic fashion plate – you know, the before-and-after kind? 'The well-dressed lady of fashion after a bucolic afternoon's canoeing on the river.'" He contemplated this image as Sarah tried to feel insulted by his ill-bred honesty. Then she looked at Will, standing in similar pose, at least as disheveled as she and breathing hard from the trip just done. She burst out laughing at both of them. All the seriousness that had built up in their race against the elements dissolved in shared laughter. They were a pair of soggy water rats. Respectable they weren't, but they made a swell team, pulling together against the odds, making the most of what there was. It was a feeling that warmed them both.

They were still chuckling as they entered the canoe house, their faces red from wind and exertion and laughter. Pop Fanning took one look at the contrast between their dripping clothes and elated faces and chalked another up to cupid's work. He didn't even charge Will for the ten minutes over, they'd had the canoe. Did a soul good to see young love in this day and age. Not too young, of course, like those pups dashing off to the altar before they shipped out to the front. But like these two. Old enough to know what they were doing. He felt a tinge of regret at the simple pleasures kept for youth.

Once in the trap again, Ebenezer docilely plodding away from the boathouse, they both agreed the Mansion Inn was a necessary stop, before Sarah set off for home. The ride through Dedham Square brought the war full force back into their lives. Memorial Hall was draped with bunting from every cornice and eave, and big-lettered posters still proclaimed the Liberty Bond rally that had taken place the week before. Stores and houses alike displayed American flags of all shapes and sizes, though the damp left the banners drooping on flagpoles and entryways. Connors' Market proclaimed its support of meatless Tuesdays and wheatless Thursdays in signs across its display windows. Khaki and drab uniforms mixed with business suits on the downtown streets.

Will and Sarah quietly compared notes on life on the home front, trying to maintain the comfortable companionship they had built. But Sarah found herself searching every window for a service flag, and breathing a prayer of thanks when it was blue, instead of gold. Dedham families were not yet mourning their men. It was a relief when the trap turned onto a curved drive and pulled up behind the Mansion Inn. The Great War did not exist beyond its chestnut door.

The tall brick Federal building on High Street had been converted to its present use after the well-known Phoenix House had burned late in the 1800s. The Phoenix House had been Dedham's meeting place for a century: dining room, dance hall and coach stop all in one. After its demise, the Mansion Inn opened, a quieter, more high-toned eating establishment in keeping with Victorian taste and Upper Dedham society. The public dining rooms at the front of the first floor were high-ceilinged and formal, their windows heavily draped with velvet and their tables set with spotless white linens and polished silver. Will considered them stodgy. The judges and lawyers from the courthouse nearby who frequented them found them suitably distinguished for weekly dinners and luncheon with important clients.

Set toward the back of the mansion was a less imposing room, however, reached by the side door and adjacent to the kitchen. Sounds of cooking penetrated the padded swinging doors, and back windows looked out on a service porch partially screened by tangled wisteria vine. This was the tea room, open from two until five o'clock on weekdays, with a light luncheon at Saturday noon. At one time this had been the family parlor. It was not a large space, only room enough for eight small tables. Yet evidence remained of its elegant past in the delicate molded chair rail and pedimented door and window frames. The woodwork had been painted white in prevailing Adamesque style, and the mantlepiece over the small coal fireplace was supported by classical columns. A welcoming fire burned there now, and Sarah moved gratefully toward it as she and Will came in. There were not many other customers. A quartet of ladies in large hats sat at a round table in one corner. Two judicial-looking men scowled over a serious discussion near the door. Sarah and Will asked the hostess for a seat near the fire, and she gave them a choice of small tables near the glowing coals. Will helped Sarah out of her wet jacket and gave it to the hostess who eyed it dubiously, but politely said nothing as she went to hang it away.

"I've always loved this room," Sarah commented, hiding a late shiver brought out by the heat. "I've been to dinner in the main dining rooms, but I much prefer to sit in here."

Will nodded. "It's a good room for imagining. I always imagine I'm part of some rich family, stopping for a spot of tea before I hurry back to international wheeling and dealing. Sitting back with my jacket loosened and my legs crossed, perusing the <u>Village Register</u> as the maid pours…, or is it the mistress…?"

"Perhaps it depends on what kind of mistress." Sarah was feeling dangerous.

"At the moment I'd take any kind, so long as the tea comes quick. My jacket's beginning to steam, but my innards aren't warm yet."

They turned their attention to the menu of tea sandwiches, pastries, puddings and light luncheon items.

"A rarebit!" Will exclaimed, eyes sparkling.

"It's a bit late for lunch, don't you think?" Sarah looked uncertain.

"Late or no, we've certainly done enough to justify a stout appetite. Besides, you've still a good, long haul ahead of you before you get to supper. What d'you say? Welsh rarebit and some good strong tea to set us up right?"

Sarah agreed, amused at the way Will could even make tea unconventional. While they waited for their food to be served, a waitress brought them a pot of Hu Kwa tea, carefully tucking a tea cozy over it after she poured their first cups. They chatted comfortably as they sipped the smoky lapsang soochong. Hands began to warm around the china cups and their faces lost the raw feeling brought on by the wind outside. Creamy rarebit arrived on browned toast points, followed by a dish of pickled apple slices and a cruet of worcestershire sauce that all crowded together on the table. For a few minutes both contentedly ate in silence, an occasional smile or satisfied comment serving to maintain social connection. When Will had made his way through most of his dish, he took up the responsibility of conversation again, letting Sarah proceed more slowly with her food.

"I guess with more weather like today ahead, we'll be spending a sight more time on indoor entertainment. Tell the truth, I'm a sucker for the moving picture shows. I get over to the theater in Hyde Park as often as I can. You ever get the shows way out there in Medfield?"

He caught Sarah with a mouthful of toast, and she swallowed with an embarrassed "mmpfh" before she could answer.

"Of course we do. At least, the serials do come to town, though I'm afraid I don't go to many of them. There's quite a posh theatre at the town house. Brocade paper on the walls, a stage with a special screen. I hear the piano player leaves a bit to be desired, but a five-cent show is still worth a nickel. Tell me," she went on, drawing him out so she could eat, and so she could listen to his voice, "have you seen any interesting shows recently?"

Will thought for a moment.

"I went up to a show Wednesday night and saw a photo play called *The Nigger*, stars Farnham in the principal role. Seems he finds out after being elected Governor of Georgia that he has Negro blood in his veins, from his grandfather's actions." He frowned. "It's a strong piece, but I don't like the ending at all. His fiancée gives him up on account of his mixed blood, resigns herself to a life of misery and pledges to meet him on the other shore."

He looked at Sarah soberly, eyes dark under beetling brows.

"If it will be all right on the other shore, what's the matter with this one?" His voice was tinged with disgust. "That kind of sentimental bosh doesn't go with me at all."

Sarah remained silent, unsure how to respond to this suddenly serious comment. How would she react, in a situation like that? Would a woman give up a man she truly loved? And if she tried to, would he not insist she stay, if he truly loved her?

"It does sound a bit difficult to believe," she said diffidently, aware of her ignorance in a town where Negroes could be counted on one hand. "But then, perhaps no more so than *The Perils of Pauline*?"

Will guffawed. "Now there's a joke if I ever saw one! Imagine traipsing to the pictures every week, just to watch a doe-eyed damsel get herself out of a burning airplane – and that with no parachute! No thank you, ma'am. I'd rather see real life any day." He went on, becoming more animated as he described the scenes in a newly-released underwater film.

"The old Boston Theatre is running a set of submarine pictures taken 30 to 70 feet underwater down near San Salvador – where Columbus landed? They show all the way to the ocean floor. And whole schools of fish, millions of them swimming like vast armies. Sharks, and one of the Williamson boys – the inventors of the deep sea machine – dives over and kills a big shark in front of the camera. Regular daredevil trick! It's the best thing in the movie line I've seen so far." He unconsciously shook his fork at Sarah as he cleaned the last of his plate. "If it comes your way be sure and see it. It's a humdinger!"

Sarah smiled at Will's extravagant enthusiasm. She was fascinated by his entertaining her one minute, and offering glimpses of his most private thoughts, the next. She was having a delightful afternoon with a delightful man, she realized. It was definitely time to go.

Her response to Will's theatrical urging was friendly, but noncommittal, and she drew his attention to the lateness of the hour. He regretfully paid their bill and they left the Inn's warmth. As Will drove the short distance to the Pottery, they kept up desultory talk of picture shows and concerts, vaudeville and local entertainments. The rain which had threatened earlier had retreated again, leaving a rawness in the air that signalled an end to gentle weather.

Will climbed down from the trap at the Pottery door. Sarah moved over on the seat, taking up the reins as she tugged the cart robe over her lap. Her view was of the top of Will's bowler shoved down tight on his head. She smiled in inexplicable amusement at the sight. Just then he reached his broad hand up across her lap, tucking the robe in snugly, protectively around her legs.

"Weather's bound to worsen before you get home. You'll get more soaked than you are now," he grumbled. "I don't want to be the cause of you catching your death of cold."

"Nonsense. I don't need you fussing over me like an old schoolmarm."

"Nah," he replied gently, looking up at her. "Family, just family. You've warmed my soul today Sadie, and I'd hate to return the gift by sending you home chilled to the bone."

"I think your imagination is running away with you, Will Robertson. I'm a country girl, remember, and I've spent lots of time in much worse weather than this. Ebenezer knows the way home cold or hot." She smiled softly. "And thanks to you, I have a store of pleasant memories to keep me company."

She flicked the reins on Ebenezer's back and the trap began to move away. Her eyes lingered on Will's broad form as he stood, arms akimbo, head cocked, his crooked smile fading slowly into the falling mist.

Dearest Chappie,

Halo-o-o out there! Cold weather is closing in and I feel as if I need to holler for you to hear me through the wind rattling about, outside. The sun was very bright today, everything crystal clear in that way that only happens during November, but the air never warmed completely, and it turned downright cold the minute the sun set. Fall still clings to a few last vestiges – a few brown leaves on the apple trees, a piece of aster here and there along the stone wall, the inevitable handful of geese who can't make up their minds to fly south. Looking at the ice along the edge of the pond, it is hard to believe I was canoeing on the river just a few days ago.

Sarah stopped to read what she had written. She'd started out all right, joking, making light of the cold beginning to creep into everything. But why had she gone on so, about weather and dead leaves? It occurred to her that one often spoke of weather when unsure what else to say. She frowned and remembered the 'cheerful tone' and encouraging words with which she should fill her letters.

The farm is pretty well tucked in for the winter. There's a good stock of fodder corn and hay in the barn. Storm windows are on – all twenty-seven of them! You should have seen me hoisting them up the ladder to Hub; my arms are noticeably stronger these days. All the winter clothes are down from the attic. Oh! speaking of winter clothes, have you received our packet of woolens yet? They were mailed out three weeks ago, and the shipping office assured us they should take no more than a month to reach France. Socks, Chappie. Lots of socks! I put in union suits as well, gloves and a balaclava in case you are stuck there longer than we both hope. Better yet, perhaps you will head home soon and you can give them all to the boys who will need them more. I have read that it has rained a lot this past month over there. It must be difficult to stay dry in the trenches.

Weather again. And warfare. She crossed out the last two thoughts. What was safe to write about?

Looking back on this past growing season, I think our little "farm stand" was quite a success. There were apples and tomatoes galore, of course, root crops and cabbage we'll continue to sell to anyone who wants them, and the Medfield apple cider. Duddy added a fine selection of preserves. (She says her portion of the proceeds are going to get her someplace warm this winter, when her arthritis acts up too badly, though I don't know what she plans to do with Hub!) Lots of people were regular customers by the time frost closed us down, and many say they'd be back if we were to do this every year. Do you think it would fly, Chappie? I've made a pretty good start as a store "manageress" and would be willing to consider continuing in that position if The Management (ahem...) offers suitable compensation. Shall we discuss this on your return?

Oh, by the way, it looks like Hub's idea of wood-for-coal was right after all. We've sold as much as we've trucked down from Rocky Woods, and have more orders than he and Jake Peters can fill. Hub promises he will be circumspect in his choice of timber.

Sarah paused to read again. Now it sounded as if his wife had become some kind of accountant, more interested in profit than in her husband. She knew how untrue that was, but she didn't know how to tread the fine line between news from home and an appearance of self-absorption. She crossed out the store manageress section. It was less amusing than it had seemed at first. Better to be straightforward.

What of you? No mail at all has come from France recently. I'm sure it has to do with Boch interference with shipping. We've heard that American naval forces are having wonderful success in countering the threat though, so God willing, this letter will cross with yours.

Are you well? Are you eating well? I had a wonderful rarebit the other day at the Mansion Inn. It reminded me of the rarebits your mother used to make, with those flaky soda crackers to go under. Mine never have managed to taste like hers, have they?

That story in your last letter, about your celebration with confiscated cognac, makes me wonder if you'll ever eat the same again! Shall I have to serve you snails and medallions of veal when you come home? I will, if you want them, my dear – though heaven only knows where I might find snails. Come to think of it, there's quite a colony in our little pond, isn't there? Now wouldn't that be something!

She smiled, pleased by the effect she'd created, hoping it would make Chappie smile as it did her. Smiles had come at odd times recently, she noticed, and laughter in unexpected places.

Here's something I've been thinking about lately, that you might find interesting. I've noticed a different mood about town since the army has really begun sending our boys overseas. Surprisingly, there's very little of the gloom you might expect from a town full of old men and womenfolk. It's very hard to explain. I wish you could hear one of the motion picture shows at the town house: the click of knitting needles is almost louder than the piano player. There is a kind of gaiety here that seems to accompany the war effort. Almost as if everyone suddenly realized how precious laughter and happy moments are, once the war came close to home. Remember, we felt that way just before you left for Europe? Only now it seems to be the general mood of society. Everywhere you go, groups of young people are partying, families are taking outings, couples are courting, 'as if there's no tomorrow.' It is delightful – and strangely disturbing at the same time.

Suddenly Sarah didn't want to write any more. Where was she going with these thoughts? Where did they even come from when, underneath it all, she knew there was nothing to celebrate? Life just proceeded as it had since Chappie had gone, used up by worry and work, coping and prayers. Occasionally, by forgetfulness.

Oh dear. I said it was hard to explain.

What a peculiar letter this has turned out to be! I think I'll do better after I read that awaited letter from you. I always hear the sound of your voice in your words, Chappie, and that sets me back on track again.

Meanwhile, ever loving thoughts from your "philosopher" wife,

Sarah

The next Wednesday's mail brought two overdue letters from Chappie. It also brought a small, note-sized envelope stamped at the top left with the Dedham Pottery rabbit. Sarah sank into the nearest chair, glancing at the framed photo on the parlor table as she carefully slit open the first envelope. She read and reread the letters from France, jealous of every word blacked out, crying when she found a full half-sheet missing. Some story, she had to assume, of one of Chappie's expeditions. He had not been circumspect enough to satisfy the censor and so she lost a moment they might have shared.

When she had spent enough time alone with Chappie's words to hear his voice inside her, she stood up, intent on finding Hub and Duddy and sharing the news. The other envelope fell to the floor. Sarah hesitated before she picked it up, fearing somehow to break the spell of her husband close at hand. Finally she clucked at her own silliness and lifted the flap. Inside was a folded sheet of paper, inscribed and laid out like a formal invitation.

My dear Mrs. Chapman,

You are cordially invited to an opening of the Dedham Pottery kiln on Saturday next between three and four of the clock. At that time the Newest Line of Art Pottery will be presented for the first time.

Yr. obedient servant,
W. A. Robertson

Sarah couldn't resist a smile at the contrast between the formality of Will's invitation and the scrawl of his handwriting. Always a joker. But the prospect of witnessing one of the fabled kiln openings was thrilling. It was kind of Will to remember she'd wanted to come.

What did Will mean by a new line? Was this the work Charlie had mentioned, the glaze experiments Will was supposed to get back to? If so, she'd be among the first to see the results. Will himself wouldn't know the outcome. A very special honor, then. More than a little brave, too. The firing might be a disaster, like some of the others he had described. This could turn out not to be such a gala occasion, but he trusted her friendship enough to include her anyway.

And how had it happened, that they had come to be such friends? If Chappie were home, it would have been different. Then she and her husband would have visited the pottery together, gotten to know Will together: Mr. and Mrs. Chapman and Mr. Robertson. The corner of her mouth turned up. Probably not gone canoeing in the rain. Or discussed the meaning of art and life. One tended not to have occasions like that with one's husband, very often. Daily life was taken up with daily events, and simple thoughts. It was not until the bonds of daily life were broken that the extraordinary might occur.

Sarah humphed at herself and put the invitation down. No good 'making much out of little,' as Duddy would have it. Dwelling on something only imbued it with an importance that it should not have.

109

A quick stop by the pottery to satisfy her curiosity, and she'd be home again. She stared absently out the window.

What did one wear to a kiln opening?

A winter trolley trip to Dedham was not a pleasant experience. Somehow it had seemed just the thing, when Sarah saw Jenny off on the train with Hub and Duddy in the morning. The great, sleek locomotive had pulled into Medfield Station with much bell-clanging and whistle blowing, and Sarah watched her daughter torn between fear of the huge contraption and unbearable excitement at riding all the way to Boston. Hub and Duddy had conceived this trip as an early Christmas present for their surrogate grand-daughter: a ride on the train, a stroll around downtown and the Common to see all the lights and decorated shop windows, early supper at Jake Wirth's and overnight with relatives in East Cambridge. Then home again with tales to tell and souvenirs to cherish through the month.

Waving at the disappearing train, Sarah had decided to follow suit on her trip to the kiln opening that afternoon. She would take the cars at Nebo Street, leaving Ebenezer warm and dry in Mr. Goldthwaite's barn at the corner. The trip would be faster, drier, and probably warmer than in the trap and besides, it would be an adventure. Was she not as much in need of an adventure as Jenny was?

By the time she descended in Dedham Square, she was having second thoughts. She had not taken into account the number of stops the vehicle would make between Medfield and the square, along Main Street and then all along High Street through Westwood as well. It picked up working girls off shopping on their free afternoon. Schoolboys climbed on with their nickels, heading to the movies. It stopped an interminable time while the conductor assisted an elderly woman swathed in Victorian black serge and shawls. The car filled with people going places. She had not mistaken the warmth of the trip. The trolley was stifling by the time it reached Dedham common, its stuffy closed atmosphere thick with smells of heavy wool, tobacco, and a shop girl's cologne.

Sarah stood beside the tracks and breathed in the damp, cold air, relieved to be off the car but anxiously checking the Memorial Hall clock. She had not realized that she would have to change to another trolley to get to Maverick Street, or else walk the further half-mile to the pottery. She glanced down at her dress shoes, carefully polished, then up at the lowering sky, and prayed that an East Dedham car would not be long in coming.

It was not, and Sarah found a bench seat at the front so she could watch for the stop. As the trolley swayed its way toward the mills she wondered what other customers might be there. Isobel, probably, perhaps even with George, her reclusive husband. Sarah had not seen Isobel since the Arnolds had closed their Medfield camp for the winter, and she was looking forward to a few minutes' chat. Was Will confident enough of this batch that he might invite some of the Boston clients as well? Why had she not chosen a finer dress?

Then common sense reasserted itself as she remembered how dirty the kiln shed was. This was not, after all, a gallery show, no matter who was coming. And if Will was working at the kiln, certainly he would not be dressed to the nines. She rubbed her cheek in the soft fox fur of her coat collar and sat a bit straighter. Will had invited her, and the Chapmans of Medfield could stand proud in any gathering. Still, she was glad she'd put new trimmings on her hat.

When the trolley reached the corner of Pottery Lane Sarah took a deep breath and stepped down. She smoothed the wings of hair beneath her hat brim, and walked quickly down to the building, hoping they had not begun without her. She pushed the showroom door open to the accompaniment of the little strap bell swaying up and down as it rang. There was no one there.

Sarah wondered if she ought to go right through to the kiln shed. She listened for sounds of activity toward the back but heard nothing. Was she here, after all, on the wrong day? Had she missed the time completely? She scolded herself for being in such a rush as not to check the invitation. A flush of confusion was rising on her cheeks when Will walked in the far door, buttoning his jacket as he came.

"Welcome, Mrs. C.!" he exclaimed. "I see the cold has brought roses to your cheeks!"

"Oh! Hello, Will." Her voice was hesitant. "I thought I'd be terribly late...?"

"No, no, not at all. You're just on time, as far as I'm concerned. I just started opening up a few bricks. Didn't want you to miss the fun, though." Will grinned his broad, engaging smile but lapsed into an uncharacteristic silence.

111

"Thank heavens for that!" she answered, relaxing a bit, perfectly willing to fill the silence now that she knew she hadn't made a terrible slip. "The shed must be nice and warm compared to what's outside right now. It's getting colder by the minute. Why, I'm guessing the ice on our pond will be thick enough to skate on in a day or two." Where did that come from, she wondered?

"Excellent!" Will's voice boomed. He latched onto the topic. "I love skating myself. And that reminds me, I wanted to try an idea out on you. You know how hard it is to come by coal these days. Jiminy, last week I near had to sell my soul to get enough for the firing. Anyway, it occurred to me I didn't need coal for the furnace that heats the building. I could make do with wood for a while, and since you folks are in the wood business, I hoped you'd be willing to sell me a cord? I could pick it up myself, bring Charlie for extra muscle. Maybe we could even take a quick turn around the mill pond while we're at it?"

It didn't matter what the occasion was. Will managed to turn it into an adventure. Sarah smiled with instant pleasure.

"Of course! We could make a party of it! Bring Maude along too, and Jenny and I will whip up some hot chocolate and roast potatoes for a skater's feast. It could be quite an event. And certainly yes, you're welcome to as much wood as you need. Just ring us up a day or so before you need it, to make sure it's accessible."

"That's swell. I'm all set for a couple weeks or so but after that I'll come calling. I'd just as soon not get scalped by the locals. They seem to think wood is worth its weight in gold this year."

"War profiteering is disgraceful!" Sarah frowned indignantly, but stopped herself from saying more before she dampened the pleasure of the day. She purposely changed the subject. "Tell me, will the Arnolds be coming this afternoon?"

Will scowled at her. "Heaven forbid! Isobel and George had their kiln opening a few years back. Isobel flattered and cajoled and talked me into it — you know how convincing that lady can be. How they wanted to be first to see a special piece I'd done for them. How she wanted George to buy into the company — on and on." He shook his head at the persuasion and what came after. "That was one of the more disastrous openings in recent memory. A good half of the wares were trash. And the special commission? Stuck smack on the middle of the kiln floor. The glaze liquefied and just glued that thing rock solid. So Isobel and George got to watch me chip it all to pieces, trying to get it out. It was mortifying."

A sympathetic exclamation came from Sarah, but Will shrugged fatalistically.

"For some reason they're still friends, but nowadays I make it a policy not to let outsiders come near a kiln opening."

"It was very kind of you to make an exception for me, then."

"I didn't. I don't consider you an outsider anymore."

Two spots of color reddened on her cheekbones.

"Oh," she said, disconcerted.

Then she rallied.

"Well, I am very flattered."

She quickly tried to rearrange her expectations. She felt special, and self-conscious, to be included in the Pottery's 'family' with Charlie and Maude, the mold-makers and casters and Will himself as they opened up the mysterious kiln. He was still explaining.

"I just thought you'd like to come, take a peek at the operation, maybe see a new thing or two. At least with you..." He sounded almost apologetic. "Well, I know you'll understand if the lot turns out to be no more than a bunch of wasters."

"Of course I would, Will. But that doesn't matter, does it? Because I'm just as sure it won't turn out like that. Now, why don't you escort me back there so I can watch all of you perform this miracle? I can't stand the suspense much longer."

It was clear that Will was still uncomfortable about something.

"There's probably one more thing you should know," he began hesitantly.

"Don't tell me there *is* a problem? The kiln?"

"No, no. So far's I know, the kiln did its job as it was supposed to do. We'll have to see that, hmm?" He smiled weakly. "But it's about the others...the Davenports, I mean, and the Boys..." The 'Boys' were the two big-muscled men who worked the clay, poured the castings, stoked the kiln, and did countless other tasks which kept the firm running. They were not famous for dependability, nor for sobriety. Will forged on with his confession.

"Well, seems Louie heard the call of Uncle Sam last week and up and enlisted. Walked out without so much as a by-your-leave – after he got his pay, of course. And the kiln firing was too much for Mike. I even sent a boy down to Riverdale to look for him this morning, but his missus says he'll be 'too sickly' to work another day or so. Ask me, *he* heard the call of the bottle after kiln-tending night before last."

A disgusted expression crossed his face as he shook his head. He went on.

"Then, to top it all off, Charlie and Maude's aunt passed on this week, and they're off at a funeral in Malden. Don't know when they'll make it back." He took a deep breath. "So I guess that leaves you and me for the opening."

Will stopped abruptly and waited for his news to sink in. Sarah studied his face, the worried look in his dark eyes. Here was a howdy-do, if she ever saw one. She had thought she was coming to a social event. Instead, they were scandalously alone. At the same time Will was making the unpleasant discovery he'd lost his workmen, leaving him with no help to manage the whole kiln opening. *Now really, Sarah,* she found herself thinking, *which is more important?*

"I promise you," Will burst out, nervous in the silence, "I didn't plan for it to be this way."

Sarah continued her study and a smile began to creep across her face. She slowly shook her head at the impossible social situation, at the sincerity of Will's distress, at the quirks of fate or circumstance that had brought them together and made them friends.

"Then we'd better get to it, don't you think?" she said, pulling off her suede gloves and putting them away. Will's answering smile beamed back at her.

As if her words had restored the companionship they had shared canoeing together, conversation was easy after that. Will talked excitedly about the kiln load as they made their way down the narrow stairs, through the storeroom whose empty shelves were witness to the importance of the wares waiting to be unloaded.

The kiln shed's heat felt good after the raw chill outside and Sarah convinced Will she was more than ready to help with the actual work, if for no other reason than to warm up. He reluctantly agreed and insisted she put on a well-worn pair of hide gloves to handle the heated bricks. Will had started opening the tall structure earlier. Its door, through which individual pieces and saggars full of tablewares were loaded, was really just a large arch in the side of the kiln, sealed up with bricks before the firing began. The outside layer of bricks was already down.

"But I couldn't bring myself to open it all the way alone," he confessed, passing two more bricks to Sarah, who stacked them to one side.

"Is there some superstition about that?"

"Oh, no. I just need company to keep me from getting nervous and dropping the best of what's in there," he said sheepishly.

Will worked steadily, and Sarah had no time to look beyond the bricks he handed her with such regularity. A year's work in the fields at Mill Farm had conditioned her to physical labor, and she did not mind the activity, but she found herself regretting the stricture of her best corset, the high collar and tight bodice of her suit that felt hotter with every load. Part of the heat came from the kiln itself, for every brick they removed was like opening a bake-oven door to check on the cake inside. How Will stood the heat of a summer's firing, she could not understand.

As if reading her mind he said, half-jokingly, "Now maybe you'll forgive my lack of etiquette the first time we met?"

He stopped work to remove his coat and push up the sleeves of his white shirt. Sarah, roasting in heavy wool, tried to discreetly slip a handkerchief out of her sleeve to wipe her forehead but Will caught her at it. Looking chagrinned, he offered her the stool that stood nearby.

"It's not right that a lady as nattily turned-out as you should be doing manual labor. What was I thinking?"

"You were thinking just what you should, Will Robertson." She defiantly unbuttoned her jacket and felt the instant relief of air on the mauve silk of her shirtwaist. "I'm a strong, healthy woman perfectly capable of hard work, who doesn't take to being relegated to the chimneypiece while menfolk do everything. Besides," she added briskly, "you seem to be quite short of menfolk today."

Will conceded she was right, but insisted she accept a work apron to keep the brick dust off. That caused another dilemma, as the man's apron had a neck strap instead of the customary pins to hold up its bib. Sarah had to remove her hat in order to slip the apron over her head. Will tied the leather strings behind her back as she returned loose strands of hair to her hairpins.

"You missed one," Will said, reaching up to tuck one behind her ear. She stood still, immobilized by their closeness.

"Can't have hair in the clay, now, can we?" he continued lightly.

Sarah gave a small laugh at the absurdity of his suggestion, and put her mind back on the task at hand.

Another fifteen minutes and the opening was large enough to step into, to reach the vessels inside. Will had been making hopeful comments over his shoulder as they cleared the last of the brickwork.

"Can't see a single saggar broken." He turned back toward the kiln.

"No sign of backdrafts." Another pair of bricks. "They smoke up the goods, y'know."

As they neared the bottom row: "Might have some good stuff in here."

Sarah smiled at his understatement. His version of knocking on wood. He reached inside and cautiously removed one of the cylindrical saggars stacked nearest the mouth. They had been arranged in a protective circle around the single pieces at the center. The saggars moderated any abrupt change in temperature caused by flaring coal or chimney downdraft. They were filled, she knew, with the crackleware which was replaceable. The hand-thrown and glazed art wares at the center were not.

Sarah moved over to the long table as Will set down the saggar, looking forward to seeing what new border might appear, but he shook his head.

"Nah, we'll let these be. They still need to be treated to crack the glaze. I'll give you a glimpse, by and by, but we're working toward the heart right now. Just let me move a couple more of these."

She stood back and watched him lift out the cylinders, appreciating the effortless way he moved the heavy saggars, and the unselfconscious rhythm of the work he knew so well. As he removed one more, Will let out a low whistle of appreciation. She stepped forward eagerly to see what they had been working toward but he put out a hand to stop her once again.

116

"No, wait!" Will's eyes sparkled with excitement. "I want you to see it the way I did once, Sadie. On a bright afternoon the sun comes slanting in that window like a spotlight. Shines in on the wares all fire and light and gleaming. It's a beautiful sight."

He looked at her as if willing her to see with his eyes.

"We're a bit short on sunlight, Will," Sarah pointed out.

He scowled briefly. Then his face cleared. "Maybe we can make do. Let me get something. But you'll promise to wait? Not to look?"

She nodded, amused. "I've worked too hard to spoil this now. I'll wait – but it's going to be hard, you know."

"Won't be but a minute."

She waited for Will to return, glancing once toward the shadowy forms at the heart of the kiln. Then she dutifully turned away, staring out the long window at the cold gray afternoon. It would be dark soon. The light was already dimming in the shed. Single bulbs on metal chains hung the length of the room, but their puddled light couldn't reach the corners, and shadows hovered behind the bottle kiln as well. Just as well Will was bringing more light, if they were to see his special pieces. It was charming of him to make such a fuss for her, like an impresario staging a great drama for her audience of one.

Will came back in a rush, a goose-necked table lamp clutched in his fist with a long cord trailing on the floor.

"Now all we need's a socket," he said. He set down the lamp and shoved a heavy work table beneath the ceiling fixture nearest the kiln. Clambering on to the table, he turned and looked down at Sarah. The Bear, she thought. The light falling on his broad shoulders, on his strong nose and bushy eyebrows, brought back her first impression of a powerful animal half-tame, unpredictable by civilized standards. But this bear grinned at her in anticipation, and his gravelly voice politely asked,

"The cord, madam, if you please?"

She handed up the end of the lamp cord. Will plugged it into the socket attached to the fixture, then lightly jumped down and switched on the lamp. Holding it by the neck, he turned its shade sideways.

"You ready?"

Without waiting for an answer he set his other hand at Sarah's waist and drew her toward the kiln.

Warm light from the lamp embraced a cluster of vases gathered at the center of a domed cave. It shone on glazes rich as gemstones, blazing purple and peach and iridescent green. It ran down trails of white ice, heightened the relief on clear celadon jars, picked out lava-flowing rainbows. The glazes pulsed with color. They glittered in the heat.

"Treasures." Sarah breathed, lost in wonder. "Aladdin's cave of treasures." She stared at the richness before her, without words. A low humming sounded deep inside, rising, echoing inside her head as if in the cave itself. The hum shimmered on a smooth lip, a rounded shoulder. It ran down the strong line of an edge, pooling at the foot of the vessels within. She stood, still and rapt; heat, sight and sound a spell surrounding her with beauty.

After measureless time, she gave a deep sigh and turned to Will. He was looking down at her, studying her with soft intensity in the silence. The ebullience he had brought in with the lamp was gone. He was very serious when he spoke.

"It's fitting that you see this, Sadie Chapman. You're a beholder and in your eyes is beauty."

Sarah nodded, speechless. If she spoke the spell would break. The hum would stop and the world come rushing in. It was very important to Sarah that this moment not end.

Will smiled gently as he continued to hold her eyes. She began to imagine that this moment could last. That they could go on always, touching while not touching, replete with the warmth and the beauty reflected in each other's eyes. Surrounded by the hum that waxed and waned with her blood pulsing.

"Shall we see what we have for treasures?" Will's voice broke into the hum. Sarah pulled herself away.

He set the lamp down and stepped to the kiln, pushing back his sleeves to keep them away from the vessels. Then, one by one, he began to hand them out to Sarah and she knew why he had broken the spell. Each bowl he handed to her, each vase and pitcher he held and admired before he passed it on was another battle won in his own private war. It was a war against shortages and weather conditions certainly, but most of all, every gleaming vase was a victor's trophy in the struggle he waged with himself.

Sarah set them all down gently in a row.

"You must be vastly proud of this collection, Will."

"Of some more than others. These here, though, they're my real treasures."

He arranged a group of simple red shapes together.

"They're the dragon's blood," he explained, "Made with pure gold."

His hand caressed one of the bowls possessively. "They came out well," he said simply.

The light picked out variations of color from one piece to another. Many had a fine white rim at top and bottom. One had purposeful spills of deeper shades running over the shoulder. Will turned back to the kiln.

"There's one more I'm looking for," he said, as he gingerly hunted among the pieces still inside. His voice echoed. Suddenly,

"Aaah." A sigh reverberated in the vaulted space.

Will backed out and turned around to Sarah. He cradled a narrow vase, his hands so big as to almost hide it. Slowly he held it out to her. He watched her silently as she placed it with the other dragon's blood and then stood back to compare. The vase was oriental in form, with a narrow neck. It curved out to a rounded shoulder, then tapered slightly down to the base. It was a delicate and light form, a masterpiece of self-effacing simplicity. The true miracle was its finish, however. The blood red glaze was flawless, evenly spread from lip to base. It glowed in unreachable depths, and the light struck golden sparks off its surface. As Sarah moved, iridescent ripples chased across its shoulder.

"It's perfect," Sarah breathed in awe.

"It's close," Will nodded in satisfaction. "And I'm glad you like it. I made it for you."

"What? Oh my. But no, Will, that's crazy! There's no need to..."

"Now, Sadie, just hush a minute. It may be crazy, but I do need to. You did something very special for me this fall and I need to thank you for it. You came along and got me thinking about what I do, and what I *can* do. You even convinced me that there is more to potting than pots. An act of creation, you said, 'valuable as bread and butter.' Since you said that, every time I've mixed a glaze, I've felt like I was some way shoring up what all those berzerkers on the battlefields of

France are trying to destroy. What you said affirms what my father spent his life doing, and what my grandfather did before him."

The words rushed out of him, spilling through a floodgate newly opened.

"We're not all made to do heroic things, Sadie. But if we're to do whatever it is we do well, then our hearts have to be in it." He paused, the words seeming to run out. "What I'm trying to say is that you put my heart back into my life. This pot is little enough to thank you for it."

Will fell silent and watched Sarah, willing her to accept. She let his words finish sinking in. Then she carefully reached out to the table and picked up the vase, cradling it as Will had done earlier.

"I'd be honored, Will. As I am to know you."

She bowed her head and studied the vase in silence, turning it in her hands and feeling the cooling smoothness of it against her hot palms. She could not think of anything to say.

"There's another gift I'd ask of you," he said gruffly, "though you're certainly not bound to give it."

Sarah set down the vase and glanced at Will uncertainly.

"And what is that?" Sarah countered, her voice sounding high-pitched in her ears.

"For a very long time I've wanted to kiss you. Just once. May I do that, Sadie?"

The blood pulsing in her ears was almost louder than his soft question. Her skin – the very tops of her cheekbones – burned. This was not a request she could take lightly, put off with a social smile and a quick word. Stunned by the panic clutching at her, she looked back at the vase glowing on the table. The hum, a whisper of sound, rose from her belly up past her pounding heart, growing louder as it reached her head. She groped for the right words to answer his question but no sound came. Her brows drew together in confusion and she nodded her head.

Broad hands settled on her shoulders and drew her towards him. He bent toward her and she closed her eyes in dread of his intensity and her own.

Their lips against each other were still at first, afraid to move, to break the spell. Sarah could not say if it was her mouth or Will's that shifted first, daring the unthinkable. Their kiss was long and many-textured. Redolent with promise, terrified by separation. Then it was done.

Sarah pulled herself away and her hand flew to her lips. She could not stop staring at Will, guilt and desire warring in her eyes as her fragile world fell to pieces. How could she have imagined she could laugh with this man and admire him and not find herself loving him and needing him as well? Imagine she might dissolve in his kiss and then walk away, Mrs. Henry Chapman again, as if nothing had changed?

"Oh Sadie." The longing in his voice was unbearable. "How I'd love to have you by me, days and months, ever and always."

Her hand moved of its own accord, reaching out to him, stroking the laugh lines on his cheek. Deep inside she had known it would come to this if she continued to see Will Robertson. Nothing would ever justify it or let it be spoken aloud. Will had brought her joy in endless months of waiting. Not Chappie. Not her husband, whom she would always love and never leave. Tears ran down Sarah's cheeks. Shaking her head at the ruin of it, she reached out again for the solid heat of his body, and pulled him close as she spoke.

"We can't," she whispered.

They held each other by the open kiln, drawing in solace. Dark closed in as they embraced, the world blacked out beyond the frosted windows. For one last time they were the only people on earth and that was enough.

Winter closed in for good just after Christmas. The winter of '18 was as bad as folks could remember, with sleet falling on top of snow, and temperatures below zero for days at a time. The days at Mill Farm were black and white. Looking across the orchard of a morning, Sarah froze in the stillness of the leafless trees and unending white. The pond was thick in ice. Even in the millrace the water barely trickled through, its burbling muffled by the frozen swags and falls that sealed the channel. For the first time in years, Hub hauled out the sleigh from the back of the barn and hitched up Ebenezer for plodding trips to the village, but no one stayed out longer than necessity required in the raw air and the ice-covered snow.

One Sunday morning after yet another snowfall, Sarah sat near the kitchen stove to write to Chappie. She was tired beyond reason, her eyelids weighted down and her arms so heavy it was a chore to raise them to the tabletop. It was the snow, she thought. If only the snow would melt a bit, back away from the house and drive; give even a glimpse of solid ground beneath.

Dearest Chappie,

Your Christmas letter finally came, six weeks in transit! It is beside me now, as I write. Hub had to fetch it from the post office, as even Mr. Sims doesn't trek out this far any more. It has snowed again. The drifts are up over the stone wall – one actually hits the top of the hitching post out front. Looking out the window there's little to see but snow and ice and more snow. The chickens barely venture out of the henhouse any more, and Ebenezer snorts indignantly whenever Hub makes him leave the barn.

Sarah raised her head at squeals of excitement coming from the barnyard. High on a mound at the corner of the barn, Jennie leaned toward the curved front of a toboggan. Her weight tipped the long sled down the slope, and it continued across the yard, stopping just short of the buried stone wall. Jennie threw herself off into the snow and lay, spread-eagled, her red tasseled stocking cap a bright spot against the white. Hub, ever ready to play along with the dramatics, tromped over and, with exaggerated huffing and puffing, hauled Jenny to her feet. The two of them towed the toboggan back to its launch point by the barn.

At least Jennie does not seem to mind the snow. She and Hub are out in the yard now. They've made a grand toboggan run from the top of the old manure pile by the barn, nearly down to the street. Who'd have thought a dung heap could provide such good clean fun?

Life has been very quiet since Amy and Roger's marriage. You did receive my letter recounting the festivities? Roger's regiment sailed less than a week later. For all the joy and pleasure of the wedding, I cannot help feeling sad at how short a time they had to love each other.

Sarah pressed her lips together and angrily wiped away tears that were escaping.

As you will imagine, our Christmas was quiet this year, but we made do as best we could. Your daughter cut out special blue stars for Daddy and hung them on the tree. I made a calico bunny for her which (I'm proud to report) she refuses to be parted from. Duddy worked her sewing magic again and made Jennie the most charming pinafore I've ever seen, complete with tucks and ruffles, and red plaid ribbons to tie in the back. Jennie had to put it right on, before dinner. You should have seen her, Chappie, in front of the tree like a Christmas angel, twirling around as if any second she'd lift right up onto the treetop. You'd be proud of how your little girl has grown.

Hub and Duddy gave her a special treat before the holiday. They took her in to Boston to see the decor and excitement, complete with a trip to Bailey's Ice Cream Parlor and overnight with Hub's cousin in Cambridge. By the time they came home, Jenny couldn't decide whether the taste of a hot fudge sundae or the sight of the Harvard militia parading at the stadium was more thrilling.

Sarah had stood on the station platform, waiting. She could see Jenny clamber down from the train, talking before she was even within earshot, but she couldn't hear a word Jenny said through the humming in her brain. The same humming was in the room now, as she wrote, as if the blood between her ears was rushing away with memories of glowing red vases and winter shadows. It was in her arms where he had grasped them. She lost herself in the heat of his body and the way it enclosed her, wrapping her up and holding her warm and alive.

Sarah shuddered, feeling her skin contract and herself withdraw from the illusion. She dragged herself back to the drafty room and the sound of her daughter, laughing outside the window, and the thought of her husband to whom she was writing. She loved him and he loved her. They had built a life together.

My own activities have been closer to home. When we make it to church on Sunday we all huddle in the vestry downstairs for services due to the coal shortage and the cold but other than that, I have seen few friends because of the weather. I seem to have too many empty spaces in my life at the moment – probably in contrast to all the activity this fall. I find myself checking in nooks and crannies of the house for things to do. I come across unexpected bits of you as I poke about, like your Harvard varsity sweater, and the old work boots I <u>thought</u> you had finally thrown out (!). Jenny and I were looking for a good book the other day and found an Uncle Wiggly with "Henry

Chapman" carefully inscribed inside the cover. Do you remember when you wrote that? Jennie's age, I'm guessing.

Mostly I find myself doing a lot of staring out the window. I am willing the snow to disappear. I keep thinking that the snow melting will mean you coming home. Is there any word yet? Any chance we might begin to count the days again? I must admit I don't feel quite as strong and independent, or any of those other things the papers keep urging 'service womenfolk' to be. I think I need you to come home, Chappie, even more than you wish you were here.

She frowned at what she had written. No 'cheerful tone' here. But what use to write it over? If it did sound slightly desperate, at least it did not give away the frantic swings of thought and mood she had battled through the winter in her own private war. War on the home front, she thought of it, and it threatened everything she touched. It had already made a great hole inside her that pretended to heal if she ever fell asleep. But freezing morning air tore the scab off again and she bled all over. She was not fool enough to think this war could end in victory. But an armistice, perhaps, so the wound might heal until only the faintest scar would be visible to outside eyes.

If she could just negotiate an armistice then the home front would be saved. Jennie, Chappie – they were too precious to engage in her war. But it was so hard. Every day the battles went on, surprise attacks from unexpected quarters, frontal assaults of memory almost destroying her defenses.

She looked down at the paper before her. Even the quiet letters to Chappie had lost their noncombatant status. To write was to reflect, and reflection was a signal for renewed fighting.

You know how winter always makes me slightly crazy. Come the first robin or a hint of thaw, I'll probably be right as rain again! I pray that all is well with you.

She signed the letter and held it briefly against her, then slipped it in an envelope. Her legs resisted the simple act of standing. She paused for a moment, then pulled herself up straight and carried the letter to the front parlor where she sat and stared at the table full of pictures.

*   *   *   *   *

Chappie came home in the last snow of winter. The flakes fell fat and soft in the dusk outside. Sarah, alone in the kitchen, was startled by a knock at the back door. She opened it to a man still in uniform, olive greatcoat flecked with white, hat shading a face so familiar it was dreamlike. Her heart stopped.

"Hello, Sarah."

"Chappie."

There was a stillness between them.

Suddenly she rushed forward, throwing her arms around him, burying her face in the wet rough wool of his coat.

"You *did* come! Oh God, you're here!" Her voice was muffled. Raising her head, she began again. "How did you...? When did...?"

Chappie gently moved her back, looked at her face. At her furrowed brow, the tears in her eyes, the shine coming through the tears.

"It was time to come home," he said.

"Oh, yes," she whispered.

Tucking his arm tight around her he cleared his throat and turned toward the pond.

"Time for the mill, too. Spring freshets pretty soon, I'd guess."

Sarah rested her head back against the knownness of him and noticed the snowflakes wet and cool against her face. Yellow light stretched across the dooryard, lighting the veil of snow which fell outside the sheltering porch. They stood for a moment together, under the round-headed arbor at the door. Flakes clustered silently on the bittersweet twining above them.

A clatter inside brought Jenny's high voice closer.

"Mommy! Mommy! Who's here? Is it daddy this time?"

Sarah looked up at Chappie and smiled.

"Time for a young lady dying to see you again."

The stream of yellow light narrowed to a trickle, then disappeared, as shrieks of excitement and long forgotten laughter echoed out into the silent snow.

The lamp chimneys gently clinked against the enameled dishpan when Sarah took one out to clean. Her hands moved automatically as she stared, bemused, at the yard beyond the kitchen window. There were a few hints of spring in the ground: clumps of crocus and early daffodils along the wall, delicate snowdrops under Nabby's Arbor. She had seen buds on the pussy willows below the dam. The last few days had been unseasonably warm. Jenny had taken to running around with just a sweater, and her boots were coated with mud when she came in. Soon Mill Farm Street would be soft ruts, and wagons would have to stick to the verge until the town's road grader made it passable again. What a contrast to the drifts of winter!

What a contrast in every way, she thought. Chappie had come home a month ago, but already it seemed, in some ways, he'd never left. He returned with a craving to work: to see the mill up and running, to clear the barn of winter's accumulation. He'd taken back the jobs she'd done in his absence, and more besides. Every day he was out checking the fields, on the pretext of mending fences but, Sarah suspected, also willing the ground to thaw, that he might begin planting the new year's crops. It was, she thought, his way of ending the war. With every stall he cleaned and every fence rail he replaced, Chappie was restoring the order he had seen destroyed in France.

He came in for supper exhausted. Then he was content to sit in the parlor and read farm journals or, with Jenny on his lap, to make up stories with her about favorite toys. He showed no interest in taking back his place in town government, or on the bank's board of directors. He made contact with few people outside Mill Farm, seeming to find the society of his own family enough. Sarah watched and waited, seeing Chappie's distance lessen a bit each day. She imagined him on a second journey back to Mill Farm, an internal journey that, in time, would bring him peace of mind. Meanwhile she had a trip to finish as well, finding her way back to him.

Often she would lie awake at night beside him, the only sounds the ticking of the clock on the stair landing, and his slow breathing. Sometimes she would think about Will, wonder how he was doing. Remember, despite herself, the one night they came together. She had seen him only once since then. He and Charlie had come to the farm for wood. She'd been grateful that a new fall of heavy snow did away with any thought of skating parties. Sarah knew she could not have pretended things were as they'd always been. But there was no time alone together either, and she felt painfully lost for words in company. It was impossible to retrieve the easy companionship she had once felt with Will. That had been changed forever. She was too aware of the unspoken questions in his eyes, which cherished her so intimately her cheeks burned and she was sure everyone must see what they felt for each other.

Sarah had watched Will drive away with a confusing sense of relief. Later she had sat at her writing desk facing a blank page. She stared out the window until dusk brought her own reflection into focus on the shadowy panes. Over her own yearning protests, she ended the affair with Will. A friendship could not survive, she wrote, when its baggage of guilt and shame outweighed its joy.

Other times in the silence of the night Sarah would lie very still, listening to Chappie's steady breath and feeling the warmth of his body in their bed. She would offer up thanks that memories of empty nights and desperate days were beginning to fade. Often still, Chappie's breathing would be interrupted by a groan, and he would turn towards her, urgently drawing her body into his arms and muttering his own litany.

"Thank God I'm home."

Sarah's musing was cut off by the door swinging open. She turned from the sink with a smile which froze as she absorbed the sight before her. Chappie had stepped into the kitchen and was dutifully wiping his feet on the mud rug. One hand held his plaid cap, while the other still held the doorknob. Behind him, filling the doorway, was Will Robertson.

"Look who I've just met," Chappie said comfortably. "Mr. Robertson's here for a last batch of wood to get him through the spring. I thought you'd want to say hello."

For a brief moment Sarah panicked, convinced that somehow Chappie knew what had happened in his absence, that he was doing this in retribution. Then she realized that was absurd, that his invitation was a simple social gesture. Judging from Will's awkward hesitation he must have had similar doubts. He stood on the doorstep as if unsure of his welcome, and there was a question in his dark eyes as he looked at Sarah. He nodded his head briefly in her direction.

"Mrs. C.; it's good to see you again."

"Hello, Mr. Robertson."

"Sorry if we're interrupting something..."

"Nonsense!" Chappie cut in. "Come join us for a bit before you head back. Sarah's always got coffee on the back of the stove." He looked at her and raised his eyebrows in question. "I figured we could use a bit of company, don't you agree?"

She wasn't sure whether Will's appearance at her door or the return of Chappie's pre-war sociability was more surprising, but she remembered her manners enough to respond.

"Company is always welcome. There's gingerbread left from last night, too, to go with the coffee."

Sarah dried her hands and escaped to the pantry to get out dishes. She stayed there long enough to calm down, making bustling noises to show she was busy. Finally a small corner of her mind even smiled at the unlikely scene in the kitchen: Chappie and Will across the table from each other, companionably talking about wood and coal, horses and motor cars. The only two men she had ever loved finding each other likeable. Briefly she wished she could just stay there listening, not break the newfound bond by her presence. Then she carried things out to the table and quietly poured the coffee.

At a break in the men's conversation, Sarah reminded Chappie that the dinnerware set for Amy and Roger was made at the Robertson pottery. He nodded appreciatively.

"Mmmf." He swallowed the last of his gingerbread, turning back toward Will. "That is a great set, Mr. Robertson. I gather your firm makes quite a range of wares?"

Will glanced at Sarah, his raised brows appraising how much of the Robertson story she had passed on.

"I wrote Mr. Chapman about the Pottery last fall," she hurriedly explained, "after your kind tour. I thought he might be interested in the different things you make."

"That little bunny you gave Jen was a real winner, did my wife tell you?" Chappie went on.

"She said Jenny liked it."

"Not just liked it! The other night Jen was spinning me a whole yarn about a tea party she was planning for her dolls. How your bunny, and the stuffed bunny Sarah made for Christmas, were going to invite them all out to the lilac grove as soon as it was warm, and they were going to have all sorts of cookies and cakes, and play hop-bunny and find-the-clover. It's going to be quite an event, I imagine." Chappie smiled fondly.

"I'm kind of embarrassed so little could be so important," Will said, self-conscious.

Chappie went on. "Now, that red vase in our front parlor is from your place too, isn't that what you said, Sarah?"

She held her breath for a moment, then nodded. "Yes. The Robertsons have a long history of making art pottery. Mr. Robertson felt that was a particularly good example." She glanced at Will.

Chappie moved restlessly, his nervous energy getting the better of his socializing. "It's a stunner," he said, nodding appreciatively at Will. He scraped his chair back. "Sarah's put it smack in the middle of the mantelpiece, and it kind of lights up the room."

Before Will could respond, Chappie had reached for his cap and stood up.

"You finish up your coffee, Mr. Robertson. I'll see if Hub's got the last of the wood on the truck yet." He dropped a kiss on the top of Sarah's head and strode quickly out the door.

There was silence when he left, a shifting of some of the tension which had made conversation stumble among the three of them. But Sarah could not bring herself to look at Will, although she felt his eyes following her as she cleared away the plates. When he spoke, his voice was wistful.

"It's good to know there's a bit of Robertson to stay in this household."

She met his eyes then. "You will always be part of this household, Will. Part of me which I never want to forget."

He frowned slightly. "He seems like a man worth keeping."

"He is."

He weighed her words.

"We'll still be friends?"

"Oh, yes! We'll still be friends."

Silence.

"It'll never be the same though, will it Sadie?"

"No, Will. It can never be the same."

"Well, then, thanks for the wood." He paused. "I guess there was something to that film, *The Nigger*, after all, hmm? About things righting themselves on the opposite shore."

"I guess there was," she murmured.

Will tipped his ridiculous bowler hat and turned away.

"Godspeed, Will Robertson," she said. "And thank you."

She followed him to the door and watched until he drove out of sight, over the frozen well-used road.

LAYER II: DIGGING IN

When the surficial layer has been removed from an excavation unit, the field archeologist proceeds systematically to remove the soil and its contents through all cultural layers... There is no formal term for this step in the process, but 'digging in' is descriptive of the mental activity involved.
— An Archeologist's Handbook

June 22, 1995

The end of June was plagued by rain. It began again shortly after Hank left Nora's on Wednesday, and was still raining Thursday morning. Nora decided it was time to find the Dedham Historical Society, a local research center, to see what above-ground evidence they might have on the Chapmans and their mill. She didn't expect any great finds, hoping at best for passing references to the family in old newspapers or account books. What she found instead, as soon as she walked through the door, was case after exhibit case of ducks and bunnies, iris and elephants, marching in circles around dishes produced by the Dedham Pottery.

The museum was empty, and she moved slowly around the quiet room, enjoying the little variations which made each piece distinct: a darker shade of blue or a baby elephant in the design, a different crackle in the glaze which seemed to change the whole shape of a bowl. She remembered a friend's long-ago teasing: who but an archeologist would get such a kick out of a bunch of pots? But she intuitively responded to the plates and dishes and mugs that were so bright in contrast to the gloom outside. There was a lightheartedness to them that made her think of Jenny Chapman, who had lost her bunny long ago. Nora shook her head to herself, picturing the tearful search that must have followed.

Absently, she turned to another display case. She must have finished the Dedham exhibit. These ceramics bore no resemblance to the cozy blue-and-white she'd been studying. Massive sculpted serving platters towered behind pitchers trying to look like patinated bronze. Ranks of vases formed a gleaming rainbow. When in doubt, she thought, start with the labels. Nora was a compulsive label-reader. It drove her friends crazy, but she argued that if someone had thought the label important enough to write, it might well be important enough to read. So she tended to take her time and meet up with friends again in the gift shop.

The label that started this case read *Chelsea and Dedham Art Wares*. Here was the range of art pottery produced by the Robertson family in addition to their commercial crackleware. As Nora read the details that followed, she kept sensing an object out of the corner of her eye. It tugged at her attention, insisting it be looked at first. She glanced up and immediately knew why.

Centered in the case, spotlit in the place of honor, was the most beautiful vase she had ever seen. It was deep, dense crimson, and the light glinted gold off the rim. It was all curves and perfect proportions, and as Nora stared at it, the color seemed to shift and change. If a piece of pottery could be alive, this would be the one. It glowed with vital energy. Finally she dragged her eyes away to read the label, like a good scholar. Her exclamation brought the curator out of his office to see what was wrong.

VASE
Dedham Pottery, after 1896
Fine example of "Dragon's Blood" glaze
perfected by Hugh Robertson

Gift of Mrs. Sarah Chapman
in memory of William A. Robertson
(1865-1929)

Later, driving back to Mill Farm, Nora marveled at the strange quirks of fate. First they had dug up that bunny, then Hank mentioned his aunt had owned some Dedham pottery, now here was Jenny's mother giving a gorgeous piece to the museum. Did she buy it that time she wrote about in one of her letters, when she was given a tour of the pottery? The Chapmans must have done a lot of business with the firm, known the owner well, for them to donate a piece in Robertson's memory. Funny it was given just in Sarah's name, but perhaps she was the avid collector of the family. In any case, Nora decided, it was exciting to find another piece of the jigsaw puzzle. Every piece brought her closer to completing the picture. Closer to understanding the real Chapman story.

She wanted to tell Hank what she had discovered.

Nora's first priority, though, was to get back to fieldwork and finding something earlier than 1900 at the site. She wasn't worried – the crew was just past basic training and still moving slowly. But it would be nice if the rain held off for a while and they could pick up the pace.

The next two days proved her right about the crew's productivity. On Friday and Saturday the checkerboard of squares by the lilac grove began to be interesting. They reached the bottom of a second soil layer – only six inches down, but deep enough to expose a straight line of flat-topped rocks. The rocks extended southward from the lilacs toward the uncleared portion of the site, and definitely formed a wall line, although it was still anybody's guess what the wall lined. Was it really part of the Chapman homestead, or just some shed thrown together by Hank's grandfather?

Andrew, working at the northern end of the line of rocks, discovered what appeared to be a corner. His fieldstones turned a right angle and began heading west, away from the pond toward Pam's square in the lilacs. Meanwhile Pam, having finally worked through the worst of the roots, exposed a large boulder which lined up pretty well with Andrew's to sketch what was probably the north end of the foundation. As she dug deeper, her next discovery was more confusing. There was a massive horizontal rock where the cellarhole should be, and it looked suspiciously like a doorstep. Nora listened to what she'd christened the Site Speculation Quotient – the SSQ.

"What's a doorstep doing inside a building?"

"Maybe we've got everything backwards!"

"You mean we're really outside instead of inside the building?"

It was very confusing.

Peg Wentworth's square, south of Andrew's, reassured them that they were still on the right track. Same exposed rocks, neatly lined up and fairly level, with more stonework showing up underneath. This was what a wall line was supposed to look like. But Peg's square had its own puzzle. The dirt inside her wall line changed from one end of the square to the other.

At the north end was loam mixed with pebbles and gravel that identified it as fill, dug up from some other spot and dumped here. That wasn't the surprising part. Open cellarholes, notorious for causing broken legs and providing cozy dens for rattlesnakes, were regularly filled in. But the south end of Peg's square looked different. It was a jumble of rocks and stones, some big and solid; others just piled in between. There was sand and clay, and one big white patch. That patch turned out to be a glob of plaster, complete with a small strip of lath embedded in it.

A piece of plastered wall! So this wasn't just a rough shed. The crew took another excitement break to admire Peg's find and exclaim over this simple evidence that they were working on a house site after all. Again, Nora checked the SSQ and threw in some cautionary questions. Where had the wall stood? How old was it? No nails had turned up, which might have helped with dating. The missing answers were enough to send the crew back to work.

On the days that followed, the crew's speculation focussed on a new square assigned to Doug, the anthro major, at the southwest corner of the checkerboard. More stone rubble appeared, along with three hand-made bricks. The bricks had shiny blackened sides and the kind of pockmarked spalling that could only come from intense heat.

"These are burned." Doug frowned over them.

"Not just overfired?" Pam, who studied pottery, asked.

Doug handed one to Nora for corroboration. She shook her head.

"These were burned in use, I think, not in a kiln. No self-respecting builder would have used bricks that were so badly damaged."

"Maybe they were part of a conflagration!" LeValliere Junior had a particularly high SSQ and a large vocabulary.

"The burning of Medfield?" Peg's eyes sparkled at the notion.

Pam stared at Miss Wentworth as she considered the reference to 1676, when Wampanoag sachem Philip led a confederated band of Indians on fiery raids through Medfield and surrounding towns. "You mean this house was burned by the Indians?"

Peg shrugged hopefully. Everyone was looking at Nora for encouragement.

"You know, plain old fireplace bricks sometimes end up looking this way."

Pam respectfully cradled the brick she'd been handed. "But Miss Wentworth *could* be right, couldn't she? Think of the Chapman family running from the flames. How terrifying! Do you think they escaped?" Her eyes were wide with the enormity of her imagining.

"Of course they did!" Andrew snorted. "They're still living here three hundred years later, aren't they?"

Pam blushed and pressed her lips together. Nora decided it was time to intervene.

"There are lots of things that could have been at Mill Farm, including some we'll never know for sure. What I *can* tell you for sure, Pam, is that these bricks are evidence of a fireplace having been here. Maybe right where you found them, Doug. Thanks to you, we now have a house with plastered walls and a fireplace."

The rest of the crew still looked unhappy at having to abandon their conflagration theory.

"Wait. There's more information in these bricks," Nora went on. "And it is actually the exciting part. See this shape? Long, thin, uneven? How the bricks don't match exactly? I'm willing to bet these bricks predate the Civil War."

Nora watched expressions change as she added the punch line.

"We made it back to the nineteenth century!"

A wave of cheers and exclamations ran through the group as they digested the significance of her announcement. Andrew was still recalcitrant.

"Only two hundred more years to go," he muttered darkly.

Sunday was June at its best, breezy verging on hot, and Nora was relieved to walk out on the bills waiting to be paid. She'd agreed to meet Hank at the dig after lunch for an owner's tour of Mill Farm. On the way she reminded herself they needed to talk preservation strategy before the afternoon ended. Hopefully it wouldn't be too complicated, just defining a party line to use against George Majors. What a character he was. A really strange guy to have on the Commission. Why on earth a consensus man like Ralph Whiting ever appointed him was a mystery.

Hank was already at the site, and turned toward her with one of those open grins she found so distracting.

"Quite a hole you've got here. Turn up any more treasures?"

"We found the 1800s. How's that?"

Hank's raised eyebrows led her to describe the crew's progress and the features they had exposed. Hank was clearly interested in the excavation, full of intelligent questions, and Nora was aware of the pleasure of talking to someone who understood more than the basics. He might not be an archeologist, but Hank understood the correlation between cellar size and building age. He frowned at the puzzle of the inside-out doorstep and enjoyed the notion of the Site Speculation Quotient.

"I'm sorry I'm out of town so much." Hank stepped back from the dig and shook his head. "I'd love to try my hand at archeologizing. My work doesn't get below ground level but it might be fun for a change."

"It has different advantages." Nora spotted an opening for preservation talk. "But think of it this way – we're just doing opposite ends of the same thing. You preserve things that are about to be destroyed. I resurrect – well, maybe 'exhume' – what's left from the destruction. Somewhere in between lies real history."

Hank held up his hands. "Wait a minute. I'm definitely not a historian."

"I don't mean textbook history. I'm talking about what actually happened in the past."

She stopped herself. The earnest Doctor Tunney tone was creeping into her voice and Hank was looking doubtful.

He squinted across the site toward the mill pond.

"Historian or not, you want to see the mill?"

He didn't waste time changing the subject, she noticed. He was the tour guide, though, she reminded herself. For now, she'd just keep quiet and learn what Hank had to teach.

"I think we'll go chronologically," he began. "Do the tour in order of building construction. That will mean in order of groundwork too, of course."

"Of course?"

He pointed toward the mill dam. "You can't put up a building until you've prepped the site. Especially when it's a mill site."

The answer seemed obvious after he'd said it.

"Show me what I need to know."

They walked downhill from the dig to the grist mill which, they agreed, stood a good chance of being the oldest building still standing at Mill Farm.

"Of course that means the dam has to be even older," Hank pointed out. "At least in its earliest incarnation. If you dug deep enough into it you could probably still find some of the old wood cribbing under all the dirt." He twisted a padlock and shouldered open the battered mill door.

The shadowy building was knee-deep in dust and cobwebs. Hank showed Nora around the mill floor, pointing out the sturdy base where mill stones had once stood. Then he drew her attention to one of the massive corner posts that framed the building.

"See that post? Just remember it for now. There's more to say about that post."

Nora nodded dutifully and followed him down a dubious ladder into the wheel pit. It was clammy with the heavy dampness of wooden structures built over water. The sluiceway was empty except for a puddle or two, but Hank talked knowledgeably about the vanished waterwheel and the complex wooden gearing that must once have filled the space.

Two ladders later, they were in the grain loft. The loft was murky, its details almost impossible to distinguish until Hank swung open the grain door on the west side. Afternoon sun streamed in through the swirls of dust they had disturbed, highlighting ropes and pulleys and a pattern of beams and rafters overhead.

"Look at the size of those rafters! And the trunnels they used. And over here ..." He led the way to a dark corner where a massive post stretched up through the floor to the roof line. Hank reached out his hand and rested it familiarly against the strong-grained wood.

"This is the post I showed you down below. Solid oak, eight inches square. Needs some work down by the sill, but the rest of it's as solid as the day it was cut. And look. You can see the adze marks. These posts are *hand-hewn*. Can you imagine how long it must have taken to make just one of these? This building's really old."

He turned back to study the beam and patted it lovingly. "Imagine the tree this piece of wood came from. Full-grown before the first white man arrived in Medfield." His voice faded off in contemplation.

By this time it was clear to Nora that Hank's knowledge of traditional woodworking was well beyond hers. "You know a lot about old mills. Have you actually worked on one, or is it in the Chapman blood?"

"A bit of both, I guess."

"So you think this is a really old building, then? Older than, say, the Big House?"

Hank grinned at her. "Oh, yeah. I'm a firm subscriber to the First Mill in Medfield theory. At least this frame."

He gave the corner post a final pat. Then he motioned Nora toward the ladder and turned to close the grain door. He continued talking over his shoulder. "Most of the frame is still in amazing shape. Sills need work. The base of that post will have to be replaced. But all in all, it's remarkably sound."

Nora's enlightened self-interest quietly cheered to hear that mill stabilization didn't sound like it would require all the Commission's money after all.

"All we'd need is a set of stones and a new wheel, and the place would make Thomas Chapman himself proud. Why, the old guy might come back from the dead just to see it run."

Even Hank applied the SSQ. He was having one of those old-mill-guy fantasies of everything put back The Way It Used to Be. Nora winced at his ignoring two hundred years of changes in the process.

Hank stepped off the ladder in time to catch the grimace on Nora's face, and misinterpreted its cause.

"You really don't think the mill's that old, do you?"

"No. I mean... That's not exactly true," she stuttered, shifting gears. "It's just that... Well, people tend to assume things are older than can be proven. And I've had a lot of clients who don't want to hear what they don't already believe."

He snorted appreciatively. "You don't have to tell me. One job I worked was a concrete block building the owner was convinced had weathered the Civil War. Forget that concrete block wasn't invented for another fifty years. Clients can be really stubborn."

A sympathetic nod, and Nora reminded herself that Hank really did understand. She needed to stop imagining trouble where there wasn't any. Too many recalcitrant clients in her past, maybe. But this was the Mill Farm Project and a very different situation.

From the grist mill they cut across the dam to check out remains of another structure located by the second spillway. The dam curved, forming a vertical half-cylinder into which the water funneled. Next to it, flat-topped granite boulders sketched a rectangular outline on the ground.

"Penstock's still here." Hank gestured toward the cylindrical indentation. "When I was a kid, the turbine was still sitting in the bottom of it."

"Was this a later grist mill?"

Hank shook his head. "Somebody said there was a saw mill here once."

They studied the boulders silently for a few minutes, looking for confirmation. Then Nora remembered the reference in one of Sarah's letters to splitting firewood, and running the sawmill come winter. She mentioned it to Hank, who nodded. He kept on nodding as he stared at the stones. Suddenly he turned and Nora could tell by the excitement in his face that something had clicked into place.

"Makes sense, too. I hadn't really looked at it before. Look." He stretched his arms out parallel in front of him, drawing lines in the air that echoed those made by the stones. "A long rectangle, built to hold the log carriage that moved the wood past the saw blade."

Nora wondered why she hadn't picked up on the outline herself. This was, after all, ground-level evidence. She should have understood.

They poked around the footings, not finding anything more notable on the surface than some stray pieces of rusty iron. Remnants, they guessed, of long-gone machinery.

"What happened to the turbine? Did it just disintegrate?" Nora looked to Hank for answers.

He stopped his poking and a gleam came into in his eye.

"Here's some real local history. When we were kids, my sister Faith and I played down here a lot. Jumping off the dam was strictly forbidden but no one ever told us we couldn't be *on* it, so after we read Winnie the Pooh we came here to play Pooh-sticks."

Nora looked blank. Pooh-sticks was not a game that had ever made it to downtown Lawrence. And its connection to the turbine was not obvious.

"You know, you drop sticks in a stream, preferably by a bridge, maybe a culvert. Then you run to the other side of the bridge and see whose stick comes out first. When we played, Faith's always won and I decided the answer was to use bigger sticks. Then I tried branches. It kind of escalated from there and we kind of clogged up the turbine."

He still looked sheepish telling about it twenty years later.

"And …?" Nora prompted.

"It started raining, and we went inside. Next morning there was such a back-up of brush at the dam that the grist mill almost washed away… It took all day in the pouring rain to clear the penstock. That's when Dad decided to take out the turbine, before any real damage happened."

"I'm guessing that was the end of Pooh-sticks?"

"Yeah. Want to try one anyway?"

Nora raised an eyebrow. He bent down and scooped up two sticks, matching up one end and breaking off the other until they were of a length.

"This is my new theory. Same size, same chance of winning."

He politely held them out for her to choose. They dropped them off the little footbridge that crossed the sluiceway, and spun around to the other side to watch. The two sticks chased each other over the fall, swirling out of the penstock and away. Nora felt a lift of pleasure riding the sticks downstream but she turned to Hank and shook her head.

"You know there's a problem with your theory. I have no idea which one was mine."

"Doesn't matter, either, does it?"

They looked at each other and grinned, sharing the absurdity. Then they decided they'd better continue the grown-up part of the tour.

"Chronologically," Hank said, "next stop after the dam and the mills should be the Big House." They wandered back to Mill Street and up toward the barnyard where Nora's apartment faced the main house.

"It's a really fascinating building," he began.

She was interested to hear why he thought so, because it wasn't clear to her that it had much to offer. The part that faced the road gave the impression of being very tall, although it was only two stories. Door and windows were regularly spaced, the chimney was perfectly centered, no shutters interrupted the even clapboarding. Some would call it 'neat and trim,' and it was. But it also struck Nora as having no personality. The side of the house that faced the barnyard was a little better. A bow window caught the light and a round-headed arbor at the side door broke up the building's straight lines. Still, there wasn't anything obviously fascinating about the place. Nora started to ask Hank what he saw that she didn't, when he frowned.

"Damn."

"Problem?"

"Well, the Downeys are away and I never talked to them about going through the house. I don't want to just walk in when they're not around."

She smiled to herself. Conscientious landlord.

"How about an outside tour?"

Hank nodded hesitantly. "I could do that." He started to move to the side of the building, considering how to begin, but he came back shaking his head.

"No, you need to see the inside. Especially the attic," he added decisively. "There are enough mysteries in there to interest even an archeologist."

"Mysteries?"

"Problems with the way the house is put together and the wood they used. Almost like three different periods at once. It's very peculiar." Then he brightened. "It's also very interesting. I'll show you when we can get in."

Leaving her with that teaser, he turned back to the barnyard.

"Now the barn, on the other hand. That's pretty straightforward."

They wandered toward the Shed, and Hank talked easily about the nineteenth-century barn, its attachments and outbuildings. The remains of a chicken coop stood nearby, where he and Faith had begun an earnest project raising rabbits, only to learn that rabbits dug excellent tunnels. Hank moved from the empty hen yard toward the arbor Nora had admired on first sight.

"Nabby's Arbor," Hank commented.

"Who was Nabby?"

"I haven't the vaguest idea," was his unsatisfactory answer.

The arbor was roofed with vines and Hank had to duck under tight green clumps of grapes to get to the bench inside. This spot, like the dam and the chicken coop, drew out memories.

"This used to be my mother's hideaway." A half-smile. "We always knew if we couldn't find Mom, to look out here."

"It doesn't sound like a very successful hideaway."

"According to her it was all she needed. She'd come out here to shell peas or fold laundry. When one of us found her, she'd buy herself a bit more time by making us sit and be quiet, 'to listen for Nabby's whisper,' she said. I never got beyond grape leaves rustling, though, or maybe sparrows."

"Didn't you ever ask about Nabby?"

He thought about that for a moment while they sat and stared across the yard. Finally he shrugged.

"When I was little, I assumed Nabby was Mom's imaginary friend. By the time I was old enough to ask, I guess it didn't seem important any more."

The scholar in Nora was incensed by Hank's perpetual nonchalance. How could he not ask? People don't name places after imaginary friends. Nabby was probably one of his own ancestors, probably had sat right here. Didn't he care about his own family's past when he lived surrounded by it, every day?

"You could ask your mother now." Her tone was crisp. "We could learn something important about the landscape if we identified Nabby. Maybe she was involved in building the arbor."

"Can't do that. My mom died a while back."

"Oh, I'm sorry..." Nora began, but Hank was still speaking, almost to himself.

"Amazing how much you don't think to ask until it's too late. Faith and I keep stumbling over questions we didn't even know existed until there was no one left to answer them."

His words held a puzzled sadness that made Nora look for something reassuring to say. "We might still track down Nabby... ."

But Hank was already moving on, unfolding himself from the leaf-littered bench and gesturing toward the road.

"If you head up that way you'll find two or three fields that are still part of the farm. Pastures, really. We still cut the hay for mulch. But I'd guess by the clear ground and the stone walls, the fields were crop land once."

The subject of family history was pushed aside again. For all Hank's seeming openness, Nora decided, he seemed to have a very private side.

During the next half-hour Nora followed Hank through orchards that lined both sides of the road north of the Big House. She was amazed that Hank knew so much about every tree they passed, since her own apple vocabulary consisted of Delicious and Granny Smiths. Hank, though, had clearly spent a lot of time getting to know these trees and was naming off Pippins and Russets, Spartans and Rhode Island Greenings. The orchards were much bigger than Nora had guessed from the road, and had been recently pruned. New saplings were growing where old stock had died out. Someone had mowed in crisscrossed swathes that widened to avenues between the varieties.

"What do you do with all these apples?" She conjured up teetering mountains of pies.

"Sell them, mostly. We ship all over New England."

"Are your orchards really that big?" She tried to keep the note of awe out of her voice.

"No. Actually they're really small. But they're some of the best old-fashioned varietals on the East Coast. Come on, there's one more section you need to see."

It was doubtful she could do justice to another apple tree. There was not a striking difference between them that she could see other than, maybe, size, but Hank's enthusiasm made it impossible to say no. Besides, it was very peaceful in the orchard, with insects chirring in the branches and late afternoon sun showering through the leaves. She might not know apples, but she knew peaceful when she felt it.

They crossed a dirt road into another stand of trees.

"This is it," Hank announced. "These are the rarest trees in the whole place, and they put Chapman Orchards in the books."

While the reason was undoubtedly clear to him, it wasn't to an archeologist. The trees were small; even the apples were small compared to others they had passed.

"You're going to tell me why?"

He beamed at her. "These are Nabby apples."

"You're kidding. As in Nabby's arbor?"

A raised brow. "Could be."

"Why didn't you tell me before? You said you didn't know anything about Nabby."

"I don't, really." His voice was matter-of-fact. "All I know for sure is that the Nabby apple's the oldest variety grown here, and that it almost died out other places. It's only been in the last ten years or so that I've grown enough stock to sell commercially again. In my dad's day you couldn't buy a Nabby."

"Geez, Hank. You're standing in the middle of history! I can't believe how... how...," she made helpless sweeping gestures as she fumbled for words. "...how *integral* the past is at Mill Farm! Don't you feel that? Don't you get shivers or something when you bring back the past – literally – like this apple business?"

Hank studied Nora long enough to make her uncomfortable. She wondered if her effusiveness had put off this man who didn't want to discuss the past.

"Not shivers." His voice was considering. "This apple business, as you call it, warms me up, the same way fixing old buildings does. Pruning back overgrowth to find the neglected old stock. It makes the blood flow faster and you know you're doing something right."

Positively voluble, as Peg had said. Nora realized he was waiting for her reaction.

"It's a good thing, rescuing what might be lost." The words seemed inadequate. "Do I gather you run Chapman Orchards?"

Hank looked relieved to be back on a simpler topic. "No, not really. I've got a guy who's a real professional doing that. We're a long way from the farmstand my grandparents used to have up the road."

"I'll bet." *Long way and a lot of family capital,* the refrain went. Nora found herself mulling over the evidence of what a little money and a lot of perseverance could do but Hank interrupted, pointing down the dirt road they had just crossed.

"Anyway, that's my driveway and pretty much the whole tour, unless you count Orchard Cottage. I'll show you that, if you want."

Nora was surprised to find it was late afternoon already and wondered if Hank's *if you want* was a nice way of excusing himself. This was his own house, after all, and she had the impression he was very private about it. On the other hand, it was supposed to be the cider mill and a necessary part of her landscape study.

"Are you sure? I don't want to be a bother."

"Of course you won't. Besides, I owe you at least a beer after all that chicken soup you gave me last week."

Nora didn't need any more convincing. They headed down the rutted driveway in the general direction of the pond, following its curves and turns to a disheveled yard. Hank's battered ambulance was parked next to a woodpile where the driveway melted into ferns and field weeds beside a shed-roofed ell. This, she guessed, was where the infamous bats lived. The main house was simple enough, story and a half, brown shingled. The front door was built into a big sliding panel that once must have opened, as the wrought iron track still stretched across the building. There were white-framed casement windows and a granite doorstep flanked by floppy hydrangeas. Unpretentious, Nora decided, like its owner.

Orchard Cottage managed to look inviting despite the dishevelment. Its location, surrounded by apple trees, was extraordinary and Nora could imagine the house, come spring, in a sea of pink and white blossoms. Now, in late June, the leaves made islands of green shade. For a moment she lost herself in imagining what it would be like to live here. Relaxing. Idyllic.

"It's safe to come in, you know. The rest of the place isn't quite as bad as the back yard."

Hank was opening the door and looking back at her. Nora blushed at being caught coveting his house, and hurried to follow him inside. Her first glance registered a surprisingly clean kitchen and a glimpse of bookcases beyond, along an end wall. The rest of the house was momentarily blocked by Hank's tall frame filling the doorway. When he moved on, Nora audibly gasped.

"It's beautiful!"

He turned to see where she was looking and agreed comfortably. "It is, isn't it?"

Across the living room a wall of French doors opened to a flagstone terrace and a field beyond. A hundred yards farther, sunlight slipped across the water of the mill pond. Nora walked through to the terrace, oblivious to the room she crossed. The view drew her into itself as if it was as much part of the house as roof and walls.

"I always think of this as my front yard." Hank's voice came from behind her. "The 'river front' of a southern mansion."

She turned to find him sprawled in an old metal lawn chair with a satisfied expression on his face.

"A modest southern mansion," she managed to joke but then lapsed into silence again, drawn back to the view and the quiet. Eventually she stirred herself enough to sit down, and tried to explain.

"I'm sorry. I'm really not usually so distracted, but this is the kind of place dreams are made of. I've never seen a spot so perfectly peaceful in my life."

Hank nodded. Then he settled his head back against the top of the chair and stared out toward the water.

"The first thing I do when I come home from a trip, is check out the view. See what I've missed, whether the ice is out, what's growing. That way I know I'm home, if you know what I mean."

Nora said she did, although in fact she wasn't sure they were reading from the same dictionary. Being home meant sitting in her mother's formica kitchen and watching ants eat the hollyhocks outside the window. It meant Mrs. Dracott's loud TV and sirens down the street. It did not mean peace and quiet and a view to die for.

"Of course, sometimes it's more comfortable looking from inside," Hank added. "Then it's very dramatic, branches whipping in the wind, or the pond fading in and out of fog."

Nora smiled wistfully. "How long did you say the cottage has been here?"

"As a cider mill, a long time. 1800's maybe. I keep thinking I'll look it up, but that never seems to happen."

Hank's smile was vaguely apologetic, but Nora knew the apology was only for her benefit.

"We should be able to pinpoint the dating. Documentation is excellent for that period."

"You really like old documents, don't you?" Hank asked blandly, but before she had a chance to respond, he held up a hand. "No, wait. Don't answer that yet. I see that turning into a longer discussion than should be done without a beer. Can I offer you one? A glass of wine?"

She had to smile at what appeared to be a smooth way of avoiding a Tunney lecture, and opted for the wine. On the way to the kitchen she inspected the room she'd ignored earlier. It was big and open, with floor to ceiling bookcases where blue and white pottery ranged alongside books and salvaged bits of buildings. Nora recognized the Dedham ware and asked Hank about the "gift of Sarah Chapman" vase in the museum. His surprise was gratifying. The crackleware on the shelves was inherited, he said, but he'd never heard of any family art pottery collection.

The whole living room was furnished with what had to be Chapman family pieces. Hank's seat was obviously the worn red-leather club chair close to a big fireplace and oriented so he could keep tabs on his view. A doorway showed an office piled with blueprints, notebooks, odd bits of wood and wrought iron. An Apple Growers Association poster hung on the far wall, along with framed certificates of some sort. Hank's voice interrupted Nora who was trying to see around the bend of stairs that headed up beside the office.

"Bath and bedroom upstairs." He filled in the blank as he held out two full glasses. "And storage over the office. That's where Sarah's letters came from."

"I wondered," she said casually, trying to keep her fascination from looking like nosiness.

147

Hank led the way back outside with a plate of cheddar and saltines. Nora followed more slowly, cautious of the ancient rug underfoot but relaxing with every step she took. It seemed so natural to have a drink and keep talking. As they settled back with feet propped on a wooden crate-cum-table, Hank surprised Nora by bringing up the topic she thought he had purposely avoided.

"So, tell me about you and old documents and archeology and such."

"Oh, I don't think there's anything very interesting to tell."

"No, come on," he prompted. "I've spent the whole afternoon going on about me and mine. Tell me about you. I'm interested."

Nora wondered what she could tell him that didn't sound like a resume, and why it was important to convey more to this man than plain facts. She wasn't sure she wanted to explore the second question too deeply, but decided to try out the story of Mr. Caton's dancing.

"If you really want to know, my archeology career really started the spring that Mr. Caton danced on the desks."

Hank looked suitably intrigued by that beginning, so Nora plunged ahead.

"I was in seventh grade, and Mr. Caton was our history teacher. He was supposed to get us all the way through ancient history in five months. He gave it a valiant try. He would stride back and forth from one blackboard to the other, drawing curves and arrows and asterisks to go with blow-by-blow accounts of the Battle of Marathon, or the siege of Masada. It was stirring, and important."

"I never had a dancing history teacher."

"Your loss, undoubtedly. Actually, I don't think Mr. Caton really danced but he did stand up there, declaiming in the agora. He had us papering classroom walls with diagrams of togas and armor, and practicing legal debates in the forum, and somehow he made the past seem believable. As if there had been flesh-and-blood people in it living real lives. Strange lives, assuredly, but still lives that could be understood, or at least imagined."

Nora paused for a sip of Hank's very good wine.

"No Mr. Catons in my education." He frowned as he thought back. "You got all this in five months? You must have been a quick study."

"That year we all were. Something to do with restructuring the curriculum, which left only half a year for ancient history."

"Lucky you."

"I was," she answered, refusing to acknowledge the sarcasm. "Mr. Caton made time race by. History became a jumble of nations running into nations, cultures melting together, whole civilizations stacking up on top of each other."

Nora caught herself in the middle of a sweeping gesture and suddenly felt acutely self-conscious. To her surprise, Hank still looked interested, if somewhat skeptical. He even smiled encouragingly.

"All those stacked civilizations got you into archeology?"

All right, she thought. Put it all out at once. Time for the Triple-Decker Theory.

"Remember, I was in seventh grade. I had an adolescent appetite and right away I decided history was a triple-decker sandwich. You see, if you chomp down through all the layers at once you get a nice big mouthful, but it's really hard to identify what's inside. But if you take your time, nibble a little here and there or gently peel the sandwich apart, you discover how complex it is. Look at those ingredients! Who would have guessed that those two would go together? And here's the same thing repeated in every layer, all the way to the top."

By now Nora's hands were talking almost as much as her mouth. She realized her left forefinger was poking at layers of invisible lettuce in the historical sandwich held by her right hand. Suddenly self-conscious, she moved the finger to her lips and almost tasted mayonnaise.

"Am I making any sense?"

Hank was studying her soberly.

"Was that the beginning of your cooking career?"

A shadow of doubt crossed her forehead before she rose to the occasion. "The dawn of the Iron Age Chef, you mean?"

"Come on, your chicken soup was a lot better than that. I was thinking Cooking Down & Dirty 101."

She raised an eyebrow. "That's better? How about Foods for the Early Archaic?"

"Sounds like an old folks' menu to me." Hank stopped grinning for a minute. "Seriously, though, I've actually thought of what you were describing, but in terms of telescope and microscope. Microscopic resolution is the close-up study you need to really understand something."

"My sandwich layers?"

"Um-hum. The big picture – the telescopic view – is the broader perspective we need to understand the *significance* of what we're doing."

She nodded eagerly. "The whole triple-decker." How ridiculously exciting it was to carry on a whole conversation in bizarre abstractions. And to have someone else do it too. "You do understand! I think I like your way of describing it better than mine."

Hank graciously toasted her with his glass. Nora thought it was time to put an end to her intellectual biography.

"Well, I was going to say that archeology eventually replaced history as my triple-decker sandwich. Knowledge at its most palatable. But I think your metaphor is more elegant. To make a long story short, I never even got to the Middle East, where I'd thought I would spend my life. My doctoral research was here in New England. But when I finally pulled together all the strands of prehistory and history on one small site, I knew I had done what you describe: I had created a telescopic view with microscopic resolution. I knew the names and dates of all the players who had camped and worked and settled and lived on that site. And I also knew the bigger picture, the 'sweep of history'," Nora gestured dramatically, "into which their life stories fit. I had finally mastered Mr. Caton's lesson."

"And turned into an archeologist?"

"One of the only jobs I know that stretches your brain while you get your hands dirty."

"There are a few others, you know."

He reached for a saltine but stopped with it halfway to his mouth.

"Hey, I'm starved. Do you want to stay and eat?"

"Sure. But don't you have other things to do? Maybe another time …"

The dent appeared in his left cheek. "We could make triple-decker sandwiches. Toasted, if you like."

Nora had to laugh. Who could refuse a man who offered toasted triple-deckers?

"All right then. As long as you let me help."

Hank unwrapped his legs and stood up. "Time for some supper music, then." He waved Nora inside and turned to a cupboard on the bookcase wall. "Something simple and melodic. Preferences? Early Miles Davis? Gershwin? We can hum through dinner and discuss philosophy over Dove bars for dessert."

"I don't think philosophy will survive a Dove bar."

"Probably not," he said agreeably.

The triple-deckers ended up a cross between Italian subs and Greek salad. Nora found bacon, salami and feta cheese in the refrigerator; Hank dug out oregano and a can of olives. He moved a heavy silver candelabrum from the bookcase to the table, assuring Nora that the flickering light would camouflage anything that dripped.

When they finally sat down Hank refilled their glasses and set the bottle down carefully.

"I'd like to make a toast," he announced. His expression held none of the laughter Nora had enjoyed as they fixed dinner.

"Here's to company. It's nice to talk to somebody who understands what I'm saying."

"Thank you." She lifted her glass. "I had the same thought earlier."

They nodded to each other, sharing the closeness with the toast.

Talk during dinner skipped from favorite CDs to college stories, from tree pruning disasters to black flies. There was an eagerness to conversation as they discovered shared tastes and more stories to swap. Nora, not wanting to rock the new boat they seemed to be in, put aside her questions about the Chapmans. Hank didn't volunteer, fascinating her instead with descriptions of Anasazi villages and dinosaur digs he'd seen during trips out west. He had a great memory for details and Nora asked her fill of questions.

After supper they sat in the dusk on the terrace and watched stars come out and drank coffee from Dedham Pottery cups. The urge to talk had wound down to comments interspersed with comfortable silence. Time to head home came earlier than Nora would have wished. They both had work tomorrow. But it had been so long since she'd had an evening like this. Ideas that excited. A place that soothed. A man she'd like to know a whole lot better. She heard whispers of regret in the darkness, at the fate that defined them as boss and employee, instead of two people on the verge of something. Nora sighed and stood up to go.

Hank didn't protest, but insisted on walking back with her, saying the way through the orchard could be found even after dark, and there was no reason she should go all the way around. It was quiet between the trees. A late robin scolded her young and crickets chirred in the long grass around the tree trunks. Nora was watching her step and soaking up the last bits of pleasure from the evening. Hank's voice surprised her.

"Remember Sarah Chapman's letter about the orchard? The one where she reminds Chappie of being there together?"

She hadn't remembered, until then. How could she have forgotten? Such a passionate, lonely letter.

"I remember."

"This had to be the orchard she wrote about. You know, ever since we read that, these trees have looked different to me. Shadows here and there. Bits of movement. Almost like the two of them still embracing." Hank's words paused. "I think they must have been very much in love."

They continued to walk. Nora was grateful the dark hid the heat in her cheeks. When Hank *was* willing to think about the past he certainly did it with a passion. His words were very evocative. Provocative? Disturbing, anyway, threatening to disrupt the easy companionship they were building. But the picture he drew, she admitted, was compelling. The night's softness and whispers brought Sarah back and involved the two of them somehow, with her and her love.

When Nora was still searching for words Hank cautioned, "Watch the stones."

She had been so lost in visions of Sarah and Chappie that she hadn't noticed they had reached the wall by Mill Farm Street. Hank caught her elbow as she stumbled, then firmly took her hand and helped her over the stones. They stayed that way, hand in hand, across the street, and through the barnyard to Nora's doorstep.

It was that last awkward moment in unfamiliar territory. Nora glanced up at Hank, to tell him how thoroughly she had enjoyed the whole afternoon. He bent down and kissed her instead. Not long. But soft, warm-lipped. Very nice. Very disconcerting. Nora retreated, beginning to stutter about not being sure… The words died as Hank's finger brushed across her lip.

"Shh. Sometimes you think too much. Good night."

A wisp of that grin again. Then he walked away into the night orchard.

She was glad when morning came and with it, an end to thinking too much. Sunday night had brought more rain and the ground was too wet for digging. Nora encouraged the crew with reminders about the site's remarkable permeability, that the ground would dry out almost before they noticed. Then, armed with the new information she'd gathered from her weekend tour, she set them to work mapping the immediate survey area.

They measured the dam and the grist mill sluiceway, and plotted the outline of the building. They cleared brush away from the footings Hank and Nora had imagined to be a saw mill. The rectangular shape he had pointed out became clearer when the bushes were removed, but what really made a difference was drawing it. Boulders and spaces were so obviously aligned. Shapes of stones took on regularity when seen in two dimensions. Nora caught herself wondering if the past could really have been as simple as it looked in black and white.

Meantime, Peg Wentworth set to work on the background research Hank had never done. She arrived at the lab Wednesday morning with copies of old Medfield maps. An 1876 map had *saw mill* labeled alongside *grist mill* at the outlet of Chapman Pond. Apparently the cutting operation had already ceased to exist before another map was drawn in 1924, however, for that one showed only one building at the dam. There was no mention in earlier town records of sawyer Chapmans either. The crew's SSQ was replaced by a reasonable conclusion that the saw mill was a nineteenth-century blip on the family business screen. Nora made a note to do some testing around the boulders to back up their theory. No urgency about it, though. It could be a second-season project.

By midweek, Nora had drafted a large scale map of the mill pond area. The Big House and its yards were on it, the orchard and Hank's cottage, the dam area and, of course, the foundation on the lilac knoll. Eventually, there would be a series of maps showing how the property changed, came and went, over three hundred years. By the end of the project, Nora knew that all the maps, documents and artifacts would come together to tell the story of generations of Chapmans' lives on Mill Farm. It was an immensely satisfying prospect to contemplate and she thanked her lucky stars that she'd finally landed a job where she could see the research through to the end.

The night before Nora was due to update the Mill Commission, she finally found time to put some of her satisfaction down on paper.

An Archeologist's Handbook
Part Two: Digging In

When the surficial layer has been removed from a test pit or excavation unit, the field archeologist proceeds systematically to remove the soil and its contents through all cultural layers until a sterile surface is reached. There is no formal term for this step in the archeological process, but 'digging in' is descriptive of the mental activity involved, if not the procedure itself.

More broadly, 'digging in' is the experience of combining above-ground research with below-ground excavation. The archeologist makes every effort to identify and investigate all available data sources, trying to verify the information from one source by corroborating it with other sources. Besides the obvious intellectual dimension of this exercise, it must be emphasized that digging in is also a highly intuitive process. The archeologist must be aware of, and prepared to accept the consequences of, finding the unexpected on the site or in other research dimensions. Unanticipated finds may significantly alter interpretation or, in extreme cases, even change the basic research design of the project.

Thursday evening, Nora tucked the new site map under her arm and set out for her second progress report to the Medfield Mill Commission. The air was just beginning to recover from sweltering midday heat and she was grateful that she could abandon suits for a short cotton shift that only occasionally stuck to the vinyl truck seat.

The upcoming report didn't worry her. She was prepared. Besides, she wasn't trying to prove anything at this meeting, just pass on information. She pictured walking into the Whitings' elegant dining room. Hank would be there. Would that be awkward after last Sunday? Nora scowled at the winding road. Nonsense. It was just what was needed. Reestablish the professional connection; avoid further detours toward the personal. She pushed aside brief regrets, then had the fickle thought that if Hank chose to put in a few hours digging alongside other Commission members, that wouldn't be all bad, either.

The evening didn't go according to expectation, from the moment Ralph Whiting opened the door. Apologizing for their old-fashioned lack of air conditioning, he led the way to the back of the house where a screen porch drew whatever cool might rise from the broad lawn. A paddle fan slowly stirred the air and a family of robins sang each other to sleep in a big maple just outside. Peg Wentworth waved a knitting needle at Nora and George Majors nodded affably.

Tonight there were bite-sized brownies to go with the iced tea. Nora remembered her nervousness last time about being caught with her mouth full. Amazing how a little knowledge could change your perspective. Jane Ogden even talked with her mouth full, for God's sake, and nobody seemed to mind. Nora set a brownie next to her map and what she thought of as her 'show and tell bag.' While Ralph answered the doorbell again, she chatted sociably with George Majors about her recent tour of the grist mill.

I know I can talk this man around, she thought. The more I listen to him, the more he'll feel obligated to hear me out. And tonight's show and tell will surely be enough to convince him the dig is accomplishing something.

Voices in the hall distracted her and she looked around to find Ralph ushering Jane Ogden into the room.

"No Hank yet?" Majors asked.

"Unfortunately not." Whiting shrugged regretfully. "Hank called this morning to say he'd been delayed in Missouri. Something about waiting for a shipment of timbers from Canada. He asked me to send special regrets to you, Nora. Said he'd been looking forward to your presentation."

Nora nodded as she weighed relief and disappointment. Hank's absence would certainly simplify the social dynamics, anyway. Then she pushed the subject aside to watch Jane Ogden tidily arranging brownie bites on her plate as the meeting got down to business.

Her progress report began well, if somewhat slowly. The two women and Ralph chimed in with details. Everyone was impressed by the way the map had turned out, although that, too, led to digressions as Ralph and Peg swapped reminiscences of stealthy midnight dips in Chapman's Pond. Nora remembered Hank's description. Perhaps it was a Medfield rite of passage? She told the Commission about a local cable reporter who had brought his high school crew-in-training to film the dig. She reported the call from a Chickering College dean, interested in possible new course offerings. She summarized the field crew's recent work. Then she opened the show and tell bag and brought out one of the burned bricks, proudly announcing they could now say with confidence that they were digging in the nineteenth century.

The rest of the summer's schedule would be dictated by what they'd already found out. Tasks would include continued work on mapping, although this was could wait until winter. They would do preliminary testing around the mill, looking for clues to its structural changes and dating.

"But most of all right now," Nora emphasized, "we need to dig, now that we really know it's a house we're digging in. We're going to enlarge the grid but primarily, we're going to dig deeper, and do our darnedest to find the seventeenth century."

She made sure her tone was confident as she mentioned the seventeenth century and kept her reservations to herself.

Nora watched the faces around the room as she talked. She felt a bit silly going over all this stuff with Hank gone. After all, Ralph and Peg and Jane had been on the scene. It did give her an opportunity to win over George Majors, though. And what she read in the others' expressions made her think the repetition served a purpose.

Encouragement, fascination, pride in participation – even George Majors seemed interested.

This is why I took this job. What a contrast. Present to a developer and I get sullen agreement – at best. But on this project, people actually want *me to find something. I'm not just a threat to fifteen building lots and a profit margin.*

She felt herself relax with the Board's approval.

This is what archeology should be all about. Excitement, anticipation, retrieving what was lost. Not defending every discovery.

"Finally, I just want to tell you how satisfying it is for me, to work on this project." Nora looked around the table. "You have all been a lot of help, and I am really grateful you're willing to devote such time and resources to Mill Farm. I'm looking forward to what the rest of the project brings."

Nora sat back, resting her hands palm-up in her lap to cool them off, and relaxed. Ralph Whiting graciously thanked her for the report, commenting that the project was more involved than probably any of them had imagined. Peg and Jane agreed wholeheartedly. Only George Majors seemed to hold back. When the others had finished he harrumphed, and shifted in his seat on the way to saying something. Little warning signals began running up Nora's spine. Majors didn't exactly look convinced of the value of archeology yet, at least not her trowel-and-dustpan kind. If she had to guess, she'd peg him as a backhoe-and-pickax, industrial type. What was he up to?

She watched him cautiously as he began a rumbling comment.

"This poking around the house is all right, as far as it goes. But I think Hank Chapman's got the right idea here, in the long run. We should restore the mill. Make it look presentable so the town can be proud of it. The way it looks now, it's an eyesore. Embarrassing. We should get it up and running. We are the *mill* commission, after all. That's what we were appointed to look after, and that's what I think we should do."

Majors' jaw was set, and he glared in Ralph Whiting's direction when he was finished. For a surprised moment, Nora's eyes shifted from one man to the other, waiting for Whiting to straighten the other man out. Hank Chapman didn't want to restore the mill. Where on earth had Majors gotten that idea? She tried to remember exactly what Hank had said. He'd said the mill was in surprisingly good shape.

He'd talked about replacing sills and repairing the corner post. But Majors was babbling about getting it 'up and running', and Whiting wasn't saying a thing. Nora cursed Hank's busy schedule, that he wasn't here to explain it all himself.

Peg Wentworth set down her knitting and frowned.

"Now George, I thought we'd been all through this."

You and me too.

"Hank's ideas are all well and good, but what Ms. Tunney is doing has to come first. We need some dates, some background."

Some common sense.

"You can't mess around with old buildings until you know for sure what's there."

And when you do know, you leave it alone!

As Nora searched for something politic to say, she noticed Ralph Whiting's agreeable, but irritatingly silent nod. Mrs. Ogden was carefully avoiding eye contact with anyone. It was time to make her own opinion clear.

"Mr. Majors," Nora addressed him as the core of disagreement. "The idea of restoring a traditional water mill is wonderful, and very ambitious. I'm sure you know what an investment of time and money it will take."

The rest of the committee were silent, waiting to see where she was going.

"I don't think I realized you were thinking of doing this in the near future. If you do, I would certainly want to pay more attention to testing around the dam this summer. On the other hand," Nora carefully looked at each of them, "if your first goal is to connect this site definitively with Medfield's founding, you're not going to do that at the mill." She knew that would get their attention. "There's a much higher likelihood of doing so around the cellarhole. People lose more things, throw out more datable trash around a house than they do at a work site. Even house shapes and sizes change more rapidly, more datably than mill buildings."

Nora looked at Majors to drive her point home. "If we can date the cellarhole, we'll have an idea how old the grist mill is, as well. And you must have that, as I believe you've said yourself, before you can do any kind of restoration."

158

Whiting frowned. "Could you elaborate a bit, Nora? I understand that dating a cellar may be easier than a mill, but what does one have to do, directly, with the other?"

Nora silently thanked him for giving her a tag line.

"In archeology we call it a *terminus post quem*, a 'point after which' something must have happened. No self-respecting colonial miller would build a mill without a house nearby to live in. He'd need to watch for flooding, be on hand to greet customers, generally keep an eye on his investment."

Miss Wentworth was nodding in agreement.

"So you see, if we can set a seventeenth-century date to the house, it's much more likely the grist mill was operating that early, too."

"Ah-ha." Mr. Whiting raised his brows in understanding.

"That's why it's really important to keep the focus of our work this summer on the house site. Then next year, with the knowledge we've dug out of the house," she glanced around apologetically at the unintended pun, "we'll have a much clearer idea how best to proceed with the mill."

George Majors' response caught her completely off guard.

"That may well be, Ms. Tunney, if there happens to be a 'next year.' But we're a local, grass-roots organization and we don't have the kind of big bucks those universities and museums and such seem to have, that start some little archeology project and ten years down the road, there they are, still digging and burying thousands of dollars in those holes. Not that archeology isn't a good idea," he declared. "It is. I'm the first one to say it. But if you've got limited funds, you have to decide. Is it going to be a new roof or a new hole in the ground? I, for one, don't think we should spend all our money on holes in the ground."

He nodded emphatically. His jaw jutted out even more than usual.

Nora's cheeks were flushed by the time Majors had finished. The heat crept over her cheekbones and began to sting the corners of her eyes. *Next year. Next year! That's the catch, isn't it? The real zinger. All this time I've been thinking and planning as if next year was a given. Just chose to overlook the 'possible second season' in the contract. Assumed what I wanted to be true. And now Majors has caught me out and it's clear he's not anxious to have me stick around.*

Resentment and distress almost silenced her for a second time. Then she realized Hank had given her another argument to use.

"Mr. Majors, I am the last one to suggest the Commission should spend its last dollar on archeology if the grist mill is in danger. Mr. Chapman led me to believe, however, that stabilization of the mill was going to be relatively simple. Not that anything having to do with old buildings is inexpensive, of course, but I certainly had the impression the work that needed to be done would not leave the Commission in an either-or situation."

"Stabilization!" Major's voice was scornful. "The Medfield Mill Commission is not just talking stabilization, Ms. Tunney. We're talking about a fully restored, working colonial grist mill! And that, as even you must understand, calls for a great deal of money."

Ralph Whiting's calm voice intervened.

"I don't believe the Commission has fully agreed on the restoration, George. But I also don't believe we have to settle the matter right this minute. If we put the very modest amount we've agreed on, toward the kind of excellent work Dr. Tunney's doing for a couple of years, we can still redirect our money after that. Who knows?" he said, his tone appeasing, "maybe we'll find other sources of funding by then, which will make the restoration go all the faster."

As Whiting talked, Nora was fast deciding the flush on her face was more anger than embarrassment. They kept missing the point. Even Ralph Whiting, bless his heart. Hank would understand, be able to explain, but where was he when she needed him? She shifted irritably on the hot, padded seat. If the Commission started messing with the mill, they'd end up with a bad industrial myth. 'Creative' reconstruction based on heaven-knows-what evidence. Chapman's Mill sterilized, just like Colonial Williamsburg. Recreated, more like, she thought disgustedly, as it never existed in real life. And the worst irony of all? What never existed in the past would be considered Authentic by generations to come.

A voice broke in on her furious thinking. Jane Ogden's high-pitched nasal tones distracted Nora as surely as they did at the site, where Nora frequently had to remind herself the woman's voice was not her fault.

"*I* think we should wait and ask Mr. Chapman what he thinks. He knows all about this sort of thing. Plus he is the donor, after all. I think we should wait to hear his ideas." She seized her iced tea glass.

There were assorted nods and hums of agreement. Nora pressed her lips together to hold in her growing frustration, and marveled at the weak-kneed posture of the whole committee. Waiting for Hank was good in one way, Nora conceded. At least then Hank could back her up on the preservation issue. On the other hand, why did everyone need to wait for him to pass judgment? He was the *donor*, for Chrissake, not some biblical prophet. Why wouldn't they listen to *her* word on the subject? She was the expert they had hired, after all.

Peg Wentworth also seemed to be wrestling with vehement thoughts. Her free knitting needle was tapping furiously against her knee, and she had just opened her mouth to speak when Whiting, ever the conciliator, stepped in.

"I'm sure Hank's comments will be useful when he comes back. We've been over some of this ground before you know, Jane, George, and I suspect we'll go over it again before it's settled. But right now it's a bit late for extended discussion. Furthermore, funding decisions, as you know, require a vote of the whole Commission.

"So I'd like to suggest we plan to take some time at the July meeting – you remember we have only one meeting next month – to revisit our long-range plans for the property, including archeology. Right now I'd like to thank Dr. Tunney for all the fine work she has been doing. The whole process is quite fascinating and I, for one, am delighted to be getting my hands dirty under her supervision."

Whiting's benevolent words met with a stone wall around the table. Nora's indignation was apparent in her flushed face. Majors looked ready to mount a major offensive, and Peg Wentworth's mouth was a thin line, holding back what she wanted to say. Jane Ogden studied the ice cubes in her glass. Without a pause, before the squabble could resume, Whiting asked for a motion to adjourn. His suggestion was greeted by expressions of mixed reluctance and relief, but the vote was unanimous. The participants escaped as quickly as manners allowed, into the hot night.

Nora had no memory of the drive back to Mill Farm, but the pick-up turned into the barnyard and the engine died. Unsticking sweaty hands from the steering wheel, she started indoors, kicking off her shoes in the airless entryway. The living room, despite wide-open windows, was just as stifling. Artie meowed plaintively at the heat. She wished she could do the same.

"Come on, fuzz. Outside. Nothing in here but suffocation."

She scuffed into old sandals and held the screen door open for the cat. Artie slipped out toward the shadows by the barn. Nora stomped off down the road, too worked up at first for the quiet footfalls she always used at night, trying to melt into her surroundings.

A breeze had begun to stir in the apple trees across the way and she remembered Hank's description of the branches black in winter. Morosely, she reflected she'd probably never see them that way. Majors and Ogden would vote her out before leaves fell.

A wisp of air brushed past her ear. Frogs trilled along the edge of the pond, and one big bullfrog voice answered across the water. Her pace unconsciously slowed as her footsteps adjusted to the slow frog counterpoint. By the time Nora reached the great sycamore she was ready to pause, leaning a shoulder against the trunk. She stared into the darkness where the mill must be. It was time to 'set a while', as her gramma used to say.

Between two of the big old roots Nora found a seat, tucked in a small pocket of stillness. At first she just listened, until the sounds outside her body were louder than the clamor inside, and the sigh that rose up out of nowhere was stronger than her heartbeat. Then it was time to think. She just wasn't good at thinking past somebody criticizing her. Obviously Majors thought what she was doing was a bunch of baloney. He thought she was throwing money away in a bunch of holes in the ground. Of course *he* wanted to throw it away on a pretty little mill wheel.

She hugged her knees tight to her chest and squinted into the darkness. A faint spot of light up the pond marked the location of Hank's cottage: a yard light, maybe, or one he kept on by the flagstone terrace when he wasn't home. The pinpoint of light interfered with her dark mood and she wanted to hit out at it, make it go away.

It was all his fault. He must have said something in the first place to plant such a stupid idea in Majors' head. One of those 'Thomas Chapman would be proud' lines. But more important, why wasn't he here now to straighten them out? He was being very cavalier. That was the word. Cavalier. What was the use of having an ally if he was never around?

A familiar voice interrupted her ranting.

Dear, you're being very snippy. I thought I taught you that snide remarks are the mark of a poor spirit.

Gramma's voice. Nora imagined she heard it sometimes, when there was thinking to be done. Always gentle, but persistent. Not always welcome, but inevitably useful. It meant Nora was beginning to think.

My snide remarks have more to do with poor bank account than poor spirit.

Nonsense. You are simply refusing to admit you admire someone else's good fortune.

'Fortune' is certainly right.

The inner voice still sounded resentful, but Nora found herself remembering the pride with which Hank pointed out the Nabby apple trees, and how he savored that view across the pond. There had been affection in the way he showed off his house. And he made good conversation. She studiously avoided dwelling on the walk through the orchard and the goodnight kiss. Hank had said she thought too much.

What are you really upset about?

He said I think too much. What does that mean? Am I supposed to just take whatever's doled out to me and go with the flow?

There is something unsatisfactory in doing that?

Of course there is! Hank's brilliant 'restoration' comment is going to mess up a perfectly lovely old mill and his selfish preoccupation is going to drum me out of a job. It's going to send me back to Somerville grime and two-week contracts.

Ahh! There's a new yearning here I haven't heard before. Are you sure you should lay all the blame on Mr. Chapman?

No, no. Of course not. It's the damned Commission. They won't give me credit for knowing how to do the job they hired me for. They think they can rush through three hundred years' history and zip on to the next project without losing anything.

And how does this differ from all those other jobs you've done? Done well too, dear, remember, considering what time and money were allowed.

The discussion came to an abrupt halt. Nora scowled, looking around the bowl of darkness for an answer to that simple question. A breeze trailed along the edge of the pond. She could hear it rustle the pickerel weed where the frogs sang their rounds. It stirred the grass at the top of the rise and brushed across her forehead on its way to the south pasture. Cooler air followed in its wake. Nora rested her head against the smooth-scaled bark and confessed.

I really love it here. I love working here. I love sitting under this tree. I love waking up in the morning to bird songs instead of traffic. I get a kick out of the crew I'm working with and there's even –as you would say – 'pleasant male companionship.'

But you're afraid?

I'm afraid.

That this is just another of your childish fantasies that will disappear if you think too much?

That's what he said, that I think too much.

Well, I don't wish to be argumentative, but I believe the proper approach might be that you think too narrowly. You are not helpless to remedy the situation, you know, my dear. If you believe the root of the problem is Mr. Chapman you need to tackle the root.

Just how am I supposed to do that?

Why, you and Mr. Chapman have a nice, sociable relationship. You are in an excellent position to enlist his support.

It's not that I haven't tried. But he's so confusing. Trying to get him involved in this project is like pulling hen's teeth. I ask him for family papers and he acts as though he's never heard of them. I ask him about a building's history and he can't be bothered to look it up. Sometimes I can't figure out where he's coming from at all. He shuts down unexpectedly. Yet he got just as involved as I did in reading Sarah's letters. And as soon as he's near a building he starts with those wonderful reminiscences...

Remember dear, not everyone is quite as intent on deciphering the past as you are.

Yeah, but something else is going on there. I don't know what, but it means I can't tell what he'll do next. Not exactly a predictable ally.

The world is full of unpredictability. Now, what do you think you might do about it?

Keep trying, I guess. Show him what background research can do. Sit him down and make him understand how far off base the Commission is on this restoration business. I need to get him whee'd up enough about the dig that he'll stop being distracted and give me a hand with the Commission. If he's really a friend he'll help me convince the Commission that this is an incredible research opportunity that can't possibly be completed in one shortened season so that they can proceed to permanently wreck the mill.

You seem to know just what you want, dear.

I do, don't I. You make it all seem simpler.

God helps her who helps herself.

A late heron squawked in the shallows across the pond and Gramma's voice retreated to the shadows where it tended to hover, just out of hearing. Nora stayed until the bowl of darkness she sat in gently tipped her out on the path home to Artie and bed.

By morning she had worked out a strategy and was ready to gently grasp the bull by the horns. First step: a pleasant note to Hank.

Dear Hank,

Belated but heartfelt thanks for the wonderful tour you provided last weekend. Fascinating information topped off with great food and a beautiful view — an unbeatable combination.

I gather from last night's Commission meeting that you're recommending an early start on stabilizing the mill building. Unfortunately it also appears that some of the Commission members misunderstood 'preservation' to mean 'restoration,' and there is now talk of extensive rebuilding of the structure and its machinery. Would it be useful for us to put our heads together and be sure we use the same vocabulary at the July meeting? It might be the simplest way to prevent any further misunderstanding. Maybe we can talk semantics as well as architecture when you show me the Big House.

> *Meanwhile, thanks again for your hospitality. Let's
> do it again sometime.*

She reread it one final time. Just the right tone. Friendly and light. Not too personal. And once the semantics were squared away, Hank would bring the rest of the Commission around. That much seemed clear from last night's meeting.

Gramma would be proud of her.

A four-day Fourth of July weekend helped Nora recover some equilibrium. There was a loud and laughing family picnic on Saturday, and an evening in Gloucester with an old college friend, watching the annual Horribles Parade and misty fireworks over the harbor. But Nora also made time to comb through her field notes, looking for bits of information she had missed, trying to understand exactly how to proceed, to get the most out of a project threatened with abrupt termination. Eventually she would need to discuss the stabilization work with Hank and find out how much ground it might disturb. Then the crew would have to do more testing at the mill. For the moment though, she told herself, at least until he responded to her note, they would continue at the cellarhole.

Because of the long weekend, July began on Wednesday for the expanded field crew that included two more Chickering College students and a Medfield high school senior. More squares were staked out west of Pam's boulder, making further inroads into the lilac grove, and the grid was stretched southward as well.

Nora decided they needed to find out more about the peculiar flat boulder Pam had discovered. After that, they would work south, checking out Peg Wentworth's rubble and trying to find the other corners of the house. If the crew stuck with it and the rain held off, Nora estimated they might even finish the house and its yard by summer's end. Two months to go. That would leave a lot of ground still untested. Permanently, maybe, if Majors and Ogden got their way. There'd be no grand series of land use maps. She already mourned the losses. Then she swore that, no matter what, at least one piece of the Mill Farm Project would be thoroughly done.

Nora moved Ralph to a new square next to Pam's, making them partners. They were a good working pair: Ralph short on energy but long on perspective, Pam working on fitness training and serious about every unglazed pot shard. Nora suggested they take Ralph's square down to the depth of Pam's, then work on both at the same level.

It was a good thing they did. The first thing Ralph uncovered was a big, squarish rock that lined up with the rest of the north wall. Then the two of them exposed the rest of the puzzling 'doorstep' inside the wall. It butted tight up against the wall-line rocks, and was absolutely solid where it lay. It had been set there on purpose, though what that purpose might have been still wasn't clear.

Ralph and Pam worked from north to south, leveling off their squares. They had dug about five inches below the level of the doorstep, finding nothing more interesting than the neck of a plain stoneware jug. The SSQ insisted that the men filling the cellar got thirsty.

Suddenly Pam let out an excited squeak and called Nora over. She arrived just in time to see Ralph pick up the tip of a white shard that lay between their squares, and pull it out of the dirt.

"Wait!" Pam squeaked again.

Ralph looked slightly guilty, caught in the act of removing artifacts. He was having a lot of trouble remembering Nora's lectures about unforgivable archeological sins. *Nothing*, she'd stressed, came out of the ground without mapping and photos.

"Well, here it is, anyway," he said defensively, holding it up for Nora's inspection.

She took the thin piece of broken ceramic and gently wiped it on her tee shirt. One edge was a finished rim, the others broken. It was beautiful. Thin, fine-grained porcelain. Plain, concave interior, but the outside was painted with a narrow geometric band near the rim, and hints of a flower cluster where the piece was broken. No color; just delicate black brushwork against the stark white. Was there perhaps a hint of gold highlighting?

Everyone gathered around, peering over Nora's shoulder, speculating about the piece.

"What is it, Nora?" Pam finally asked.

"A tea bowl, I'd guess. You know, a cup with no handle? They stopped being made by the mid-1800s. But this is a really special one. Chinese porcelain decorated in *encre de chine* – "Chinese ink." As I remember, you don't find that on tea wares after 1820 or so. It was all the rage during the early Federal period: elegant, understated, very urbane."

"What's it doing out here in the country, then?" Andrew wondered.

"Someone must have been really upset about breaking this one." Miss Wentworth shook her head.

That reminded Nora that the little shard really didn't help push the cellar date back, at all. It could have been dumped any time after 1800 or so. She reminded the crew of this and sent them back to work. Ralph and Pam's first assignment was to put the shard back and take down the rest of the level around it for a nice, tidy picture of the artifact *in situ* before it went to the lab.

What Pam and Ralph painstakingly uncovered in the next hour was fascinating. It turned out that the shard they put back was not just a single piece, but one of half a dozen shards that lay, face down, fanned out around a rock on which they had clearly broken. The entire tea bowl was there, wanting only a little glue to make it whole again. After the Edison job's lack of artifacts, Nora was as thrilled as the crew to see a second, genuine, exhibition-quality find emerge from this dig.

The surprises continued. As Pam was carefully leveling the dirt in the area of the cup, she exposed smooth rock surface just below the shards. Ralph found the same in his square, and eventually it dawned on everyone that they were not working south of some doorstep.

The 'doorstep' was the top slab of a set of stone stairs. The tea bowl lay on a second stair. If the steps continued downward, there would have to be a sizable room at the bottom: big enough to house the stairs, and big enough to justify all the work involved in building them. It was very strange, and very exciting. Nothing Nora had read about early colonial buildings supported this. Cellars, if they existed at all, were small storage areas with interior trap doors and ladders for access. Building a stone stairway called for an effort and a level of expertise which seemed totally out of keeping with the modest house that must have stood on this site. It was another puzzle to keep the crew thinking.

A short while later, when Ralph let out a rolling "A-l-l-l right!"

He was hunched over a corner of his square, furiously brushing at something while Pam anxiously hovered over him.

"Don't touch it, remember," she scolded. "You've got to leave it for Nora to see."

"What have you come up with this time, Ralph?"

He stiffly sat back on his heels, half-glasses sliding down his nose, big smudge on his cheek from pushing them up with a dirty hand. He gestured grandiloquently with his whiskbroom and beamed at her with all the pride of fatherhood.

The rim of half a teacup shone white in the dirt. Its delicate black border was a sure match for the shards already found. Not one, but two *encre de chine* dishes had been dumped in the Chapman cellarhole.

The lunch break that followed was more talk than eating. Peg reminisced about dumping in what she termed the *old days* – her childhood, when trash and brush on a farm were used to fill unwanted dips and hollows in the land. Nora gave an impromptu talk on ceramic chronology. Everyone discussed the Chapmans and what led them to throw away two perfectly good and probably valuable tea bowls. Maybe the pattern had gone out of style. Some Victorian-era Chapman wife wanted newfangled china and got rid of these pieces to clear the shelves. The crew shook their heads and bemoaned the taste of their ancestors.

In the end, they congratulated themselves on the treasure they had found. This was, they all agreed, bound to be the high point of the summer.

ENCRE DE CHINE

July, 1796

Abby Chapman sat straighter between the Chapman men as their carriage neared the Charles River. She quietly applauded her insistence that she come on this expedition. Father and Luther tended to assume she had no interest in milling since it was they, after all, who carried on the business. Yet she often thought Chapman's gristmill was as important to her life as to theirs. She had grown up beside it, hearing its rhythmic thunking every spring and fall, sharing the family's fear of wash-outs, and working the flour which was her father's pay for his services. Only too likely she'd stay beside the mill too, she thought. It seemed there'd soon be no young men left in Medfield, so many were off to the cities or the West. Abby and the mill. Unassuming workhorses of the family. The thought did little to cheer her day.

What was a business call for the men of the Chapman family was a rare outing for Abigail. Her days and weeks were filled with the thousand chores of householding, tending Luther and Lucy's babies, seeing to Lucy herself – weakly by birth and, more often than not, pregnant by marriage. Abby's lost childhood, taking her mother's place on the busy Chapman farm, made her forget sometimes, that she was still only twenty-two. That there was time and to spare for her to make a match of her own, begin her own family. Though in darker moments she wondered, briefly, where the benefit might be, trading one workplace for another just as hard. Abby blinked to dismiss the fruitless thought, and turned to the scene around her.

The Chapmans were driving toward Fisher's Bridge, five miles from Medfield, where the Charles River slid round a bend in Dover. Old Deacon Fisher's saw mill was up for sale, and Luther had spent long evenings convincing his father that they should consider buying it and removing the business to Medfield. Abby had been surprised to hear her older brother argue so persistently. For a quiet man, he had been positively eloquent. Perhaps, she thought, Luther saw this mill as a way to make his own mark on the old place.

Meanwhile, rumor was spreading that much more was going on at Fisher's Bridge than the sale of a decrepit building. Some kind of iron works was to take its place. Abigail had come to see what truth there was in the rumor. And, she acknowledged, to snatch a few hours to call her own.

Noises grew louder as the carriage topped the rise above the river. The air rang with hammering, against the steady counterpoint of a mill saw at work. Luther gave a low whistle of astonishment and pulled the team to a halt to take in the view. Mr. Chapman, dour as ever, snorted in disapproval at the raw landscape of construction spread below them. Abby felt an anticipatory smile tug at the corner of her mouth. Astonishing. The scene at Fisher's Bridge would never be the same.

Fisher's sawmill was something of a monument in these parts. No one knew how long it had been in operation. But now old Deacon Fisher had finally died. His relatives held no particular attachment to the homestead. Besides, in these first decades of the new Republic, land was money. A gentleman from Boston had offered to buy up the place. The price was more than fair, neighbors agreed, considering the buildings' run-down condition and the equally run-down soil in the fields. But no one could have imagined what would happen next. Woodsmen were paid to cut and clear the riverbank. Young men in town were hired right off the farm to widen the millrace. Experienced builders and expert stonemasons came from as far away as Rhode Island to supervise the extensive construction.

"Not much sense to all that fuss, as far as I can see."

Ebenezer Chapman looked down the hill at the swarm of activity and scowled. Everyone knew the deacon's mill was old. If the new people wanted to rid themselves of the old equipment, fine. The Chapmans could buy it up cheap. Then Luther could play at this sawyering business without frittering away what little cash they had. Privately, Ebenezer admitted he was proud of Luther and his ideas. Not that he was about to say so, but his son's notion might just have some merit. Put this saw alongside the Chapman grist mill, and you'd get two for one. Not that he, himself, was about to learn a whole new trade, not at his age. But the boy was young and eager. Might just work. If the cost wasn't too high. Ebenezer still controlled the Chapman fortunes, and he wasn't about to let go of them, certainly not until Abigail was set up and young Daniel, though that was years away still. Maybe after that he'd let Luther take over Mill Farm. By then, though, Ebenezer'd be one foot in the grave, and more concerned with prayers than portions.

The aging miller looked out at the river curving around a spit of land. No doubt about it, Fisher's location was the best in the region. There was that narrow channel, cut right across the neck of the peninsula, diverting a stream of water from the river. A constant supply for the sawmill that sat on its bank. And come high water, you just dropped in a few flashboards and all that extra water went roaring around the river bend, leaving the mill sitting high and dry. Pity the Chapmans couldn't come up with a site like that. He shook his head. What power there was in Medfield lay up crooked little brooks like theirs: a nice small fall, a good swamp upstream. Not perfect maybe but, he cheered himself up, enough to serve the trade. Folks who fooled with rivers courted their own destruction.

Ebenezer spotted a pair of broad-shouldered oxen straining to move a sledge piled high with boulders near the riverbank. Why was there so much activity on the river? Why were they building footings out into the main channel? Abby's voice cut into his ruminations.

"Why the place looks like a great desert."

It reminded her of a new plow field back home, where Luther had cut the wood and heaped huge mounds of brush to burn. It stood dry and bare under the July sun, an occasional lone tree left here and there for shade. Abby scanned the area, trying to make sense of what she saw. One gang of men worked right in the river bed, where the summer's low water had bared the mud bank. They were levering boulders into a row, lining the river's edge with a protective wall.

Other teams of men and work animals were busy along the roadway approaching the bridge. A cart path was being filled and leveled, leading toward the new stonework at river's edge.

One man on horseback rode between the work gangs. He would briefly sit apart from the confusion, then move forward and comment or gesture to the gang foreman before moving on. He was the only man there, Abby noticed, in frock coat and high hat. Apparently a gentleman. Even the foremen wore worker's smocks or shirts and slouch hats. Their sleeves were rolled up against the heat, already becoming oppressive. Abby loosened the shawl around her shoulders and speculated on the gentleman's role in this endeavor. He was interesting to watch.

"Looks to me an awful lot like they're building a dam," Luther Chapman muttered incredulously.

He narrowed his eyes against the bright sun to see more clearly. It was a dam. A vast dam, twenty-five feet thick if it was an ell. A monumental dam, going to go right across the whole Charles River, harness the power of a whole river to run...what? He paused in his thinking. What kind of mill would need all that head to make it work? And what made a group of city merchants think they could tame a river to do their bidding? He scanned the scene with a practiced eye, and decided it was a harebrained venture. The river was a good two hundred feet wide. Besides, he'd seen the water, of a rainy spring, rise right up over the bridge and flood most of the point. What made them think they could build a dam to withstand that? It went against laws of nature, against centuries of experience, against any kind of common sense. No, trying to dam this flow would never work.

Just the same, Luther grinned as he watched the oxen tug the stone boat closer to water's edge. Something was bound to come of this. If, by some miracle, this folly succeeded – if it even survived the next flood season – then Luther would study what they'd done. Whatever was being built on Charles River could undoubtedly be copied small on Mill Brook. He would return, and watch.

But first there was a sawmill to be bought. Luther studied the swaybacked shed beside Saw Mill Creek. The building was a ruin: its flat board siding rotting, the roof gaping open in spots. He could hear, inside the shed, the mill saw tearing its way through a log, so at least that was still working, though how well it would survive removal to

Medfield was one more concern. He offered up a brief prayer that it could be managed. This was his chance – maybe his one chance – at a future that promised more than repeating his father's past. What with the current lack of imports, a man would have to be a fool indeed, not to make money provisioning America. Already, the Chapmans had turned a tidy profit shipping flour down Maine. If they could branch out, to lumber – even shingles – they could get top dollar right next door. Dedham, the new county seat, was carpenter's paradise. A lot of plans began with this sawmill.

Suddenly Abby gasped and Luther's train of thought was broken. He glanced at his sister's clasped hands and followed her stare to the ox team straining on the riverbank. A panicked shout went up.

The oxen's pulling had swayed the sledge to one side and forced it toward the river's edge. Three workmen waved frantically below. They were sure to be hit if it tipped. Already a metal runner was edging over the bank. The young teamster in charge of the oxen had panicked, his well-known commands forgotten. Speechless, his head turned back and forth from sledge to men as the oxen strained to keep their footing against the backward pull of the stones' weight.

Abby, watching in fascinated horror, saw a roan horse gallop toward the sledge. Horse and rider made a matched set: powerful and controlled, concentrated energy seeming to throw them across the ground. The horse slewed to a halt, its rider swinging down and onto the sledge runner in one unhesitating motion.

"Haw!"

A deep-voiced call carried to the watchers on the hill.

"Haw!"

The oxen, attuned to the sound of control, heard the repeated command. They heaved against the inert stones. One step. Another. They gathered the massive muscles of their forequarters and threw themselves against the yoke; determined, dragging the swerving sledge by inches away from the riverbank. The young drover recalled himself to action and, picking up the commands, guided them a few last steps to safety.

Abby watched the rider step back to calm his anxious horse. He summoned a workman to hold the roan, while he and the teamster together carefully backed the stone boat into position. Then he remounted and sat watching, still and tall until the waiting crew unloaded the last stones. Finally he spoke a few words to the teamster and rode off. The young owner of the oxen stared after him, then brought his switch down against the dirt so hard the near ox startled. With a high-pitched, angry yell, he drove the team away from the site. Abby guessed he would not be back.

"Whiting's got a nice hand with the animals." Ebenezer Chapman's grudging compliment interrupted the silence of the hilltop. "Funny he didn't stick to farming like his father."

"Not so strange," Luther commented. "All that time working at his uncle's mill in Dedham must've rubbed off. Even if he was born in a Dover farmyard." Luther added laconically, continuing to stare at the scene before him as he spoke.

"Is Mr. Whiting the one on the roan horse?" Abby asked, looking from father to brother. "He seems remarkably quick-witted," she observed. "And strong," she added quietly.

"Strong!" Luther snorted dismissively. "The oxen were strong. He was just the drover."

"But yes," he answered after a moment, "That's Colburn Whiting. They say he's to run this new mill. Company agent. He must have met some powerful men when he was in Dedham, to get in on an enterprise this big. Wonder what he did to impress them."

"Surely, if what we've just seen is any indication, he has a most commanding presence." Abby considered. "Would that not make him a suitable director of men?"

Ebenezer snorted. "Eyes are too close-set, just like his father. More like a ferret than a fox. Sure sign he'll look out for his own before the other fellow's. Why, Old Squire Whiting would chivvy the pants off a beggar if he took a mind to them. Don't doubt the son'll be like the father." He lapsed into judgmental silence.

Behind her bonnet brim, Abby raised an eyebrow at her father's pronouncement. Much as she respected him and gave him her devotion, she was sure the man wasn't born who could outscheme Ebenezer Chapman. He was a master of control, and knew just how and when to get what he wanted. Quite likely, she thought, his perception of Mr. Whiting was strongly influenced by his knowledge of himself.

Luther's voice interrupted.

"Be that as it may, it's Colburn Whiting we need to see about Fisher's Mill. Best get on with it."

He gathered up the reins and headed the carriage downhill.

Abby had learned long ago to take her family's judgments with a grain of salt. Quick to criticize and slow to praise. She had also learned to reserve her own judgments. This Mr. Whiting had surprised her though, with his air of command, his quick movements and control. Such a contrast to father's considered ways, or Luther's slow and steady work. Perhaps she saw in him the way she would wish to behave in such a situation. Decisive and strong.

There was an unfamiliar tension in Abby's narrow shoulders. In a rare gesture of self-consciousness she straightened her brown silk bonnet ribbons. Then she clasped her hands together in her lap and scanned the busy scene for Colburn Whiting.

Abby wasn't born strong. She started being strong when she was eight. Not right away. When her mamma birthed that baby boy, Abby was still just a little girl, soft and a bit scared, loving the tiny determined baby the midwife showed her, worrying that her mamma was so sick. Seemed so far away somehow, even though she was lying right there, on the big bed, hair slicked back off her forehead. She was very pale, and very still. Mama opened her eyes though, and turned her head to Abby, and gave her a little smile.

"You have a little brother to take care of now," she whispered. "What do you think we should name him?"

Abby, who'd never been asked a big question like that before, stared wide-eyed at her mother. Her mama was silent, looking at her. Abby suddenly knew that this really was an important question she was to answer all by herself. Her big brown eyes stared solemnly at mama and she considered.

Father was named Ebenezer. Luther was her older brother's name. There were Chapman uncles and boy cousins, but none with a name that seemed to suit the expression of intent, concerned wonder on this baby's face. Abby blindly stared out the window. Her fine-lined brows drew together in concentration, as her mind sifted through stories mama had told her.

"Daniel."

"Daniel? Not Thomas, or your father's name? Or my father, John?"

"Daniel is the right name for him."

"Then Daniel is his name," mama said firmly. "Daniel Chapman. I put him in your special charge until I get better."

Mama had smiled again and Abby had felt the love and reassurance in that smile. Then father had told them it was time for mama to rest, and the midwife had shushed her out the door. Abby felt very important, and very excited that she was big enough to watch over Daniel herself, if only till mama got better.

Mama never did really get better, though. A few days after the baby was born she tried to be up and about, but something was wrong. At first she sat down a lot more than she used to. Pretty soon she took to resting a lot. Mama and Daniel, curled up together on the big bed, sleeping right in the middle of the day. After that came the time mama didn't get up at all, and Abby really had to take care of the baby, trying to do it the way the midwife and her mama had showed her. Daniel knew it wasn't the same, just as Abby did. He fussed and cranked a lot when she put him in the cradle so mama could sleep. He smelled bad and looked worse when she had to change him, which she did have to do even though she hated it, because Father and Luther were planting and the midwife had to go home sometimes and mama was asleep.

After a while Abby got used to the smell, and Daniel seemed to get used to her. Sometimes caring for him was almost like playing with her doll, dressing him and talking to him, singing little songs as she rocked his cradle. Sometimes she even forgot that mama was so pale and weak in the next room but then she'd feel guilty at forgetting, and tiptoe to the door and peek in. Listen for her soft breathing and pray fervently that the sickness would go away and things would go back the way they were supposed to be.

But four months after the baby was born mama died. What Abby remembered most was standing by the bed and trying to get her father to do something. Shouldn't he get Dr. Gerauld to come, or maybe Mrs. Wilson? Maybe mama needed a drink of water, or a cool cloth on her head to make her better?

But her father just sat there, holding mama's hand, stroking it very gently.

177

No, Abby it's all right. I'll just sit here for a while. Go on outside. I'll stay with her.

She backed out the door and desperately wondered what to do? what she could do? why couldn't she make things better? Then Daniel mewed faintly in his cradle and she gathered him up, blankets and all, and carried him out to the big granite step out front. There she sat, rocking back and forth with the baby asleep in her lap, until father came and sat next to her. He put his arm around her shoulder and said mama had gone. He drew a very deep breath and let it out slowly. Shakily. Then he reached out his other hand and softly stroked Daniel's cheek, not even waking the baby. It seems our Father needs her in heaven, he said. So we are left to do the best we can here. He gave Abby's shoulder a squeeze and kissed the brown hair that hid her downturned face, then stood up. I need to find Luther. He slowly walked away toward the barn.

The Chapmans were not a demonstrative lot. They swallowed their grief and fought off sadness with work. They never spoke of matters of the heart. So when, in the months that followed, a pang of loss would stab one of the family, it would be beaten back: a impatient shake of the head, a moment of silent distraction, a fugitive tear brushed away. There was no good accomplished by crying. Mama would not have wanted it so. They struggled through the harsh change in their lives, expressing the love and sympathy they felt inside by silently lending each other a hand, each one trying to ease the others' burden of work as they carried their burdens of grief alone.

Over the next year or so Abby completed the process she'd begun when Daniel was born. She found out all the things her mama had done so easily, had started to teach her daughter but had not finished. Abby struggled with the steaming water and lye soap of wash day, the wet clothes too heavy to wring out. The butter churning she'd always been allowed to stop when it got too stiff, she now saw through to the end. Three meals a day, every day. The kitchen garden. Sweeping. Chickens. Spinning. The fire. And always, the need to see to Daniel, tend him, feed him, watch out for his safety.

Luther and her father tried to help, but they had the whole farm with its fields and animals to tend. Father's attempts at meal preparation were poor excuse for food. The wash that Luther set out to dry came in a mass of dusty wrinkles. Abby soon found it simpler to do it herself. Especially in the first months, neighbors and church lent a hand. Puddings and breads, clothes for the baby, generous gifts of goods and labor. Mrs. Wilson, down the road, came by nearly every day, or she would bid Abby bring the baby to their house, and there Abby would serve as 'apprentice in huswifery,' as Mrs. Wilson cheerfully said, while one of her brood watched Daniel.

Abby found domestic work easy enough to learn. It taxed her physical strength more than her mental powers. Even so, every month she felt stronger, and less in need of help from the grown-ups around her. Her father, man of few words though he was, let her know he was proud of her, and the way she was managing. Luther stopped teasing her, and even allowed as how her bread beat out Mrs. Collins', of which he'd become especially fond.

"You may not wish to climb down, madam."

The warm voice interrupted Abby's thoughts.

"I'm afraid the dust grows deeper with every wagon coming through. Your slippers would be bound to suffer."

Abby found herself torn between amusement that Mr. Whiting could think the rough brogans covered by her gown could be damaged by dust, and surprise that a man would be so thoughtful of her convenience. She silently added good manners to the list of Colburn Whiting's pleasing attributes as she nodded her thanks to him.

The Chapmans had tracked down the company agent and explained their interest in buying the old saw mill. After driving across the construction site with Whiting riding alongside, they were about to dismount in order to inspect the building and its contents.

"I appreciate your concern, Mr. Whiting," Abby said as she gathered up her skirts, "but you will see that I have come prepared for the occasion." She accepted his proffered hand and stepped down, sturdy shoes much in evidence. "I am, after all, a miller's daughter," she reminded him with a brief smile of amusement.

Whiting bowed over her hand and grinned without embarrassment. "I see I have not given you your due, Miss Chapman. You should perhaps be first to tour the Deacon's mill."

He opened the door at the end of the weather-beaten building and ushered her inside, followed by Ebenezer and Luther. The smell of

179

fresh-cut pine filled the barnlike room, and a haze of sawdust blurred the shapes of men working at the machinery inside. The noise was deafening.

Despite his acknowledgement of Abby's presence, Whiting turned his attention to the Chapman father and son, shouting to them over the saw blade's whine, pointing out features and identifying the auxiliary planing and shingle machines which came with the mill. Abby did not mind remaining in the background, for there she could watch without interruption. She liked the precision of the vertical blade slicing up and down through a whole tree trunk, and the steady rhythm of its movement. After a few curious and appraising glances at a female in the mill, the workmen returned their concentration to their work, and added their rhythms to that of the great saw.

She found herself watching Mr. Whiting. He fascinated her. His forceful gestures and expressive voice were such a total contrast to her family's restraint in word and motion. She was surprised, too, at his concentration, the unflagging attention he gave her father and brother, though surely there must have been a thousand other tasks and decisions which waited on his presence outdoors. From time to time he sent a sympathetic glance in her direction, a silent apologetic lifting of his eyebrows for keeping her waiting in the noise and heat and dust. She was not used to such consideration. And his eyes were not too close-set at all.

Eventually, the discussion moved outdoors, to the relative silence and calm of a shade tree under which the horses stood. Abby waited by the carriage and observed the negotiations. It was clear to her that her brother was ready to buy.

"We might just have some interest in the operation." Luther looked determined

Ebenezer, stone-faced, began grumbling. "Hmmph. The whole works are too antiquated to be worth more than a few pounds."

Colburn Whiting nodded, listening solemnly to both men's words. Then he shook his head.

"Unfortunately, gentlemen, it is out of my hands. I've been informed the stockholders have voted to auction the mill, come the end of this month. There's been quite a bit of interest in the place, all things considered. But I'm sure, especially now you've had a good look around, you'll know just how high to bid."

180

Ignoring Ebenezer's scowl and Luther's crestfallen look, he shook their hands and unobtrusively began moving them toward the carriage.

"I hear Mr. Gay will be bidding. Maybe Mr. Clark, who of course you know. I'm not sure about the fellow at the Lower Falls or some of the others but, all in all, it should be an interesting turnout."

Whiting smiled ingenuously and wished the Chapmans well in their efforts.

As he handed Abby up to the seat, she silently marveled at the way this perfectly polite and attentive man had managed to put even her father right where he wanted him: ready to buy and price be damned. Ebenezer Chapman rose to competition like a fish to bait, so any doubts he might still hold as to the wisdom of Luther's enterprise would be submerged in his desire to win out over his neighbors at the auction to come.

Abby met Whiting's gaze as she sat down. His light blue eyes were cool, carefully hooded to cover the thoughts within. For a moment though, as they met hers, his eyes warmed and his brows rose slightly. Almost as if he were checking with her, maybe sharing a small joke. Recognized in her an ally. She blinked and dipped her head down.

The ride home was quiet. The two men were busy with thoughts of the mill and its sale, as shown by occasional muttered comments they exchanged over her bonnet. Abby sat very still in the middle, eyes open but sightless, as she studied again the fascinating sights within her head. Most of all she studied the image of Mr. Whiting, and a very small, faint hope began to glow deep inside her.

Abby did not go to the auction. Daniel was down with a summer ague, Lucy's late-term pregnancy had brought on sciatica so excruciating she was bedridden, the raspberries needed picking before they rotted, and it was bread baking day. Besides, Abby consoled herself, she was not at all sure she wanted to be in the vicinity of the Chapman men if their bid for the mill was unsuccessful.

When the men walked in the door mid-afternoon, it was clear she needn't have worried. There was a swagger in Luther's walk which, she guessed, was part pride and part the celebratory bowl of punch he must have offered round at the Dover Tavern on the way home.

"You bought it, then?" she asked him.

"Lock, stock and barrel!" Luther was uncharacteristically talkative. "Sometimes it pays to work on your own," he went on, momentarily overlooking his father's involvement. "There was one of those new Dedham *corporations*, they call 'em, bidding, but the gang of them couldn't agree to bid higher, for all their money. And Ellis & Gay, from the Clapboardtrees, dropped out before the bidding had barely begun. They didn't have a chance," he finished with satisfaction.

"Hmph. Didn't have a chance for all that money you kept throwing at them!" Ebenezer muttered, but the corner of his mouth twitched up in pride at his son's successful bidding.

Lucy carefully walked through the doorway in time to hear Ebenezer's grumble. She smiled softly at her husband and quietly commented,

"Our children will thank their father for what he did. Chapman's Mills will draw business from miles around, I have no doubt."

Luther stared at her and repeated,

"Chapman's Mills." He savored the words.

The pair exchanged a long look of shared vision, a future they had planned for many years. It was very intimate and full of love.

Abby quickly glanced away, blushing as if she had intruded on private affairs. As if a curtain had lifted, exposing one of the mysteries of wedded life. She found herself wondering at the incomprehensible bond between husband and wife. It pained her to realize she envied them. And for what? They were only seeing to their family's future. As they should. As they must. Nothing so enviable about that.

She picked up a wooden spoon and impatiently stirred the cornbread she was making for supper. Luther stopped dreaming and turned to his sister.

"Oh, and Abby, you'll have a chance to show off your cookery, Friday. Whiting's bringing the papers over here to sign." He sounded a bit puzzled. "I told him I'd head back over there with the rest of the money, but he insisted. Said it was his pleasure, he was indebted to us."

Luther turned to Ebenezer. "Whatever you may think of those close-set eyes, Father, you can't deny Whiting is a gentleman in business dealings."

Ebenezer snorted. "Gentleman and business are contradictory words." He shook his head. "Don't get me wrong. I don't know a thing against the man himself. But the family has a long history in these parts. A Whiting may be a gentleman in polite company, but he's no better than a Barbary pirate, when it comes to money matters. I see no reason to believe anything different about this one."

Abby kept her silence during this exchange, hearing nothing she hadn't heard from her father before. But as she scraped the batter into a baking pan she tested the image of Colburn Whiting as a Barbary pirate, lawless and wild, storming the Atlantic and destroying the peace and dreams of quiet-living men. This wasn't the man she had met.

She smiled at her father's penchant for exaggeration and set the skillet by the fire.

The Mr. Whiting she had met was far more likely to set sail for some distant shore than raid the one he knew. He would run a tight ship, but it would be a respectable one, and its complement of sailors would be full, made up of men who would follow him anywhere, drawn by his commanding presence. Her father would never understand a man like that.

The dinner and the land transaction went well. Mr. Whiting was polite to the point of formality, patient with the children's comings and goings that could not be avoided in the Chapman's old, crowded house. He was especially attentive to Abigail. His compliments on her cooking made her realize how rarely praise came from her own family. His private admission at dinner's end, that her bread surpassed any he had tasted for delicacy and flavor, prompted her to wrap up the remaining loaf, and shyly press it on him as he took his leave. He bowed low over her hand, and thanked her for her generous hospitality.

As she cleared the table, Abby caught herself stroking Mr. Whiting's napkin, as if to draw from it some essence of the man himself. Bending over the wash pan, she found herself listening for echoes of his voice, hearing again the telling comments he had made at dinner. The man had talked easily with Luther and Mr. Chapman, about subjects with which they were comfortable. But Abby caught glimpses of a much broader knowledge at work in his mind, glimpses of ideas far beyond the thoughts of the Chapman men.

Lucy took note of Abigail's distracted silence, and nodded optimistically.

"Luther, I do believe your sister has taken a shine to Mr. Whtiing."

Luther snorted in brotherly amusement. Next morning he passed the word as he and his father yoked the oxen together.

"Seems Lucy's got it in her head that Abigail's making eyes at Whiting. Think there's any interest there? She could do worse, to my mind."

"Might be she could do worse, but as to eyes, you know my opinion."

Ebenezer shook his head at Mr. Whiting's close-set eyes.

By the end of the week, when they began dismantling and moving the Dover sawmill, Lucy had convinced Luther to invite Mr. Whiting to return for another meal with the Chapman family. He accepted the invitation with alacrity.

After that, a week rarely went by, that Mr. Whiting did not dine in Medfield. Sometimes it was on pretext of advising Luther on reconstructing the mill, or installing a second sluice in the Chapman's dam. As often, it was at the express invitation of one or another family member. He always arrived with some small token which he presented to Abigail in appreciation, he said, for her delicious food and kind hospitality. Abby blushed frequently, flustered by his attention, and stole surreptitious glances at him when she thought he would not notice. Sometimes he would catch her at it, sharp light blue intercepting wide-eyed brown in mid-glance. For a moment, it seemed to her, the entire world stopped and he looked right into her thoughts.

Not that she was sure what those thoughts were. When he had left, and Abby was cleaning up, she could quietly consider Mr. Whiting and his effect on her. She found him quite an attractive man, she admitted. And his conversation was interesting. He had brought more animation to the Chapman table than had been seen in years. More confusing, though, was his attention to her. Surely it was beyond mere politeness? But that would suggest there was something in her which he found out of the ordinary agreeable? While Abby wished that might be so, she knew herself well enough to recognize that she had little to offer beyond what any country girl might: a well-enough looking face and figure (her hair was too fine; her form perhaps too slight); some years' experience in household management, and an aptitude for cookery. Oh yes. And her bread. Abby shook her head at the irony of her least favorite household duty resulting in the most effusive praise. If nothing else, she decided philosophically, Mr. Whiting's visits added an element of excitement, of anticipation, to a daily routine which had little enough else to recommend it.

It came as no surprise to anyone except Abby, when Mr. Whiting formally requested permission to keep company with Miss Chapman. Once she had digested that astonishing information, though, it came as no surprise to her that Mr. Whiting pursued his courtship with the same decisiveness he brought to his business affairs. Colburn Whiting was a man of quick decisions. He would consider a matter thoroughly before acting upon it, but a decision once made, he would lose no time seeing it through.

There was a proper courtship, of course. He came again to Mill Farm, drew Abigail out of the kitchen for slow strolls about the pond, or a brisk trot to Sunday meeting in his snappy new gig. Abby was so tense with the exhilaration of going about in public with this extraordinary man that she could barely breathe. She felt the envious and appraising stares like pinpricks on her skin and wondered how Mr. Whiting could maintain such an air of calm detachment from the gossip that whispered around them. When he handed her down at the church, he caught her eye and gave her such an warm encouraging look that she felt buoyed up, and she placed her hand on his arm with a rush of confidence which carried her all the way to the family pew, where she lost herself in the sound of his vibrant singing as the opening hymn began.

Sometimes, after the midday meal, they would walk out to the shade of the great sycamore which overlooked the mill pond. These were the times she cherished most, when she could sit and listen to Mr. Whiting's impassioned discourse on the issues which concerned him. Concerned them all, he would say, as citizens of the new American republic.

Luther couldn't get over how the man just kept on talking. To Abby, however, raised in a household where a dozen words together made a speech, Colburn Whiting's observations opened a whole new world. He was well versed in the issues of the day, the debates between free trade and tariff protection, or the opening of the Northwest Territory. His observations encompassed the local, as well as the national scene. He had made it his business to know the world of industry in Norfolk County. He knew the rural landholders and the Boston merchants who were investing in new manufactures. He knew the extraordinary men, many of them English-trained, who called themselves millwrights. Not, he told Abigail, like Luther and her father, men who knew the traditional ways, who could put together a grist mill or dam a brook with logs and dirt.

"These men will lead America into the future," he declared, and his eyes shone with excitement as he described to Abby the engineering miracles they performed. Rushing floods of water diverted by vast stone dams; three-story buildings constructed strong enough to carry heavy looms and tackling, forges and presses on every floor. And on the heels of the millwrights came another novel trade.

"They call themselves *mechanics*."

"But surely this is no new trade?" Abby asked gently.

"Indeed you would say so if you saw them work. They are equally at home with metal and wood. They fabricate – often with no more pattern than memory and imagination – those machines which will set America free."

Abby could not let that comment pass.

"But sir, was our independence not won two decades ago? My father and men like him fought for independence…"

Colburn cut her off.

"That's where you are wrong, dear madam. America is only now on the verge of true independence. Our nation will be free only when it frees itself from economic dependence on Europe. First control our own manufactures. Only then can we bid the Old World goodbye."

His eyes narrowed, and he frowned with the intensity of his vision. Even though he directed his comments toward her, Abby knew his thoughts were rushing on alone.

"Do you see?" His voice was urgent. "Americans will make our own! Our own steel, our own textiles. Everything from bricks to porcelain, carriages to glass. Our young men will have work aplenty. Our merchants and landholders will have room to invest. Even our farmers will have new markets for their crops."

And Abigail fell under the spell of his passion. Whiting, on his part, found Abigail Chapman refreshingly intelligent, a female who listened with interest to his thoughts and opinions. Furthermore, her quietly considered comments suggested an earnestness of purpose to match his own.

"The poet had it right, Abigail, this is a brave new world. We are embarked on the greatest voyage of discovery since Ulysses departed Ithaca. The greatest challenge, the greatest danger certainly, but together with these, the greatest chance of reward the world has ever known."

"Yours is an inspired vision, Mr. Whiting," Abigail responded, lifted up by his enthusiasm. "Surely so eloquent a proponent as you, must be in the forefront of this daring voyage."

Then she dropped her gaze and looked down, studying her hands which lay, work-roughened, in her lap. She glanced back up, searching Colburn's face for reassurance.

"But where is there a place for such as I in this enterprise? I have no special skills to bring, no knowledge of this world that you so eloquently describe. You have offered to make me your wife and I am honored by such consideration. But I cannot fathom how it is that I might fit into your brave new world?"

She nearly held her breath as she waited for his answer. Colburn Whiting was a man she could believe in. He was a man she thrilled to be near. But she needed to understand her place in his life and his dreams. It would certainly not be the same as her place at Mill Farm.

Colburn contemplated her intent face for a moment before he replied.

"My dear Mistress Chapman, you have seen that new world beginning at the iron works. You know my part in it, the worry, the disaffection, the bustle of it. Truth be told, I cannot conceive of carrying the responsibility of this role without knowing that there is someone who understands and cares for me more than a little – for Colburn Whiting with all his qualms and dreams, not the agent on the high horse. You are just such a kind and understanding person. I see in you the helpmeet that other men long for. There is about you such an air of calm competence, of attentive kindheartedness. I see you as my Penelope, anchoring my soul when the gods blow me about the seas of fortune."

Abby continued to stare at him soberly as she considered the mythic Penelope, ever-faithful, ever-patient wife. She glimpsed the woman endlessly carrying the burdens of everyday life, while her husband lost himself in voyages of adventure. But that was only myth, she scolded herself. If she were to marry Colburn Whiting, theirs would be a shared adventure – husband and wife, Abigail and Colburn. She dismissed her qualms and smiled brilliantly up at him.

"You, dear sir, do make a most perfect model of Ulysses."

The day had not begun well. Perhaps it was breaking the season's first ice on the rain barrel that had put her out of sorts. Perhaps it was knowing that Mr. Whiting was due for noonday dinner that had distracted her, so she'd knocked the jar of yeast right over into the waiting heap of flour. No way to measure now. No way to salvage enough of the frothing liquid to get bread set today. Then, just as she'd cleared the worst of the sticky mess, Daniel had slunk in the door, casting hangdog looks in her direction, his mouth pulled down in anticipation of impending doom.

"You brought the eggs?"

"Sort of."

"Daniel Chapman, I need half a dozen right now," she snapped. "Now go wash them off and bring them to me. You won't even sample the maple pudding if they're not here inside of a minute."

"Won't sample it anyway," Daniel muttered.

Abby turned and gave him her full attention. "What are you talking about?" she said sharply. "What's wrong? Aren't they laying?"

Daniel's answer was barely audible, his chin was sunk so low on his chest. "Hen house door got left open last night, I guess. No eggs there." He cast a quick glance in her direction before he studied the floor again.

Abby's voice was shrill with indignation. "And who closed them in last night, hmm? How many times have I told you to check the

188

latch before you go? What were you thinking that was so important you couldn't even do your chores right?"

Daniel's eyes flashed defensively. "It's Marmalade's fault! I saw her in there this morning. She had yolk all over her whiskers."

Abby interrupted. "Marmalade," she said scornfully, "didn't leave the latch off. Marmalade wasn't the lazy soul who couldn't even drag himself to the henhouse till this morning was half over."

She suddenly thought of Colburn Whiting's coming to dine and her shrillness turned to panic. "How do you expect me to bake without eggs? What am I supposed to serve company when you ruin everything?"

Her face flushed with angry frustration. "Why can't you ever do what you're told?!" Suddenly she screamed, "Get out of my kitchen before I take a switch to you!"

Daniel glared at her defiantly for a moment, opened his mouth to say something. Then instead, he ducked quickly out the door, being sure it closed with a heavy slam.

In the sudden silence Abby heard her rushed breathing keeping frantic time with the pounding of her blood. She stared horrified at the door which Daniel had closed so thoroughly. Daniel had never glared at her like that before. With such despite. Such anger. What was wrong with him these days, becoming so intractable, so hard to reach? Hadn't they always been best friends? The loving little brother and his devoted big sister.

The shrillness of her recent words echoed still in the room. She thought again. One might better ask what was wrong with her these days. Raising her voice. Losing patience. Snapping at the children like a shrew. Fumbling through the day. She considered her situation. Nothing remarkable had changed. Luther and Lucy's newest baby had brought a few more wails into the house, a few more clothes for her and Lucy to scrub clean. There were extra chores from harvest time, but nothing she hadn't done before.

She did fritter away more time socializing than she used to, more time and effort on the frequent meals prepared for Mr. Whiting. Abby felt her anger waning. More time seeing to her clothes, her hair. Staring at the looking glass on her chest of drawers. Wondering what Mr. Whiting saw when he looked at her face. Could he see the same thin nose, the mouth too small with lips a bit too full? Or could he see beyond the deep brown of her pupils into the soul which yearned inside? Surely he knew to stir that soul. Inspire it with dreams of change and the hope that life itself could be as fulfilling as dreams.

Fulfillment and change. She tested the words. Two rarities she'd never thought to call her own.

When Abby was ten, two years after her mama's death, Father had married Mrs. Collins, the lady whose bread Luther liked so much. Mrs. Collins was a plump and sociable woman, a widow herself, who lived in the village with her daughter and son-in-law. She had made something of a business out of her bread-baking ability, and folks referred to the son-in-law's house as "Collins' Bakery", because they came there more often to buy a loaf, or a sweet cake, than they did to call on the taciturn son-in-law. Mrs. Collins' chattiness and her easy sympathy for those in need, immediately drew her to the Chapman family. Nor was she above noticing that Mill Farm was a handsome piece of real estate and its owner, Ebenezer, a well-favored man, despite the quiet grief that continued to pinch his brows in a constant frown. Then, too, there was all that flour the Chapmans ground: grist, as it were, for her own mill.

Abby was confused when this new lady came into the family's life. Luther said it was just because Father wanted a housekeeper. Father stroked Abby's hair and said it was so she could be a little girl again, and so Daniel would have a mama. But Abigail knew she wasn't a little girl anymore. Privately she insisted to herself that she was as much Daniel's mama as Mrs. Collins ever could be. Then she admitted that she wasn't much of a mama, wouldn't ever be, the way she remembered her own mother being, all warm and gentle, softly loving. But she was also sure that Mrs. Collins would never be that way either, whatever Father might think.

Despite her reservations, Abby eventually acknowledged that Mrs. Collins (she never could think of her as "Mother", or even "Mrs. Chapman") made life easier at Mill Farm. Mrs. Collins cleaned and cooked. She scolded Daniel when he was being naughty, so that he would run to Abby for solace and Abby could be the loving, understanding big sister she really wanted to be. Abby and her stepmother worked out a satisfactory, if wary, relationship with each other and faithfully, twice a week, they would bake together.

Beginning right after breakfast they would lay a fire in the deep beehive oven and listen to it roar as they measured and mixed, kneaded and set the bread to rise. When the fire died down they would scrape out the coals and test the heat. At first it was Mrs. Collins who tested the temperature. Later Abigail learned to stick her hand in the opening and try to count to forty before the heat became too much to bear. The rye bread went in and baked while Abigail peeled apples and Mrs. Collins rolled out flaky crust. A pie went in when the oven was emptied, along with fat loaves of white flour bread. Abby always slipped in a few twists of sugar-sprinkled pie crust. These she hoarded as treats to share with Daniel. Before the day was over a thick pudding may have browned in its earthen pan, custard if the hens were laying or when the men took sick. Next morning, Abby pulled out a black pot full of slow-baked beans for breakfast.

Hot weather brought the baking down to once a week, but it was a day to dread, as they worked at the kitchen table with hands so sweaty the dough stuck to them. When she could not stand the heat another instant, Abby would slip out the door on some pretext and sit down for a moment on the shady side of the house, facing the pond. The water would wink at her, cool despite the heat. She could almost feel it drawing her away. Away from the endless loaves of bread, away to sink her feet in the cool shallows by the shore. But the pastry twists hadn't been done yet, or the next batch of yeast set to work. Or Mrs. Collins would call her with that trilling voice of hers, pleasantly insistent that Abby return to finish her chores.

Six years after Mrs. Collins' appearance in their lives, she was gone, carried off by an unexpected weak heart. On a damp April day, the Chapmans laid her to rest as befitted her station and family. Ebenezer shook his head in puzzlement at the confounding ways of Providence, then went back to the mill, its wheel turning overtime in the spring high water. Luther's face was expressionless as he returned to setting fence posts in the north pasture. Daniel was upset, hovered near Abby for days thereafter, as if afraid that she, too, would suddenly disappear.

Before the week was out, Abby realized things were really no different from six years before, when it had been up to her to cook and clean, garden and care for the chickens. Only now she was sixteen, and could add spinning and sewing and baking to the endless household chores needing to be done.

After that, nothing much changed in Abby's life. Luther brought Lucy into the household. The couple took over the room Luther and Daniel had always shared and Danny had to make shift with a pallet in the storeroom upstairs. Luther and Lucy got busy making babies right away, and young Thomas, soon joined by George, slept on a second pallet in the store room as soon as they could be trusted up and down the steep back stairs. Washday was longer, bread disappeared faster, and little children distracted and charmed her with prattle about "Nabby" as they got underfoot. Six more years went by, measured in Abby's life primarily by the change of seasons, though even those tended to blur from one year to the next.

Abby's thoughts drifted back to the small disaster at hand. Her eyebrows went up at the memory of her scolding. What a tempest in a teapot! There was more to life than fussing over spilled yeast and broken eggs. This year, she suddenly realized, there had finally been a change. Mr. Whiting had appeared and suddenly she might look forward to more than a routine that had turned her shrewish at the age of twenty-two.

In fact, Mr. Whiting was the one piece of her existence that bore no resemblance to the commonplace. He was as near a paragon as one might hope to find on earth. She listed his virtues to herself. Strong-minded and unafraid. Quite handsome in a stern way. He enjoyed lively conversation, unlike her taciturn father. He felt her worthy of consideration, unlike Luther who seemed to think she was part of the household furniture. And he had a drive, a bursting of energy about him directly opposed to the careless nonchalance of Daniel.

She moved the tin baker onto the hearth and stirred up the fire. Why did she hesitate to link her life with his? Everything she had learned of Colburn Whiting simply confirmed the impression she had formed that first day, that he was a gentleman of many admirable qualities, whose life she would be more than pleased to share.

Besides, there was little to look forward to in years to come at Mill Farm. She set her jaw determinedly and measured out corn meal. She would do something about that.

When Colburn Whiting knocked at the door an hour later, corn bread was cooling on the kitchen table, two pies browning in the bake oven, and the room smelled of roasting capon and onion sauce. Abigail let him in, her family being conspicuously absent. Colburn noted the starched cap perched on Abigail's smoothly dressed hair, and the stiff baize gown that showed beneath her spotless white apron. He smiled warmly and bowed over her hand in exaggerated fashion, to which she responded with a blush and a breathless, "Do come in."

"I believe Luther and Father will be here presently," Abby rushed on. "I'm not sure what has kept them so long at the mill, for they knew you were expected at noontime."

Colburn shook his head in dismissal. "It makes no mind to me, when I meet up with the Chapman men. I am here as much on your account as theirs."

He reached out the small burlap bundle he had been holding in one hand and offered it to her. "And besides, I rather hoped you would find a moment soon to open this. I came across it just this week in Boston. At Clark's warehouse on the wharf. I thought of you."

Abby continued to stare at his outstretched hand without moving.

"Please open it." Colburn pressed the bundle into her hands and motioned her toward the table. "With care," he cautioned gently. "The contents are delicate, like their bearer."

Sometimes, Abby thought, when things are just right, just as they should be, you have to stop to take it all in, to freeze it all in place preserved forever. This man who came for her, his intent blue eyes, his cajoling voice, the small brown bundle with promised magic inside… She suddenly realized what a dolt she must look, standing there gaping at Mr. Whiting and his bundle. Summoning a polite smile, she moved to the table and thanked him in advance for his kind but quite unnecessary gift.

"Necessity, dear Miss Chapman, is, I believe, in the eye of the suitor, who sees embodied in the slightest thing some cherished aspect of his beloved. This gift cried out to be given."

Silent again in the face of his gallant turn of phrase, Abigail turned her attention to unwrapping the package. Her smile deepened.

While Abigail worked at the string and spread open the burlap, Colburn leaned on his cane and studied her. He cherished the flush on her neck and cheeks, marveled at the concentration and care she gave to everything she did. She was so small and fragile, yet so full of energy, of determination. He frowned briefly. The navy baize of her gown was all wrong. It washed out her pale skin, dulled her fine brown hair. *Serviceable.* That was the word; serviceable and dull. And due, no doubt, to the lack of gentle example the poor girl had had in her life. But it would take little study for one as quick as Abigail to learn the gentler side of womanhood. For one as eager, as open...

It would, Colburn admitted to himself, be a delight to teach her in many ways. Yes, and sometimes to stand back and watch as she learned. To begin, he could introduce her to some of the gracious women and forward-thinking men of Boston society. How surprised, how delighted she would be to discover a world where people enjoyed discussion, where they savored the finer things of life. Not like the Chapmans' self-enclosing universe, their narrow minds which sought answers from the past for tomorrow's problems. Abigail would blossom away from all this. She would soon be example to them all.

"I bought these as token of the life we might share, Abigail. A life enriched by the broader world beyond our doorstep. Though it may be initially austere, yet we can count ourselves wealthy in the conversation of sophisticated men. And in time, if indeed God helps him who helps himself, you shall have all those material goods you have done so long without. For I assure you, I will never require of you the extreme financial restraint practiced by your family."

Pennypinching, Abigail thought to herself. He's politely describing Father's pennypinching ways.

The rough burlap held a mass of straw inside, which spilled across the table as Abby unwrapped it. Nestled in the straw were two white dishes, and two deep-dished saucers to go with them. Abby gently lifted one out and held it up for inspection. It was a thin porcelain tea bowl, the graceful curve of its silhouette unmarred by the inelegant handles which some English china men had recently begun putting on their wares. At first the decoration seemed so plain as to be severe: a narrow leafy band below the rim, a wispy sprig of rose and leaf on each side, all in black relieved only by the smallest touch of gilding.

"*Encre de chine*, the ship's factor called this: Chinese ink decoration," Colburn explained. "A new style, they tell me, and quite the rage among knowledgeable circles. These were shipped direct from the orient on one of Mr. Clark's swiftest vessels. I doubt you'd find a newer fashion this side of the Atlantic," he ended proudly.

Abby reached into the straw nest and retrieved a matching leaf-rimmed saucer, set it gently on the table, then the tea bowl on top. A touch of smile came and went on her lips as she silently repeated the process with the other set, then stood back to admire the result. She would not be rushed. The delicate brushwork and fine line of the black ink brought out the pure white of the porcelain. Such a contrast to the earthy pots and mugs, the cream-colored plates and colorful servers of the Chapman household. Surrounded by all the packaging and food, the utensils and trappings of mealtime in a crowded kitchen, the pair of cups glowed quietly on the table. Serene, Abby thought. Nearly untouchable in their perfection.

"Will you have them, Abigail?"

Colburn seemed to step into her thoughts. An unexpected question. Of more weight than first appeared. The bowls were not untouchable, were they? They were hers for the taking. Like this man and his new world. A great glow of delight rose up in her and her expression, when she looked up at him, was radiant.

"I will, Mr. Whiting. I will treasure them always as emblems of your kind regard for me."

He came closer and took her hand in both of his. His hands were so full of warmth, she thought. Colburn raised her hand to his lips and kissed it, staring at her the while.

"And will you have me as well, Mistress Chapman? Will you be my Penelope?"

No more hesitating, she thought. No more making do.

"I will, Mr. Whiting."

Later that day, when congratulations were done and wedding date set, when the children were in bed and the last clean dish set on its shelf, Abigail retired to her chamber and sat by the small table that held her writing box and a handful of books. She removed all the large, stiff sheets of writing paper from the box and carefully folded them, first lengthwise, then three times across. Slitting the sheets along the crosswise folds, she sandwiched them together in a folio, then covered the whole with an bit of brown wrapping paper. Leaning near the candlelight, she carefully sewed the spine with small stitches, binding the pages together. The small booklet complete at last, Abby dipped her pen in ink and began to write. Inside the brown cover she inscribed her name and the date. Then, across the blank first page she wrote, in careful schoolgirl script: JOURNAL.

She did not even pause to consider the next entry.

This day I begin the record of my new life. I am to be wed in three months time, to Mr. Colburn Whiting, a gentleman of Dover. I cannot say what drew this admirable man to my side, although he is most gracious in his flattery of me. But for my part, I find in him such a multitude of virtues and attractive qualities as will furnish a quantity of food for thought – yea, food for heart and soul as well – which needs must be writ down, else I shall burst from all the words within.

So shall I begin, that I may forthwith record those thoughts which he inspires in my brain.

"Now! Madam, prepare yourself to view a great wonder!"

Colburn's eyes glinted with excitement as he flicked the reins, urging the cart horse downhill toward the new dam. Abby turned her head just enough to secretly study her betrothed beyond the edge of her bonnet. She marveled at the enthusiasm in his voice, at the energy which seemed to lend urgency to everything he did and said. She was certain that whatever he had to show her could not compare with the wonder of the man himself. Except, perhaps, the wonder that he had found her to be a suitable companion for his brave journey toward tomorrow.

She glanced back at the scene around them, and was surprised to see that they were driving right past the raw new mill building. Was this not the "great wonder" then? Surely something as novel as an iron-working enterprise was worthy of admiration. Indeed, as word had spread of the Dover Nail Manufactory and its sophisticated machines, not a day went by but some party would arrive to admire the works and the massive dam that stretched all the way across Charles River.

Their gig continued across the bridge, however, and began the short climb up the facing hill. Abby noted a long, new rooming house. She saw another crisply-painted building. That was the company office. The new manufactory had space demands that were filling in the yard room between the few old buildings at Fisher's Bridge.

Workshops and storage sheds, cottages and larger houses were spreading away from the river's edge, forming a village where for centuries, there had been only a handful of structures.

At the top of the rise was another bare, raw-looking house nearing completion. It was spaced apart from the rest. Stiff granite posts marked the lot corners and the muddy path which would one day be a carriage drive. The house itself, set back slightly from the road, was stark white, with windows carefully balanced each side of the front door, which was crowned by a small fan window and framed with fluted columns. The building seemed tall, all its familiar features attenuated to lend grandeur to what was, in truth, a quite ordinary-sized structure. A stylish house, Abby thought, built to the new taste for all things classical. Certainly the most elegant one on that country road. She dismissed it. Never be one of her favorite designs. More than anything the house reminded her of a straight-laced dame with brows permanently raised in disdain at inferior surroundings.

Whiting pulled back on the reins as they came abreast of the hilltop building. He studied the house for a moment, head tipped to one side so that his top hat looked precarious. Inexplicably then, he jumped down from the gig and turned to Abby, barely-controlled excitement lighting his eyes.

"May I present you the great wonder I promised?" He reached up, inviting her to take his arm and descend.

As she gave him a questioning look, he bowed briefly and said with great pride and affection, "Madame, I bid you welcome to the new home of Colburn Whiting, Esquire, and his lovely bride to be. May they always be as happy here as they are today."

Abby gasped in astonishment. Once again she found herself tongue-tied by one of Colburn's surprises. Silently she reached for his arm, but found herself caught at the waist by his strong hands, instead. He set her down, eye level with his shirt front, and continued to hold her close. His stunning announcement and the intensity of his light eyes, when she dared to look up at him, spun together in her mind and mixed with the warmth of his hands holding her so familiarly as to leave her lightheaded.

"*Our* house, sir? For you and me together?"

He smiled at her fondly. "For you and me and a brave young family of entrepreneurs." His smile faded and his voice became earnest as he went on. "Ever since I walked into your father's house, Abigail, I've wanted to give you a home to call your own. No more the drudge to someone else's family. You've served that stint for much too long. It's time and beyond for you to take your rightful place. Mistress of your own home. I see you inside already. I picture you quietly sitting there as the clamor of work below becomes too loud. I will come home to this house of an evening, and find you waiting." He briefly touched her cheek. "You, with your gentle smile in the calm of our own home, will be a balm to take away the worries of the day."

Colburn paused, and looked at her seriously as he held her just within arm's length. Abby felt her face turn hot as she carefully studied his neck cloth and listened to the passionate sincerity of his words. No one had ever made her part of their private vision. That a man would devote such forethought, such attention to her, was beyond experience or understanding. This was a new world indeed. She briefly prayed she need never leave it.

"Truly, Abigail," Colburn went on solemnly, "I believe you are my Penelope. You will give me a port to sail home to. I do not think I should survive without your loving care."

In the silence that followed his declaration Abby, on the edge of tears, gathered herself together and looked directly at Colburn. This was a man truly worthy of her devotion. She chose her words carefully.

"You shall always have my loving care, sir. And in truth, I must be Penelope, so closely do you resemble that Ulysses of old, braving uncharted waters and unforeseen foes in search of great reward."

She glanced down at the manufactory, then turned her eyes to the house that waited across the road. She nodded toward its orderly facade and continued, as if thinking out loud.

"But come." She freed her waist from his grasp and took his arm. "If this is to be the palace where I am to wait, please, will you show it to me, dear Ulysses?"

Colburn leaned forward and kissed her cheek. Then he clasped her hand tightly and led her across the road to their new home.

Abby moved in silence through the first-floor rooms, barely hearing Colburn's enthusiastic narrative of cajoling an up-to-date builder to work this far out in the country. Colburn's boot heels echoed on the hardwood floor as she studied the carved woodwork in the front parlor. She was struck by the high-ceilinged elegance of the dining room and thought of the crowded, worn spaces in the Chapman house. Colburn spoke of Mr. Lyman, a Boston gentleman and one of the ironworks' proprietors, who was even now building a country retreat not unlike this very house – though of course on much grander scale – in Waltham.

Wherever Colburn led her, Abby was struck by the newness and the thorough attention to detail. The mantels were fine, the walls carefully finished; windows were large and every room was rich with its own fireplace. Many rooms even had cupboards for storage of clothing and other goods. Nothing was missing, nothing had been left out.

Her greatest shock came when Colburn drew her into the kitchen. The fireplace was perhaps half the size of the massive chimneypiece she'd grown up with. She wondered how they'd keep warm on a frigid winter day. Even the oven was smaller, handily built into the front of the structure. A soapstone basin was actually set permanently against the window wall, held up by stout wooden legs. Colburn proudly showed her the hole he had especially required drilled at the back so, he explained, the wash water could drain directly outside. Here was a room to work in with pleasure! Space enough for all the needs of domestic economy. And, she silently added, for children underfoot as well.

The last room Colburn showed her upstairs was nearly as fine as the front parlor. Delicate moldings defined the door and windows, and a carved chair rail tied the room together like a ribbon on a package. This, he told her tenderly, was the conjugal chamber. Abby blushed at the intimacy of his words, and turned to stare out the window while she collected her thoughts. In the awkward pause which followed, the workmen's hammering was loud outside. She looked down to glimpse what they were doing, but saw only the muddy path leading to the front door.

"So, my Penelope, what do you think of our home?" Colburn considerately changed the subject.

Abby turned back from the window with a small puzzled frown on her face. "I find myself at a loss for words. You have considered and planned so thoroughly... It is beautiful..." She lapsed into silence again. Colburn raised his eyebrows in question.

Abby made a helpless gesture with her hands and blurted out, "But surely this is too grand for us? We are but two, and two just starting out. This work must cost a fortune! I know it's not for me to say...but are you not stretched beyond your reach?"

Worry and embarrassment warred in her face as the questions tumbled out. Before Colburn could answer she was already apologizing.

"I know is not a wife's place to wonder at a husband's expenditures. It is certainly no way to express my gratitude."

Colburn cut off her stammering with a short laugh.

"A true housewife's concern! I number practicality high among your virtues, Abigail." He took her by the shoulders, watching her face in wry amusement. "But this time you need not fret. The house is a dower gift from your esteemed father. It was he who insisted on a proper home for his beloved daughter, and set me to getting it done before we were wed."

"My father!" Abby could not conceive of penurious Ebenezer Chapman relinquishing so much money for anything, particularly when his land was not involved.

"Squire Chapman himself," Colburn nodded. "His dower gift to you. But there's more. It seems this gift is not just a pretty notion to him. This house, my dear, and every foot of land it stands on, is entailed solely in your name." His smile was stiff. "We are standing in *Mrs.* Colburn Whiting's house."

"I do believe, madam," he concluded, "your father does not wholly subscribe to my faith in the future of manufactures."

Abigail could not decide whether the bitterness in his voice mocked her father's old-fashioned ways, or his own far-reaching dreams.

That evening, Abby settled herself at the writing table in her room. She moved the candlestick closer to the page and tried to order the thoughts which tumbled over each other.

I am afraid I have behaved unconscionably today. But truly, I was
so angered by father's high-handedness.

Mr. Whiting took me out driving this afternoon – an innocent enough pass-time, one would think, 'til we arrived at the new village and he discovered to me that he had engaged to have a <u>house</u> built for us! A house to marvel at, for its size and elegance and situation on the hill crest. Only to think that my betrothed would do such a thing – and with such timeliness – for me and for our life together! Thus I was doubly – nay, trebly confounded when he let out that this remarkable building was <u>my father's</u> gift to us! not even to <u>us</u>, it would seem, but to me alone, without any regard for the sensibilities of my husband-to-be. And the act did hurt him. Not that he much let on, but I could hear it in the sharpness of his voice, the way he made mock of his own fondest dreams, just as I believe my father does. I was in a fine temper by the time we returned back home, and hard put to graciously bid farewell to Mr. Whiting.

"So, Abigail. How was your ride?" Ebenezer Chapman asked carefully.

Abby found him sitting by the kitchen window with his *Village Register* and his clay pipe. He was, she was convinced, waiting for his supper to magically appear, and the thought added further to her indignation. She was too absorbed to notice the uncharacteristically tentative look he gave her as he spoke.

"My *ride* was most enlightening. And yes, Mr. Whiting showed me our new home. He told me about it too, Father."

Ebenezer raised his eyebrows. He knew his daughter well enough to recognize that her emphatic tone did not bode well, though he was hard-put to fathom why that might be so. Abby drew in a deep breath.

"Father, what on earth were you about, making such arrangements behind my back? Mr. Whiting might be excused from consulting with me, for he has not had experience of female company, but you! I have kept house for you my whole life. You know I have some appreciation for what is involved in a house – in the running of it. Enough for you to afford me some bit of respect and consideration…some small say as to my own future home? But no! You go about this – you and Mr. Whiting – wholly behind my back!"

She stopped to catch her breath and Ebenezer protested.

"Now wait a bit. There's all the difference in the world between knowing houses and knowing the running of them. Mr. Whiting's greater experience of construction and style …"

Abigail cut him off, picking out of her father's protest the other root of her indignation.

"And there's the other rub! If you intended this house as a betrothal gift, then surely it should be in Mr. Whiting's name. What can he think at your insistence otherwise? What *were* you about, Father? I was ashamed to look my future husband in the eye! You've as much as said Mr. Whiting is good enough for your daughter, but not for her money. Truly you do the man great disservice!"

Abigail stopped for a moment, then blurted out, "And me, as well. Have you no faith in my judgment at all?"

... Father was remarkably patient through my tirade. Although I do admit I gave him little chance to respond. On the other hand, he has never been known to tolerate what he considers insolence from any of us. Thinking of what came next, I must question whether I might have misread his sternness all these years. Our father is a surprising man ...

"Like your mother after all," Ebenezer murmured.

Abby's irate silence stretched painfully as he scrutinized her hot face and clenched hands. His study was long enough for her to begin to return to her senses, to dread her father's reaction. Then Ebenezer did something to confuse her even further. He smiled. A rare smile of affection which softened the strict line of his mouth and spread to the weathered wrinkles of his cheeks, although his eyes were – what? Sad? Abby could not read their expression. Ebenezer shook his head.

"When she got riled up, not that she did it very often, she'd put on her stubborn voice and come up with more questions than a body could answer. Just swamped the culprit with questions. And every one as sharp as a blade."

Abby was too surprised by Ebenezer's words to take offense. Father never mentioned his first wife. Abby could barely remember the mother who died when she was eight. She longed to hear about this woman whose loving hold on her father cast so long a shadow even after death. She held very still, not wanting to break Ebenezer's train of thought.

Chapman shifted, and his voice became more businesslike. "It was your mother, Abigail, decided what was to be done with you, you know. Before she died. She insisted I secure your dowry in your own name. 'A woman needs an independence,' she said. She had on her stubborn voice and I always knew with your mother not to gainsay that voice no matter what."

He frowned briefly, and shook his head. "I'm not sure yet, that I agree with her. A woman needs a man's brain to handle financial matters, despite what she thought. But Mill Farm goes to Luther some day, and there's a respectable portion set off for you, as well as for Daniel. Certain sure, you've more than earned your keep around this place, even as far back as when she was sick. And done it again, these past years since Mrs. Bessie Chapman passed away." Ebenezer never referred to his second wife except by her full name. "Your mother would be proud of you."

And you, Father?

Ebenezer didn't hear his daughter's silent question. He was deep in his own thinking.

"I thought, this way, with the house, you could bring a fair portion to your marriage. Mr. Whiting would have the wherewithal to set you up suitably, despite all his fooling around with those manufactures. And I'd still satisfy your mother by an 'independence' for her daughter."

Ebenezer turned toward the fire. He was talking more than he'd done in a month of Sundays, and talk was tiring. But he frowned in concentration and it was clear he had more to say. Abby eased herself onto the edge of the nearest chair and waited.

"You haven't had much out of life yet. Pray Almighty God that Mr. Whiting does well by you, gives you what you won't find here. You know I don't care much for the gentleman, myself."

Abby knew that. She also knew that his one judgmental comment was as much as she would hear of her father's dislike. Ebenezer was old-fashioned, a Yankee farmer, with little patience for 'talking out of turn', as he called it. Little patience for unsolicited opinions founded on a slim basis of truth. She was sorry he could not see Mr. Whiting as she did, but thanked heaven that he would not come between them. As if in response to her thoughts, Ebenezer continued grudgingly.

"But no one speaks ill of him, I'll say that. And he certainly has powerful men behind him in this manufacturing business. And you seem to think he's what you want. So I'll answer your question, Abigail. I do trust you. Enough to let you choose your own life. I guess that house you're all riled up about is your mother's and my way of furnishing that life a bit, that's all."

He shrugged, and stood up to signal the end of his long speech. "I can't do more than that, and wish you godspeed."

... It was as if Father was saying goodbye. Bequeathing me some final patrimony. As if I were off for the western territories instead of the next town. Or as if – God forbid – he were on his deathbed, rather than giving his daughter in marriage. Such a long speech, and so personal. And truly he moved me to tears as he spoke of Mother. There was such a tenderness in his voice. I never realized how deeply he must have loved her, and how he must have missed her companionship, even when he took another wife. It is such strength of feeling I trust I shall come to share with Mr. Whiting. Colburn. My husband.

I do believe my father was trying to convey the affection he feels for me. Both by what he said this afternoon, as well as by the sorry business about the house. I do love him for that, and for the honor he bestows on my mother's memory. I pray I may be worthy of their trust.

Abby had risen from the seat across from her father and kissed him on the cheek.

"I am so ashamed. I have little excuse for my outburst but amazement." Her words were as stiff as his had been, two people equally unused to speaking what was on their minds.

"Your care for my future... The great expenditure..." She tried again. "Do not think I am ungrateful. The house Mr. Whiting has commissioned is splendid, but it was so unexpected, so unthought of. It took me completely by surprise!" Abby's voice softened. "And I never dreamed, either, that Mother thought to provide for me before she died. That is as great a gift as any I can imagine."

Ebenezer looked down at her without speaking. Suddenly it was very important for Abigail to soften the stern line of his jaw and the sadness of his eyes.

"Oh, Father, you must believe I never doubted the charity of your intentions! You've cared for us – Luther and Daniel and me – seen to our welfare all our lives. You've kept us together. You, of all people must know, Father, that that won't ever change. Even though I'm to be Mrs. Whiting, I will never cease to be the Chapmans' daughter."

Her eyebrows lifted in question. "I trust you're willing to have that so?" she ended lightly.

Ebenezer nodded and drew her into a brief tight hug. Then he cleared his throat and walked stiffly out of the room.

But my thoughts are ever drawn toward the future now. With Colburn. (I think in this journal's privacy I shall use his given name. It has such strength, and vigor – like the man himself). Together in the house of his fond imagining. I do – very privately – regret he did not consult with me before he approved the plans, although I can say nothing against the fashionable design and great scale of the building. I do think perhaps Mr. Whiting was caught up by his enthusiasm for all things new, however – for this new style does not show that vitality which he himself embodies so well.

As for myself, I will be well enough content with it – no – enraptured might be yet a better word, for it is what my heart's desire desires, and that must be enough.

Perhaps time and love will soften the structure's sharp edges a bit...

Summer 1797

Abby carefully smoothed a few stubborn wrinkles from the fashionably striped gown and laid it in a drawer. A transparent embroidered apron went on top, and she smiled at the delightful irony of this delicate garment bearing such a utilitarian name. She could just see herself prancing about the kitchen in this, swiping her greasy hands down the front of the spotless lawn. Fashion, it seemed, made all things new, transforming the familiar into something never imagined by its practical inventor.

What a long way from standing at the wash kettle in Mill Farm's back yard to where she stood now, in this chamber she shared with her husband. From her skirt hem tucked up out of the way in her waistband and petticoats protected by coarse tow apron, to the narrow-cut dress she wore today, with so little petticoat beneath she'd catch her death, were it not a summer's day.

Abby's mind wandered as she paused to admire her image in the looking glass, then laid away the other garments that Anna had washed but that she herself had carefully ironed. The fine chemises and imported stockings which Colburn insisted she must have, that time last winter they visited the modiste in Boston. The white shirts and carefully starched cravates about which he was so particular. They were handsome garments all, and Abby thanked heaven for Anna's help every wash day, when the older woman's big, capable hands grasped the near-boiling laundry and wrung it out, passing it over to Abby to spread out to dry. Abby's own hands were not quite so red these days, or so sore.

Abby turned from the chest of drawers to tidy the rest of the chamber, although again Anna had accomplished much of what needed to be done. She shook her head and marveled. Who would have guessed Abigail Chapman would have a housekeeper for herself? Wayward pangs of Chapman frugality still bothered her but she did not miss cleaning out the fireplace ashes. She needn't even empty the slop bowl on the wash stand.

She did insist on trimming the candle wicks each morning, keeping the brasses and the handsome pieces of wedding silver polished. She tended the back yard chickens and pigs and saw to provisioning the household. She and Anna together prepared the meals and served them. Breakfast was at dawn before Colburn walked down to the mill; a hearty dinner at noon, often for unexpected guests, gentlemen come to the mill on business, whom her husband bid to dine without warning. After the first times, when Abby and Anna found themselves scrabbling for dishes to fill out a company meal, or Abby picked at a pastry in polite disinterest as a voracious guest devoured the last chop, she had learned there was some merit in apparent extravagance. From then on, the noonday meal always included at least one portion more than should be needed, and often two or three. More times than not, there were takers for the food, and Mrs. Whiting began to have a reputation among Colburn's circle of acquaintances for setting a tasty table. The compliments outweighed the awkwardness of her lesson in domestic economy.

Supper wasn't always quite such a success. It was simple, just enough to tide them over, but Abby had not yet resolved the struggle between a thrifty upbringing where good food was never wasted, and her husband's adamant dislike of leftovers. Shepherd's pie was *poor folks' food*, to his way of thinking. Corn cakes made from the morning's mush were *hand-me-downs*. Where he had developed this aristocratic posture was beyond Abby – certainly his own farm family could not have eaten thus. But she made an effort to accommodate his wishes, reminding herself that he might have leaned toward much more expensive tastes. At times though, she still shook her head at the money expended on food.

And after all the food was done, the sewing always beckoned. Stockings to mend and linens to hem, shirts to make or a collar to turn on Colburn's older coat. Like other gentlemen, he sought out a tailor in Dedham for new suits, but she would need to set about working on her own winter wardrobe soon, a new afternoon gown for the social occasions which were becoming more frequent, and certainly changes here and there to make last year's wardrobe fresh again. Fashion had unexpected demands, Abby thought ruefully. Clothing herself at Mill Farm had been simpler, and much less time-consuming. She noticed a run in one of the stockings she was about to put away, and pulled it out of the drawer again, to be consigned to her workbasket.

Abby wandered across the landing to the upstairs sitting room where she kept her sewing and her writing desk. Some day soon, God willing, the desk would be crowded out by children's things. Her mind's eye furnished the room with a trundle bed and a well-loved rag baby on it, a chest to hold toys, a shelf for the books from which they'd sound out their first words. There would be a rocking chair, perhaps, where she could sit and hold them, snug them to her as they read and rocked, laughed and cuddled close.

For reasons known only to the Almighty, she was not breeding yet. Abby stopped by the window and touched her forehead to the glass, cooling the flush that came with thoughts of Colburn's nighttime attentions. A small smile played at the corners of her mouth as she admitted to herself that sexual congress was not a bit as she had imagined; was, in fact, a brave new world all of its own. That vitality which she had loved in her husband from the first, was not left at the chamber door. Rather, it was committed entirely toward her, and the alternating patience and urgency which he displayed inflamed her with a pulsing sense of her own bodily demands (and charms) of which she'd been entirely innocent. Here was a meaning of womanhood she could never have conceived. A meaning and a satisfaction.

Thank goodness six months' experience of wedlock had tempered her first astonished delight. In those first days of marriage, an evening's loving could give the world a whole new, disconcerting aspect. Abby would catch herself in truly lascivious and thoroughly unseemly speculation as she went about her daytime, ordinary life. *Look at that woman on the street,* she'd think. *She has just been thoroughly loved. You can see it in the way she sways her hips, in the lower neckcloth at her bosom. There is about her a bodily pride, which matches my own.* Or she would catch a couple exchanging glances in meeting. *Their minds are clearly not on the hereafter! I know quite well where their thoughts are taking them.* And she would wholly lose the Reverend Mr. Caryl's admirable train of thought. Or she would talk with the stiff and formal spinster up the street and later, when Colburn returned from the mill, Abby would find occasion to see him alone, and press herself against him in urgent gratitude that she need not deny herself or him, as that poor singlewoman must.

Abby recalled herself to the present and lifted her forehead from the glass. Children would come in God's good time. She should not wish upon herself too soon the difficulties Lucy suffered, nor the dread of following her own long-gone mother. No, this was time appointed by Providence for husband and wife to come together, to learn to live with and sustain each other so that later, when children did appear, they would have a solid base on which to build a family.

She stared down at the sparkling river's bend and resigned herself to patience. All in due course. From this window she could see the broad dam, and the industry that lined both riverbanks. This was the only window – this and the one in the parlor below – where she could see the mill and, in seeing, feel closer to her husband during the long hours they were apart. She shook her head in gentle mockery at behaving like a moonstruck girl. There was plenty to fill her time when she and Colburn were separated. And if, as today, she found an hour to spare, why surely she might put it to good use.

Suddenly she had an inspiration. It used to be, when the house was too quiet and the work could wait, she'd walk down the hill to Chapman's Mill. She'd pass a few words with Father and gossip with the townsman who'd brought grain. She'd listen to the satisfying rhythms of water and mill stones, and breathe in the fresh, powdery smell. Somehow the little visits made the work she returned to seem part of a greater whole. The Chapmans working together, each in his or her own way.

Abby turned from the window and hurried back to the bedchamber across the hall. Inside its shallow closet, looking out of place beside the calfskin and fabric slippers she'd had made in the new fashion, Abby found the heavy leather brogans she had brought from the farm. She used them rarely now, making an effort instead to slip her delicate shoes into the wooden pattens that stood by the back door, if the lane was muddy or the chicken yard particularly dirty. On this occasion, however, solid brogans suited better, disreputable though they might be. It was time for a reminder of the Whitings working together. She was going to pay her husband a visit at the mill.

Whiting's commanding voice bid "Come!" at Abby's tentative knock on the little office building's door. Just as she reached for the latch the door swung open, and Mr. Cates stepped back to allow her to enter. Abby smiled warmly at him in greeting. She liked Cates. She gathered he was indispensable to her husband: secretary, bookkeeper, and man-of-all-work at once, always ready to see through some new chore which Colburn created in the mad rush which was his business day.

"Mrs. Whiting." Cates nodded politely. Behind him, Colburn glanced up from the papers that covered the top of his worktable. A brief frown passed over his face.

"Abigail!" He rose and came to meet her. "What brings you here? Is everything well?"

"Oh yes, thank you." She looked up at her remarkably handsome husband and gave him a smile somewhere between shy and challenging. "I hope I do not disturb you too much, but I have come to see the workings of the mill."

Colburn raised an eyebrow in question. Abby rushed on.

"That is to say, I recognize that you showed me about, when we first came here. And you introduced me to the workmen. But there was no opportunity then to really *watch* the forge or all the great machines in operation. And since that time I have been quite taken up with putting the house in order, and all those small details of domestic economy which so absorb a female's time…"

"You have accomplished miracles, madam, in short space," Colburn said gallantly. "As I knew you would."

"Yes, well, thank you." There was a thrill of pleasure in his compliment, but Abby was not to be distracted. "But I now find myself with some moments of free time, and wondered if you…or Mr. Cates perhaps," she said hurriedly, "for I know you must be busy with a hundred tasks…might show me the operation of an iron mill, that I might better understand what occupies your days."

She paused briefly, then shrugged one shoulder in embarrassment and added very quietly, so Cates would not hear, "When you are away from home and me."

A range of expressions chased across Colburn's face: surprise, amusement, irritation. They resolved into a short chuckle, a shake of the head and a knowing look meant for Abigail alone.

"Surely, Mrs. Whiting, there must be more appealing ways to pass your time than tromp through the noise and dirt of a manufactory. Not that I'm not flattered by your interest. And delighted to see you so unexpectedly."

A quick knock sounded on the door behind them, interrupting Whiting's thought. He turned and opened to a blue-frocked workman, a carter apparently, for a handsome team of Percherons waited patiently by a heavy wagon just outside. The carter tipped his hat and swiped his sweaty forehead in one practiced gesture.

"Morning, Mr. Whiting."

"Jepson! Good to see you here at last. This the stock we've been expecting from Clark & Son?"

"Yes, sir. But there's a new wrinkle this time, I'm afraid."

"Wrinkle? Hmm, come in." Colburn frowned, then turned to Abigail. "I'm sorry, my dear. Let me just see to Mr. Jepson here, and I'll be right with you. I'd be happy to show you what I can." He turned back to the deliveryman. "Now, Jepson, what's the catch to this shipment?"

"Well, sir." Jepson held a paper out in Whiting's direction. "Seems Clark & Son have started asking for payment on demand. They tell us we're not to deliver until the buyer pays up. In *full*," he added, his emphasis stressing the extraordinary nature of the demand.

"Pay up front?" Colburn bridled. "What's this all about? Our credit's always been good. Surely Clark & Son has no complaint about our credit?"

"Oh no, sir." Jepson hastily assured him. "It's not Dover Nail alone. Seems they're doing this to all their customers."

"Jepson." Colburn's eyes narrowed slightly. "Are you telling me there's trouble in the wind for Clark & Son?"

Jepson frowned at the floor, and slid the brim of his hat between his fingers as he thought for a moment. He shook his head.

"Can't rightly say, Mr. Whiting. Don't seem to be no problem on the money end. Their credit and their silver's good as ever." He paused. "But y'know, sir, there's more of these here iron mills every day, it seems, around these parts. And what with all the fuss going on across the Atlantic, I don't see the stocks of iron down on the docks the way they was a couple years ago…" He drew himself up and met Colburn's eye. "You ask me, I think Clark & Son are coming up short themselves. There's not so much supply, and a whole lot more demand. Tell the truth, I'd guess they're making hay while the sun shines, if you know what I mean."

Whiting's expression was grim.

"I'm afraid I do, indeed, know what you mean. And I don't like it. Not a bit! They can't just expect us to pay on the barrelhead, like some part-time ironmonger. We've got deadlines to meet, and our own invoices outstanding. It's unfair dealing, the way I see it. And if I have my way, things will change around here in the next few years. The Dover Nail Manufactory is going to be so big that no chivvying middle man is going to drag us down. Clark & Son can just go to perdition trying!"

Abby listened, fascinated, as her husband's voice grew louder, and more vehement, in his indignation. He was, she thought, a very convincing speaker. Of course he had convinced her six months ago, she reminded herself, so she should not be surprised that his talents extended to the field of business as well.

Mr. Jepson was a voice of practicality breaking into her thoughts.

"I guess you must be right, Mr. Whiting but, meaning no disrespect, for now I need to collect before I can unload."

He pushed the invoice in Colburn's direction again.

"Yes. Oh, all right!" Colburn snatched the paper impatiently and tossed it to Cates, who stood silently writing at a tall clerk's desk by the window.

"Draw him up a bill of credit on the Dedham Bank," Whiting ordered. "And get that wagon over to the mill. We've got customers waiting as far away as the Carolinas for our nails!"

Without another word he grabbed his tall hat off the peg by the door, took Abby's arm and pulled her outside, the edge of her straw hat tipping back with the force of their departure.

As they strode away from the office, Abby could feel the anger in her husband's grip. His mouth was drawn in a tight line, and a frown of concentration warned her not to interrupt the tense silence, despite her eagerness to understand what had just transpired. Instead, she waited for the moment to pass, and turned her attention to the crowded mill yard they were crossing. The space was filled with buildings of all shapes and uses. Just downriver, cut into the bank itself, stood a long, partially open lean-to. Smoke rose from three tall chimneys sticking through the roof, and Abby could hear a resounding clang of hammers on metal. The blacksmith's forge, Colburn said. A dirty apprentice disappeared into the shed, shoulders pressed down by the yoke of full water buckets he carried. Hard work for a hot day, Abby thought, even in shirtsleeves.

Across the river, on the little peninsula where Deacon Fisher's mill had once stood, she caught glimpses of a small village growing. A long narrow boardinghouse for some of the mechanics – some had left families as far away as Rhode Island for a chance to learn how the new machines worked. She spotted a man vigorously wielding his whitewash brush. John Woodward was working on the new dry goods store.

Colburn propelled Abigail across the yard toward a long wooden building stretched along the riverbank. This was the rolling and slitting mill itself, and it dominated the other structures. Abby was astonished at the noise. So loud and insistent. Great barn doors stood open to let in air, and she could see a massive stone forge outlined inside. A blossom of flame illuminated sweat-streaked faces as air from hidden bellows fanned the coals. Underscoring all other sound was the thud of a great waterwheel, ominous and deep, while cogs and gears creaked and thumped in urgent counterpoint. Abby's first step through the doorway was met by a great hiss of billowing steam and Colburn jerked her aside until the cloud passed. Abby wondered what devil she tempted by entering this infernal place. She was grateful her husband protected her.

"What was that?" Abby had to raise her voice over the clanking around them. Her eyes tried to adjust to the flares and shadows.

Colburn bent near her ear and yelled back. "They're cooling the rollers between passes."

He pointed at a massive set of iron cylinders lying stacked on one another. Wisps of steam still rose around a leather-aproned machine tender who adjusted a crank alongside the rollers.

"Watch there. They're doing a second press."

Abby watched as two other apron-clad workmen, kerchiefs tied as sweat rags on their heads, grasped a plate of glowing metal with long heavy tongs and fed it between the revolving steel cylinders. A horrible screech rose in the air as the hot iron plate was squeezed between the rollers. Sparks flew out from the tortured metal, rollers shrieked, men yelled across the machine. Under it all the wooden gears kept up their heavy thumping. Just as Abby thought she could not bear the noise another instant, the plate emerged at the other end, wider, longer and thinner than when it had gone in. The workmen carried it outside and began a new stack of sheet iron.

Even as they did so, the machine tender and his boy were dousing the rollers with water to cool them down, clouds of steam rising and swirling in the flares of forge light where other ingots were heating. Colburn bent low again.

"Are you ready to quit this hell hole?"

Abby flashed him a strained smile. "Nearly so. But please tell me first what those other rollers are for." She pointed to a second machine, sitting idle at the other end of the shed. "Are they not the same as those in use?"

"There is one vital difference," Colburn began. Just then a new plate was fed between the rollers and he had to stop. Abby covered her ears, for what little good it did, but stared in fascination, amazed at the transformation of a seemingly immutable substance.

As the flattened sheet came out the other end, Colburn spoke quickly.

"See that those other rollers have ridges around them? They line up, one with another? Now come." He drew her outside into the sunbaked but relatively silent yard. Before he could go on, Abby interrupted, her eyes bright with interest and excitement.

"Wait! That must be the slitting machine, is it not? The ridges somehow cut those sheets they're making?"

Colburn was surprised at her quick understanding of mechanical matters.

"Ah! Masculine wit in female form! You are quick to comprehend." He nodded appreciatively. Abby flushed with pleasure at his compliment as he went on with his explanation.

"The ridges are a series of steel knives, which slice through the hot metal as it is forced at them." He drew her over to a metal stockpile at the end of the shed. "And here are the results. Barrel hoops for a cooperage in Portsmouth. These, here, are going across the river," he gestured toward the peninsula, "to the triphammer shop. Farnum's making them into reinforcing plates for Mackintosh's carriage manufactory."

He turned last to the biggest heap, of long, narrow rods.

"But these will be our fortune. Nail rods." A screech behind them announced the rolling of another plate. Colburn frowned and grabbed Abby's arm again to hurry her away, down toward the chimney-topped lean-to she had noticed earlier. A broad-shouldered workman caught up with them partway across the yard. He was outfitted a cut above the others, she observed: waistcoat and neckerchief in place despite the heat. With a nod and a low word of apology, he drew Whiting aside for some business that couldn't wait.

The relative silence was a relief, though steady hammering came from the long shed in front of them. It was almost musical in contrast to the clamor behind. Abby was not sorry to leave the mill building. From this distance she could appreciate the drama unfolding within it. Briefly, she remembered that first glimpse of construction, that time she had ridden with Father and Luther. How they had sat on the brow of the hill and marveled. Who could have guessed then, how much more there was to marvel at than met the eye? In her own life too, not just the scene around them. Twelve months and all was changed. A married woman. A home of her own. A husband whose word controlled dozens of people, whose vision could change the future. She felt a rush of pride at being part of such a grand scheme.

Abby focussed again on the bustle around her. Small wonder visitors continued to come and stare. Needham farmers and their wives, smart young blades in fancy gigs, whole parties of businessmen from Dedham or Boston. They all came to admire the great dam across the Charles. They wandered through the yard and marveled at the flares and steam emanating from the rolling mill. Like a dragon in its lair, she thought, then frowned at her silly flight of fancy. What she had felt, scorching flame and stifling clouds of steam, ear-splitting metallic screams and the roar of dangerous machines was not to be wished on any man. It was a far cry from Chapman's Mills.

Colburn was shaking his head as he returned.

"Something is amiss?" she asked gently.

"The gods are making mock again."

"Who was the gentleman who came just now?"

"Richards. Calvin Richards." He spoke impatiently. "You've met the man before."

"Oh! Mr. Richards." Abby hurried to smooth out the situation. "I confess I did not know him right away in working garb. Could you assist him with his problem?"

Colburn shook his head again and began to walk away, talking as he went. "I could not. Not that I know any who could do better…" He suddenly realized Abigail still stood where she was. Colburn spun around and glared at her, his anger apparent in the sharpness of his words.

"It seems, according to our highly knowledgeable foreman Richards, that we are in danger of losing power to the mill." He gestured abruptly toward the river. "Our perpetual water supply is drying up."

"But how can that be? The Charles River doesn't dry up!" Abby tried to imagine such a thing. "A mill stream perhaps… I've seen it happen at Father's mill. In fact, more likely than not, there are only mosquitoes and frogs in his raceway by this time." She smiled at the contrast as she turned toward the river. "But here, the wheel continues turning. The current still moves along, no matter how far the water is down along the banks."

215

"Madam," Colburn cut in impatiently, "If there is not substantial rain before the week is out, the water level will be too low to turn the wheel at all or at least, too slow to work the gearing for the slitting machine."

"Then Mr. Richards will raise the flashboards in the gate at night, will he not? Surely by morning the water will have ponded sufficiently to run the mill again. Father regularly extends his grinding season up to a month by this."

Abby's confident words faltered as she watched the transformation in her husband. Whiting's face drained of color except two flushed spots high on his cheeks. His jaw clenched and his answer was tight-lipped.

"Mrs. Whiting." He emphasized her name. "This is not some backwater tub wheel run by an aging farmer. These machines require the full power of an overshot wheel – a wheel bigger than any before seen in these parts. You can't just whip a few boards into a two-bit sluice gate and make it all better. In fact," he gestured impatiently, "we can't put in any boards at all because the damned farmers upstream have a damned contract which forbids us to raise the water till their damned haying season is over! As if a few stacks of hay bear value against a fortune in iron!"

Abigail opened her mouth to speak but was cut off before the words came out. Whiting's close-set eyes narrowed and his low-pitched words were scornful.

"It was my understanding that your unorthodox visit today was in order that you might *learn* something of this business, not so that you might *instruct*. Your small experience of one upcountry grist mill, madam, does not pertain to the difficulty at hand."

He rushed on, the words gaining momentum in a flood of scorn. "Your comments are, at best, naive. They are out of place and I only thank God that you did not utter them in front of Mr. Richards. They would have been patently embarrassing to us both! In the future I would ask you to confine your comments to those subjects with which you are familiar."

Abby was so stunned by Colburn's unexpected condemnation that she just stared at him at first. A ringing filled her head; words tumbled about, but mostly it was the tone she heard, the scornful, hateful tone coming from a person she loved more than anyone in the world. He disapproved of her thought. Surely more than that. He rejected her offer to help the only way she knew how. Her ill-judged words had only been intended to support her husband. Yet he rejected her very support. What was she to make of that?

Shame and indignation fought inside Abby as she dropped her eyes from Colburn's unbending scowl. At the same time it seemed essential that she set things right between them. Her brain desperately searched for words to temper her husband's flash of anger, to make him recognizable again. Staring at the ground, Abby prayed her down-turned hat brim would hide the tears.

"I apologize, Mr. Whiting, if I overstepped my bounds in speaking as I did." The words hung between them in a painful pause. "I spoke merely out of concern for you, and did not in any way intend to question Mr. Richards', nor your own, far greater knowledge of the current situation."

Abby blinked at her shoes, hoping her husband might say something – anything – to break the tension. Colburn remained silent.

"Perhaps it would be better were I to leave you to your work."

Still silence. It was becoming unbearable.

"Might I return another time to have you complete the tour of the mill works?"

The question hung in the air for such a space that Abby dared to glance up, desperate to glean some response from the unmoving man before her. She caught him staring, but not toward her at all. His head was turned toward the river, a brooding look on his face as he contemplated the falls. It was as if he had already forgotten her presence.

Eventually he realized she had spoken, and roused himself to answer her last comment.

"I think there is little enough else here worthy of your time and discomfort, madam. Indeed," he added distantly, "there are moments when I wonder if they are worth my own..." Bringing himself back to Abigail he went on. "I would hate you to think your obligation as my wife extends to dirtying yourself about the millyard. Why, look at you! I had not appreciated the shabby gear you'd forced yourself to wear in order to come here. Those brogans! I thought never to see them again, except in the henhouse."

His eyes drifted back toward the dam and he drew himself even more erect, lifting his chin and tugging down the hem of his waistcoat. "We must never fail to remember my responsibility as representative of the proprietors of this concern. My greatest charge is to see to its commercial success. All the dirt and discomfort we must endure will result in greater prospects for the future. Bearing all this in mind, I aim always to present myself in a most respectable fashion to all men, high and low alike."

Colburn looked down at Abigail and spoke carefully, "I am certain, Mrs. Whiting, you wish to do likewise. Much as I appreciate your attention to my concerns, I do not believe you should trouble yourself further with the turmoil of the mill yard. Over dinner, perhaps. You might ask me for more information then, if your lively mind seeks still further enlightenment. Surely this would be a better forum? You need not suffer the heat and distress of the mill, nor" – he gave a dismissive glance at Abby's shoes – "ever have to wear those shoes again. Do you not agree?"

Colburn's look was earnest, certain that his spouse must see the merit of his point of view. Abby tried to separate his words from a new feeling of unease. Colburn did not wait for a response. He took her elbow and began to walk away from the mill buildings.

"But now, dear madam, I am short of time. Richards and Jepson and Cates all require my attention before the day is out and, much as I might enjoy attending you, I fear the press of business calls. Will you forgive me if I leave you to see your way home alone?"

Whiting's solicitous words were made merely formal by the absence of any warmth in his voice. She was being dismissed. Her husband was sending her away because she was an interruption. Of course she should have anticipated such a possibility. This was not a slow-paced rural mill. Why did she not recognize how busy he would be before she set out on this foolish errand? Why did she not stay at home to begin with?

Abigail studied her husband's face, her brown eyes wide and serious. She chose her words carefully.

"I did not realize until now, how fully occupied your time is. I am sorry to have inconvenienced you. You need think no more of it, however, for I am certainly as capable of seeing myself home as of coming here in the first place." She raised her chin a bit and tilted her head, tried to make the next words cheerful. "Shall I expect you, then, at dinnertime?"

Colburn bowed briefly over her hand. "Of course, my Penelope. Just as soon as work allows." Then he walked away so quickly that Abby's goodbye fell to the ground between them. She studied his purposeful bearing and his tight, quick stride, knowing his thoughts had left her faster than his feet. She frowned.

Clenching her hands in her skirts, Abby turned her back on her vanishing husband and the mill yard. Quick steps became a near run as she rushed to escape the humiliating scene which had just taken place. How could she have been so foolish as to interrupt her husband's work? *Or beard the lion in his den*, she thought irreverently. Why, for an instant, did she imagine her presence would be welcome? Why, for an instant, could he not have shown her a bit of that affection he demonstrated at home? Even a bit of the respect?

In all fairness, it was clear that he was under great pressure in his role at the manufactory. She had not realized before how many facets of the business ended on his shoulders. Not only the normal agent's concerns of commercial dealings but, apparently, control of the mechanick end as well. And this business with the river and low water! Surely that was enough to distract the most devoted spouse.

Abby's flight had taken her off the main road to a cart track along the river. The river moved slow and steady to one side, its bank lined with pickerel weed and cowslips. Across the path a hayfield stretched into the distance, grasses tall and near to harvest, the air a tactile substance in the August heat. The drowsy surroundings finally slowed her pace. Somehow the heat did not oppress here as it had in the machine shed. And the steady whine of cicadas soothed away the pounding echoes of metallic noise. Abby perched on a shady stretch of stone wall at the edge of the hay field. Perhaps the calm around her would help to sort the jumbled feelings that still disturbed her peace.

It seemed there was a side to her husband which had hitherto lain hidden. An impatience, an anger at that which impeded the progress of business. This man she loved was so clearly driven by his crystalline vision of what *should* be done, that he resented anything which interfered with his vision – be it man, like Clark & Son with their unreasonable demands, or God, whose unaccountable ways brought the river so low that the work was apparently threatened.

Was it really so unreasonable to look for payment on delivery? She wondered. Surely her father thought not. But that, as Colburn pointed out, was up-country dealings. She supposed they might not pertain, here. And the low water problem. Something to do with gearing, presumably. The speed with which the massive rollers turned. Insufficient head, they would have said at home. But Colburn implied that the workings here were much more complicated than she was able to fathom.

There was nothing to be done, on her part, to remedy the errant ways of God and businessmen at the nail manufactory. And she would be the last to dream of changing her husband's behavior, as if that were even possible. What was left, but changing herself? She sighed. She had changed so much already. Sometimes it seemed she had left everything that was familiar behind. Her home and family, her daily routine. Even baking the endless bread. Nowadays Anna picked up a loaf at Mrs. Woodward's, in the morning on her way up to work.

Abby idly swung one leg back and forth, making a furrow in the dust with the toe of her shoe, imagining what her delicate new slippers would look like after a few swings. A breeze brushed past her cheek bringing the clean, simple smell of warm grass. She lifted her head to watch some early goldenrod waving at the field's edge. That was familiar, at least. She looked further down the path and noticed black-eyed-susans and Queen Anne's lace. Just like the fields at home.

Abby walked over to a clump of the yellow flowers and ran her palm over them, absently stroking the soft, fuzzy blossoms. If what was required in this marriage was for her to change, then she would do so. It was her duty and it would be her challenge. Her marriage to Colburn Whiting was the most important element of her life, and she would do all she could to smooth over any roughness in it. Today had made one thing quite clear. No matter how much she cared for him – and cared for the business which occupied him – she would have to show it at a distance from the mill. Here, it seemed was a situation of absence making the heart grow fonder. Colburn thought more kindly of her at home than at his side, at least when his side was in the mill yard.

She wandered slowly along the track, absently reaching out and touching flowers as she passed. So be it. She would do all in her power to make their home the haven he so clearly wanted, the welcoming harbor for which Ulysses must yearn. With sudden determination she bent down and broke off stems of goldenrod. Moving on, Abby uprooted two or three delicate Queen Anne's lace, wishing she had a knife to cut them properly. Black-eyed susans, a few spice-scented fronds of tansy, even a spray of seed heads from the hay itself. An unorthodox bouquet, perhaps, but it would fill the house with scent and sight of gracious summer days.

Abigail's return to their house on the hill was optimistic. She refused to dwell any longer on the painful scene in the mill yard. Her husband must be forgiven a few sharp words and she had learned a useful lesson of matrimony. She would manage differently in the future. Besides, she thought whimsically, she carried a sheaf of summer in her arms and it was redolent of home.

As soon as she walked in the door Abby climbed the staircase to their chamber. Removing the offending brogans, she wrapped them thoroughly in brown paper, and with a hint of regret, buried them in the far corner of a drawer. The armload of meadow flowers greeted her as she rose, overflowing the wash stand where she had dropped them. She smiled at the profusion of yellow and white and green, delighted by their freshness. Suddenly an idea struck her and she laughed aloud with the pleasure of it. Hurriedly Abby searched out her scissors from the sewing basket, and set to work. She would make this room a bower of summer delights.

Aug 15, 1797 – Mr. W. – peels down some <u>golden-rod</u>, which I had carefully prinked round the looking-glass, in contempt, as he said, of its being placed there, either for ornament, use, or a sign of domestic economy. As he strewed them over the floor: "<u>do</u> make as much work for me, as you can!" says I, in a voice half insolent and half angry. – Immediately he went about feeding the pig; and contrary from his usual custom, he returns the swill-pail not, indeed, to its usual place, but right upon the kitchen table! Some other things he removed out of their usual places as well, indicating thus, I am sure, his silent disapproval of my behavior. I found myself without words to *express my aggravation at his petty revenge. If he chooses to banish me from <u>his</u> chosen venue, then surely he has not the right to so criticize my small attempts at prettying that sphere which is mine! And then, as further insult, his senseless disruption of <u>our</u> household, all in a fit of pique!*

I know not how to withstand such unconscionable behavior! Nor can I fathom its source. Can it be some egregious fault of mine, that provoked him to it? And if so, how can I know it, when he will not speak, but rather stomps about displacing things?! I am resolved to hold fast against his foul humor. He shall learn that I, as well as he, can play the mute, and we shall see which one takes first for stubbornness. 'Twas not for naught I became his Penelope, that most persevering of females!

But truth be told, I am hard pressed to comprehend just how to model myself after that heroine. So many venues seem closed to me in this new life. Certain I am, I shall not take up weaving, as did she! Although I warrant my husband would disapprove of that as well, it being such a menial task. But I, like she, shall somehow persevere.

Abby woke the next morning to an empty bed. She hurried downstairs in search of Colburn, fearful that her silent condemnation of the evening before had gone too far, horrified at the thought of their feud continuing.

She stopped in astonishment at the kitchen door. There stood the swill pail, back again on the work table. This time, however, it overflowed with a mass of fresh field flowers. Goldenrod and daisy, Queen Anne's lace and tansy: all the blossoms discarded the night before. Beside the bucket was a sheet of paper. Abby recognized her husband's writing.

> *My dearest Penelope,*
> *Our disagreement of this past evening brought me such distress that I could not sleep beyond first light. I beg you to use these flowers as you see fit though indeed I would be justly served, were you to treat them as unkindly as I treated the little blooms you gathered yesterday. I know not what to say, to excuse my behavior, but that the present difficulties of the*

*business distracted me from right behavior toward my
most cherished wife.*

*I would that you might find it in your heart to
forgive your impetuous and profoundly apologetic,*

Ulysses

Abigail smiled softly at her husband's notion of apology. She
tucked the note away in her pocket, then caressed the flowers he had
gathered. Finally she searched out an elegant creamware vase, an
unused wedding gift, and began to carefully arrange the stems.

Over the course of the morning, Abby tried four more vessels and
countless arrangements before she was nearly satisfied. When
Colburn appeared for the noonday meal, he was greeted by the sight
of a small, neat posy of tansy in the entryway. A pair of matching
urns stood on the parlor mantel, filled with matching yellow and
white bouquets. He cautiously complimented his wife on her artistry
and the subject was dropped. He did not dwell on the new set to
Abigail's jaw nor the regret in her eyes.

*August 16, 1797—R. looked favorably on my poor attempts at
flower arranging today. It is not a skill that I shall ever master, I fear.
The blossoms have minds of their own, and do not bend easily to my
human will. I must bear in mind that this is but a small experiment,
however, which I shall strive to improve upon in time. May our
marriage do likewise.*

October, 1797

Colburn was in Philadelphia on business when Ebenezer
Chapman died. Daniel drove to Dover to tell Abby and take her back
with him to Mill Farm. Their father had died as he had lived: with
very little fuss, and without consulting anyone. He had not appeared
at breakfast that morning, and Luther went to search him out, finding
him crumpled on the floor, hands still clutched to his chest, a lifeless
stare of shocked indignation still on his face at having to meet his
Maker without prior warning.

Abby found the news impossible to take in. She went about collecting her belongings in a state of numbness, spoke to Anna without hearing her own words, and was surprised to find herself in the Chapman's carriage an hour later, heading for Medfield and the burial to come. Daniel had remained silent during much of the intervening time, unsure how to ease his sister through her obvious shock, wishing she could make him feel better and wishing he were anywhere else, at the same time.

It was his voice that finally broke through her stunned silence.

"Luther says he must have gone right away." Daniel hesitated. "That he didn't suffer much, or anything."

Abby turned to look at him, forehead wrinkled in puzzled disbelief. "Did none of you know there was anything wrong with him? Had he made no complaint at all, earlier?"

"Not a word."

"Why could we not see that this was coming?" she exclaimed querulously. "He was a perfectly healthy man!"

"Oh, come now, Abby. He was hale enough, that's true, but he was coming up on sixty." Advanced age, it seemed to Daniel's fifteen years. Daniel searched for other clues to explain his father's abrupt departure. "I guess his left arm had been giving him some trouble for a while. But nothing in his chest."

They lapsed back into silence as the horse trotted steadily toward Mill Farm. As Abby began to comprehend her loss, she felt a weight of sadness spread out within her. Like a dull gray blanket, she thought. The blanket that covers his face. That covers his body lying at rest. So unlike him, to rest in the day. He should be out at the mill. Or striding down to the lower pasture on some urgent matter. No, she stopped herself. His blanket is deep blue. And the coverlet our mother made on top to keep the chill away. Her mind wandered on between pangs of loss and gently familiar details.

Eventually Daniel cleared his throat to draw his sister's attention.

"I guess things'll be pretty different now, around home."

Abby agreed dully. Daniel tried once more.

"I guess it's time for me to make some changes, too."

That caught her attention. Puzzled, she looked over at him.

"What do you mean, Danny? What kind of changes?"

Daniel carefully stared between the horse's ears. Abigail noticed the set to his jaw which had always warned in advance of her little brother's mind being made up. A first flicker of alarm hit high in her chest.

"I'm heading out."

He rushed on, before she had a chance to react to his announcement. "I spent a lot of time talking to Asa Richards when he came back east last month, and he says there's work for everybody, and land to be had cheap out in Ohio Territory. Good land, too," he said earnestly, "not like the woodlots and played-out pasture you know I'm going to get from Father's place. Besides, Luther could use that land, the way I see it. You know, keep it with the rest of the farm. And if I can talk him into buying up my share, I'd have enough to make a start out west and who knows, before long maybe I'll end up with as big a spread as he has – a better one, at that!"

He rushed on, half to himself, caught up by his own enthusiasm. Abby realized with a shock that this was not a new idea for her brother.

"Why, Asa says the soil out there is two feet deep, and in places it's as black and rich as sin. He says the fields will almost plow themselves and there are so few rocks you have to put up *wooden* fences! And all the while there are settlers passing through, ripe and ready to buy whatever you might fix to sell: food, wood, almost anything. And Asa says he's pretty sure he can fix me a place with a neighbor of his who needs a hand, till I can set up on my own, so I won't even be out away by myself until I'm good and ready."

Daniel seemed to think his last point would reassure Abby.

"But Danny, you're just a boy still! And what about our family? How can you conceive of leaving Mill Farm?"

His expression turned stubborn.

"Father's the only one who's kept me here since you left. Don't get me wrong," he hurried to add, "Luther and Lucy have been nice enough and all, and the kids are fine when they aren't being pests." He paused to search for words to capture his feelings. "But *you* should know, Abigail. If anybody can understand, you should. There's a whole world out there, and most of it is new and looks like the Promised Land. I want to see it! I don't want to see my life dribble away on the same farm, plowing the same fields my great-grandfather did. I want to be part of the future." He suddenly found the connection to convince his sister. "Like Colburn is, Abby. I want to make a difference, the way he does. You understand that, don't you?"

An incoherent sound from his sister made him glance to the side to judge her reaction. Her brow was furrowed and she concentrated her stare on the road ahead. If it had been Father, that expression would have meant a tongue-lashing. When Abby spoke, though, there was none of the scolding in her voice that he expected. If he had to put a name to it, her tone sounded more like pleading.

"Oh Danny, there are lots of ways to make a difference in the world. You don't have to do it all at once. Especially so young." She shifted to another tack. "I know you've been wanting a change for a while now, but surely there's plenty of time. Won't you at least wait until you're of age? That's only…"

"Three more years. I know, Abby. But I'm ready now," he insisted. "There's nothing to gain by staying. I can't stand waiting, and waiting. For what?"

Abigail groped for words. "But what will Luther do without you? Especially without Father as well? He cannot manage both farm and mills on his own. What does he say to your going?"

Daniel chose to ignore her last question, continuing with an explanation that he had clearly spent some time and thought on. "Luther can hire help cheap enough. The Cheney boys have barely enough work to feed themselves. They grew up farming their uncle's land so they know well enough what to do. And Goudy's old mill finally washed out in last spring's thaw. He's still at loose ends, too. Why, just last month he came nosing around, looking to help out, only then Luther said we didn't need any help. So, now we do, that's all."

Abigail returned to her question. "And what does your brother say to all this?"

Daniel adjusted his chin a bit higher and scowled. "I haven't had much chance to talk it over with him yet."

He saw one eyebrow go up. "You had in mind that I might, didn't you." It was a statement.

Daniel nodded.

His sister sighed. When she spoke again the words came out slowly, as if she were working through her thoughts aloud. There was pain in her voice.

"Oh, I don't know, Danny. It's too much to ask. Just this morning I woke up thinking today was like any other. Now in a space of hours, you tell me Father is gone and you want to leave as well." Her hands drew together at her breast as she pulled her cloak tighter around her. "When you came this morning, and told me about Father, I felt as if a great hole opened up in my heart. Always before he'd been within reach, just a few miles away from me. But suddenly he's gone beyond reaching ever again." Her voice had risen until she stopped herself. When she went on, the words seemed weighted down by her confusion.

"I don't know what to make of that. I don't even know what difference it should make in my life. But there is a hole right inside me. And already you want me to enlarge it; want me to help you go away too." She shook her head.

"But I'm not *dying*, Abby! That's the difference. I just want to start life on my own!" Daniel protested. "Don't you understand?"

She stared at him. "No, Danny. *You* must understand. The 'life on your own' will be so far away that we shall barely exist for each other. Time will pass – not just hours or days, as now, but months or even years – and everything we share will change. You will grow up without my ever seeing it, and I will grow older without your knowing how. And when we meet again we will be strangers. *Strangers*, Danny! Just as if we came from foreign lands. Daniel Chapman and Abigail Whiting would be two different people, no longer kin except in name."

Abby seemed to withdraw into herself as she spoke. As she went on, Daniel had to strain to hear her voice. Her look, when he dared to glance toward her, was sad and distant.

"I do not know if I can bring myself to help you go away, Daniel. Sometime soon, perhaps, but not today."

Daniel tempered his impatience, recognizing the finality in his sister's voice. The end of their trip took place in silence.

Two days later Ebenezer Chapman was buried. The large number of townspeople who came to pay their respects were duly entertained following the interment. Luther, proud and stiff in his new role as squire, saw to the distribution of mourning tokens: discreet gold rings for the pallbearers; black-embroidered handkerchiefs for the women whose pies and hams had covered the table and whose quick stitching had made up the necessary black accoutrements. Abigail had engaged a local dressmaker to copy one of her new gowns in black silk faille, despite the fact that the dress she had worn at Mrs. Bessie Chapman's death was still perfectly serviceable. It was, however, five years and a lifetime out of date and Abby did not want to shame her husband by dressing in country clothes.

Colburn Whiting returned home in time for the funeral. He was a consoling presence for Abigail, who felt the hole inside her heart draw nearly closed when her husband walked in the door.

"Your father was a good, upstanding man, Abigail. I know you will feel his loss."

Abby wondered what her husband really thought of Thomas Chapman and realized she didn't know. Colburn was difficult to fathom sometimes. But the grief of the moment outweighed all other thoughts and she was grateful simply for his presence, strong and reassuring by her side. Later, as they stood in the graveyard waiting for the somber prayers to end, Abby drew close beside him, drawing warmth from his nearness. The words of the prayer echoed and briefly, she was eight again, holding baby Daniel tight against her, praying he would sleep until the minister's endless words were over, trying to keep the tears from slipping down her cheeks as she desperately wished her mother would come back to help her through it all. The same helpless desperation began to build in grown-up Abigail. Now Father. Soon Daniel as well. *Too many people are going away,* she cried in silent protest. *They're leaving nothing behind.*

Her husband stirred at her side, a tangible reminder that that was not true. She glanced about her at family, young and old, and neighbors known since childhood. Even the burying place itself was familiar, scene more often of peaceful Sunday strolls than of the grieving taking place today. She drew a deep breath. She would not cry this time.

Following the burial, Colburn assisted Luther in the necessary obsequies that accompanied the passing of a respected country gentleman from this world to the next, and by his charm and attentiveness he reinforced the local opinion that Abigail Chapman had made herself a worthy match. When it was over, he returned to

228

Dover and the work waiting at the mill while Abigail stayed on a bit longer at the farm, to sort out Ebenezer's things and visit with her family. Abby waved him off at the front gate. Watching him ride away, become more distant and then disappear around the bend, brought an instant of dread. It was too much like the other unwanted farewells. Then she reminded herself how soon they would be together again, and dismissed her qualms as foolishness.

During the days that followed Ebenezer Chapman's death, Abby found herself returning often to her conversation with Daniel. Danny had always had his sights set beyond the bounds of Mill Farm. Even as a young boy, he would disappear of a summer's day, returning only as evening and serious worry settled on the household, so full of excited tales of his adventures that even Ebenezer's stern threats of punishment evaporated in the night. She resigned herself to the inevitability of her younger brother's departure.

So Abigail told Lucy of Daniel's plan. Abby mentioned it to her brother as well, choosing a moment when he was distracted by funeral arrangements. She slipped it into a conversation when she knew he would be too busy to give it much thought. Later, Abby knew, Lucy would broach the subject again, providing her own arguments in favor of the plan. By the time the two brothers had a face-to-face discussion, the worst of Luther's protests would be defused, and he and Daniel would reach an agreement of their own. Abby and Lucy shared a certain understanding of the way men's minds worked – especially Chapman men.

With Ebenezer's funeral past and Daniel's journey approved and planned, Abigail felt changes were done, and she was ready to return to Dover. The family crowded around the table for a last noonday meal together before Daniel drove Abigail home. Baby Sybil was sitting on Abby's lap. Thomas and George were pleading for one more piece of 'Aunt Nabby's bread,' as they called it, while Lucy dished out beans beside the meat stew. Abby was enjoying the comfortable clamor when she caught Lucy exchanging a significant glance with Luther, who suddenly made himself busy pouring cider. As he came to Abby's place, he cleared his throat.

"Now, Abigail," he began ponderously.

"Luther." She responded in an even tone, knowing he was leading up to something, waiting to hear what it was.

"I know you think we've been through quite enough the past few days. And I certainly agree with you." He nodded definitively as he bent over Daniel's cup. "But Lucy thought you might want to hear about our own plans before you go on back home."

Lucy looked mildly surprised at being assigned responsibility for what was coming, but held her peace. Abigail wondered what on earth her brother could be getting at, guessing it had something to do with the mills. Luther ran out of cups to fill and sat down heavily at the head of the table.

He finally looked her in the eye and announced, "We're going to build ourselves a bigger house."

"You are? How exciting!" Abigail could see that her enthusiastic response surprised Luther, and she briefly wondered why.

Lucy's soft voice took up the story. "Now Abby, you don't need to be told that this house is small for a growing family." She glanced around the crowded kitchen and toward the cavernous fireplace. Her voice became wistful. "And seeing your house made us realize how simple it would be, these days, to improve on its conveniency."

Luther interrupted with more urgent concerns. "To say nothing of its solidity." He shook his head. "I've started seeing signs of beetles in the front sill. And the south side of the roof'll need replacing soon as winter's over. In fact, if we don't do something pretty quick, the whole place'll come down around our ears, like as not!"

Abby raised her eyebrows at Luther's exaggeration. "Oh, come now, surely Father would have done something if it were that bad?"

Luther snorted. "He refused to believe it *was* that bad. Didn't look any different to him, he kept insisting, than it ever had. 'This house was around long before I was born,' he'd say, 'and it'll be around long after I'm gone.' Can't you hear him, Nabby? He had this blind faith that it was just the way it was supposed to be. Never could get him to look square at the problems."

Abby smiled softly in memory of her father's determined resistance, whenever possible, to change.

"Well, you're right about that. And you certainly could use more space. But where will you add on, then? There isn't a whole lot of yard room between the road and the drop-off to the pond." She paused, feeling sorry for Lucy having to make do with even less space during construction, while the addition and repairs were going on.

Luther looked surprised. "Oh, we're not adding on, Abigail. We're building new. Up the road by the barn. We'll start fresh, dig a real cellar, close in a good big yard between the house and the barn. We'll build bigger; face right on the road and the pond across the way, with ceilings high enough I don't have to duck and fireplaces small enough we don't watch all our heat go up the chimneys."

"My goodness! Sounds like the new saw mill has gone to your head, Squire Chapman," Abigail teased. "And will there be any timber left on the wood lots after you build your palace?" She winked at Lucy to include her in the joke.

Luther took his vision too seriously to hear Abby's joking. Like Daniel, he wanted his sister's approval. He hastened to reassure her of the plan's soundness.

"We're not out in the wilderness, you know," he insisted stubbornly. "We'll use what wood we can, of course, from this house." He nodded to himself, thinking aloud. "That's another reason we need to work fast. Need to get the good beams out before the beetles spread."

Abby suddenly understood where her brother was leading. Her voice was shrill with the need to be told that she was wrong.

"You don't mean you'd take this house down?"

There was a dreadful silence while her question hung in the air. Even the baby stilled in her lap, staring up in wide-eyed puzzlement at her unfamiliar voice.

Luther frowned. "I can't see any other way to do it that makes sense. The place is rotting. It's old and cramped and not much use. Seems to me, it's put to better use being parts for a brand new house, than trying to save those same parts from falling down on our heads."

"But this house has been ours for generations. You can't just tear it down!"

Luther gave her a long, sober look. "The way I see it, Abigail, you got your new house when you married Whiting, there." He hurried to clarify his feelings. "That's just as it should be. You've got a good place to raise a family, a place that tells the world who you are and that you're worth reckoning with. But Lucy and I, now, we haven't had that, living here with our dad and all the Chapmans before him."

231

His voice took on an unfamiliar defiance. "For all we cared for Father, Abby, he's gone and it's our time now. Time for the Luther Chapmans to stake their place in the world. We're going to build a place that says *we're* worth reckoning with."

There was a finality about the way he spoke. Abby found herself speechless in the face of it. She looked to Daniel for support, but he kept his eyes on his plate. Lucy's look begged her to understand.

"I'm going to build a new house," Luther declared, "and Abigail, there won't be many who'll mourn, when this old place is gone. I'm sorry if it pains you to hear it, but that's the way it's going to be." He hunched forward over his cooling dinner and began to eat, signalling he was done with discussion.

Abby shook her head in the silence that followed, then buried her face in the soft wispy curls on Sybil's head. The fresh scent, the silky feel of the baby's hair, the very solidity of the child sitting peaceful in her lap, suddenly overwhelmed her with a longing to go home. Home to her husband who took her feelings into account, home to their future together and their own children. It was past time to leave this place of goodbyes and endings.

November the 1st, 1797 – It gives my heart ease to sit once more at my own writing table, in my own chamber. So much of import has transpired within a week's time that I cannot, even yet, take it in, only to acknowledge its passing. My dear Father's untimely death – so fast we never even said goodbye – And then the news of Daniel's imminent departure for the Territories – I cannot convince myself that he is of an age to manage without family, nor that I am ready to have the younger brother I raised go so far away. Then, of course, this business with the house. I do recognize (to give Luther his due) that the Mill Farm house has arrived at an age where 'quaintness' may better describe its charm than does 'comfort'. And I have little difficulty comprehending my brother's wish for a larger and finer residence. Still – it was the home in which we all were raised, and I feel strongly that it is deserving of a better fate than to become a stockpile of used timbers. I left that hearth with yet another passing to mourn. Helpless to prevent the destruction of my birthplace – the birthplace of my brothers and our father, and his father before him as well.

Truly, it drains the soul to feel so utterly helpless. And so alone in one's thinking.

One momento I did bring back with me, to remind me of early times. It is the old caneback chair which Father used to say was as ancient as our house itself. I have set it in a place of honor in our parlor, by the window where I sew. The needlework seat shows decided signs of fraying, and the scrolled crest rail is nearly black from age and polish. It is, I admit, a somewhat dowdy piece. I am sure Colburn cannot approve of its old-fashioned quaintness, but he has been so mindful of my tender feelings on this point that he has made no mention of his opinion, for which I am thankful.

I am not thankful, however, that his business goes forward so well as to demand his absence from here frequently in the months to come. The proprietors put such stock in his powers of persuasion that they have commissioned him to secure grand new markets for the mill's products. Mr. W's travel itinerary over the winter months would serve for a geography lesson of the seaboard – even as far as the islands to the south. At least I shall not worry that he might catch a chill in those more moderate climes! Tho' I dread the cold days here and, I confess, the nights which I must spend without his warming presence. I must remember that when I agreed to be his wife I agreed to be his helpmeet however that might be possible. I must not grumble. Rather, I shall strive to occupy myself with such improvements as will make my husband's return that much more pleasurable. For us both.

PINK LEMONADE

July 15, 1995

Taped sheets of yellow legal paper stretched in all directions, flopping over the edge of the desk and threatening to slip off altogether. Nora's arm had smudged some of the pencilled names, but not so badly she couldn't read them. Extra slips of paper were stuck here and there, corrections for which there was no room left on the original pages.

Nora was spending an absorbing evening trying to finish the Chapman family tree she had patched together from vital records and the research done by Peg Wentworth. There was something quietly magical about reconstructing the skeletal history of a family over nine generations. From the first Thomas who was born in 1640 to Hank, the present Mr. Chapman, born in 1963. She could even assign owners to some of the artifacts they had found: Jenny's doll dish, George's marble. It personalized the objects, she mused, gave them voices.

The yellow sheets traced the Chapmans of Medfield and Dover and Dedham. But it also recognized the more mysterious Chapmans who went away, whose artifacts were buried in distant pieces of ground. Sometimes the records pointed a way. *Chapman, Daniel, b. 1783; moved to Ohio Territory after 1797*. Elsewhere, bare facts read as haikus of family tragedy. Great-aunt Amy Blake's husband died just months after his return from World War I, of complications from gas poisoning. The couple had only been married two years.

Nora scowled at the entry. *[_____] Blake, d. 1919.* His was not the only blank left on the chart. There were a frustrating number of unknown names and dates. Some of them were due to a single family living on a single piece of land for such a long time. There just weren't the reams of recorded facts that built up as property changed hands. She wished Hank Chapman would get around to finding the family papers he 'guessed' he 'might have somewhere.'

Nora shook off her irritation and went back to studying the chart. She started looking for birth patterns, the natural rhythms of childbearing in which a syncopation of a year or two predictably meant a family crisis. Right in the first generation there was something unusual. There was Comfort Chapman, married in 1675, six children all regularly spaced including her last, charmingly named *Waitstill.* But the very first child, named for his father, Thomas, was not born until a full five years after the wedding. Nora contemplated problems of the marriage bed and wondered if a couple could really take four years to sort things out between them, then seem to be so compatible for the rest of their lives.

She stirred uncomfortably and frowned at the smudged lines. Of course there was another explanation. Living on a frontier might have been enough to sidetrack their sex life. The poor woman had barely been married when Medfield came under Indian attack. Half the town destroyed; no assurance they'd live until tomorrow. It was hard to even imagine how traumatic life in Medfield must have been then.

Nora contemplated her own reflection in the night window and wondered if either explanation was right. There were no clues in the records or the ground. No way she knew of, to get at the answer to this particular question. She was just going to have to live with not knowing. It really wouldn't make any difference to the project. Still, she hated having to settle for not knowing.

She carefully set the question aside and left Comfort and Thomas to sort out their own relationship. Skimming over the next generations, a corner of her mouth curved up at the reassuring patterns that emerged. Lots of children, lots of survivals; marriages and second marriages. Even deaths had a predictability to them. Each family part of a larger pattern, yet each one unique: genealogical fingerprints of the past. There was a satisfaction in spelling it all out, as if by so doing Nora became part of the family herself, instead of just its recorder.

Nora stopped on the fourth generation, at another of the irritating blanks left on her chart. The Mill Farm lineage was clear enough. Luther Chapman, eldest son, inherited the farm. He and his wife Lucy had a flock of children, and eventually they were buried in the Medfield cemetery beside their ancestors. Nora was briefly distracted by the realization that the *encre de chine* tea bowls dated from this generation. Lucy Chapman might have bought them herself. Another piece of the puzzle dropped satisfyingly into place.

Luther's sister Abigail married Colburn Whiting from Dover. Peg had found Whiting in a volume of local history. The man had been notable for having built the first iron mill in Norfolk County. *"A pioneer of modern industry,"* the book said, but the standard death information was missing. Other sources were no more useful, and his death date remained blank. Nora had finally found Abigail's death, listed in Medfield, rather than Dover where she was expecting it. What was Abigail Whiting doing back in Medfield? There were no children. Was she a helpless widow? Had she been forced to return to her brother's family, ending her days perhaps tended by some reluctant niece? How demeaning that must have been. And where did her husband die?

The reassuring pattern of Chapman lives seemed to end in this generation. Nora looked ahead and saw smaller families, more moves, war and disease, marriages without issue. The prolific family tree of yellow legal sheets that stretched so wide in 1800 narrowed to a single page before the end. At the very bottom were Hank and his sister, Faith. She lived out of state, and Hank, the ninth generation Medfield Chapman, had just given away the very piece of land that had anchored his family for three hundred years. Nora could not begin to understand a family that threw away their past, like broken tea bowls. It was such an incredible rarity, being able to lean on the strength of nine generations. The Chapmans had persisted, and in doing so had made themselves a permanent place in the history books and on the land. How could Hank turn his back on his own inheritance? The rows and lines of names and dates were silent.

Suddenly the telephone began a shrill ring. Nora fumbled under the chart to reach it, finally shoving the yellow pages off the desk in mixed frustration and relief.

"Hello?" She scowled at a clock unearthed by the falling chart. It was ten thirty at night. The sound of Hank's voice at the other end of the line almost made up for the time.

"Nora? Hey, I'm sorry to call so late, but I just got in. I didn't wake you, did I?"

Fleeting glimpses of walking through a nighttime orchard mixed confusingly with remembered frustration at Hank's absence from the last Board meeting.

"No, no. I'm just trying to get some work done. What's up?"

"Coming home just now, it occurred to me I could show you the Big House tomorrow. The Downeys said they'd be off at church, so we wouldn't be in their way. You still interested?"

"As long as you don't mean the crack of dawn."

"It can't be much after nine. The attic is pretty awful later on."

"That's not a problem. Meet you there?"

"I'll come by your place. No reason for you to hang around waiting."

"Okay. See you then."

Just as Nora was thinking the whole exchange was too abrupt, that she should be more conversational, Hank saved her the trouble.

"So what was important enough to keep you working on a Saturday night?"

"I'm trying to piece together your family tree. Did you know you're the ninth generation of Chapmans in America?"

"Oh yeah? I knew there were a lot of Chapmans, but I never spent much time with the specifics."

"Maybe you should. It can be pretty interesting stuff, you know."

"You're probably right." There was a shrug implicit in his words. "I tell you what, tomorrow we can trade people stories for building stories."

"That should be quite a swap. Don't you mean *house*-story?"

"Nora, that is too bad a pun to acknowledge. Besides, I do mean 'buildings.' I've got something to show off to you, that I'm very proud of."

"What's that?"

237

"An article that just came out. But it'll wait till tomorrow. The pictures are half the fun."

"Fine then. I'll just sit here in suspense until tomorrow."

"You do that," he said with unmistakable satisfaction. "Oh, by the way, I got your note. Sounds like I missed an interesting Board meeting last week."

Nora light-heartedness promptly crashed. She caught herself before she said something she would regret, but she had to wonder if Hank could be as immune to local politics as he appeared. It seemed highly unlikely. Nevertheless, she silently vowed the topic would come up before the next day's tour was over. It was no good having an ally on the Board if he didn't know he had to take sides.

After she hung up the phone, Nora found herself puzzling over Hank's contradictory signals. What *did* he care about anyway? Obviously he cared about old buildings, his own family's as well as others. Yet he seemed to avoid talking about Chapmans as much as possible. Even the reminiscences that had cropped up last time they were together seemed to sneak into the conversation, rather than come by choice. Why did he shrug off this family whose roots were so long and so fascinating?

She wandered over to the screen door where a yellow bug light lit tall hollyhocks and silhouetted a moth spread-eagled on the screen. Staring at the pool of light she tried to match up the Tunney family tree with the Chapmans'. The Tunneys' would be short and broad. Only four generations in America, but prolific ones. It was hard to keep count of cousins and second cousins and nieces and nephews. No one else in the family would even think of staying unmarried into their thirties, like her.

Her Aunt Ethel was getting worried. *You'll end up an old maid like poor Aunt Mary. She was just too fussy.* As if Nora was supposed to grab the first guy who came along. Nora silently acknowledged she'd be more likely to do so if more men bore passing resemblance to Hank. There was a lot to like about Hank. Even if he didn't care enough about long-gone ancestors.

Her mind wandered back to last week's family birthday that had taken her back to Lawrence for a Sunday of big food and everybody minding everybody else's business. The relatives had sat around the kitchen table and lectured her on isolating herself out in the country.

If she lived in the city she'd meet more nice men. Nora couldn't actually think of many nice men she'd met in the city, but it seemed futile to tell them that.

In the Medfield night she shrugged at the moth and tried to picture Hank at the Tunney's kitchen table. Aunt Ethel would love him.

The moth suddenly detached from the screen and Nora strained to follow his flight into the rustling dark. Most of the time, though ... most of the time I'm pretty content with life as it presents itself. Especially here. Evenings are very soft here. The breeze drew her outdoors to a seat on the big fieldstone step. There was more to contentment than summer evenings, of course. There was getting up in the morning and looking at the same view through the same bedroom window. A rural view, no neighboring Somerville triple-deckers. Nor the range of parking lots that landscaped the economy motels which were her short-term field accommodations. Here she had watched a whole family of mocking birds grow up and fly off from the maple behind the Big House. She had stayed in the same place long enough to see Nabby's Arbor leaf out and form tight clusters of grapes. Nora wondered what it would be like to make grape jelly some weekend.

There was a quiet stability here, a continuum that smoothed out the wrinkles of everyday life by putting them in longer perspective. Mill Farm had changed, certainly, but so slowly that she could imagine herself involved, evolving, like everything around her without the frantic rush of life in urban places. She loved the slowness of change that allowed her to keep pace with it, to be part of it.

Nora reached out to run her hand down Artie's tail as he circled back from yard patrol to check in.

I think this is what home must feel like.

A last bedroom light went off at the Big House and the small barnyard world was almost dark, except for the bug light's yellow glow. She toyed with the idea of staying outside to look for distant stars. But her discovered sense of belonging was as much of a reach as she could manage for one night. Stretching up with a contented sigh, she ushered Artie in the door and flicked the switch that left the yard in darkness.

The next morning Nora took Hank by surprise by opening the door before he knocked. Anticipation had pulled her out of bed, knowing today she would track down another piece of the Mill Farm puzzle. Clearly Hank was key to the tracking and Nora chose to accept that as enough explanation for feeling good. By quarter of nine she was sitting at the kitchen table, cradling an untouched mug of coffee and staring off into the orchard when a glimpse of white tee shirt caught her attention. Her eyes followed Hank's weaving progress through the trees until his shirt's apple tree design became clear, above gray shorts and nylon-strapped sandals. His leg muscles tensed and stretched rhythmically as he strode into the yard. No sunglasses, she noticed, despite the glare, and a tan that spoke of long days outdoors. When he was nearly at the door she stood up for a quick mirror check. She tucked a strand of hair more firmly behind an ear and made invisible adjustments to her collar. Then she reached for the doorknob.

"Good morning!" Hank stepped backward in surprise. Nora silently thanked Gramma's voice for scolding her out of worn cut-offs. Hank took in the khaki shorts and chambray shirt she had picked instead, knowing as she did so that the sleeveless top would show off the tan line on her upper arms made by her work jerseys. His grin was appreciative.

"Looks like you've had plenty of time to wake up. Ready to go?"

"Any time. Unless you want some coffee first?"

"Later, maybe. Feels like it's going to get hot fast today. I'd just as soon get going."

"That's fine. Is that the article you mentioned last night?" Nora gestured at the magazine folded under Hank's arm.

"Oh! Yeah. Can I leave it here? Maybe you'd be interested in it after the tour."

A glimpse of old mill building on the cover piqued her curiosity but the shirt was already beginning to stick to her back and she knew enough about attics to imagine the heat already building inside. With only a small grimace of regret, she agreed and they headed across the yard.

Hank's guided tour of the Big House put all thought of the mysterious article out of Nora's mind.

"There's nothing surprising about the front of this house." Hank's running narration had started before they even went in. "Long windows, tall sidelights, corner boards." He gestured as he talked. "Everything they could think of to elongate a house that's really just a three-bay colonial underneath."

"Is this a particular style, then?"

He worked on an answer. "Not really. A country style, I guess, somewhere between Georgian and Federal. Probably built because of some local boom after the Revolution, before the real Federal style got sorted out. You see a lot of them around here: Medfield, Dover – all over Norfolk County."

A bell went off in Nora's head. "Norfolk County – of course! You're right about the boom. All sorts of things were going on here by 1800. The county had just been set up, Dedham was the county seat. Medfield was on the main road to Hartford and New York." As she warmed to the subject her voice became animated. Puzzle pieces fit into place. "New industries were cropping up all over the place – on little streams in the woods, along the highway, right in downtown Medfield. And there was a population boom of sorts, too, all those newcomers working at new jobs. But a lot of people left. Some of your own family headed west. To Ohio, I think, and New York."

She stopped when she realized Hank was staring at her. His expression was either admiring or tolerant, she wasn't sure which, but it made her self-conscious.

"You know a lot about my part of the country."

"Well, it's my job, you know. Besides, Medfield's not so far from Lawrence. Geographically anyway."

"Lawrence. Wasn't Lawrence becoming a big industrial center around the same time?"

"No." She shook her head emphatically. "All that was later, a decade or more later. That's what's so ironic. People study places like Lowell and Lawrence to learn about the beginnings of American industry, about urbanization, demographic change – oh, all sorts of things. Nobody seems to realize most of those changes began *here* ten or twenty years before they did anywhere else. It's amazing."

"So why don't we get some credit, then?"

Nora hesitated. "Maybe the changes around here didn't go far enough. Not enough resources. Too much too early. I'm not sure."

Her expression brightened. "But from an archeologist's standpoint, it's great. There's still a lot of information in the ground around here, that more successful towns bulldozed into oblivion."

Hank was studying the front of the house again as she finished.

"What did you say the difference was between Norfolk County's boom time and these other places?"

"Prime time for this area was 1790s to 1820 or so. After that Waltham and Lowell – even Springfield to the west – stole the glory. I bet life was pretty tame around here after that."

Nora stared off toward the pond, imagining the slow-moving life of Mill Farm, trying to populate it with people from the family tree. Was Abigail, the aging widow, living here by then? Suddenly she remembered Hank's question hanging in the air.

"I'm sorry — why were you asking about dates?"

He didn't seem fazed by her distraction.

"Because it explains the house. And the other ones like it around here. If you look, you won't find a lot of Federal houses here, the way you do around Lowell. Instead, there are these slightly awkward, *almost* Federal ones. Built the old way, massed like good eighteenth-century buildings, but trying hard to look thin and elegant and modern on the outside."

"Conservative-progressive generation gap?"

"More than that, in this house. This house is more like *three* generations all slightly at odds." Hank was shaking his head. "And yet... Yet it doesn't feel like additions put on in different generations. There seems to be a sameness to the whole building that suggests a single period of construction, despite its inconsistencies. Come see."

Hank unlocked the front door and waved Nora inside. As they peered around children's toy boxes and under braided rugs, into empty fireplaces and behind the washing machine in the cellar, Hank pointed out details of construction and finish that made the house both an example of its era and an anachronism. He interpreted window moldings and floorboards, comparing as he went, the ones they saw with earlier and later ones, until Nora began to see every piece of wood as a sign of its time.

She was fascinated and thoroughly confused by the time she reached the door to the attic. Hank's familiar use of obscure architectural vocabulary had left her floundering and she wanted to ask him to say it all again in layman's terms, but Hank was already halfway up the attic stairs, talking as he climbed. His voice floated down the stairwell.

"This is where the really good stuff shows up."

She started up the narrow flight and felt the heat descending, like a heavy cloud settling around her, slowing her progress as she climbed. By the time she reached the top, Hank had twisted the hanging light bulb so it turned on, and was standing head down, apparently studying his feet.

"See what I mean?"

Nora's earlier fascination was already being snuffed out by the heat.

"No."

He glanced up in mild surprise at the tone of her voice.

"The floorboards. Actually, come on back down for a minute. You'll see it better."

He took her arm and drew her back down the first steps, until they were eye level with the attic floor. Cooler air from below swirled enticingly around her legs and she suddenly wished they could just forget the attic. Then she remembered Hank saying the 'good stuff' was here. She drew a deep breath and rallied.

"Tell me what I'm looking at?"

"If you sight along the floor, like this," Hank tipped his head sideways and squinted into the shadows, "the floor boards have a sheen to them. See?"

Nora followed his example and saw what he described. The boards were smooth, almost polished-looking, with occasional rounded bulges where knots were located.

"I do, but I don't know what it means."

"These are floor boards."

She scowled at him.

"Hank, even I know that much."

"No, no. I mean *finished* floorboards. Reused. Recycled from some room where lots of feet walked. They've been planed, and scrubbed and polished. They're not the rough-cut leftovers you'd expect here. They're worn from years of heavy use in some public room. They definitely didn't start life in this attic."

"Are you saying the Chapman who built this house got his boards from someplace else?"

"Um-hum. I'll show you some more."

Hank trotted back up the stairs and Nora silently groaned. Didn't he feel the heat? How could he maintain his enthusiasm against the weight that hung around them? She thought it might simply push her backwards down the stairs. She followed him with slow steps.

"See that big rafter next to the chimney?"

Nora looked where he was pointing.

"See those notches along the side? The round holes that are empty? That timber's recycled, too. You're looking at part of a roof plate from some other building. And the damned beam's hand-hewn, just like the ones in the mill. But look: right next to it, the very next rafter, has perfectly clear vertical saw marks the whole length of it. No one in his right mind would hew his own rafters when there were sawmills all over town by 1800."

Nora's head felt fuzzy in the heat and she was having trouble following Hank's thinking.

"So...?" she asked hesitantly.

"So whichever Chapman built this house must have had an old barn on the property, maybe even an old house, and he wasn't going to let all that perfectly good wood go to waste."

"There's more?"

"All over. Floorboards reused as partitions, beams with empty mortises. Check out this window frame."

Hank moved down to one end of the attic where a small window stood partway open. Nora swam toward him through the thick air and realized a cool draft slid through the opening. She stood as close as she could to the moving air.

"This window frame isn't even Georgian," Hank went on. "If I had to guess, I'd say it was seventeenth century with new sash put in."

"That doesn't make any sense, Hank. Why would they go to all that work? Surely lumber wasn't that scarce?"

"Of course not, but we're talking Yankee here. Waste not, want not. Penny saved is a penny earned. For all we know they could have cut their own at the Chapman saw mill. But you gotta love 'em for it. It's their penny-pinching that left us with two completely different eras of woodworking all in one place. What a survival!"

He turned from his contemplation of rafters and boards and challenged Nora with a grin.

"Now, that's my idea of history!"

Her eyebrows went up but she rose to the challenge.

"I'm perfectly willing to go along with that. Just the way Dedham Pottery and porcelain tea cups are history. You know they go together, don't you, the *encre de chine* cups and this house? Somehow. They were from the same period. I think probably Lucy Chapman used the cups, although I'll never be able to prove it. Do you suppose her husband built the house?"

"Could be." Hank shrugged. "Maybe he was one of Medfield's movers and shakers. Showing the town how up-to-date he was, even if he was a penny-pincher. Wonder where he picked up the idea of federalizing his house..."

His mind wandered off in another direction and he changed the subject.

"There's one more thing I have to show you. Over this way."

He plunged back into the furnace heat. Nora followed him reluctantly, assuring herself that there could not be much more to see, as Hank led the way between cardboard cartons and stacked furniture toward the other end of the attic. She was just thinking the place was remarkably neat, as attics went, when he suddenly wheeled toward her, a worried expression on his face.

"Hey, you don't mind, do you, tromping around up here? I forget the heat, sometimes, when I get caught up in the construction."

His apologetic consideration was almost as soothing as the open window had been, and it made Nora want to listen.

"I'm fine. And old wood is fascinating, especially when you tell me what I'm looking at."

"Well, we're almost done. I just don't want you to miss anything."

He purposefully guided her through the rest of the Downeys' accumulation. They passed an overflowing rack of summer clothes and a crib piled high with bedcovers.

"You should have seen this place when my folks lived here. We couldn't have made it from one end of the attic to the other. I don't think anyone had ever cleaned out anything since the house was built."

Nora was surprised he had brought up his family, but she certainly wasn't going to let go of an opportunity to learn more. She searched for a question to keep him on the subject.

"Was it junk? Or was it wonderful?"

"When I was a kid it was all wonderful. I remember a couple of swords wrapped up in flannel. They lay on top of a big dark table and my Dad never let us touch them unless he was there. He did let me put on a moth-eaten World War I uniform. I pretended I was part of a Chapman regiment, saving the world from the Hun. Faith's favorite was a box of old dishes. She opened it every time she came up."

"Encre de chine?"

"Nah. Some flowery printed stuff. There was a batch of little doll dishes on top that actually matched the set."

"How charming."

Hank gestured back toward the stairs and the single bulb that shadowed as much as it illuminated.

"Between here and there were cases full of old books. Magazines too; years of *National Geographic*. And furniture, except stuff had been piled on it, and more stuff on that. You never could tell just what was underneath. We were told not to step on the rolled-up rugs and not to open the trunks all the way because the hinges would break."

For a few moments Nora forgot the heat as she pictured the attic full of unwritten Chapman history. Three-dimensional stories just waiting to be read, if one only understood the language.

"It must have been a treasure trove."

Hank shrugged.

"Nobody knew what was here. Oh, a few things, like the swords. But mostly it was the stuff nobody wanted. You know: too old to use, too good to throw away."

"But, Hank, what fun to explore! So who sorted through it all?"

"I did." There was a sudden flatness in his voice, as if the pleasure of his memories was washing away, being replaced by something harder. "I cleaned out every last carton."

"It wasn't so much fun after all?"

Even in the gloom of the attic corner, Nora caught the tight look Hank shot her and knew she was right. There was something more to this attic business than pleasant nostalgia.

"Yeah. It wasn't."

He briefly studied the cobwebbed rafters again.

"I thought it was going to be. For years I'd itched for a chance to go through what was here. Sort through the piles, explore all the chests and boxes. It was all going to be treasure. All the Chapman family past in one room, a time capsule for the taking. Then I started really doing it. Had to, when I decided to rent this place, and you know what? It was overwhelming.

"Most of the time I felt as if I was just intruding on other people's lives. Over by the chimney, for instance. At the bottom of a pile over there I found a whole box of scrapbooks, maybe a hundred years old. Full of programs from musicales, picture postcards without any writing, news clippings about no one and no place I'd ever heard of. Books and books full of totally meaningless bits of paper."

"Who had they belonged to?"

"I don't even know that." He swiped tiredly at the sweat on his neck. "Totally meaningless. I threw them all out."

"Oh, no!"

This time the look he gave her was almost defiant.

"What else was I going to do? Nobody else was around. *You* weren't around to tell me they were important. Matter of fact, I don't really believe they were important. But you see, I won't ever really know, will I? The same was true of every single thing I unearthed. Every time I had to ask, is this important? Why should I save this? And then, you know what? I felt this pang every time I threw something out. Felt *guilty*, as if I was betraying my own relatives by throwing away something that had, at some time, for some reason, been important enough to save."

"You didn't throw everything away, did you?"

"No, of course not. We ate dinner on the old table the other night. Most of the furniture ended up at my place. A bunch of local stuff went to the historical society. Couple of pieces even ended up at the MFA in Boston. But there isn't a whole lot of storage over at Orchard Cottage. Thank God," he muttered to himself. He scanned the half-empty space where they stood. "It was time, I guess. Somebody had to confront the attic sometime; I'd just as soon it hadn't been me."

"I can imagine," Nora said, wondering if she really could. One thing Hank had said bothered her. "I mean, I can imagine the throwing-away part being hard. But didn't you feel good about what you did save? Your refined collection, so to speak?"

Hank was pulling his sweat-soaked shirt away from his chest and seemed to be only half-listening. Then his eyes swung back to challenge her.

"No. I didn't. I took the things that absolutely had to stay in the family – papers, bible, stuff like that —and stuck them in my own attic and closed the door. I hadn't had to open it for ten years until you came along asking for information."

She felt an urgent need to change the subject.

"Ten years. Is that how long you've lived at the cottage?"

"Since my mother died."

Nora nodded, struck dumb in the dusty silence that followed his words. There was a moment of understanding hovering just out of reach, a moment that would resolve the seeming contradictions of this man who was already turning away from what he had said. But the heat pressed against her chest and made it hard even to breathe, much less to take the intuitive leap that would clarify it all.

In the background Hank had abruptly changed the subject, discussing a complex of beams and rafters that formed the corner between main house and ell. Nora only half heard his explanation of another case of mixed construction eras. She was back in the attic of ten years ago, with a younger Hank Chapman frowning over papers in his lap.

Saying goodbye. He was saying goodbye with every item culled from the attic. Stumbling over ghosts of a dozen dead Chapmans. It certainly wasn't playtime anymore. She found herself grateful that the ghosts she dug up at work belonged to other families, not her own.

Hank swore as he burned his fingers unscrewing the light bulb, and led the way back downstairs, away from the memory-filled dust of the attic. Nora followed in silence, down a second set of stairs at the back of the house, through a narrow door to the Downeys' well-used kitchen.

Her first impression was of dishes piled by the sink and cereal strewn across a high-chair tray, but the long, narrow kitchen still felt welcoming. Was it the comfortable mess? Then Nora noticed the windows set opposite each other. Half of them, over the sink, were facing the barnyard and shaded by green awnings. Across the kitchen were more windows, wide open to let a cool breeze in from a shaded porch.

Her reaction was immediate. "What a great place to cook!"

Hank looked at her with amusement. "More chicken soup?"

"No ..." Nora contemplated the alternatives. "Jelly, maybe ... No, pickles. Gramma's half-sours in big crocks."

"This was the summer kitchen, you know." He squinted in thought. "At least, I guess it must have been."

"What do you mean?"

"Well ...I keep thinking it's too early for a summer kitchen. Not that there's any very definitive dating for them, but I'm pretty sure this whole ell was built not long after the rest of the house. The weird set of sistered beams I showed you just before we came down is where the ell meets the main house."

Nora was struck by how thoroughly Hank had seemed to put away the bitterness and the memories that had emerged in the attic. As if just talking about construction had built a cage to keep them under control. Now here he was, apparently perfectly content to talk about Chapmans as long as they were engaged in some kind of *building* project.

"... Peculiar, really – almost as if they forgot something the first time around and tacked it on afterward."

"Maybe they came up with more money?"

"Maybe. I don't know. But the other unusual thing about this addition is that the rooms here are nicer than in the main house. At least I think so."

"What do you mean?"

"They have character. They were thought out. Just look at this room. Lots of windows for cross-ventilation; doors out to the barnyard and the back porch. Even so, when you raise that awning in cold weather, it stays pretty warm in here. And the porch serves as an extension of the room, too."

"Extension?"

Hank frowned in contemplation of the shady space.

"We used to spend a lot of time out there. Faith and I would set up in the shade. Then one of us would call inside to Mom, and she'd come out to keep us company." A small smile lifted one corner of his mouth. "Other times I remember standing there in my snowsuit, hands up, turning in circles while Dad swept snow off my back."

His voice turned in on itself, fading as other memories slipped out of the cage. By the softened expression on his face, Nora thought they must not all be bad. Then he shook himself, like a dog shaking snow off his coat.

"Anyway, this ell is a great design."

"Why did you give up living in this house, Hank, if there's so much you love about it? Was it just too big?"

"Yeah, there was that. And I never liked the front of the house that much." He looked around the kitchen as if the walls might offer further explanation. It came out hesitantly.

"And here … I don't know. Too many memories here." He shook his head. "It was crowded, like living with a bunch of ghosts."

Hank pulled open the back door, gesturing in silent invitation for Nora to precede him outside.

"Better the way it is now." His voice was decisive. "Kids, toys, food, mess. It keeps the place alive. Ready to go?"

His voice said the subject was closed, but Nora resisted, thinking about the extraordinary collection of souvenirs that Hank kept trying to lock away, for some not-entirely-comprehensible reason. She paused in the doorway and looked up, noticing the set of his jaw and the faint smile that didn't make it to his eyes.

"Tell me, Hank, do you think a place like this *is* alive, somehow? I guess it sounds absurd, but I can't believe the dozens of Chapmans who lived here didn't leave something more behind than boxes of paper. Something more essential."

"I try not to think about it at all," he snapped. "I'd a whole lot rather do something in the present than worry about the past. You know, Nora, sometimes I feel as if Mill Farm doesn't even *belong* to me. As if I'm some sort of glorified caretaker hired to maintain dead buildings."

Hank abruptly let the door he'd been holding slam shut and strode off across the dusty barnyard, leaving Nora to follow as she might. She was surprised by the vehemence of his words, and began to wonder if that was her fault. She couldn't seem to stop asking questions, simple questions mostly. She'd just been trying to learn more from this man who knew so much. Still, she'd kept gnawing away even though he'd made it plain he didn't want to dwell on family. Couldn't she ever leave well enough alone?

She hurried to catch up with him and make amends.

"Hey, Hank. Sorry if I raised a sore subject. But listen, you give a great tour of a dead building! Sure you weren't a teacher in a former life?"

Hank snorted and shook his head. "No way. I've just had a lot of experience."

"My gramma always said experience was the best teacher. Of course there were lots of things she felt strongly that I shouldn't experience ..."

Nora was rewarded by a chuckle of understanding from Hank. She reached for the handle of her screen door.

"Listen, you want some lemonade? The heat is getting to me and you must be parched after all those purlins and joists and rafters."

Hank agreed, promptly heading for the dish cupboard while she took out ice and the juice pitcher. It pleased her in some small way that he knew her kitchen well enough to help. They chatted companionably about the virtues of air-dried lumber as they poured lemonade, then agreed to go outside to find breeze and shade. Hank picked up both glasses and the forgotten magazine he had brought. Nora, feeling empty-handed, grabbed the pitcher.

She followed Hank around to the back of the Big House where, by unspoken agreement, they moved together toward Nabby's Arbor. Nora set the pitcher on the ground and settled next to Hank on the bench, sighing in relief at the cool greenness of overhanging leaves. For a moment they sat in comfortable silence. *Listening for Nabby's whisper*, Nora thought whimsically.

Eventually she broke the spell. "So what's this article you have to show me?"

Hank's face became animated as he pulled out the magazine and handed it to her.

"It's a brag piece, really. My company made it into *Smithsonian*."

"C'mon! Is there a picture of you?"

"More than one, actually. Check it out."

The cover Nora had glimpsed earlier was a picture of a wooden mill building. Not like Chapman's Mill; a sawmill, she guessed, against a rich green backdrop of forest. In the foreground a frothing stream poured past a huge exposed water wheel. Off to the side were the italic words *Wrighting the Strong*.

"That's a weird title."

"Actually, you're looking at Abraham Strong's sawmill in North Carolina. It's a pretty well-known historic landmark in those parts."

"You worked on this?"

"Yup. But look inside. The pictures are great."

He reached over and flipped the magazine open to a page with the corner folded down.

The title repeated itself, followed by a subheading: *New England firm responds to demand for old-mill expertise across the nation.* There was a picture of a work crew standing by the Strong Mill waterwheel, one of them unmistakably Hank. *Crew of Spokeshave Enterprises poses before the great wheel turns again*, the caption explained.

Nora studied the picture as she tried to understand just what she was seeing, but Hank urged her on.

"You don't have to read it all. Just look at the rest of the shots. They're more interesting than the story."

She began to thumb through the article, stopping again at a striking end-on photo of a newly cut log coming off the carriage at the sawmill.

"I'm confused," she said hesitantly. "It looks like there was a lot more than building stabilization going on here."

"You got that right! Should have seen the place. Most of the wheel was rotten; we had to put up a whole new sluiceway, make a bunch of adjustments to meet safety regulations." Hank's voice held an unmistakable note of pride as he went on. "But Strong's Mill can turn out four hundred board feet a day now, if the water holds."

"Why on earth does it operate at all?"

"There's a big market for old-growth timber, and North Carolina's one of the few places you can still get it. Besides, vertical sawn lumber's appropriate for a lot of rehab projects. Strong's Mill could work full-time and not meet the demand."

Nora nodded, reluctantly acknowledging that this was an exception to the rule; that there might be real need here for the mill to be actually set back up and running, rather than simply stabilized to weather the next century.

"At least you could preserve most of the building intact. Though I would think all the modern regulatory requirements must have been really frustrating for someone who thinks like you."

Hank's shrug seemed fatalistic.

Nora glanced at the next page to see a swarm of fresh-faced children peering at an early broad loom. *At Bruchner's Mill, now a living history museum, Milwaukee third-graders participate in the manufacturing process. Spokeshave Enterprises, working with state and local sponsors, restored the building from a burned-out shell.* She glanced up at Hank with raised eyebrows.

"I'm surprised Spokeshave does so much work on industrial sites – or is that just the article? I thought you worked for an old-house firm."

It was Hank's turn to look puzzled. Then his expression cleared as he grasped Nora's misunderstanding.

"Spokeshave Enterprises is my own company. See?" He pushed over another page as if the next picture would explain it all.

Hank Chapman, founder of Spokeshave Enterprises, investigates early industry throughout the United States. At Red Cliff Tin Mine, shown here, Chapman contemplates the challenge of reopening the cog railway that used to serve the mine. The railway is scheduled to reopen in two years.

"Let me get this straight. You *own* a nationally-famous preservation contracting firm?"

The dent in Hank's cheek appeared as he nodded proudly.

"I do. We specialize in old industrial buildings."

"I'm impressed! But Hank, don't you go crazy having to do so much gut-and-replace restoration, rather than leaving these beautiful buildings alone?"

"Well, we tend not to 'gut' very often …," he contemplated the idea. "But restoring mills is our specialty."

"What do you mean? You said you were a *preservation* carpenter."

"Preservation. Restoration. You brought that up in your note the other day, didn't you? I never spent a lot of time on the semantics. But putting industrial sites back in working order is what we do. Buildings, machines, the power train to run them. If I had to stick with a label, I guess I'd pick 'millwright' before anything else."

Nora carefully set down the magazine. Her whole body was tense. She reached for the lemonade to buy time but found her arm was shaking too much to pour. Instead, she grasped the pitcher firmly in her lap, her hands drawing cool from the icy glass while the rest of her felt hot.

"You okay?"

Hank's voice was concerned. Her own answer sounded distant in the silence.

"I need to be clear about this. When George Majors talked about you restoring Chapman's Mill, that wasn't a misunderstanding on his part, was it?"

"Not at all."

"And when you suggested to the Mill Commission that the grist mill might be restored you had in mind overseeing it yourself, right?"

"Doing it, actually. I've offered to do it if they're interested."

"Why didn't somebody tell *me* this? Why didn't you tell me about this whole thing? Didn't anybody think I was important enough to be in the loop?"

Hank's expression was puzzled as he tried to respond to Nora's obvious distress.

"I don't think anybody meant to leave you out. I mean, the mill restoration is a whole separate project from the archeology you're doing."

"Of course it isn't! It's an either-or situation as far as they're concerned. George Majors, for one, is all set to throw me out, along with all the work that hasn't been finished and all the training that's going on. And what about the issue of bastardizing your own inheritance, turning it into Historic Disneyland? Doesn't that bother you at all?"

"What's so Disneyland about a working mill?"

"Hank! Listen to yourself! You're talking about rebuilding this and putting in new that. You're talking about compromising the integrity of the whole site to satisfy fifteen different codes just so a bunch of kids and tourists can spend ten minutes being bored. How can you do that? You *are* caretaker of your family's heritage, like you said back inside, whether you want to be or not! And here you are, talking about twisting the past out of all recognition!"

"Wait just a damn minute. You're carrying on as if Chapman's Mill is a piece of the holy grail. What makes these buildings so sacrosanct, anyway? They were built by regular people – some of them not even very good at what they did. Lived in and worked in and run down by regular people too. And I, for one, am not going to tiptoe around them with kid gloves on."

Nora tried to interrupt but Hank overrode her.

"Especially mills. Mills are *working* buildings, more than any other structure I can think of. There's not a single thing so important to the life of a mill as its work. And when the work stops the mill dies. I don't care how solid the roof is or if the sills are sound. It's a dead building if it doesn't operate."

Nora glanced up briefly but looked away again. He was glaring at her, daring her to say something, but she was dumbfounded by the intense rush of words.

"So don't talk to me about distorting the past," he said with finality. "My company doesn't turn old houses into fairy tales. If old buildings have 'souls' the way some people claim, then I'm doing what I can to restore the souls of these mills by restoring their reason for being built in the first place. And I don't think that's any more peculiar than your trying to find the past in a hole in the ground."

She knew he was still glaring at her in the silence that followed. Her cheeks burned with the insult of his last words, as if he had hit her instead of deriding her profession. Where had all this come from? Why had this man beside her suddenly turned from ally to enemy? How she could have gotten so much wrong? Anger and confusion beat inside her skull. Humiliating tears stung the corners of her eyes and she knew she had to get away.

"I guess you've said it all, then, haven't you? I need to go."

She stood abruptly, sloshing lemonade out of the pitcher, and escaped across the back yard, ignoring Hank's calling to her. With every stride, lemonade ran sticky down her leg. It was getting hard to see where she was stepping. *Damn him anyway. Damn him!* The tears almost held off until she reached the door. She pulled it open and stumbled into the kitchen, slamming the pitcher down in the sink so hard it shattered. A sliver drew blood at the base of her thumb.

Nora leaned on the sink and cried for everything gone wrong as reddened lemonade ran down the drain.

LILACS

March 1798

The sun finally showed its face the second Sunday in March. It seemed to Abigail that winter had gone on forever, that every time she thought to go out, the weather took a turn for the worse. The last three Sundays she had even kept away from church, the first day being blanketed in heavy, wet snow; the second one coming at the tail end of a thaw which flooded the frozen stream beds and made the deeply rutted roads impassable. Last week the heavens had opened again, this time to let down sheets of rain which froze on contact with every surface in Dover. Abigail had spent the morning at her parlor window, bible dutifully open on her lap, but her eyes turned more often to the bleak gray and white scene before her than to the heavenly mysteries within. The view, she decided, was the harshest she had ever seen. Every branch, every stray weed that still dared stick its head above the snow was frozen stiff, sealed in a capsule of ice. As if, she mused, all that she beheld would remain as it was to eternity, never moving again, never growing or changing. Her examination shifted to the patch of river she could see, above the dam. *No*, she thought, *I am wrong. There is a more terrible view yet.* The force of the current at the dam kept the water open: a rough-edged crescent of shiny black, smooth, apparently motionless, severely beautiful. *But so very deep and cold*, she thought, *so deadly cold.*

A shiver broke her meditation, and she drew a paisley shawl closer around her shoulders. *Too much sitting about listening to myself,* she chided. *High time I got up and did something, made myself useful instead of entertaining gloomy fancies.* She headed for the kitchen where, she knew, there was always something needing to be done. *And a good visit would be in order, as well. Someone to talk to besides myself. With Colburn gone I rely far too much on Anna's company. Such a solitary day as this encourages me to make wider social effort.* She took down a string of dried apples; she would put together a pan of dumplings for the Ellises down the hill who, she had heard, were struggling with a bout of winter ailments. Abigail vowed she would not be so shy about visiting on her own in the future.

After such gray solitude, the pale sun that rose the next Sunday was doubly welcome. Abby walked briskly down to the Woodwards' house, the wooden pattens strapped to her shoes crunching nicely on morning ice in the cart tracks. She rode the rest of the way to church with them. Abby and the Woodwards had come to this arrangement early on in her married life, for there were almost as many Sundays that Colburn did not go to meeting as ones when he did. The mill might be closed but business was never finished, he reminded Abby when she dared protest. And recently, there had been many weeks when he was away, traveling somewhere to promote the company's business.

So most Sundays, Abby would ride with the Woodwards, listening to Joanna's retailing of mill village news, while John drove in the uncharacteristic silence he reserved for Sunday. According to Joanna's laughing assessment, John spent his whole week talking at the store, so silence was his way of resting on the seventh day.

The three of them lingered after service to greet acquaintances and compare stories of the damage caused by last week's ice. As the Woodwards were shaking their heads over a description of Luther Richards' devastated apple orchard, Abby felt a light touch on her arm and turned to find Henrietta Chickering hovering next to her.

The Chickerings had been among Dover's first settlers, and Henrietta took the responsibility of that position quite seriously. She observed the formalities, made clear distinctions between newcomers and 'real townsfolk,' and kept track of the complex hierarchy of occupations and family ties which defined Dover society. Abby was quick to admit that Henrietta Chickering also had a generous sense of christian charity, offering aid wherever needed, soliciting donations for the distressing number of poor who were an increasing burden to the town. Mrs. Chickering was also known for her outspoken belief that females were competent to assume all sorts of responsibilities reasonably assigned to men. It was laughingly whispered that in the Chickering home, the chick ruled the roost. Aloud, community members were much more respectful in what they said.

This morning, as Abby greeted Henrietta, she entertained a brief irreverent image of the dowager as a pouter pigeon fluffed up against the cold. A voluminous gray velvet cloak enveloped her and matched a velvet bonnet, folded back like a ruff around her neck. A gauzy kerchief billowed in fashionable fullness at her bosom. *Even the woman's nose is somewhat beaklike,* Abby noted, then chastised herself for thoughts ill-becoming in one as little favored as herself. She gave Mrs. Chickering a particularly warm smile to make up for unworthy thoughts. The older woman's response was effusive.

"Dear Mrs. Whiting, I did so hope I would find you here this morning!"

"I am certainly glad to be so, Mrs. Chickering. What a relief to be about again after such a long spell of impossible weather."

"But I am sorry not to see your Colburn here, as well. I do so enjoy that young man. His Uncle Whiting was telling me just the other day that he is often absent with this iron business. I trust all goes well?"

"Oh yes," Abby replied. "Indeed, marvelously so, I believe." She found it a bit peculiar that Henrietta, whose husband was among the mill investors, thought it necessary to ask for such information. Then again, she thought, it was likely the woman was simply being polite.

"It is hard to keep track sometimes, is it not?" Henrietta commented vaguely. "I find that Mr. Chickering becomes so absorbed in the endless details of his work that he has been known to forget my presence altogether – to say nothing of telling me what transpires in his days. In fact I believe that men quite unjustly assume we poor females could never take an interest in their doings."

Abigail found it encouraging to hear an echo of her own recent complaint in Henrietta's comment. Then she hurried to amend her thought by recalling times when Colburn had, indeed, spoken of his work to her. Less now, perhaps, than in the past, but this was surely but a temporary lapse. Henrietta's voice recalled her from her internal debate.

"I do propose we put a stop to this situation, at least momentarily," she announced decidedly. "I think perhaps it is time for a small supper party where husbands and wives are required to speak with each other. It might go some way toward reminding them that we, as well as they, have heads which can be turned to worldly affairs. What do you think of such a plan?" she asked Abby disingenuously. "Might I include Colburn and yourself on our guest list?"

"The plan" was not new to Dover society. Abby was more than a little flattered that she and her husband had achieved the social status in Henrietta Chickering's eyes to be included in one of their intimate supper parties. Chickering suppers were known to offer at least as much good conversation as good food. The parties frequently included out-of-town guests of some consequence, such as Dr. Ames from Dedham, or Samuel Colburn, president of the new bank. The ladies, it was rumored, often remained at the dining table for after-dinner discussions ranging from international affairs to the latest industrial experiments. Both intellectual and social levels were of the highest. Abby was delighted.

"Why, Mrs. Chickering, I am confident I may speak for both of us in saying we would be most pleased to attend. Have you an evening in mind?"

"I have just cajoled Mr. Bussey, of Newton, and his wife into coming out on Tuesday week. A small celebration of the first of April might be amusing, don't you think?"

Abigail started to agree, then paused as she remembered Colburn would be away much of that week, including Tuesday. *But I have vowed to be more gregarious on my own,* she reminded herself. *Perhaps a milieu such as this, which does not rank humans by gender first, is as good a place as any to start .*

Affecting a confidence she did not feel, Abby returned Mrs. Chickering's smile.

"And shall you serve Tipsy Fool pudding to honor the occasion, Mrs. Chickering?" They shared a brief laugh and Abby went on with more confidence.

"I have, naturally, heard much of Mr. Bussey's textile venture on Mother Brook, and would be delighted to make the acquaintance of him and his wife. I believe my husband and Mr. Bussey have met more than once in the course of business and he speaks very highly of him." She took a deep breath. "Regrettably, Mr. Whiting will not be in town that week. Your husband and others of the proprietors have charged him with negotiating for new markets in the western counties. I would be honored if you would consider including me, however."

The silence that greeted Abby's suggestion prompted her to add, "If that might be appropriate?"

Henrietta pursed her lips. Her brows drew together in concerned sympathy for a wife's plight.

"Oh! What a shame! Would it not be a better world if wives were able to conform their husband's actions to a decent social schedule?" She smiled briefly, then shook her head as if thinking better of it. "But truly, my dear, I would not want to inconvenience you by asking you to come without Colburn. It might be quite discomfitting." She brightened. "And there are sure to be countless other occasions when we might get to know each other better."

Henrietta's voice rushed on before Abby could respond.

"Why don't we just plan another time in the near future?" She arched a disapproving brow. "And whether we would or no, we shall just have to consult your husband's daybook when we do." Her eye shifted to someone beyond Abigail's shoulder. "Oh my, would you excuse me for a moment? I must catch poor Mrs. Larrabee before she leaves. I do regret our little plan was not to be."

Henrietta Chickering quickly adjusted her bonnet over her head, gave a tight smile, and moved on. Abby followed her bustling path through the parishioners with carefully expressionless eyes.

The ride back from the village seemed excruciatingly long. Abby answered only vaguely Joanna's friendly questions, lapsing finally into such grim-visaged silence that Joanna was prompted to comment that she traveled with two, rather than one mute today.

On the walk back up to the house, Abby repeated yet again the argument she'd been having with herself all the way home. Mrs. Chickering was perfectly correct. A wife had no business going about socially without her husband. Yet had not Abby been included in social invitations when she was still a singlewoman back in Medfield? Why should she be a less suitable guest now that she was wed? Of course, it was quite likely that Mrs. Chickering's invitation was directed primarily at her husband. Henrietta apparently had a fondness of long standing for Colburn, and of course, she was well acquainted with his family. Not with her, Abigail. But was there not at least some rule of sympathetic decorum that bade hostesses include those females temporarily bereft of spouse? Surely there must be.

Abby thought of a lifetime of tittering afternoon teas and well-meaning work parties, of church affairs for families and evening musicales she might attend with a woman friend. But not suppers, she thought to herself. Not interesting conversational suppers where a solitary female might be a drag on lively conversation. Would she be such a female? Nonsense. Although she had to admit she had not had trial of like situation. Why should she believe she was any more capable of interesting discourse than any other of her sex? Than *many* others of her sex, she amended. She was, after all, still in large part rural bumpkin. Clothed fashionably enough, she supposed, but with little experience of sparkling repartee. Where then, was she to acquire conversation if she was forced to sit at home in solitude? Insufferable position indeed!

The house that had seemed so large just yesterday was suddenly too small to bear. Abby walked right through. Through the entry hall whose dish of potpourri smelled stale and dusty. Through the parlor with its gloomy formal chairs. Through the empty kitchen where a damped-down fire only served to emphasize the chill. She pulled open the back door and stepped into the back yard. It was full of sunshine. The chickens glanced in her direction, briefly entertaining the notion that they would get a second breakfast, then went back about their business. A chickadee called nearby. Its spring song, Abby thought. The fieldstone slab she stood on, which served as a back step, radiated heat upward. She could feel the warmth beneath her skirt. It made a pleasing contrast to the still chilly breeze around her shoulders.

Abby noticed that the sun against the south-facing house wall had warmed the strip of ground by the foundation. There was a place like that at home, she mused, by the front step where long ago someone had planted snowdrops to emerge and charm the senses into thoughts of nearing spring. This was a good spot for planting, too. Warm enough for early greens. It was time she set to work making a kitchen garden in this place. Colburn would never do so. He had left all interest in the soil when he left his parents' farm, and though he might appreciate the fruits of agrarian labor, Abby guessed he would go to great lengths to avoid doing any himself. Colburn Whiting was no gentleman farmer. She sighed at one more bit of distance between them.

She studied the patches of ground on each side of the step a while longer. There were humps and valleys where the dirt had frozen and thawed and where stones had worked their magic way to the surface. Even so early, the first dandelions were poking up through the soil. It was peaceful, and familiar. She suddenly nodded her head in decision. Henrietta Chickering could go to Hades.

Abigail stepped back into the empty house and traded her cloak for the short, worn jacket hanging by the door. Almost immediately she felt better. Crossing the yard, she located a flat-ended spade in the carriage house. She clucked sociably at the chickens on her way back, and they squawked in return. Abby carefully lined up the spade parallel to the house, eight feet from the wall. Then she stepped down on it. She was immediately grateful she still had on the wooden pattens, for beneath the soft surface the ground was still partially frozen, and she had to stomp to get the spade any depth into the dirt. Abby was not about to be bested by an inch or so of frost, however. She set her jaw determinedly, pushed the handle back and forth to loosen the soil, then drew the spade out and repeated the process.

There was a satisfying violence to the work. Set the spade. Stomp. Push it in. Yank it out. Set the spade… Abby worked along a line and found thoughts coming unbidden to her mind. Set the spade. Henrietta Chickering. Stomp. Yank it out. Set the spade. Colburn's absence. Stomp. Yank it out. Set the spade. All alone. Stomp. Yank it out. Set the spade… Long before she was done she had run out of complaints and the forceful rhythm of the task worked its own healing.

An hour later, Abby stood back and surveyed the results with satisfaction. The spade line was a barricade closing the world's disappointments out of her garden. Large squares lay outlined in the ground on each side of the back door. It would be a week or so, she allowed, before the frost was out enough to turn it all over. But meanwhile, she could clean the henhouse and have a place to deposit the manure. She could talk to Anna's husband about a fence to close in the beds. John Woodward would have seeds, or at least tell her where to obtain them. And after that... She smiled. After that it would be no time at all before vegetables and herbs started sprouting, and she and Anna could use the produce of their own back yard.

Before that, Abby reminded herself, Colburn would be home. She wondered briefly what he would say to her garden – or, more problematically, to her gardening. She would have to ask in the village for a boy to give her a hand. Colburn would not be likely to mind, she thought, if there were a young man to do the heavy work, to get dirty and cart things about. She would make sure Colburn did not find out about cleaning the hen house.

And after that, she would have a most satisfactory occupation. Nothing extraordinary, she reminded herself, just some useful plants. But plants she had grown and tended, in soil she had sweetened and rid of grubs. A small corner of the world where use and comfort came together, and where she understood exactly how to proceed. As Abby scrubbed the dirt off her hands, she recalled the intensity of her distress earlier that day. She was surprised to find how little Henrietta Chickering's rebuff still stung.

Over the next three weeks the garden took shape. Colburn finally returned home and Abby immediately drew him out to the back yard to give him a tour of her project. Her feelings wavered between pride and trepidation over his reaction. He looked somewhat askance at the patches of dirt with their rows of puny seedlings, but Abby's description of the harvest to come was enthusiastic. There was such eagerness in her voice, such silent pleading for understanding in her upturned face, that Colburn found himself moved to put aside his own preferences and forget his own concerns for the moment. This was the youthful enthusiasm which had drawn him to Abigail at the start, he reminded himself, the eagerness which had been suppressed by Mill Farm's drudgery, which he had so delighted to bring to light in conversation and – his body warmed – in their marriage bed. Of course, the dirt was no place for his wife, any more than the wash tub, but it would take time, yet, for her to come to terms with that and meanwhile, the Penelope he loved stood happy before him. She was very exciting.

Colburn gave his wife an unrestrained kiss on her surprised mouth. Then he smilingly approved her project, and complimented her on her sound choice of young Larrabee as garden boy. Abby began to tell him the names of the young plants already showing, and those dormant in still-bare rows, until she realized he was only half-listening. He was, rather, staring at her. Studying her, she guessed. His intent look made her self-conscious and she wondered briefly whether she had, yet again, done something inappropriate. Then it occurred to her that Colburn's look was rather admiring than critical, and she felt a flush rising in her cheeks as she began to understand where his thoughts were leading.

Colburn took her firmly by the hand and, without breaking his stare, drew her away from the garden toward the house.

"My lovely Abigail, I have something in mind other than roots and salads. Many times this past month I missed more than your sweet voice, and I believe you must have done too. Did you not?" His voice teased her.

Speechless pleasure and embarrassment warred in Abby's wide-eyed gaze as she nodded. The smile on Colburn's face broadened. He chuckled deep in his throat and drew her into the house. The garden would wait, she thought briefly.

After that first day of Colburn's return, however, Abby found she had more time for gardening than she had hoped. Her husband immediately became engrossed with the affairs of the mill again. She gathered his trip to Berkshire County had not been wholly successful, either. A wilderness full of rocks and needy people, he had described it. That Shays Rebellion business a few years back had done nothing to improve trade, and the western half of the state was cursed with a bunch of backward-thinking farmers who didn't know their own good when they saw it. The outcome, Abby deduced, was that they would not consider buying from a firm they didn't know, and Colburn had returned empty-handed, outmaneuvered by well-known merchants from New York.

By June the Whitings had eaten their first home-grown salad. Crisp chard leaves and delicate baby lettuce combined sweet and tart in an exquisite taste of summer which thrilled Abby. Colburn was less appreciative of the rare treat. Abby had to force his attention to his plate before he took sufficient note to comment. He left the table abruptly after the meal, and she did not welcome him home again until the sun had set, well into the evening.

In the middle of the month, the Whitings went on an outing which had caused Abigail great concern from the moment her husband delivered the invitation. She fussed over her costume, primped endlessly before the mirror, and even practiced gracefully sipping tea the day before they went. In her desire to behave appropriately, Abby attempted to anticipate whatever might transpire, but found all her guessing left her in a state of dread by the time Colburn handed her up into their gig.

June 10, 1798 – Mr. Whiting and I journeyed to Waltham this afternoon, to the country estate of Mr. Theodore Lyman. Mr. Whiting was to attend a meeting of the mill proprietors there, and Mrs. Lyman was so gracious as to bid the gentlemen's wives to take tea with her, while the males resolved – or ought I to say attempted to resolve? – those Affairs of State which ever engross them.

Mrs. Lyman is a seasoned hostess, and valiantly attempted to put this rural Penelope at ease tho' the same could not be said for some of the other ladies. I felt too often their high-browed stares turned in my direction, and confess I was not so comfortable with them as I would have liked. Perhaps with more exposure to this elegant company I shall overcome that useless vanity which drives the mind to fruitless competition with others. Then too, Henrietta Chickering was there and, much as I might regret such mean-spiritedness in myself, I do find it difficult to wholly forget her manner toward me this spring.

Be that as it may, I would do well to derive what lesson I might from my own discomfort. I regret that I am of such a withdrawing nature as to stumble so in polite society. I shall do well to study the behavior of Mrs. Lyman and model myself on her, for she combines gentility and kindness in a manner which benefits us all. I am resolved, then. I shall strive to amend those faults which are most obvious, and to discern those more hidden from the outer eye. Shall I not, then, more closely approach that image of womanly virtue which my husband envisions? And in so doing, fulfill as best I may my marriage vows?

E'er we departed The Vale (as the estate is aptly named, for the mansion is set in a pleasant green meadow, bordered one side by a gentle brook, on the other by a quiet country lane) the gentlemen joined us ladies and, it being a seasonable afternoon, Mr. Lyman invited us to stroll the gardens and planting beds with which the house is surrounded. What wonders awaited my unsuspecting eyes! It would seem that Mr. Lyman belongs to that small group of gentlemen whose <u>acquisitiveness</u> is informed by <u>inquisitiveness</u>. He has made it his pastime to study the native flora of these parts, and, in correspondence with like souls here and abroad, has exchanged slips and seeds, cuttings and whole plants between Europe and the New World. Mr. Lyman has planted a virtual Garden of Eden about his house, and he served as nature guide as we went about the grounds. Here at last, I felt at ease, and less sensible of my social limitations, for though many of the flowers and shrubs were new to me, certainly the broad needs and habits of plants I understood, and I could maintain an acceptable level of conversation as we strolled. In truth, I fear I was overly forward, but Mr. Lyman was more than patient with my incessant questions, though Colburn more than once was moved to press my arm in gentle reproach of my enthusiasm.

I do wish he would be more forbearing in his criticisms. I do not truly believe I overstepped the bounds of polite conversation. Our host was certainly most encouraging of my interest, though some of the others (including my husband) had lost their taste for the exercise before we were quite through. As for myself, I could have tarried some time more. The beauty of the surroundings was matched by the inherent interest of Mr. Lyman's discourse.

I wonder how Colburn would take to my performing a few modest "experiments" about the small grounds of our house? Perhaps a hedgerow along the eastern border, or a grape arbor to the rear? A planting of perennial flowers might serve to hide the more commonplace herbs. Dare I suggest it? I am resolved to ask. They would go far to relieve the newness of our home.

A week later, Abby left dinner preparation in Anna's capable hands while she set out perennials in the garden. The first edging row was half planted when a rumble of cart wheels distracted her. Brushing off dirt as she went, Abby walked around the side of the house and stopped in surprise as a two-wheeled cart, drawn by an aging horse, pulled to a stop by the carriage barn. A smock-shirted driver jumped down from his seat and headed toward her. Abby caught a glimpse of long, green-leaved branches sticking out of the cart behind him, along with a burlap-covered mound.

The driver nodded casually and asked if Mistress Abigail Whiting be about. It occurred to Abby that dirt-caked hands and coarse apron did not lend themselves to easy identification of the mistress of the household. Somewhat self-consciously, she wiped her hands on her apron and acknowledged she was Mistress Whiting. The young driver turned red and stammered embarrassed apologies. But Abby recovered her aplomb and smilingly stopped him.

"Please, don't apologize! You would need second sight to know who I might be." She held up her hands. "Especially in this state. And there is no harm done, in any case. Rather, tell me what I can do for you?"

The relieved driver visibly relaxed and gestured behind him at the cart.

"These are for here."

Abigail shook her head, puzzled.

"I don't understand. We are not expecting anything. Certainly not any shrubbery or such, if that is what you carry."

"Well, ma'am, Mr. Lyman told me to deliver these here. Mr. Theodore Lyman," he added, as if the further identification would clarify everything. Abigail looked more confused.

Suddenly recollecting the rest of his charge, the driver gave a brief exclamation and reached into the big pocket on his shirt front. He drew out a rumpled letter and offered it to Abby. She noticed the fine-quality paper as she broke the seal. Inside was a brief note written in hasty script.

Honor^d Madam –

I beg you to accept the items which accompany this note as small tokens of my esteem. I gathered from the interest you expressed this past week that your enthusiasm for horticulture mirrors my own. Surely this is a trait to be admired in the Fair Sex, and, I believe, most appropriate to that traditional female concern for domestic economy and solicitous attention to all small growing things.

The cart contains two lilac bushes (Syringa vulgaris) which I dare to think might grace the lawn of your new home. Their bloom is just done, and you will wish to have the spent heads removed to encourage next year's flowring. These are my own cultivars of a Syringa brought over long since by a Lyman forebear. Further, I am sending a more delicate plant, an orange tree in topiary form, which you will wish to keep within doors, as it is native to more southerly climes and cannot withstand the rigors of our N. Eng. winters.

I trust you may find pleasure in these small things, and that you will continue your horticultural inquiries. Pray extend best regards to y' estimable spouse, Mr. Whiting, whose indulgence I beg.

Y' Brother of the Spade, T. Lyman

"What in heaven's name is all this shrubbery?"

Whiting's impatient voice interrupted Abigail just as she was finishing the note. She was so delighted by Mr. Lyman's gift that she had forgotten her own dishevelment. Even the disapproving scowl on Colburn's face was not enough to detract from her pleasure.

"Oh, Colburn! See what Mr. Lyman has sent over for us!"

She held the note out toward him and went on talking at the same time.

"Lilacs! For our 'lawn', he says, though perhaps 'dooryard' might better suit our situation," she said with amusement. "And some exotic planting to grow inside the house. The parlor perhaps. Here," she rushed on, "See what he says while I investigate the plant."

She pressed the note into his reluctant hand and walked over to the burlap-wrapped object in the cart. With the driver's help, Abby carefully unwound the cloth to expose a carefully pruned and luxuriant topiary bush. Its leaves gleamed dark green with star-shaped white flowers scattered among them and, here and there, a small green ball. A clean sweet smell rose from the blossoms as they came to light.

"Oh!" she exclaimed. "Could this be? Is it truly an orange tree? But in so miniscule a form!"

She did not really expect an answer, but the young driver, who had kept his distance during her exchange with Colburn, stepped forward and nodded eagerly.

"Indeed it is, Ma'am. Master Lyman done the clipping himself, too, I can tell you. He threatened all kinds of trouble if this one got damaged on the way."

He reached over the side of the cart and carefully lifted the plant up, resting it on the top edge so she could get a better look. The tree in its clay pot had been set in a handsome Chinese blue and white urn. Plant and pot together formed an elegant whole. A living sculpture, Abby mused, as she stared at it in satisfaction. Then she remembered Colburn, and turned back to gauge his reaction

"What is your opinion, Mr. Whiting? Do you not think this a magnificent gift?"

Abigail's tone was hopeful, but in fact she was not at all sure how Colburn would take to his wife's receiving gifts from another gentleman. He had given no evidence of a jealous nature during their time together. On the other hand, Abby reminded herself, he had had little occasion for jealousy, founded or unfounded, since they were wed. Not that the aging Mr. Lyman presented the slightest cause for jealousy to her mind. He and Mrs. Lyman were clearly devoted to one another, and these splendid gifts were no more than they purported to be: a gesture of amity between two like-minded gardeners. Still, she reminded herself, it was an unconventional gesture, and Colburn might well take exception to it.

She waited in some suspense as he finished reading Lyman's note and lowered it. For a moment he just stood, hand on hip, inspecting the cart, its contents, and his wife. There was a peculiar expression on his face, which Abby was at a loss to interpret.

"Well?" she prompted. "Are they not beautiful?"

Colburn stirred, and gave a nod of sorts.

"They look well enough," he said grudgingly. "At least the potted one does. It's anyone's guess what those trees look like." He gestured toward the heap of branches hanging over the back of the cart and shook his head. "It is beyond me to understand how anyone can be excited about plants. Especially plants that aren't good for much of anything." He searched for something more to say. "They are green, I'll give you that. And Theodore Lyman seems to think they're worth attending to – which in itself is worth attending to, given his position."

Finally he walked over to Abby and looked down at her upturned face. When he spoke again his voice was tolerant, if unconvinced.

"And for whatever reason, you seem to think they're beautiful. If they bring you pleasure, Abigail, you should do with them as you will. Get young Larrabee to dig them in for you somewhere."

Abigail beamed up at him in relief and tried to engage him further.

"Where do you see the lilacs placed? Should they be at the front door? Or better each side of the carriage way?"

Colburn shrugged. "Wherever, my dear. I am sure you are quite capable of these significant decisions on your own. As for me, I am in need of my dinner."

He turned his attention to the carter and handed him a coin. "If you would unload the shrubbery on the side of the drive, there, my wife will direct you as to the potted plant." He started to go, then caught himself. "Oh, and on your return to The Vale, do convey our deepest appreciation to Master Lyman for his gift. Undoubtedly my wife will express her thanks in more suitable form before the week is out."

Then he turned back to Abigail and dismissed the subject.

"Now, Mistress Whiting, what have you and Anna concocted for this day's meal?"

Abby found it hard to shift attention from lilacs to roasted chicken. Trying to stifle a twinge of annoyance, she reminded herself that her husband's needs must come first, that he had little time to spare for midday horticulture and that the tall and healthy bushes being lifted off the cart could bide their time as well as she. Most important, he found no fault with keeping the gift. The jealousy she had dreaded in her husband was nothing but a chimera, after all, quickly banished by Mr. Lyman's support of her innocent pastime.

She smiled engagingly at Colburn and took his arm to go inside. As they walked through the kitchen garden, her eye went to the half-seeded edging of tansy and she had to suppress a brief urge to finish the row.

Instead, she regaled Colburn with the menu for the noonday meal to come.

An unseasonably raw Sunday afternoon at the end of summer found Abigail at loose ends. She set herself at the writing desk and opened her well-thumbed journal.

Sept, 1798 – Colburn travels again, in a southerly direction this time, ever on the look-out for new markets. Mr. Ellis, who serves in his stead as local agent, bears little resemblance to my husband in drive or enthusiasm. Tho' I cannot doubt his steadfast devotion to the company, yet Mr. E is apt to err in all things on the side of caution. He is one ever to hobble the horse, rather than give him his head, for fear of what – in his timorous brain – he conceives might possibly occur. I would imagine that workman and proprietor alike give thanks each time my husband returns, rather than answer to Mr. E another day. I shall give heartier thanks than they for his return, tho' not for the same reason. I do confess to struggling with solitude, and missing the guiding hand and caring heart of my husband.

On another topic altogether, visited Mill Farm yesterday. What should I discover but the new house Luther is building bears every resemblance to our own house here in Dover! (tho' he insists this is not so). Luther may be infinitely knowledgeable about farming and his mill, but he is too quick to be swayed by others' advice when he doubts his own abilities. I do believe my brother is quite irrationally taken by Colburn's ideas.

Abby stopped writing and reread her last sentence with surprise. What on earth made her write that? Surely Colburn was a sterling mentor? Luther was wise to follow his lead, even as she did herself? But there were a distressing number of occasions on which she did not do so. Could not do so, in fact, for what her husband did pertained so little to her own life. Was there fault therein and if so, must it not necessarily be hers? She moved restlessly in her chair and frowned. She did not wish to pursue that train of thought. She searched for another topic.

Our ancient house is now a partial shell, a dusty ghost of what it was, for L. has taken many of the stoutest timbers for use in the new building. It saddens me to see the past so irrevocably destroyed. Perhaps I should seek to find satisfaction in this process. Luther and Lucy are, after all, doing no more at Mill Farm than what I see transpire around me here: they are making all things new and fresh, starting clean. But I cannot dispel the thought that Lucy will suffer all the same inconveniencies as I – more fires to keep up, more rooms to clean, more east-facing windows to collect road dirt in summer and let in the gray drafts of winter. I confess to harboring some doubt about Newness as a solution.

Abby humphed at herself as she dipped her pen in the inkwell. Heavens! The first gusts of autumn must be drawing out bad humors, for her to write in such discouraging fashion. Perhaps her time would be better served by more constructive activity.

She impatiently wiped the nib clean and pushed back from the table. Fresh air would help. Dropping her shawl, she hurried down to the kitchen and pulled on the old jacket that waited by the door. Once outside, she paused, searching for something to fight off the grayness that seemed to weigh her down. Her search stopped at the bundles waiting by the barn. She nodded and moved purposefully toward them. She had work to do.

When Abby returned to her desk she had to ease herself onto her chair. She was stiff, and her shoulders ached from overwork. But there was a smile of satisfaction on her face.

Mr. Lyman sent 3 young apple trees this morning. How kind he is to continue his encouragement of my small efforts. I have just planted the saplings myself, across the driveway. Digging like a groundhog in the dirt. Surely no blacksmith from the mill can have appeared more rugged than I as I coaxed the bundled saplings into their places! But I can picture the softening effect of apple blossoms in 6 months time, when we are all sick to death of winter's gloom. Will they bloom first spring? I must make note to inquire.

What a great relief it is to dig in dirt! The earth, at least, remains immune to fashion's foibles. I give thanks there are some things which do not change.

Three years into the marriage Abby still had not conceived, much to Anna's concern and head-shaking. Abby's own attitude fluctuated unpredictably between regret and momentary flashes of resentment that her husband held her solely responsible. Then she would lapse into guilt at her failings both in thought and deed. Colburn was out of the house more than he was in it, between time at the mill, meetings with the proprietors, and increasingly frequent travel.

He spent long hours attempting to set up deliveries from their sources direct to the mill. 'Cutting out the middle man,' he called it, and went on at length at dinnertime about its being the only way to make a profit from ironwork. At the same time Colburn was running into problems at the other end of the manufacturing process. Nail rods cut at the manufactory were jobbed out to local farmers for heading. It had seemed like a convenient arrangement at first. The farmers, always short on coin, had time to spare some months of the year, and the job of pounding the top of a nail flat was certainly within their capabilities. From the company's point of view, the outwork arrangement eliminated the need for blacksmiths and forges. But something was going wrong.

"These Jonathans forget that nail rods even exist, come planting time!" Colburn was impatient with agricultural cycles. "If it's not planting or haying or harvesting or some damn other thing, then it's lambing time. Bloody stock men only turned in half what they contracted for last month. How are we supposed to fill a fistful of orders if these yokels don't care about being paid?"

When Colburn carried on about farmers Abby kept her own counsel, thinking it somewhat strange that he was tarring his own family with the same brush.

"I sent Ellis out yesterday to collect the unused blanks around town. Do you know he came back with half a cart full, all of 'em supposed to be headed and ready to ship out by now? I've had enough of farmers. If they don't have their head buried in the dirt, they're heading off for parts unknown, completely without warning. Just like your brother." He spit the words out, ignoring the evident pain on his wife's face as she suffered Daniel's leaving all over again.

When Colburn was not talking about manufacturing problems, Abby struggled to overcome his increasing distraction. He seemed more distant with every aggravation of the business. He was never consciously rude or mean to her. Rather, she thought to herself, he was *absent*. As if his preoccupation was so great as to leave little room for a wife in his thoughts and his attentions.

Abby also found that her experience with Henrietta Chickering was not an isolated instance. The more her husband tarried from home, the fewer invitations came for Mr. and Mrs. Whiting to attend a city ball or even a country supper party. Rather, Abigail's social life was characterized by chatting after church and sipping endless cups of tea with female acquaintances when Colburn was away.

She had more time for reflection than she appreciated. Some of it she spent in the garden, though even that outlet was denied her during the long winter months. From time to time Mr. Lyman would send a book on horticulture by his driver. She valued these, and read them avidly, absorbing what she could of advice on soil improvement and planting conditions, pruning and pollination. Abby's initial efforts at landscaping met with success: the lilacs bloomed profusely, the apples less so, though the books advised that this was due only to first-year transplant shock. Mr. Lyman was kind enough to stop in one afternoon on his way to the manufactory. He complimented her on her success, and encouraged her continued efforts. Abby decided to conduct some "little experiments", as she wryly called them, and made first trials of grafting from the fruit trees he had given her, onto ancient apple stock which had self-seeded nearby.

And always, she quietly prayed for patience to attend the time when the ironworks would become settled and her husband would come home to her for good.

Oct 1799 – Mr. W caught the tide today for Bournemouth, in England. From thence he intends to visit a number of cities to the north – on the Continent as well as England, seeking, he says, a supplier of higher-grade ore than can be had hereabouts, that one aspect of the business over which they have least control but on which so much depends. He has been so concerned, so distracted of late… I pray that this voyage will settle the worries which have haunted him. He does not know how long he will be gone, the time being entirely dependent, he says, on the temperament and greed of those he meets. I fear he may be further delayed by storms, given the season. By now I should have schooled myself in patience to await his homecoming. Yet I discover I must still do so, and not anticipate his return much before spring. Instead, I must trust his letters to see me through this *Premature Widowhood*.

I did make tentative inquiry as to whether I might not accompany him on this long journey, but he made it clear that the unpredictability of stops and stays would make travelling extremely inconvenient for me. Then too, I must remind myself that this is a costly undertaking, even just for him alone. I have heard that staying in even the most modest inns can empty one's pockets in no time. He was exceeding irritable and brusque before he left, complaining that even the proprietors were hampering his efforts, but in the end he assured me they saw to keeping him in funds for the necessary length of his stay.

I must turn my thoughts to gratitude for his taking my comfort and best interests to heart, and banish my impossible longing to accompany him. In his absence I shall remember him as he looked this morning, his face flushed with anticipation, boyish in excitement at the start of an adventure. I was put to mind of his likening himself to Ulysses, back when we first met. He still has that energetic quality about him which has, I think, been suppressed of late by the concerns of the iron works. Am I too fanciful in believing the salt wind blew his cares away? Certainly the smile he sent back with his last wave held no reservation. He is, I believe, swept along by his vision of our new American republic, and his place as a pioneer in it.

As for me, I cannot help regretting that his fervor draws him farther away from me. Truly, from a female's standpoint, this pioneering vision leaves much to be desired! First it takes my dear Daniel to the farther end of the settled continent. Then it removes my husband across an ocean for unknown time and to what avail? Yet I think they delight in pioneering, in daring all to be first and gain most. As for me, I find myself striving to make a new life right here at home, with few guideposts to show me the way. Another form of pioneering, I would wager, but I find myself less than enthralled by this particular journey.

Alas, I fear I may be taking on that crankiness which Colburn left behind when he put out to sea. I cannot feel a single smile hovering within me, nor find a single pleasant thought to while away the endless time until we are reunited. I shall pray that the Lord keep close watch over him, and give him a swift wind to bring him home again.

The butchered carcass still steamed in the cold December air as Abigail and Lucy completed the work Luther had begun in Mill Farm's new barnyard. Luther had slaughtered and bled a hog for winter use. Soon there would be hams hanging in the smokehouse over a smoldering fire until they were cured. The meat would taste as much like hickory as pork. Abigail had ridden over to help with the work, and to have a good visit with Lucy and the children. The two women worked with their sleeves rolled up despite the chill wind blowing across the pond, for removing innards was a messy business, at best. Shortly, however, they could retreat to the relative warmth of the kitchen and begin grinding the meat for Lucy's sausages.

"Would you have use for a head cheese if we fixed one up this time, Nabby?" Lucy knew there would be another hog butchered before the winter was out. The boys, growing like weeds, were clamoring for meat and besides, Luther would want part of the second animal to sell for cash money when tax time came around.

Abby raised her eyes to heaven.

"Lucy, if I never tasted head cheese again it would be too soon. I confess it is the one part of a pig for which I have no liking at all. And with Colburn gone, there is little enough call for delicacies at our house. Make one for your own family, if you like, but thank you no, not for me."

"Indeed it is a process I'd be just as happy to forego. Our own tastes run more to sausage than sweetbreads any day. Perhaps we'll give the dogs a winter treat." The Chapmans' hounds were always interested when butchering took place. Lucy had made the two boys take them off on a prolonged scouting expedition around the pond, to prevent mishaps during butchering.

"Your sausages are well worth waiting for, Lucy. The best I've tasted, and I'm delighted to help put them together. But more important, I am so pleased to find you well enough to make them – to do all this –," Abby gestured with a greasy elbow. "Truly, you seem in better health now than any time since you and Luther were wed."

Lucy smiled gratefully and nodded.

"It's true. But you know, Abby, it comes as a peculiar coincidence. I mark my improvement from that summer I miscarried, when Sybil was still a baby." She shook her head, and her voice held the sadness that still remained from the loss of an infant so near term. "Perhaps it is God's way of compensating our loss. Giving me the strength to play with the young ones I do have…"

Lucy plunged her arms into the bucket of hot water that stood nearby and determinedly shifted the conversation.

"But what of you and Colburn, Abigail? It may not be my business to pry, but we cannot help but wonder when there will be young Whiting cousins to play with ours?"

She kept her tone light, but the look she gave Abby mirrored her real concern. Abby kept her eyes on her work.

"You cannot wonder any more than I, Lucy. I have no cause to think we would not have children, nor know of any reason why I might not conceive."

"Your flux comes regularly? There's naught amiss there?"

An embarrassed flush rose up Abby's face and she shook her head.

"Well, what then of your relations with your husband?" Lucy persisted.

Abigail gathered herself up and met her sister-in-law's determined look.

"There can be no complaint in that area, other than rarity, since Colburn is so often from home. Our intimate relations are all that I could ask. Indeed," she continued in a burst of confidence, "They are more pleasurable than I ever expected when I went to him as a bride."

Lucy giggled appreciatively and continued her quizzing.

"Then how do you let him get away on these perpetual travels of his?"

Suddenly the pleasure went out of Abby's voice.

"It is not by *my* will he does so!" she shot back, then faltered. "He must go, you know. The business requires it of him. I cannot see that I can have much to say in the matter."

"Do you not miss him sorely when he's gone?" Lucy's voice was sympathetic.

Abby's hands stopped moving and her eyebrows drew together in an intense frown. The silence went on for so long that Lucy thought Abigail was not going to answer. When she did so, the words forced themselves out.

"There is nothing on this earth I hate more than Colburn's absence." She stopped. Then she drew a deep breath and continued her unwanted confession.

"Unless it is the very moment of his departure. That moment feels like nothing so much as a piece of my soul being ripped from my body." Abby shook her head in self-reproach. "I try to overcome it. I try to reassure myself that each time is but a moment in all the time we shall be together. I seek solace in labor. In digging and weeding." She turned an anguished look on her companion.

"But oh, Lucy! His going leaves such emptiness behind! And I cannot think how to make it any better. Perhaps if there were babies… But I am so alone."

Abby blinked back tears and pressed her lips together as if she could stop the hurting by stopping the words. She turned desperately back to the carcass, fumbling with her knife as she tried to see through blurred eyes. Lucy moved close and reached an arm around her shoulders in a tight hug.

"Dear Nabby! I am so sorry I brought this on. I had no idea how sorely Colburn's going hurt you." Giving an awkward laugh, she tried to lighten the mood. "Of course I find myself in the situation of wishing your brother would just disappear from time to time. I firmly believe there's such a thing as staying *too* close to home!"

Abby tried to smile in appreciation, although she was sure Lucy was wrong. Lucy went on.

"But in all seriousness, Abby, I do think your husband might be more considerate of the demands of wife and home. It seemed quite clear that he was enamored of you when you were wed … Surely this has not changed?"

"I ask myself that more often that I like to say. Especially when I don't hear from him for a time. Have I done aught to weaken his love? Am I less than I first appeared to him? Certainly I am no more than I was. I am as barren as the day we met."

Lucy broke in indignantly.

"Oh, nonsense, Abigail. There is more to marriage than children, you know, despite what this household leads you to believe. Just look at you! You are a wonderful woman. And beautiful. Skilled in all manner of things; able to converse about the affairs of the world *infinitely* better than I ever shall be. The children love you; Luther and

I love you. Why even the dogs love you – and they barely get along with anyone!"

"Well." Abby stammered at the praise. "Thank you," she said simply, then collected herself and repeated for Lucy the explanation she had painstakingly worked out for herself.

"But it would be wrong of me to let you think any fault lies with my husband. I'm afraid I have let you hear the worst of my self-pity. I do know he cares for me. Indeed, as soon as he returns home from one of his sojourns, I am instantly reassured of his affection. I have come to believe that this less-than-satisfactory situation derives solely from Colburn's necessary attention to the affairs of the ironworks. After all, Lucy, Colburn is working on a manufacturing venture as great as any in England. What sort of wife would I be to stand in his way?"

Although the question was meant to be rhetorical, Abby feared it would be answered anyway, and she dreaded what she might hear. She carefully set down her knife and rinsed the last of the sweetbreads. Her sister-in-law stood arms akimbo, studying Abby silently, unconvinced by her protestations. Then Lucy humphed and shook her head.

"Sister dear, you are the sort of wife that heaven must be made of, for I believe you belong there with the martyrs. It is not my place to be critical of your husband, and for all I know, what he is doing may change the course of history. But I think the true question concerns what sort of a *husband* Colburn Whiting might be! For to my mind, as a husband, he leaves much to be desired. He has hurt one of the finest, most loving people I know."

Abby opened her mouth to protest, but was cut off by Lucy, who picked up a trencher of innards to carry indoors. She looked uncharacteristically stern.

"Now enough of this. If I say any more we shall end in a quarrel, and that is the very last thing you need at the moment. Bring in the sweetbreads and we shall set to work on sausages. I do agree with you about one thing, at least: hard labor can clear the head of many woes. And we still have our share of good hard work ahead of us today."

Driving home the next morning, a packet of roast pork on the seat beside her, Abby tried to keep her mind on the pleasures of the rest of her visit. She and Lucy, between them, had mixed up sausage meat enough to last the winter, stuffed the casings and tied them off, to be hung beside the hams in the smokehouse. Pig's feet were cleaned and put up to simmer for the nourishing jelly which Lucy would store in fat-sealed jars the following day. Slabs of fat were rendered down and added to the barrelful which would go for soap one smelly day later in the winter.

When it was all done, the family had sat down to an impromptu celebration. They feasted on fresh roast pork and cracklings, apples brought up from the cold cellar and baked alongside a pan of root vegetables which Tommy had been bullied into peeling while the women finished their work. Luther was in an expansive mood, joking straight-faced with his two sons, who fell all over each other giggling as they endlessly repeated punchlines. Sybil, who, at two and a half had no notion of what they were saying, squealed in sympathetic delight until Lucy finally had to smilingly insist that her husband quiet things down.

Abby had been bone-tired. Her back ached and her hands were raw from their time spent in wash buckets, but the warmth of the Chapman family had relaxed her like sitting by the fire. At first she shook her head at the silliness, but as supper went on, she found herself caught up in the spirit of the moment, teasing Lucy that she was too much the old sobersides. By the time Abby quietly slipped into bed beside the sleeping Sybil, she was smiling to herself, savoring the warmth and love that passed among her relatives, sustaining them as much as the food they ate.

It was this sustaining warmth she tried to hold onto as she rode home the next morning. But fragments of yesterday's conversation with Lucy kept intruding, and their parting replayed in Abby's head.

Lucy had given her a last warm hug and said, "This is your home too, you know, and you are a special part of the Chapman family. You know you are always welcome here, Nabby." The words were no more than gracious. Why then did they keep ringing so portentously in Abby's head? Was it Lucy's somber tone, perhaps, so unlike her normal soft and comfortable way of talking?

In truth, she had never known Lucy to be so forthright in her opinions. Or so uncharitable. And to have it be about *her* husband.

But then, Lucy could not be expected to understand how things had to be. Lucy had never listened to Colburn's glowing plans. Or experienced the passionate enthusiasm of his homecomings. Surely these were times worth waiting for!

A glimpse of last night's laughter crossed her mind. A different way of life, that was all. Some day. Perhaps some day she and Colburn would sit at supper like that. Would joke with their children. Would share the lives they led, and the food they made. Although Abby admitted it was hard to picture Colburn telling childish jokes or helping a toddler cut her meat.

Some days it was just hard to picture Colburn.

Abby was struck with horror at that unintended thought. What monstrous sort of wife was she, to ever lose the image, deep within, of her husband?

She flicked the reins in her hands, and the surprised horse broke into an unwilling trot. Abby was just as glad to have a diversion, and kept up the quickened pace for the rest of the return home.

When she arrived, she was greeted at the door by Anna, who thrust a note in her hand before even saying hello.

"This came just this morning, ma'am. By Master Lyman's man. I was thinking it might be more to do with your shrubbery?" she said hopefully.

Abby removed her gloves and broke the seal. She quickly scanned the note, then frowned and reread the brief paragraphs. When she looked up, the housekeeper knew from her expression that the subject was not shrubbery.

"Mr. Lyman writes that he would like to call at my earliest convenience. With Mr. Ellis and Mr. Chickering. Something about the iron works, I assume, they all being proprietors and coming together." Her voice was puzzled. "Though I cannot fathom why they should wish to speak with me. It is not as though I know aught of the business."

"Maybe they're coming to pay a friendly visit, then," Anna speculated. "Out of consideration for all the trouble they've made you, snatching your husband away!" she ended pointedly.

Abby sighed.

"Anna, we've been through this before. They, and he, are only doing what they must to see that the business prospers. Better we put our minds to properly receiving the gentlemen than to chiding them." Her voice was purposeful, and the discussion moved to answering Mr. Lyman's note and planning tea, but the edges of Abby's mind continued to worry at the reason behind this unexpected request.

The gentlemen appeared on her doorstep at three o'clock the following afternoon. Tall, gracious Theodore Lyman greeted Abby warmly, and went through the formality of presenting Joshua Ellis, Colburn's temporary replacement as company agent, and George Chickering, Henrietta's husband. Abby thought briefly that Ellis and Chickering presented a perfect contrast in face and form: the agent narrow-shouldered and dour; Chickering large and emanating a self-confidence that only came with long roots and good investments. She noted uncomfortably that none of the men was smiling.

Abigail showed them into the parlor where Anna had set out a table of cakes and sweetmeats, dried fruit and cheese toasts. Conversation proceeded awkwardly as tea and hot water were brought and Abby inquired if the gentlemen preferred a glass of madeira. Mr. Lyman complimented Abby on the health of her topiary orange tree.

Abby and Mr. Chickering commented on the Reverend Mr. Caryl's latest sermon. Mr. Ellis drank his black tea in silence and nibbled a cheese toast.

Finally, mindful of her duty as a hostess, Abby turned to Mr. Ellis.

"I trust, Mr. Ellis, that all goes well at the iron company during my husband's absence?"

Ellis glanced furtively at Lyman and Chickering.

"Hmm." He began noncommittally, giving the others an opportunity to step in. They remained silent. Mr. Chickering busied himself with another slice of pound cake.

"As well as might be expected," Ellis answered cryptically.

"I am sure it must be challenging to step into another's place as you have had to do," Abby said politely. "The company must be grateful that you have been able to do so." She glanced at Chickering and Lyman for agreement, praying that her tone did not betray the unreasoning dislike she had for this dour little man.

"Grateful in more ways than they expected." Ellis nodded vehemently, then looked to Lyman to elaborate.

Mr. Lyman carefully set down his tea bowl and straightened his plate. It seemed to Abby that he was uncommonly reluctant to enter the conversation, but she wished he would, as she was having little luck drawing Mr. Ellis out.

Lyman finally spoke.

"Mrs. Whiting, have you heard from your husband recently?"

"Why, yes," she replied quickly, relieved to find such an easy explanation for the visit. The proprietors must not have received a letter by the same packet as Colburn's last letter to her. They were calling for news.

"Indeed, I heard but a week ago, by the *Columbia*. The ship put into Newburyport on its way back to England." Smiling slightly, she shook her head. "Of course you know how out-of-date such messages can be. My husband's letter was all of two months old. Written, I believe, not long after he disembarked at Bournemouth. I gather the *Columbia* had called at a number of Caribbean ports before sailing up here."

Abby reminded herself that she was digressing, and cut herself short.

"But may I ask what you gentlemen wish to know? You must have had word from him yourselves?"

Mr. Lyman responded reluctantly.

"We have, Mrs. Whiting. Just yesterday, in fact. Mr. Ellis received a letter by direct mail from London."

He paused as if wondering how to proceed. Suddenly Abby froze with the appalling thought that something had happened to Colburn. That these men appeared so somber because he was hurt. Or in pain. Or dead. But then, she thought desperately, they would not have heard from him themselves. Was that not what Mr. Lyman had said? A large bass voice cut into her panic. Mr. Chickering took up the questioning.

"According to the letter Ellis had, your husband plans to head off for the Continent, Mrs. Whiting. Might you know anything about that?"

Abby was so relieved to realize Colburn was unharmed that she missed the edge in Mr. Chickering's normally mellow voice.

"Oh! Of course, Mr. Chickering. He led me to understand that was one of the charges you gave him before his departure? To seek out sources of better iron ore? He did explain that much of your intent. Though of course he does not speak to me in any detail of company matters."

Abby did not want the proprietors to think that Colburn had confided in her inappropriately, and it was still quite unclear as to what they were getting at. She was beginning to suspect, however, that they were definitely getting at something in particular. And as she was sorting through her thoughts, she noticed a quick exchange of glances among the three men.

Mr. Lyman stepped in.

"No, of course not. But Mrs. Whiting, we are concerned that there may have been a misunderstanding here and, speaking directly, we have come to you in hopes that you might help us clear up the situation."

"I cannot imagine how I might assist you gentlemen, though I am most happy to oblige." Abby's heart was still racing after her brief panic, and she was having trouble attending to Mr. Lyman's words. He went on.

"It appears there has been some disagreement among the proprietors as to the nature and extent of Mr. Whiting's charge abroad, Mrs. Whiting. We felt it was incumbent upon us to rectify the problem, and felt you might be able to shed further light on Mr. Whiting's plans."

There was a mutter of disbelief from Mr. Ellis.

"Whiting himself probably couldn't shed light on them. The man goes off half-cocked..."

Mr. Lyman briskly cut him off. "Mr. Ellis, please! There is nothing to be gained by casting aspersions heedlessly. I beg that you let us proceed as we had discussed."

The gentlemen's words had recaptured Abby's attention, and she began to have an inexplicable sense of dread that was not related to her husband's health. Misunderstanding? Problem? Colburn going off half-cocked? What was making Mr. Ellis so much more unpleasant than usual this afternoon? She put up her guard.

284

"Please, gentlemen, I do not know what you are looking for, nor why, but I would ask that you tell me why you are concerned about my husband?"

"Well, Mrs. Whiting," Mr. Chickering began reluctantly, "It seems your husband has taken on more responsibility than some of us might have intended. Of course, you know how such things happen. Growing company, lots of demands. Have to make decisions on the spot, sometimes, to get things done..." His words petered off in a series of confirmative nods. He cogitated for a moment while the others kept silent. Then he went on.

"The proprietors' disagreement seems to center around just what Colburn was meant to accomplish with this trip of his. Now you say he is off looking for first-hand sources of ore. A good idea, I've no doubt about it." He nodded his head again, thoughtfully. "But some of us didn't exactly understand that that was what he was going to do. You see, Mrs. Whiting, some of us thought your husband was taking a short trip to England just to firm things up with the same supplier we've been buying from all along. And after that he'd be coming right back, and settle right back into his place as agent here. For of course you know how much we depend on him to handle things." He nodded once more. "Good man, Whiting. Can't do without him."

"Mr. Chickering, I must admit I am surprised to hear this. Surely the proprietors approved my husband's plans before he left? He would never undertake such an extensive trip without the company's backing."

Mr. Lyman grimaced. "That is part of the dilemma, my dear. You see, he did present the proprietors with a proposal. It was very forward-thinking, and quite grand in scope. As I remember, he suggested visiting a number of European countries and, at the same time he was arranging for more direct supply of ore, he would research the likelihood of American firms actually supplying finished product to the Old World. A revolutionary concept! But what with establishing contacts, and negotiations and the like, even he would not estimate the duration of this foray." He looked at Abby and shook his head. "And that, of course, is one of the reasons a number of proprietors disapproved of the proposal. Mr. Chickering is quite right in saying the company depends on your husband's sound guidance here at home."

"But they did eventually approve, did they not?" Abby prompted. "For surely what you describe is just what he has gone off to do?"

"They did not." Ellis spat out. "Nobody in his right mind would approve such a fantastical scheme. Spending away the company's profits on a long-shot gamble with no guaranteed benefit. No sir, we voted him down!"

"Mr. Ellis." Lyman broke in with quiet authority. "I must remind you that the proprietors did no such thing. The proposal was tabled for further discussion at a later date." He turned to Abby. "The concept seemed to be one for future consideration. Some of us told your husband that the idea had merit, but would better wait because of its significant expense."

"It's true," Chickering rumbled. "No vote was ever taken, one way or the other."

Abby's mind twisted in confusion. What were they saying? She suddenly remembered his complaints about their hampering his plans. Did Colburn act without proper authorization? Where was this leading?

"Gentlemen, please! Has my husband done something wrong?"

The three spoke at once.

"Yes!"

"Not exactly."

"Mrs. Whiting,"

Lyman's voice rose above the others, curbing them as he summarized the company's situation. "Your husband has taken rather more upon himself than we would have wished him to do. In his position as agent, he is given a great deal of leeway in making decisions on his own – of course with the understanding that such decisions are in the best interests of the company. Apparently Mr. Whiting chose to think that his European 'campaign,' shall we call it, was of sufficient merit, and urgency, to be acted upon immediately despite the strong counsel of the other proprietors toward patience and delay. As a result, he has withdrawn significant sums from the corporation to cover his anticipated expenses. He has departed for a trip of unspecified duration at a time when production is most demanding. And Mr. Ellis finds himself in the position of trying to fulfill large contracts made by your husband without guidance as to how to accomplish that end.

"To answer your question briefly, then. No, Mrs. Whiting, your husband has not done anything which is clearly unlawful. We *are* forced to call his judgment into question, however, and are disappointed at his disregard of the opinions of those whose investment he puts in jeopardy."

Abigail had never heard Mr. Lyman speak so grimly. She was shocked. The disquiet caused by his words became worse as she looked from one to another of the men in the silence which followed. Ellis's mouth was pinched and he glared at her indignantly. Chickering looked acutely uncomfortable, as if he wished the whole matter would disappear.

Abby knew they were waiting for her to say something, to protest or plead or deny what Colburn had done. Then she heard again his voice as he told her his plans; the determination in it, the firm belief that what he did was right. *But they will not understand, Abigail*, he had said. *They cannot understand you have to risk to gain, and risk greatly at that!* His eyes had glittered with what she thought of now as defiance. *Men of small minds and small imaginations. They will only be convinced when it is done!*

At the time she hadn't understood what a dangerous voyage he was setting out on. She had never thought to question Colburn's words, his plans. Now it seemed, there were more questions than answers. These gentlemen wanted answers. Some of them, like Mr. Ellis thought they knew the answers but they didn't understand. A cold determination settled over her. She might not understand her husband either, no matter how hard she tried, but she knew he was not a criminal. She would deal with the gentlemen first, then confront the confusion within. Determination drew her upright in her seat and she clenched her hands together in her lap. That way they didn't tremble. Then she raised her chin and met each man's eyes in turn as she answered them.

"I am greatly disturbed to hear your complaints against my husband, gentlemen. I have no wish to further the apparent discord among the proprietors, but neither am I willing to hear Mr. Whiting maligned for what, as you present it, may be ascribed more to your own manner of proceeding than to aught he has done wrong. I feel quite certain that Mr. Whiting would never deliberately do anything to endanger the iron works –" Abby turned toward Chickering, "a venture, I would remind you, in which he himself holds shares, as well as you. You have seen fit to trust his decisions in the past, and I see no reason why you should do less in the present circumstances. Unless, of course," and she looked pointedly at Mr. Ellis, "those who have been chosen to manage during his absence are not capable of such weighty responsibility."

Ellis twitched forward but Abby stood up before he could speak.

"I am certain there is nothing more I could say to 'clarify the situation', as you put it, Mr. Lyman. So perhaps it would be best for you gentlemen to leave now. I must respond to my husband's last letter and, I would suggest, you might be better advised doing the same, rather than searching for potentially incriminating information from your own agent's wife."

She turned her back on the men and walked out of the room, leaving them no choice but to follow her to the front door, which she silently held open. Ellis and Chickering both left, muttering in their different ways as they went. Lyman held back, standing before Abby until she was forced to meet his eyes. The look he gave her was sympathetic, and regretful.

"Dear Mrs. Whiting, your husband is an extraordinary man. He thinks great thoughts, and dares great things. Unfortunately, he sometimes leaves others behind in his breakneck voyage toward the future. Let us hope we shall find a happy resolution to this dilemma, and that you will forgive us for burdening you with it."

He bowed formally and went to join the others.

For a long time Abby just stood in the doorway, holding tight to the door at first; then, when the worst of the tension ebbed, leaning against it in exhaustion, staring at nothing. *Burdening her with it.*

Colburn had gone too far this time, had he not? With his vast schemes. Gone beyond what other men would sanction. Taken money. Taken control. Chosen to overlook the limits imposed by normal life.

Still, her thoughts veered, his actions would prove him right. He would be vindicated on his return, when all the shrewish Ellises of the world acknowledged the soundness inherent in his plan.

It was sound, wasn't it? The money would prove to be well spent, would it not? But how was she to know? What did she know about business affairs anyway, since he had, in effect, shut her out of the mill's workings? And that left her with no evidence of her own, nothing to judge by but the words of panicked men against her husband. For all that they were worth.

How dared they come and accost her? How dared they challenge the man who had led them so far? And seek to lay the blame on him, for their own weaknesses? How dared they... She was so infuriated, she could not complete the thought.

"How dare they!" she hissed, and slammed the door.

Over the next few weeks, Abby spent a great deal of time sitting in the parlor, trying to think. She would settle in the old Jacobean chair of an afternoon, and sip her tea from one of the *encre de chine* teabowls Colburn had given her all that time ago. Then she would relive her conversation with the proprietors.

She had written to Colburn and mentioned the interview with Lyman and the others. Yet she had trouble telling him about their suspicions and mistrust. As if just writing the words was libelous. Every time she tried, the phrases seemed to shout Treason, seemed to leap off the page and proclaim her guilty of doubting her husband's wisdom, of failing him as a wife. She had no reason to doubt Colburn. She knew what he intended. He had told her somewhat of his plans, and of their necessity. So what question was left for a wife to ask? And what answer would a husband give, beyond what had already been said? If the proprietors chose to find fault, then they must proceed as they saw fit. Nothing she might ask, or he might say, would change that until he returned. The success he brought home with him would be his vindication.

In the end, Abby left most of the conversation out of her letter, settling for a brief caution that Mr. Ellis was fault-finding once again, as he had been wont to do on former occasions. As she sealed the folded pages, Abby allowed herself to hope that Colburn would be sufficiently struck by the proprietors' visiting her, to read between the lines and write back, unasked, offering reassurance and further explanation. Surely he must do so, she encouraged herself.

The world entered a new century on January first. The weather responded by besieging New England with a long and unusually cold winter. Even Boston Harbor froze, and shipping all along the coast came to a near standstill with the foul weather. It did not help Abby's state of mind that the letters she so counted on from Colburn were delayed, some for weeks at a time.

When they did come, sometimes more than one, she would hug them to her, savoring them even unopened while she performed a ritual of fixing tea and settling herself in the parlor. Then she would open them up, and smooth them out, study the dates and cities written at the top, carefully arrange them in order before she read, as if the motions would prolong her husband's long-awaited "visit", as she'd come to think of these occasions.

Each of Whiting's letter began *Dearest Penelope –*. She did not mind his using that name for her, because the sound of his voice as he called her that, echoed in her head. It was a voice that had cherished and admired her, radiating warmth and love. The letters were short, much taken up with description of impressive manufactories he visited or important men of business with whom he had dealings. But sometimes he'd write as she had known him to talk – wittily, with ample use of exclamations and opinions. And sometimes he'd remember to tell her of an unusual "clump of shrubbery" he'd come across. Abby was always torn between regret she could not share the scenes in person, and gratitude that Colburn thought to entertain her. She looked for those sentences, feeling him close by as she read.

In the weeks following the prioprietors' visit Abby looked for evidence in Colburn's letters that he was concerned by it, but there was no mention at all. Of course her letter with its implicit plea for reassurance might have gone just as far astray as his were apt to do. Still, when she put the pages down in her lap, doubt sneaked back into her thoughts, blurring the images of urbane drawing rooms or snow-dusted hedgerows.

Was he succeeding yet, in the business he was about? Could he show them proof and defend his reputation?

She sighed heavily and stared down toward the mill. It was so tiring, trying to know what to think. Resisting the unkind thoughts of others about her husband. Holding onto her faith in Colburn by love alone, without him there to strengthen and reassure her. So tiring to be alone.

As the winter dragged on, Abby took to her bed earlier and earlier in the evening. Some nights she felt so tired that the supper Anna left out for her was too much work to eat, and she slowly dragged herself upstairs to the big bed in the chamber. She would curl up under a mound of blankets and coverlets, and bury her head beneath the covers to make a dark and warm cocoon. Finally, ever so slowly, she would begin to feel warm, herself, and she could listen to the words from Colburn's letters whispering in her head, and remember his voice whispering in her ear as he lay beside her in this bed. Abby would lull herself to sleep with her husband's warm reassurance tucked away inside.

The next morning always dawned just as cold but Abby, refreshed by dreams, determinedly tracked the days going by. Every one, she told herself, brought spring closer and with spring, the reopening of New England's ports. Through the frozen months Abby nourished a small hope deep inside where she stored the sureness of her husband's love. At first she barely acknowledged its existence, as if to do so would tempt fate and preordain its failure.

When the harbors open, she would chant to herself, *when the harbors open...* Out loud she would finish, "a letter will come." But silently, in the nighttime cocoon or in the orange-scented parlor, the hope had a different ending. *When the harbors open, Colburn will come.*

It would be just like him, wouldn't it? She would muse on, and smile tolerantly at her husband's impetuousness. To come without a warning, like Ulysses coming home all unexpected. Making all things well. And never sailing away again. Then she would smile in pleasure at her own whimsy and sip her tea or, nighttimes, stretch out warm and fall asleep.

Long and cold weeks later the ice did break and the harbors reopened to shipping. Abby's anticipation built, almost beyond bearing, and she jumped at every knock on the door or rumble of cart wheels on the driveway. Then April came, and dragged on through endless rainstorms which kept Abby from the garden. Anna would find her pacing in the front room. "Wearing a hole through the carpet," she would scold, yet when she tried to distract Abby with a bit of work, like as not the mistress would stop in mid-stir, and let the pudding burn as she stared out the window. Anna had a good idea what was eating her, and she shook her head in worried sympathy.

Another rainstorm was finally letting up when Abby's waiting came to an end. She pulled open the door to find a sodden carter on the doorstep, rain dripping off the brim of his hat. Her hopeful glance behind him showed only a canvas-covered wagon standing deep in the mud, its draft team breathing steam and shaking the water off their forelocks.

"Ma'am," the driver muttered politely, touching his hat.

"What is it?" Abby snapped, tension overriding manners.

"I'm looking for Mistress Abigail Whiting? Be you she?" the man persisted.

Abby took herself somewhat in hand.

"Yes! I am Mistress Whiting. What is this about?"

"A letter, ma'am. I've a letter here –"

The carter reached under his soaking cloak and fumbled about in his weskit. Abby thought the wait was interminable.

"– Came on the brig *Atlantis* put into Boston yesterday. Mr. Clark said I might as well deliver it here since I was heading for the mill." He gestured with his chin toward the ironworks, as he finally pulled the letter out of a deep pocket. Abby almost grabbed it from his hand in her impatience. Then she caught herself and thanked him warmly, tipping him twice the usual from relief. She pushed the door shut and hurried into the parlor, calling to Anna for some tea as she went.

Colburn's well-loved handwriting looked up at her as she settled herself in her chair. *Not my husband in person*, she thought with a brief pang of disappointment. *Not yet*, she quickly amended, *but perhaps he will say when.* She sat absently, her hand resting on the paper, anticipating the long-denied pleasure for a moment. By the time Anna brought tea, Abby was engrossed in reading. The housekeeper quietly set the tray at her elbow and left the room, relieved that Mrs. Whiting had word at last.

My dearest Penelope – Abby smiled at the words' familiar ring.

> *It has been too long since I have had opportunity to take pen in hand. Be sure you are in my thoughts, but these past weeks have sped by, with little time left aside for the pleasures*

of correspondence. At last, however, I have a respite, and I welcome this chance to share my inmost thoughts with you, my dear wife.

I am finding Europe a truly remarkable place to be in this new century. On the one hand, the state of manufacturing here – indeed, of many of the mechanick arts – is so far in advance of what our country can yet aspire to, that it is not to be believed. Yet I hasten to counter this glowing comment with the observation that the state of <u>manufacturers</u> – those wretches forced to make their living by these trades – is so deplorable as to nearly overthrow any benefit that might be attributed to Europe's more "advanced" production.

There are great changes coming here, Abigail. They are coming in the aftermath of the endless wars and turmoils which have shadowed this continent. I can see them in the eagerness with which even the most experienced businessmen greet my news and views – almost as if they were seeking fresh answers from our New World. I have received significant encouragement for my direct trade proposals. Better still, one mill owner – engaged in iron manufacturing himself – has invited me to make an assessment of his company, even to the extent of taking a hand in managing the firm for some period, so as to improve its production!

Would that the cautious proprietors of our Dover company could be schooled to think likewise. I am coming to believe it is a mistake to form a company of investors from country gentlemen and farmers. They simply do not have the <u>breadth</u> of vision to know that they must be daring. At least from this distance, they cannot squabble with me over every thought and every penny!

And it is here, I am sure, that I will find the resources that we need – our raw materials, our piece of the Atlantic trade. Indeed, I believe that, if I take what time is necessary, and am thorough in my investigation, I could bring offers home for more than just the Dover iron works. Imagine, Abigail: contracts negotiated for the nail works in Dedham as well, and Canton. Even firms farther afield – Pennsylvania, say, or Delaware. There is no limit to what might be arranged!

But, dear wife, this in turn brings me to dolorous news. In order that I may accomplish these great goals, we must remain parted for some time more. For, much as I would delight in having you by my side, I do not foresee having any settled dwelling place within the months to come. Certainly I cannot see you being dragged about the continent, inconvenienced every few weeks, without friends or the home I know means so much to you. Thus I believe it to be for the best, heartache tho' it must be for us both, for you to remain in Dover, close by what is near and dear to you, until such time as I may find a settled place here.

I have given careful thought, dear wife, to your welfare. I do not wish you to lack for anything in my absence. I have written this same day, instructing my attorney Mr. Jakes, to permit your signature on whatever legal papers may be needed to protect our assets and provide for your material wellbeing.

No one, my dear Penelope, knows my mind so well as you, and I am confident that you will understand the necessity of this painful arrangement. I shall sorely miss your loving companionship and your charming form. But when your wandering Ulysses is too brought down by lonely circumstances, he shall restore himself by thinking on your image. There you will be, sitting by the window in the parlor, as is your wont. Mr. Lyman's strange tree presides over the table at your side, and you are quietly sipping tea from one of the cups I brought you when we were first betrothed. A pleasing scene indeed, to carry me over many rough seas.

When at last I find a settled shore, be assured I shall send for you with all haste. Then you shall come to me again, and we shall travel the world together, beyond the confines of ordinary men.

Until then, you will ever be my Penelope and I,

Y' *most obed'* *& loving*
Colburn Whiting

Abby lowered the sheets of paper she had been holding up to the light. At first there were no thoughts at all in her head, just Colburn's voice echoing off the pages. Slowly she came back to her surroundings and saw herself, suddenly, as Colburn would see her. Sitting in the Jacobean chair, next to the window where the late spring light delayed the need for candles. Her pale blue gown fell in soft, ladylike folds around her feet. The teapot Anna had quietly brought in as Abby read sat untouched on the table beside her, and Colburn's prized *encre de chine* teabowl was empty and waiting.

She stared at the tea things for some time. Then her gaze moved to Mr. Lyman's orange tree silhouetted, graceful and green, at the window. Slowly a noise of blood beginning to pound in her ears blotted out the silence of the room. She began to tremble. Desperately she looked back to the last page of Colburn's letter. Looked to draw from it the reassurance her husband intended. The hope he seemed so sure of, that they would be together again. Instead, she found an image of herself frozen in time and space. Never to move, or love, never even to <u>be</u> except as he described her.

Suddenly Abby was desperate to leave this scene so perfectly like the one in Colburn's brain. She thrust his letter off her lap and nearly ran from the room, throwing open the door he had always insisted be closed. She stopped momentarily, wild-eyed, in the hall, trying frantically to think of where to go. What to do to escape the pressure threatening to burst her apart? Then she gathered up her skirt and ran up the stairs to her chamber. She jerked the bottom drawer out of the tall clothes chest and pushed aside shawls and petticoats as she searched.

There it was, thoroughly buried. From the very back of the drawer she drew out a bundle, wrapped in an old rag. What fell out were the brogans she had carefully packed away that day so long ago.

Shod and cloaked, Abby rushed out of the house and strode downhill toward the river. She had no idea where she was going. She knew she had to keep moving, walk, run even, go as fast as she could to escape what was up there on the hill, screaming from the pages on the parlor floor.

Abby was gone for a long time. The storm was finally over and nothing slowed her down except the streams of run-off in the cart ruts. She walked as far as the village center and back, avoiding people, skirting settlement wherever she could. She followed a wood road part way home, fording the storm-born brook that crossed it, welcoming the damp that soaked through even her brogans; turning her face up to showers of drops shaken loose from the trees overhead. Their cold wetness was a compress on her hot forehead. When she came in sight of the house again, she cut across a pasture and down to the riverbank path, still unable to face what waited inside.

It was dark when Abby finally came home. The desperate demons which chased her through the countryside were finally exhausted. Talkative, mothering Anna met her at the door, scolding and clucking at the same time. She took in the grim line of Abby's mouth, the stiff control which kept her wet shoulders from sagging, and she silently worried at the sadness which pooled in Abby's eyes.

"...near frantic with worry, Mistress Whiting. Where did you disappear to? You had no bad news, I trust, in that letter today? Look at you! What were you about out there in the wet and the dark?!"

Abby gave her no answers. She let Anna drag off her sodden cloak, and remove her soaked shoes. It was too much effort to do so herself. She soon sent the woman home for the night, however, firmly refusing repeated offers of hot broth and bed warmers. Anna went off down the hill, scowling and muttering to herself that the lady should not be alone so much, that any right-thinking husband would see to permanent companions for the poor soul. Or children. Children would be even better.

Abby, carefully avoiding the parlor, closed up the house for the night and went upstairs.

She got as far as the bedchamber door before the familiar nighttime routine broke down. The big four-poster bed seemed hung with memories. She stared across the room at it, watched the memories flare and shift in the candlelight.

Her marriage bed. Everything she knew about being a woman was there. Or so she had believed. About being with a man, feeling him warm beside you and hot within. With Colburn. So vibrant, vivid. She could almost feel his presence wrapped around her, cherishing her as he dreamed.

Dreams. All dreams. So vivid they rushed ahead and left reality behind. Abby sadly shook her head. When did Colburn lose sight of what truly existed in the glare of dream light? When did he lose sight of her in a fantasy wife eternally weaving a web of dream?

She shook her head again and frowned in concentration. No. When did she lose sight of herself? She'd been swept away on a cloud of love and dream. Four years believing she could be – wanted to be – what Colburn wanted for her, and for them. Pioneers of the new Republic. New ideas, new status, even new fashion. She glanced down at her wet and mud-splashed skirt and grimaced. Too tired to stand there any longer. But too awake to lie in that bed and wrestle with thoughts that wouldn't go away.

Abby sighed and turned away from the door. Slowly she walked to her room across the hall and lit another candle from the one in her hand. Then she set both down at her writing desk and drew up a chair. The room was very dark around the flickering light.

The pages of her open journal were blank. She had avoided them for weeks now. They were empty of words like her mind, suddenly, which had just been so full. Words had tumbled madly around in her head since she'd read Colburn's letter, those thousands of hours ago. Her husband's words: his confident assurances, his defiant explanations, his assumptions about her and her future. Her own words: panicked denials, questions screamed in desperation, plaintive cries which would never reach a husband so far away.

She roused herself and sighed. It was time now to think clearly. She had lived long enough by Colburn Whiting's thoughts. Now she must work this out on her own.

Apr the 28th, 1800 – Today I received at long last a letter from my husband, assuring me that he is well and safe abroad. He wrote of many other things also, of such a serious nature as to give me pause and disturb me profoundly concerning what is to come in the future – for our marriage and for me. Let me try to compose my thoughts on these matters with such order as will lead me to understand what course I must take from here on.

First off, I believe wholeheartedly that my husband had no intent to damage the interests of those proprietors whom he has represented so capably over the past four years. I am confident of his innocence of any but the most minor wrongdoing. By this latter I refer only to his unfortunate tendency to paint every picture in the brightest hues, so that those who did not know him well might be misled into thinking there were no concerns which needed attending.

This outlook of Colburn's is both one of his most attractive features and the source of his undoing, I think. It is what drew me to him from our first meeting, that summer day so long ago. He is a man of strong purpose and resolve, with a vision of progressive improvement for the world and mankind. He is willing to dare all and in his daring, sweeps all before him.

But I do confess that I sense in him, too, in his essential character, a terrible flaw. I can no longer overlook this flaw as I have done – have, I admit, chosen to do – as it has changed my behavior, nay, my very life, so profoundly as to make me a stranger to myself. How to put a name to it?

This afternoon, when I had read his letter, memorized its contents beyond what I would wish, I walked for miles about the countryside. I do not know what drove me, whether I sought more to flee from the dark thoughts which assailed me, or searched for some new and clearer-headed path to take.

In any event, at last I found myself on the bridge which crosses below the milldam. To one side, water splashed out the tailrace, roiled up because of the storm just past. But over the dam itself, where it stretches across the river, the water flowed dark and smooth, and the force of it curved the flow over the wall like a billow of black satin. I watched the stream for untold time, mesmerized, I think, by the sound and the deceptive, nearly solid look of it. It wholly disguised the sharp fall of the downstream side of the dam.

After some minutes a pair of mallards rounded the turn above the dam and moved into the shallows opposite the mill. They foraged for supper in the pond weed swept downstream by the rain. The drake kept edging ever farther out into the stream, balancing on the very lip of the dam, boldly stretching out his neck to grasp at one more, and yet another, tiny bit of weed. The duck followed dutiful behind. I fancied that she dreaded every step, knowing full well the weed ashore was just as sweet as that desired by her mate, and ten times less dangerous, to boot! Why do they risk so much for a morsel of green? I thought. They do not conceive how close they come to destruction.

Strange, is it not, how we can see clearly the traps and follies that beset others, yet be so blind to our own occasions? That drake turned not one glance toward his mate as he searched for the prize. And the duck apparently never thought of staying where she was, to feed.

So has it been with Colburn and me. But I am certainly not the prize he searches for. And I truly believe that he, like the drake on the dam, is so caught up in his own great adventure that he can be no help to me.

I find I must thank God for many unexpected things. I was not born a mallard, nor must I follow my mate.

How this realization may work itself out tomorrow, and in the days to come, is not to be conceived tonight. I dread that the outcome may be more painful than I would choose to bear. But this marriage is not a marriage. In my spouse's idyllic imagining, Penelope may forever weave a life about Ulysses, but Colburn and Abigail can no longer be.

Abby laid down her pen and bleakly stared. Then she closed the book, as if to trap inside the burden of what she had just written. Pushing back her chair she rose, snuffing one candle as she picked up the other to light her way. She crossed the hall and set the taper down beside the bed from which the memories were briefly banished by exhaustion. Ignoring her daytime clothes and mud-stained stockings, she crept under the heavy coverlet and slept.

It took two weeks for Abby to work out her plans. When she had, she drove the trap over to Mill Farm, timing her arrival to coincide with the noonday meal, for Luther was in the middle of plowing, and would be hard to catch otherwise. As she turned into the barnyard she marveled again at the irony of this house so closely resembling her own, the house that Colburn had built.

Then the children tumbled out the door, yelling for Aunt Nabby. She arranged a pleasant facade on her thoughts and was swept up in greetings and news of teeth lost and frogs found. Lucy watched the commotion from the doorstep as she dried her hands on her apron. Eventually she shooed the children away and gave Abby a hug and a warm welcome.

"But I warn you ahead that all is in disarray within!" she said with laughing chagrin. "I cannot seem to get the gist of juggling babies and dinner and springtime mud all at once."

"Oh, Lucy! Don't tell me the last girl you hired didn't work out?"

"Work out? She was a delight, Abigail. But she's off to Salem and the big world. Family connections, I gather: she found a place in one of the grand merchant's houses up there – and well you may believe Mill Farm offers little to compare with *that* grandeur!"

Abby's facade cracked slightly and she spoke with vehemence. "I do *not* believe so, Lucy, not at all!" Then she recovered her aplomb and went on. "But truly, you have had such trouble keeping help."

Lucy shrugged.

"It's always something, isn't it? The young ones get married, the older have ailing relatives to tend." She gave a tired little smile. "No one ever succeeded in taking your place, Abby. But then you know that. Come inside and we'll set another place."

When dinner was cleared and the children banished, the adults remained in the elegant small dining room, talking over a cup of tea. Luther delayed his return to the south planting field for a bit, in consideration of his sister's visit. This was the moment Abby had planned for, and she started in to speak her piece before she lost her nerve.

"Luther. Lucy." She began hesitantly. "I've come here with something very important to say." She paused between each thought. "I am leaving Colburn Whiting."

The Chapmans' response was shocked. Abigail was too steady-natured for this to be some momentary whim. Lucy uttered a sympathetic exclamation. Luther was instantly indignant.

"What has he done to you? When did this happen?"

Abby held up a hand.

"Stop, Luther! Please let me explain before you work yourself up to false conclusions. Colburn has done nothing. Not in the way you mean. To the best of my knowledge he has broken no legal marriage vow. I know of no other woman. He has not beaten me."

She paused and, in the puzzled silence, the sigh she let out seemed to fill the room.

"He would be hard-put to beat me, even if he wanted to, so rarely does he come within arm's distance. And this is the crux of my complaint." She shook her head and looked from one to the other of her family. "I find it difficult to explain, even to myself, why I must take matters into my own hands. Lucy, I know you've had some inkling of my unhappiness. Luther though, I do not know if I can begin to convey to you how untenable my marriage is. I am almost afraid to try."

Luther's scowl softened as he met his sister's pleading brown eyes. He nodded.

"I'm listening."

So Abby told him and Lucy about her husband's increasingly frequent absences. She tried to explain how he could be absent even when he was present, distracted by the mill to such an extent that she might as well not be there. Last, she described Colburn's latest plan, full of enthusiasm and no place for her. Her New England upbringing got her through the telling: a lifetime of self-control and contained emotions laid out the saga of four years' disappointment and disillusion with only hints of the despair that Abby worked so hard to hide. A bit of it crept out as she ended her tale, driven by the urgency of convincing her brother.

"You must think I am a dithering female, Luther, to carry on at something which so many wives expect. Wives of soldiers and whaling men suffer through long months without their mates. But Luther, I have come to learn that I cannot be like them."

She stirred uncomfortably and gave a short laugh. "In one way I am fortunate. I do not need a husband in name only. I have Father to thank, financially, for that. Emotionally," Abigail stopped to touch her brother's hand, "I have all of you. For whatever reason, the Lord has seen fit to deny our union children." She could not keep a hint of bitterness out of her voice. "And there is small chance that may change, with a husband who finds his dreams more alluring than his wife. But I cannot bear a life without family and work to summon me from bed in the morning. I cannot survive on the faint hope of love."

Luther had been frowning at his teacup as Abigail spoke. When her words stopped he glanced up and briefly met her gaze. A worried "Hmmph" expressed both his attention and his sympathy. He had no idea what he might say to stop his little sister's pain. While Luther was still at a loss, Lucy stepped in decisively.

"Abigail, you cannot stay with that man! In all the years I've known you, I've never seen you so overwrought. Truly this is insufferable! Have you thought what is to be done?"

Abby sent her sister-in-law a grateful look, then turned again to Luther. It was he, she knew, who must be convinced of the next step.

"I did not come here to burden you with a melodramatic tale of woman scorned. I am really here, Luther, to ask that you let me return to Mill Farm."

"You can come anytime, Abby. You know that."

"No, that's not what I mean. I am quite sincere about the marriage being over, despite the lack of grounds for legal separation, did I even wish to pursue that route. I am asking to *live* here. For good."

Lucy's quick exclamation was clearly one of delight. Luther's reaction was not so easily read. He studied her soberly as he thought.

"I would not be coming empty-handed, you know," Abby argued. "I have just made arrangements with my husband's attorney to sell the Dover house."

"You think you'll get his consent to such a thing? He prizes that house."

"Ah, but Luther, you forget that Father insisted it be put in my name." The trace of smile on Abby's face was bitter. "It seems he did have some grounds for wanting to protect my welfare, if for all the wrong reasons."

Luther snorted. Remembering his father's stand on Colburn Whiting made it easier for him to know where to place the blame.

"No wrong reasons I see. Father used to go on about Whiting's close-set eyes. Saying that he'd always look to his own best interests, and everybody else be damned. Never thought to see my own family bear the brunt of that man's selfishness though. Should be a way to haul him up before a judge for what he's done to you!"

Abby stopped him abruptly.

"No! Luther, don't say another word. Whatever has passed between my husband and myself, I will not have you – or anyone else – seeking ways to malign him. He is a man of many good parts. If being a husband is not one of them, I will not have that serve as cause for finding fault with all that he does so well. In fact," she ended adamantly, "I would prefer not to speak of Mr. Whiting at all, unless absolutely necessary, and insist you respect my wishes in this."

Luther shrugged in obvious frustration at having to abandon his defense of his sister. Abby returned to her immediate concern.

"Now, I ask you again if I might come back to Mill Farm?"

"We would never turn you out, Abigail. You know that. But where would you stay? You're used to a whole lot better than sharing a bed with Sybil. There's not a whole lot of room in this new place, despite the fancy exterior." Luther shook his head, muttering. "Pity there's nothing left of the old house."

Abby was relieved to see the discussion turn to practical matters. Here, at least, she knew she could be persuasive.

"I have given some thought to this, Luther and you're right. I have become spoiled in a number of ways the past four years. But you forget: there should be a substantial sum coming to me from the house sale, even with debts to pay." She spoke with assurance, then paused to see if Luther saw where she was leading.

He did not. Instead he bristled.

"We don't need your money, Abigail! We need space! And besides," he went on with defensive belligerence, "What is there on Mill Farm for you? You know what your life would be like here, how hard it is. I thought that was half the reason you headed off with that man in the first place?"

"Luther!" Lucy quietly remonstrated.

But Abby put a restraining hand on her arm and answered the question.

"It was, you're right. But I've learned a number of things over the past few years, Luther. I've learned that our brave new society offers women few choices in life. I've learned that I'm lonely. And that there is nothing for me in Dover."

She drew herself upright and set her hands together in her lap. This was her last chance, the only offer she had left, to convince Luther and salvage what she could of her life.

"I am here with a simple business proposition. I am willing to take up my old role again in this family: spinster aunt, household domestic. I know Lucy needs the help."

Lucy sent her a grateful but dubious smile.

"You both know you'll get more than your money's worth of work from me. But in exchange I have three stipulations."

Abby caught the narrowing of Luther's eyes as he adjusted to thinking in terms of bargaining.

"First, I will give you the money to put an ell on this house – a full two stories."

Luther's eyebrows went up.

"And that ell will have all the elements I've missed ever since leaving the homestead. I have thought very carefully about this, you know." Abby ticked off specifications on her fingers. "It must have windows on the south side to bring in the sun. And opposite, on the north side, a porch for summer afternoons." She glanced at Lucy. "You could move the kitchen into the first floor room if you like, or make it a dairy room. But upstairs – upstairs I wish for a chamber of my own."

She sat back in her chair as she finished, an expression of calm determination on her face as she waited for their response.

Luther snorted good-naturedly.

"Don't I seem to remember you going on about my having high-faluting ideas about this place, Sister? Seems like you want to add another whole house to this one, by the sound of it."

Abby smiled in recognition of the fact that he was teasing. "I like to think of it as adding a branch of a house, Brother, like adding my branch of the family to yours."

"Would you really come back to us, Nabby?" Lucy asked hopefully. "You would be such a wonderful addition – yourself, I mean, not the ell, though that is nothing to sneeze at!"

"It would be no more than taking you up on your own offer, Lucy dear. You remember? You said there was a place for me here?"

"I meant that, you know perfectly well, Abigail. *We* meant that. Is that not so Luther?" She turned to her husband for agreement.

He nodded with growing assurance. "Of course it's true. Though she might be going overboard a bit with her notion of homecoming presents."

The mood of the three had lightened, and they jokingly began to imagine the elaborate trimmings with which they could gussy up an addition. Abby interrupted, voice sparkling with relief.

"But wait, there's more! I told you I had three stipulations. I am asking that you let me set out planting beds about the house. You know I have been doing so in Dover and find I have some handiness at it. They would be with your approval of course, Lucy. The children shall help, too. A new kitchen garden first," Abby gestured as she elaborated. "Imagine a grape arbor by the stone wall. I have lilacs I could bring with me! Roses!"

Lucy giggled at Abby's enthusiasm.

"And shall you turn all our children into horticulturists, too, like your Mr. Lyman?"

Her question stopped Abigail for a moment, and she turned to Luther with some seriousness.

"The last favor I ask is that you agree to let me put the head-of-the-pond pasture to different use. I shall, of course, pay you for the property."

"Now what on earth do you think you need a pasture for?"

"Not a pasture, Luther. An orchard. My 'friend Mr. Lyman,' as Lucy calls him, was kind enough to give me excellent graftings of some apple strains he is developing. I have been experimenting with others on my own. In time, we shall know which to save and propagate, until the whole orchard is full." Her voice radiated new confidence as she explained her plan.

"One thing my husband did teach me was to look to the future. I am quite certain there will always be a demand for apples – and for cider – which is more likely to grow than to diminish in the years to come. I think of an orchard as my way of looking ahead."

Luther shook his head again. He found himself doing that a lot today. This time it was in surprise at his sister's business sense.

"Why are you doing all this, Abby?" he asked admiringly.

Her answer came slowly, as if she were thinking aloud about a part of her soul she'd always kept hidden.

"You run Chapman's mill – two mills, now – and the farm, Luther. Lucy, you raise the children you two have made. Both of you are bettering things. Creating. Building. I will not have children of my own, I know, or build a mill. But I need to create as well, as every person does. I need to know that my life was good for something more than baking bread. You might think of those trees as...well," she shrugged in embarrassed admission, "my heritage. My own bit of earthly immortality."

Lucy, ever one to be easily moved, went to Abby's side and knelt to wrap her in a tear-splashed hug. Luther nodded his head in silent understanding.

The scene of Abby's removal to Medfield resembled nothing so much as some pagan triumph over the dirt road through Dover. In the three months it had taken to put up the ell Abby had packed up her belongings, carefully leaving out those things which were Colburn's portion, selling others for which she saw no use. Still, there was quite a bit left. Luther brought his farm cart to carry her possessions from Needham, and Abigail had hired another large wagon on her own.

Back at Mill Farm, Lucy set the younger children to watch for their arrival and, at their excited shouts, she ran out to the bend by the old cellarhole, to greet the procession. The road stretching west from there was surprisingly busy. Neighbors, even townspeople from farther away, had come out or up from the fields in an impromptu welcome. Lucy watched the wagons draw closer, past the clustered gossips and well-wishers along the road.

Luther's cart led the way: a heavy, two-wheeled conveyance stacked high with trunks and barrels, furniture and carpets. The cart carried an impressive number of things, it seemed to Lucy, and she was thankful that the new ell had been completed on schedule, for surely they would not have room for such an embarrassment of possessions otherwise.

Then her attention turned to the second wagon, moving slowly behind Luther, drawn by two plodding oxen. The sides of the wagon were nearly hidden by foliage spilling over the edge. Young trees, carefully balled and tied, waved in a mass of branches behind, and late-blooming lilies filled one corner with orange.

Sitting straight beside the driver was Abigail, dressed in one of her most fashionable Boston costumes. She acknowledged the waves and greetings of curious neighbors and acquaintances with a slight smile and a brief bow of her head. Much of the time she was still, looking neither to right or left but gazing at some scene ahead which only she could see. The women all agreed Abigail looked terribly sad. Such a pitiful look in those great dark eyes. The men silently admired the girl's gumption, sitting up there in plain sight, facing down the rumors like she'd picked her own fate.

By the end of the week, life at Mill Farm was beginning to settle into its new routine. Abby was out back, supervising the older children as they stripped long strings of scented bark from a pile of cedar logs soon to become an arbor for Mr. Lyman's grapes. Luther stepped down from the recently completed back porch and came over. Giving Thomas a hand with a particularly stubborn strip, he spoke to Abby.

"Going to borrow the boys away from you for a while this afternoon."

"Oh? What are you up to?"

"It's past time to fill in the old cellarhole. Been meaning to do it for months now but something always seems to come first. Almost lost my best rooster in there last week – fool bird wandered into the brush we'd tossed down there and got himself all tangled up. George had to crawl in and drag him out – crowing and pecking all the way. Just be a matter of time before some other fool animal gets stuck."

Abby nodded emphatically. "Or baby, I'd warrant. I noticed little Sybil was trying her best to clamber over the stone wall in that direction yesterday."

"Hmmph." Sybil was Luther's pet. "Past time. Anyway, I need the boys to help with clearing a mess of old gear out of the barn. I've set the men to breaking up the last of the timbers and such from the house." Luther was thinking out loud. "We'll pile it all in, maybe the top course or two of the cellar wall. Guess we'll haul up some of the muck from the dredging piles by the dam to top it off." He recalled himself to his present purpose. "Don't suppose you've got any cleaning out left to do, do you?"

Abby looked at her brother strangely for a moment in silence. Then she nodded in decision.

"As a matter of fact, yes. Why I brought along some of the things I did is a mystery. I'll add a few bits to your treasure trove."

Later that afternoon Abby made her way across the road to the cellarhole of the house where she had been born. Her apron skirt was gathered around a small bundle and there was a set expression on her face.

The small rectangular space was already filling up with trash and brush. Tom and George crookedly rolled a derelict barrel across the yard and, as Abby watched, they reached the edge of the pit. With one last shove and a yell, they toppled the barrel in. Staves and hoops jarred loose as it landed hard against a pile of broken bricks from the chimney. The men joined in a chorus of laughing cheers at their success.

"Come on, Aunt Nabby, now it's your turn," George encouraged her. "Make a big crash!"

Abby smiled at him and began to enter into the spirit of the moment.

"Oh, I'm not sure there's enough here to be good and loud. But here it goes!"

She stepped to the top of the stone stairs leading down and grasped the edges of her apron, intending to fling its contents into the pit. A fold of cloth impeded the action, however, and only a few objects made it to the bottom. Among them, a small booklet fluttered open on its face, its brown paper cover blending in with the leaves and brush already lying there. The rest of the contents fell only a few feet away from where she was standing, onto the stone steps. Those made a satisfying crash, and the boys cheered again at her success.

Abby took one last look at the uselessly exotic tea cups, nodded her head with finality, and walked away.

LAYER III: BOTTOMING OUT

At some point in every test pit and excavation square, there is an end to cultural deposits. Sterile subsoil is exposed, in a process casually known as 'bottoming out.' The investigator has removed all the evidence of human activity in that particular location.
— Dr. Nora Tunney, **An Archeologist's Handbook**

July 17, 1995

During the week following Hank's career revelation, Nora managed to lose herself in site work. Monday morning was difficult: she found herself studying every crew member. *Did you know he destroys old buildings for a living?* Sometimes she already knew the answer. Jane Ogden and Peg dug as industriously as ever, but Nora eyed them in disbelief. *Why didn't you tell me!* When Ralph Whiting drove up she almost confronted him with her accusation, but a remnant of common sense kept her quiet. It wasn't as if the crew had done anything wrong, after all.

As she tried to control her frustration, however, Nora became increasingly impatient with the friendly, slow-paced routine the crew had established over the past month. Pam and a new girl, Marilyn, talked too much. Andrew was so slow he would never finish his first square. Ralph's frequent rest stops were a white-haired excuse for laziness. Nothing was getting done. Nothing was being accomplished.

Rather than say something she couldn't take back, Nora finally grabbed a trowel and dustpan and stepped over the grid line into a deserted square. It had been worked reluctantly by Levalliere Junior, who hadn't found sweat and dirt half as appealing as his brother did. Senior continued to dig and photograph with equal intensity, but everyone had been relieved when Junior was hustled off to a more distant vacation. Given the snail's pace everyone was working, however, the other crew members might never get to Junior's square, and Nora felt a driving need for accomplishment before the Commission's next meeting. They only had a week and a half.

Nora had done very little digging during the summer, choosing instead to keep moving around the site, helping to pick through a screen load of pebbles and artifacts, identifying a shard just uncovered, making a comment on someone's technique. At first, the job of field director had called for constant crisis-prevention as the novices were broken in. But she had to admit they were learning. They had caught on to the delicate work of removing dirt an inch at a time, of double-checking the sifting screen to rescue rusty nails that looked like roots, of remembering to record before they forgot. Finally now, halfway through the season, Nora found she had some leeway that hadn't existed earlier. She welcomed the chance to escape her frantic thoughts in an old, measured routine. She crouched down in the abandoned square and the crew's comments began.

"Hey Nora, you joining the field school?"

"Nah, she'd taking an in-service day. You know, to keep her certificate up to date?"

She shook her head and grinned half-heartedly.

Ralph Whiting peered over his spectacles. "Perhaps we have a demonstration in store."

Peg Wentworth chuckled. "My guess is, she knows there's something good in that square. Isn't that true, Nora?"

Forced to respond, she shrugged. "Just want to keep my hand in, I guess. So let's see if we can keep out of trouble for a while, hmm?" She tugged the brim of her baseball cap lower and set to work.

Over the next few days the dig worked its familiar magic on her. There was a pattern to it that closed out outside thoughts, like a mental scanner tuned to a narrow band, constantly roaming back and forth, seeking connections, listening for telltale sounds that signaled a find. The rhythmic shuffle of stones across a sifting screen. Stones and artifacts. Brick chunks and coal clinkers, fragments of pots and the higher-pitched clink of a sharp shard of glass. The regular scrape of trowel across dirt, then a metallic ring as it struck intrusive stone. Nearby, a decisive whir as measuring tape snapped back into its holder. All layered on top of cicada whine and occasional whoosh of passing cars.

There were some interruptions, fewer toward the day's end than in the cool of morning. A cough. The thump of pebbles falling into the screened dirt pile, a camera's clicking shutter. Voices too, but not often. Energy was conserved to maintain the rhythm of work and combat fatigue as the day wore on and the heat rose.

"That's it?"

"Yup. The end of Level 2."

"We going any deeper?"

"I'm not sure. Check with the boss."

Nora would stand up slowly, unbending her knees and refocusing her eyes on a flat square of dirt across the cellarhole.

"You still finding artifacts?"

"Oh yeah," Doug answered. "We came up with a whole bunch of nails in that last sifter load. You think we found a wall or something?"

Ralph sat back and pushed up his spectacles. "I'd guess someone dropped a bag while he was working. I've done it myself."

"We ought to be able to tell whether they were used or not," Nora observed. "Don't forget to look for use wear when you get to them in the lab."

The nails were an excuse for a social intermission in the day's routine. Everyone stopped for a water break, stretched sore muscles. It served to restore the bonds of excitement and purpose that tied the dusty crew together. Then the crew dispersed back to their assigned tasks. The sifter's rocky shuffle set a rhythm again as work proceeded in companionable silence.

Below the level of the two *encre de chine* tea bowls, the Chapman cellarhole proved to be a time capsule of two-hundred-year-old activity. The bowls were only the beginning of a delightful assortment of broken tools, building remnants and other rejects which, as artifacts, became imbued with a significance they never had in life. It was fortunate the tea bowls had turned up, because they were among the few solidly datable artifacts that were appearing. The crew was finding lots of redware storage jars and milk pans whose shapes didn't change over two centuries. They found a heap of broken window glass.

"Look! This one's cut at a sharp angle. You think it's a diamond window pane?"

"Nah. It's just broken that way."

"It could be, though. Look how wavy the glass is."

The glass was passed back and forth, spit-polished and examined. It was definitely old, but had it come from a seventeenth-century diamond-paned casement? Maybe yes, maybe no. No thin strips of leading appeared as confirmation.

Where is the seventeenth century? An annoying whisper interrupted Nora's concentration.

"One thing's for certain," she said aloud, as much to encourage herself as the others, "somebody was certainly renovating something. You've discovered that much."

Following the nail discussion, Doug's next puzzle was a crumbling white heap that took up the middle of his square. Small strips of rotting wood. Bits of brick. Finally whole bricks, some with mortar still attached, some with blackened signs of burning. Had the house burned down? The Site Speculation Quotient soared. Had the Chapmans many years ago been forced out in the middle of some cold winter night, rushed frantically to the pond for leather buckets-full of water? Peg, whose knowledge of local conditions informed her imagining, wondered if instead, they had watched, helpless as the fire raged, because the pond ice was so thick there *was* no water.

Each successive discovery fueled the crew's speculation. The melodrama was the focus of lunchtime discussion and as usual, Nora played devil's advocate.

"I think you may be getting carried away with all this imagining."

"Nonsense, Nora." Jane Ogden's enthusiasm was audible even through her egg salad. "It's fun to make up history sometimes."

Pam took the whole discussion more seriously. "At least doing this makes me feel closer to the people whose things we're digging up."

Andrew snorted and crushed his soda can. "You mean whose trash we're pawing through, don't you?" Pam slanted a disapproving glance in Andrew's direction, but Nora was amused by his iconoclasm, which did nothing to hide his passion for archeology.

By the end of the week, reality won. Doug had uncovered enough wood and brick and "white stuff" to recognize the remains of a chimneypiece. The bricks lay tumbled into the cellarhole, roughly in a line, and they were interspersed with wood lath and disintegrating horsehair plaster – the white stuff – which had once faced the fireplace wall. On close inspection the crew admitted there was not much sign of burning after all, other than what you'd expect on well-used bricks. They reluctantly adjusted their fantasy to envision a few strong men with sledgehammers and a solid old horse, working together to pull the chimney down, to tumble it into the hole with all that remained of the house itself.

"You know," Nora mused, pushing her cap back, "I think the lack of melodrama here may be one of this site's greatest assets."

"Oh, c'mon Nora. Where's the fun without some excitement?" Marilyn Faxon, one of the later high school additions to the crew, was a proponent of frequent, if not constant, excitement.

Nora glanced around the crew and noticed a lot of nods at Marilyn's words. Much as she hated the interruption, she decided it was time to emerge from her shell long enough to put the work in perspective. She climbed out of her square and brushed powdery dirt off her knees.

"All right. Maybe we need to talk about this. Can I have everybody's attention for a minute please?"

Younger crew members sat back on their haunches while some of the Commission took the opportunity to sit and stretch their legs. Marilyn's eyebrow rings drew together in a worried frown as she wondered if she'd gone too far. The boss lady was known to have very definite ideas about things.

"If you think about what we've found so far, it all fits together really beautifully. The stuff from the recent past on top, like aluminum foil and acorn caps. Then the early twentieth-century lost-and-found mixed into the upper layers." Her hands unconsciously sketched the levels as she talked. "The blue bunny, for instance, and the doll dish." There were nods of understanding. "And now, since Pam and Ralph found the tea bowls, we've been digging up a real time capsule. The chimney bricks and the fact that building materials are all mixed up with domestic trash is good solid proof that this cellarhole was filled intentionally."

Nora's voice lost its impatience as she contemplated their incredible luck.

"I've got to tell you, time capsules like this are really rare. Especially in the country. Oh, people have dug urban privy pits that had been sealed up. Wells are famous for holding treasures from some period or other. But a whole layer in a cellar hole. This is incredible!"

Andrew, picking up his self-assigned role as skeptic, stopped Nora's rush of enthusiasm. "I don't see how this is such a treasure. I mean, it's cool and all, but so what?"

Nora looked around the site silently, pulling its strands together. When she spoke again, her voice was reasoning, and patient.

"Let's see if I can explain. Because the infilling here was intentional, because the Chapman family went out and found trash to take up all that space, the artifacts we are recovering in this layer constitute a carefully selected sample of what a farm family decided was 'disposable' around the year 1800."

Andrew was frowning in concentration. He shrugged that he still didn't understand and Nora went on.

"Take all the lead-glazed redware you're coming up with. What kind of dishes are they?"

"Pots, mostly. Milk pans."

"Pickling crocks," Pam stuck in.

Nora nodded. "And almost every piece has a scabbed interior where the glaze has flaked off, right? That is proof right out of the ground that a farm wife by 1800 already knew lead glaze could be poisonous in contact with acids. We haven't found any stoneware crocks, have we? But some of the lead-glazed ones are *whole*. No right-thinking housewife would throw those away without good reason. And fear of poisoning is a pretty good reason."

"So you're saying we can learn about their thinking from their trash?" Andrew's voice still held a tinge of disbelief.

"Absolutely. You have to consider what we do find, and you also have to ask yourself what we're *not* finding, and by the time you're finished you should have a pretty good idea of what was important in these people's lives."

"But Nora," Peg Wentworth drew her attention. "That can't explain the tea bowls, can it? I mean, one didn't have even a chip missing."

"You tell me why else they're here then?" Nora asked, her tone flippant. She was playing devil's advocate again, enjoying the challenge of thinking through a puzzle.

"*Surely* they're not just trash!" Jane Ogden sounded personally offended by the idea.

"Remember the blue bunny, too," Pam put in. "He seems to have just gotten lost."

A derisive snort came from Andrew. "Yeah, but that's completely different. A grown-up doesn't just 'lose' two perfectly good tea cups on the cellar stairs, nowhere near where they would have been stored."

Nora had kept silent through this last exchange, struggling with the uncomfortable realization that she had been jumping to conclusions about just how tidy their time capsule was. Andrew was right. There was no obvious explanation for those tea bowls being thrown away.

I don't have an answer. She strained to hang on to the optimism that had fueled her impromptu lecture.

"Anomalies." The word burst out of her. "Every archeological site has its anomalies. You know, the single item that doesn't belong? That has no logical explanation? Like the nineteenth-century deposit that has one broken arrow head in it? I think, for the moment at least, we need to assign the tea bowls to the 'anomalous' category."

Her voice was confident, bringing nods and words of agreement from the crew, signs of relief at finding an official archeological context for the puzzle piece that didn't fit. There was a general move to return to work. Lecture time was over. Nora pulled her digging gloves back on as she discussed next steps with Ralph and Doug, but her mind wasn't finished yet.

Unfortunately that's not an answer that satisfies me. Got to keep going. Find out what's below this layer. Maybe there are answers here I haven't even considered. A glimpse of Hank superimposed itself on her thoughts and she frowned at the reminder of her immediate challenge. *Find the seventeenth century.* The blade of her trowel sank deeper in the soil than it should.

315

The end of July came with frightening inevitability. Nora rang the bell at Ralph Whiting's door and caught a wistful glimpse of the last time she had been there. She'd been so confident. The plot plan of Mill Farm, her show-and-tell bag, her conviction she could talk Majors around. It had been very hot then, she remembered, and she'd worried about what to wear. At least that didn't seem like an issue anymore. She grimaced, glancing down at her jeans and sandals, thinking about how much more was at stake now.

Last time her heartbeat had quickened over the thought of seeing Hank Chapman again. Tonight she already knew he was here. The ambulance loomed incongruously in the driveway. But she wasn't in a hurry to see him again. Fifteen times, at least, in the past two weeks she'd thought of calling him. Maybe things weren't as bad as she'd imagined? Maybe something she could say would make a difference in … what? His profession? His beliefs?

Other times she'd gone as far as pulling out paper to write a note. Maybe she'd overreacted. He really was a nice guy. A guy who'd had too much of family responsibility. She should admire him for finding his own way of making peace with the past. The orchard, the restoration business. 'Bringing it back to life.' Wasn't that what he'd said? Of course she didn't believe you could bring things *back* to life. You gave things a whole *new* life, maybe, a twentieth-century life, but that wasn't the same, was it? By the time she'd thought that far she had put the paper away again and gone back to staring at nothing.

He certainly hadn't contacted her in the past eleven days.

Between moments of confusion over Hank and hours of intense work at the site, there had still been a lot of time to think about this meeting. Nora had weighed a lot of options. She had invented and rejected any number of plans to convince the Commission to see things her way. But in the end, as far as she could see, it all boiled down to a single choice. The Commission could see the light and choose to limit work at the mill to careful stabilization, thus freeing money for completion of archeological work at Mill Farm. Or they could follow George Majors' lead, opting for the fancy restoration Hank was promoting. If they did that, sure as sunset, there would be no further talk of a second season's dig. Nora could pack up her bags and go away. The choice was clear, but she was desperately worried she wouldn't be able to talk those members around who didn't already agree with her. The other problem was, she wasn't a hundred per cent sure which side most of them were on.

Ralph's warm greeting as he opened the door was lost on her. She was trying to gauge where his sympathies lay. Nora automatically followed him down the carpeted hallway into the dining room, vaguely absorbing his comment about the chill that had come with the weather front. Even so, she sat near the one open window, already feeling the sweat that she knew would get worse as the evening wore on.

Hank's were the first eyes hers met. He was stretched out in his slouch position despite the upright cherry chair and he was looking intently at her, while making some semblance of listening to Jane Ogden. Nora thought his expression was meant to be friendly, given the tentative smile he bent her way. She nodded coolly, wondering what new, unpleasant surprise he might be about to spring.

Nora tried next to read Jane Ogden, whose enthusiasm for fieldwork this past month might well have swayed her to the side of archeology, but the woman was concentrating on pouring a glass of water. In the background Ralph Whiting apologized for the lack of refreshments, due to his wife's being off visiting. Nora remembered with some bitterness the chairman's skill at sidestepping responsibility when he chose to do so, and her hope of his support began to sink. Of those at the table, only Peg Wentworth was a sure ally. The gray-haired historian had made her opinion clear from the start. Nothing should get in the way of archeology, whether anything was ever done to the mill or not. Tonight it looked as though Peg had come armed for battle. She was urgently tapping a pencil against the notepad in front of her and there was no knitting in sight.

Nora was greeting her one staunch supporter when it dawned on her that George Majors was missing. Could he possibly not be coming tonight? Last time discussion had been tabled because financial decisions required a full board vote. If Majors was absent, she had just won another chance. Her mind leaped ahead. By this time next month, who knew what miracles she might perform? What unexpected proof she might uncover? For the first time in days she felt a glimmer of hope that, despite every appearance to the contrary, she might be able to stay after all. And if she stayed, she might talk them out of restoration.

The doorbell's chime put an end to wishful thinking. As Nora set the last of her papers on the table Majors strode into the room in front of Whiting, his expression all business. He immediately confronted Nora.

"So, have you gotten to the seventeenth century yet?"

She almost laughed, a nervous giggle brought on by Majors' frontal attack as much as by his question. She controlled the urge but her reply was still cocky.

"Not quite, Mr. Majors. We've been having a good time along the way, though, as I'm sure you'll hear from a number of people tonight."

He eyed her flippant remark coldly and took his favored seat at one end of the table. Hank's eyebrows had risen at Majors' peremptory tone, but otherwise his position did not change. Ralph Whiting pulled a chair up to the other end and set both hands on the table top.

"Well! We have a lot to talk about tonight. A great deal has gone on at the site, as Nora mentioned, since our last meeting. We also need to spend some time this evening looking ahead, deciding the course the Mill Farm Project should take after this summer's discoveries. With that in mind, I'd like to suggest we just accept the secretary's report and move on, unless there is any objection?"

"So moved," said Majors, barely glancing at the page before him.

"All those in favor?"

Whiting proceeded with other administrative details as Nora's concern grew. Majors was being particularly brusque tonight, even for him. If he had decided he was in a hurry, he was not going to have an open mind to anything she had to say. And if he voted against her, he'd drag at least one member – Jane Ogden – with him.

"Next on the agenda," Whiting's voice cut into Nora's growing pessimism, "I think we would all like to hear Nora's perspective on the field work to date. I must say, Dr. Tunney, working at the site this month has been a wonderful experience for me. I have a whole new respect for the challenges you archeologists face every day. To say nothing about knowing a whole lot more about ceramics!"

Ralph smiled at her benevolently and Nora sent him silent thanks for his upbeat introduction. She realized Peg and Jane Ogden were also making enthusiastic comments. It was unexpectedly heartening to think the outcome of tonight's vote might not be a foregone conclusion.

"Thank you, Ralph. This has been an exciting month for Mill Farm, I think you'll agree. But first we need to explain to Mr. Majors, and to Mr. Chapman," — it sounded strange to refer so formally to Hank – "what it is that's keeping us from the seventeenth century."

Nora looked straight at George Majors, about to challenge his one-track mindset with the best argument she knew, which was also the only one she had.

"What has delayed our 'finding the seventeenth century', as you put it, Mr. Majors, was a rare piece of archeological luck. In the course of this month's excavations we have determined that the cellarhole where we thought we might find a small assortment of scattered artifacts, is actually an extraordinary time capsule of late eighteenth century life."

Nora saw Hank's eyebrows go up again, this time in interest at the carefully chosen words of her announcement. There was no visible response from Majors. Nora took a deep breath and forged on, telling the board all she could about the sealed deposit that was the Chapman cellarhole. But as she spoke, she wondered what effect her words could possibly have. Three of the members – Ogden, Wentworth and Whiting – already knew most of the story. She couldn't improve much on their first-hand experience, except to reiterate the significant research value of new archeological data. As soon as she said that she winced at her own words. Too academic. They might convince Peg, but Nora couldn't see George Majors – or Hank either, the man who avoided his family's past – being swayed by academic research value.

She plunged back into the presentation, describing the lead-glazed pots and the hand-made bricks, the imported teacups and heaps of building material. She argued for their value as teaching tools, even going so far as describing an imagined scene of Chapmans two hundred years ago, filling the cellar to protect the livestock that grazed nearby. Ralph was nodding vehemently. Hints of appreciation came and went on Hank's face as he listened. Jane Ogden was staring with rapt attention. Maybe, Nora thought in wonder, they might come around after all. She should wrap up quickly, while sentiment was running in her direction. Her smile was all-inclusive as she looked around the table.

"I know you want to know what impact finding this treasure will have on the rest of the Mill Farm Project. The crew and I believe we are almost through the cellar-fill deposit. Underneath and around the edges of that will be whatever original construction evidence exists. It is that evidence which will lead us to the date – seventeenth century or otherwise," her eyes flicked to Majors, "– that the Board originally charged us with finding."

Nora paused to let the information sink in. Ralph Whiting's gently encouraging voice asked a question.

"And will that be it? You think the fill we're working on now constitutes most of the archeological story, then?"

"Actually, no. Given our success so far, I have to believe the chances are good of finding more 'treasures' as we near the cellar floor. But it is also important to understand that, once the Mill Farm date is firmly established, quite a bit more research needs to be done. Even when the cellar's empty," she added jokingly.

"What does that mean?"

Majors' grumble. Nora had known he wouldn't sit still through that announcement. She collected herself for a last piece of persuasion.

"Once we know for sure what century to attribute to Mill Farm – better yet if we can narrow it down to a few decades – we can make informed predictions of other features that might be important on the property. We can be much more efficient, sampling around the grist mill, for instance, or looking for other buildings. We can accomplish more testing in less time, with less money, based on the fact that every period of colonial development had its own land use and settlement patterns."

"How soon can you get it all done?"

Nora silently cursed Majors' unrelenting antagonism, the tone that made it perfectly clear to everyone around the table that tomorrow would not be soon enough for him, and drew a breath to steady herself. It was time to lay her future on the line.

"At the rate the crew is proceeding now, I'm hoping we can complete work on the cellarhole this month. But as you know, many of the crew members are students and they'll be back in school after that, so August is pretty much the end of our field season. I can't see the rest of the testing being done without a second season on the project."

"Hmph." Majors didn't even need time to reflect. He pinned Ralph Whiting with his scowl. "We've heard enough. It's time to vote on this whole business."

Ralph bridled at Majors' autocratic behavior and overrode his impatience.

"Yes. Well. First I would like to thank Nora for her presentation. I thought I knew what was going on out there, Nora, but you gave us a very useful perspective on the project, and what we're aiming for. Thank you."

Having reestablished his authority over the proceedings, Whiting reluctantly turned back to George Majors.

"Now then George. We need to be clear about what decision we are trying to make tonight. What exactly is the vote you're asking for?"

"I move that we begin work on restoring Chapman's Mill as soon as possible." The first part of the motion was self-evident. Majors' second clause caused more of a stir.

"And that the resources of the Medfield Mill Commission – *all* the resources – be directed to that end, from this point forward."

Miss Wentworth did not even wait for Whiting to invite discussion before she jumped in.

"Nonsense! Nora has a contract through September. 'This point forward' isn't even an option."

Majors shrugged reluctantly. "Fine, then. Change it to 'from the end of the 1995 season'."

"Hank," Whiting asked, "when were you thinking of beginning your work on the mill?"

For the first time since the meeting started, Hank changed position, slowly drawing himself up and then forward in his chair until his arms rested on the table. His answer was as slow as his movement, as if there were something more occupying his thoughts than the immediate question.

"Pretty soon, actually. I'm finishing up a job, and then I want to get the crew here, to work on footings while the water's low. So best guess ... week after next, I'd say."

"Oh!" Jane Ogden exclaimed excitedly. Peg Wentworth shook her head. Nora felt a sharp pain, as if she'd been stabbed near the heart. So this was the surprise she'd been wary of before the meeting began. Too bad being wary didn't ease the hurt.

Whiting was speaking again. "Well! We'd better get a vote recorded, then. For the sake of simplicity, I'd like to propose we split George's motion into two separate votes. The first vote will be a decision on supporting restoration of the mill. Then, if that vote passes, we should vote on redirecting our money, since that affects Nora's contract and a number of other budgetary considerations."

"Shouldn't we ask Dr. Tunney to step outside while we vote?" Jane Ogden's voice echoed the nervous fiddling of her hands.

George Majors snorted. "Come on, Jane. It's not as if this is some big secret. She should be pretty clear where we stand by now anyway. Let's just get on with it."

There was general agreement and the Board proceeded to reword the motion. Nora forced herself to sit very still, working at maintaining a carefully passive face as she heard the voices around her deciding her fate. *This is it, then. And if they vote Aye, the next vote is inevitable. They can't support the mill without money. They don't have the money for it and for me. So Dr. Tunney is expendable and I'll pack my bags and slink away. Goodbye archeology. Goodbye Mill Farm.*

Two voices whined and rumbled together. "Aye." A third vehemently stated "Nay!"

Ralph Whiting felt a need to prolong the agony by sorting through his own thoughts aloud.

"This is not a simple decision. I must say I am fascinated by archeology and convinced that Nora has unearthed a great deal of valuable information at Mill Farm. However, I don't see how we can turn our backs on Hank's generous offer, so I feel I must vote aye. Do I assume we know your vote as well, Hank?"

It occurred to Nora that Hank had been silent during the polling. She carefully shifted her eyes in his direction to find him scowling at the table, as if embroiled in complicated thoughts.

"I guess I'd better vote aye," he finally said, "since I'm doing the project. But I'd like to suggest we table the vote on whether or not to renew Nora's contract, until she comes up with a firm date from the cellarhole."

What on earth for? Nora silently protested. Hank continued hesitantly.

"I don't understand all the reasoning behind it, but I'm convinced the date is important for all of us. I just have this sense it may bear strongly on the future of Chapman's Mill."

He finally glanced at Nora and she was surprised by the unsure look in his normally self-confident face. She was astonished by his irrational, intuitive explanation. Most of all, she was moved by Hank's trying to buy her time. As if he cared about what she did, or even about her. Not that it would make any difference, in the long run. The money would not magically appear, to pay for both projects at once. Why, she silently railed, did a vote for Hank inevitably have to be a vote against her? More than anything else right now, she didn't want them to be on opposite sides.

Peg spoke up at last.

"Seems to me you're talking too little too late, Hank. It seems perfectly clear there won't be any money left for Nora after this year. Next month's stabilization work alone should pretty much wipe out our bank account. Why keep the girl dangling any longer when the outcome's inevitable!"

Hank leaned farther forward over the table as he answered.

"I don't see any inevitability right offhand. I mean, my time's not costing anything, and I've already said I'd cover the crew's expenses."

He was stopped by a chorus of surprised exclamations.

"Didn't I say that?"

Ralph Whiting gave an emphatic shake of his head.

"Hmm. I was sure I'd told somebody … And the timbers we need are coming from the Strong Sawmill. We worked out a barter, sills for labor, last spring, and they owe me." This time there was teasing in the glance he sent Nora. "Good old American tradition, you know."

Hank returned his attention to the listening Board members. "Look, I know that doesn't solve the problem of money for next year, but maybe it makes enough difference to let Nora finish the archeology, anyway. I'd sure like some archeological back-up to fix a date on Chapman's Mill. You don't come across seventeenth-century mills every day and there's bound to be a lot of nay-saying when we go public. Besides," he finished abruptly, "I think Nora's still got treasures to find."

It was clear that Whiting and the two women were delighted with Hank's proposal. Enthusiastic comments about his generosity and problem-solving overlapped questions about project schedule and immediate plans. Above it all, Nora heard her own relief echoed in the others' words; relief that a sticky problem had been solved so simply.

"Just a minute." George Majors' voice cast a shadow like a crow stretching its wings. "I still think we need to set a limit to this archeological business. Just because Hank Chapman is willing to bail us out for a month doesn't mean the treasury's got unlimited funds. We've got big expenses down the road and we need to conserve every penny we can to meet them."

The earnest, responsible tone with which he had begun shifted slightly, hardening.

"I say we vote now – so as not to 'keep her dangling,' Miss Wentworth – that renewal of Ms. Tunney's contract is absolutely dependent on her finding proof of seventeenth-century occupation of Mill Farm." Majors' cold glare challenged the other Board members to disagree.

"You're being ridiculous, George!" Peg Wentworth exclaimed. "You know that's not the only reason we hired her. This is so unnecessary."

"It's the only way you're going to get me to go along with it."

Ralph Whiting frowned in exasperation. Majors' stubbornness was going a long way toward ruining the pleasure of Hank's announcement. But the announcement, Whiting suspected, was itself the root of Majors' intractability. The man resented Chapman's easy generosity. Moreover, based on past episodes, Majors would continue to be obstructive until he managed to get some semblance of control. Ralph clenched his teeth and thought ahead to getting this man off the Board. Meantime, however, something had to be done.

"Nora," Whiting began. "Are you willing to continue working under the terms Mr. Majors has proposed?"

The evening's meeting had taken so many twists and turns that Nora felt stunned. What choice did she have, anyway? She shrugged and gave him a half-hearted smile.

"I'll do the best I can. I can't promise to come up with the date you want, any more than I could when the project started, but I'll try."

"Then let's vote," Whiting said briskly.

This time the vote was unanimous, without further discussion, to satisfy George Majors and shut him up. The group adjourned with a collective sigh of relief and as they moved toward the door, the hallway echoed with renewed enthusiasm for Hank's plans. Even Majors, mollified by the recent vote, congratulated Hank on finally getting the real work off the ground.

Nora followed behind, a polite smile on her face. She nodded and made appreciative comments. Finally she slipped out the door, leaving Hank enumerating sills and joists to four eager listeners. She felt superfluous. She felt gray, as if somehow her essential color had been sapped by the meeting's madness.

The wind had picked up along the front that Ralph had said was coming through. Nora stopped beside her truck and sucked it in, delighted briefly by the shiver that was so much clearer than what had just gone on indoors. At least she still had a job. For the moment. Stars shone very bright in the darkness far beyond the front porch light. Fast-moving streaks of cloud erased the Dipper, then revealed Orion in its stead. The seventeenth-century bugaboo was still rearing its eternal head. But that was nothing new. A small moon climbed the western sky, haloed by approaching weather. Nora stared at it and wondered why her brain had no answer to the question *What about Hank?* She was too tired to think; that was all. It had been an exhausting meeting. Time to go home and sleep it off.

"Nora?"

Hank's approach was surprisingly quiet on the gravel driveway.

"I know you want to go, but I wanted to catch you for just a minute. I've been trying to call you all week."

A disbelieving sound came out.

"No. I mean I've been trying to talk myself into picking up the phone all week. About the article and what happened after." He gestured helplessly at Nora's continued silence. "I'm sorry about what I said about archeology. It was a cheap shot. You mean more to me than that, you know. And I have a lot of respect for what you do. I guess I was just being awfully defensive."

Hank shifted uncomfortably as Nora shaped a response.

"Defensive? *I* was acting about as childish as George Majors back there." She suddenly stopped, remembering the others not far away, and went on in a lower voice. "My grandmother always told me I had a problem with people who didn't hold the same opinions. I'm just sorry you got to see what she meant. I usually have better luck controlling myself."

"Hey, it was hot. We'd both just spent an hour in attic hell…"

"Come on. It wasn't bad enough to excuse *that* scene."

"Another opinion we differ on, then. I told you what I think of attics."

Voices moved outside the front door and down the steps. Hank finished in an undertone.

"Anyway, I'm sorry. Maybe we could try again?"

"I'd like that."

He reached over and gave her shoulder a quick squeeze before moving discreetly around the front of his ambulance. Nora backed her pickup out and headed home, less tired than she'd felt for days.

The next morning Nora walked down the road to work in a confusion of emotions. Relief at the Board's continuing to support her – for the moment – warred with resentment at their knuckling under to Majors' peremptory demands. The pleasure of making amends with Hank stumbled against the clash of their thinking on old buildings. All in all, she thought ruefully, she was thoroughly confused. Taking a deep breath, she hiked up to the cellarhole and consciously cleared her mind to make room for the day's work.

Pam and Ralph's work on the granite stairway was chugging along. Actually Pam was making good headway thanks to a large boulder, part of the cellar wall. The deeper she dug, the farther it intruded, so she was only removing dirt from about half the square right now. That wouldn't last long, Nora suspected, but every half-day gain increased the chance of finishing this summer. So far they were only down four feet from the top of the wall, and even if the Chapman's cellar had low overhead, Nora estimated another foot or more to go before they reached the floor and bottomed out.

Jane Ogden and Peg were working squares along the east wall, overlooking the pond. Doug's pit was staggered between theirs, close to the center. Andrew, to his delight and Pam's chagrin, worked on the west wall near her, where he could scoff at her serious remarks and, when he thought no one was looking, admire the pull of her shorts across her backside.

Nora was comparing the looks of their two pits when he arrived for work.

"Morning, Andrew. Take a minute before you start to tell me what's going on here."

Nora found that someone else's perception of what she was looking at often made her see it in a different light.

"I can tell you I'm getting sick of hoisting rocks, for one thing." A growing stone pile sat outside the edge of his pit, threatening to fall back in if he added much more to it. Andrew had also sifted more pebbles than dirt over the last few days, complaining loudly. "And that big boulder in the wall still doesn't show any sign of a bottom edge."

Nora nodded. "That doesn't surprise me, given the drill marks you found." There had been a great stir earlier in the week when Andrew's trowel had exposed semicircular grooves running vertically down the face of the boulder. They were the evidence left by a mason's working to split the boulder down to size. "Looks like the Chapmans were stuck with really big field stones for building blocks. But I am surprised by all the little stuff." She shrugged. "Well, keep at it, and keep asking questions. You never know what may turn out to be important." Nora moved on to the next square and left Andrew to contemplate the rocks and Pam.

By early afternoon, the boulder in his square showed signs of curving outward below the drill marks, as if the mason's splitting had succeeded only so far, before being foiled by the granite's irregular structure. The curve paralleled the bulging stone in Pam's square as well and everyone was briefly at a loss to understand why. In the last hour of the day's work the answer finally emerged. Andrew lugged the last stone rubble out of his square as Nora kept a sharp eye out for unexpected artifacts. Then he wiped a dirty arm across his brow and joined the rest of the crew, who had long since abandoned any pretense of work, to contemplate the peculiar sight before them.

Along the cellar's west wall, a course or two of foundation stones had resisted the conflicting pressures of frost and gravity to remain remarkably upright, their stability due in large part to resting on an uninterrupted face of granite. The Chapmans had made clever use of the site's natural features, locating the cellar – and thus the house – on the edge of a bedrock slope, shaping the bedrock to form a solid wall. The house was built along one side and on top of it, resulting in a perfect subterranean storage space.

"This is brilliant!" Doug, normally the most laconic of the crew, was the first to get excited. "The house was literally pinned into the hill! I'd been thinking this was a pretty iffy site for a foundation, smack at the edge of a bluff, but it's not going to shift if the wall's part of the bluff itself. Thomas Chapman was a smart guy!"

"Thomas or some other Chapman," Nora, devil's advocate, cautioned.

"It certainly makes for a cool spot on a hot day." Ralph picked up the thread of admiration. "Even open to the sky, the way it is now, it's not bad to dig here if you're in the shade."

Marilyn gasped, her eyes glowing with excited imagination. "Think what a great place it would be to hide from the Indians!"

That prompted another SSQ round as the crew conjured up the first Chapmans cowering in the dark, beneath the floor of their isolated house, while vengeful red men burned half the town of Medfield in 1676.

"Hold on, hold on!" Nora, cheered by their enthusiasm, resisted nevertheless. "How could you prove this is true? You need some evidence, you know, that this is first-generation defense. At the moment it could just as well be a very sensible cold cellar, as Ralph was noticing."

"We'll just have to find some artifacts." Peg's voice was positive. "How about musket balls, are they the right period? Or arrow heads?"

Andrew frowned pedantically. "From what I read, half the local tribes seemed to have guns of some sort by then. Besides, why should arrow heads be in the cellar?"

"It would depend on who won, wouldn't it?" Marilyn's eyes opened wider.

Nora's thoughts were still back at the farmer's cold cellar. The fun of playing devil's advocate was running out. This was not just an intellectual exercise anymore. It was the devil who was winning.

"We need to get back to work," she announced abruptly, and turned her back on the crew's surprised looks. She walked over to Doug's square, halfway across the cellarhole, and studiously examined it.

Unlike Andrew's bedrock intrusion, Doug's square seemed to go on forever, producing a steady supply of unexciting but satisfying mid-colonial artifacts: wrought nails, a plain brown stoneware jug, a nice bit of slip-decorated redware. Doug was good at keeping things intact while he worked around them. His trowel didn't jab into fragile chunks of plaster. He didn't scrape the glaze when he worked around a pot shard. He could be infuriatingly slow but Nora often appreciated the results of his patience. It was Doug who managed to maneuver around a long iron strap, leaving it sticking out of his pit wall until he discovered another below, and another below that, and they finally identified surviving remnants of a barrel whose wooden staves were long gone.

Doug's square was clearly not like Andrew's, and Nora felt reassured just looking at it. She glanced up to find most of the crew still watching her instead of back at work. Ralph and Jane Ogden were discreetly picking up tools. Nora suddenly realized it was quitting time and she laughed self-consciously.

"Hey, Doug. You've found so much stuff in here – maybe you'll unearth vital evidence tomorrow. Find a coin or two, why don't you? How about a cache of Spanish *escudos*? We could use some good dating about now."

"Spanish *escudos*?"

"Sure. You'll become famous for finding the Chapman Hoard. Think of the publicity!"

She made her way out of the cellar and grabbed her own tools.

"But right now, we need to put these tools away and then it's time for a beer. Anyone want to join me?"

Her offer broke the uneasy spell and discussion of the Chapman Hoard grew loud as the crew lugged buckets and screens into the barn for storage overnight.

When Artie purred in Nora's ear the next morning she opened her eyes to dark clouds and the heavy stillness that presages rain. There would be no digging today. Her impatience to finish the cellarhole was countered by awareness of the growing stash of artifacts needing to be cleaned. All the good weather had put them behind on lab work, so rain would provide them with a catch-up day.

She met the others in the barn and they spent a comfortable morning washing artifacts. By lunchtime, the shelf of screening that ran the length of their work table was covered with pot shards and rusty nails, oyster shells and food bones, carefully laid out in discreet clusters to dry. With any luck, Nora thought, most of them would be dry enough to catalogue in the afternoon. Some would be individually labeled. Then the fun of matching and mending could begin.

The morning's spates of rain had let up and there were even patches of blue showing when Nora walked outside to stretch. Ralph Whiting joined her in the yard, rubbing stiffness out of his neck. They were alone for a minute as the others dumped wash basins of dirty water and found their lunch bags.

"I've been meaning to speak to you since Thursday, Nora," Ralph began uncomfortably.

Nora raised her eyebrows.

"Are you all right with what went on at the Board meeting?"

She was surprised at the directness of his question, but decided it required an equally direct answer.

"I'm certainly not thrilled. You know that. I realize George Majors just thinks I want to milk the project for more money..." Whiting began to protest but she went on. "But I hope that you and the others, at least, understand how important I think Mill Farm is. It's an incredibly untouched source of information on so many different aspects of history and archeology, rural development and ... well, I've been through this before. The point is, it remains so, whether we ever come up with a nice, tidy seventeenth-century date or not. I'm just sorry it all ended up being tied to that date."

"Hmm." Ralph's look was sympathetic. "I understand your distress. On the other hand, I hope you can appreciate the ... um, ... political machinations that are involved with even so small a board as ours."

"It's nothing new to me, Ralph." *It's just this time I thought it would be different.* Nora shook her head and gave him a half-hearted smile. "I'll just have to work some miracles, won't I?" She didn't want to discuss the subject any more. For one thing, she was afraid Whiting would bring up the mill restoration and Hank's part in the project. She wasn't at all sure how she felt about those particular political machinations. Doug and Miss Wentworth were walking toward them and Nora seized the opportunity to change the subject.

"Anybody want to walk over to the site before we eat? We need to check out how much damage the rain did."

They all agreed, Ralph's expression of concern mixing with relief that he need not pursue the awkward subject any further, at least for the time being. The sight that met them when they reached the edge of the cellarhole completed the distraction.

Puddles of water stood in nearly every pit on the site, and the rain had eroded the neat edges of the walls and baulks that divided the squares. Outwash was not surprising. In fact, the crew's first job back on the site after every shower had been to clean up the dirt washed into each square, so as not to confuse it with the soil level they were actually working.

Puddles, though, were unexpected. Back at the end of June, the last time there had been substantial rain, the soil's permeability had amazed them all. Standing water had drained away almost as fast as it accumulated, the crew returning to work within hours of a rainstorm. For some strange reason this was no longer true. Nora frowned at the inexplicable scene, then switched to practical considerations.

"Looks like we'll be bailing after lunch."

The crew spent an hour that Saturday afternoon with buckets and dustpans, lifting most of the water out of the pits. Their efforts combined with clear, dry air the rest of the weekend, made the site workable again by Monday morning, although pockets of damp remained, especially alongside the bedrock of Pam's and Andrew's squares.

Doug went back to his square, cheered on by the others who were taking bets on his finding the Hoard. He concentrated on the area outside the ghost barrel and reported to Nora on conditions as he dug deeper.

"Texture's changing here, Nora. Still damp like everybody else's, but it's getting compacted. Really tough to dig."

He was talking as he scraped away the surface of the soil. Just then his trowel blade ran into something.

"Not hard, exactly, but not as soft as plaster, either. You want to check it out?"

Doug squinted up at Nora anxiously, and she restrained herself from jumping in next to him.

"Not yet, Doug. You're doing fine. Work around it. Try to outline it if you can."

He tried to do as she said, but was only partially successful. The edges kept flaking away despite his care. His puzzling find was rectangular, measuring perhaps five inches across. It was sodden and, as far as they could tell, brown. Nora thought at first the object might be leather, but the texture was wrong. As always with an interesting discovery, Doug's lump attracted the rest of the crew's attention. They peered over at his square, commenting and kibbitzing as work on their own squares slowed to half-speed.

Nora's impatience at Doug's slowness increased with her irritation at the lack of progress elsewhere. He agonized so long over his find that she was on the verge of taking over his pit, something she never did on principle, but her principles had reached the straining point. Suddenly Doug announced he had done all he could to clear away the dirt and save the object. A collective sigh of relief, it seemed, rose from the site as others chipped in to do the requisite recording. The area was swept clean, photos taken, the object mapped. Nora finally climbed into the pit and helped Doug remove the lump intact, laying it gently on a board. The others crowded around.

"What on earth is that thing?"

"Looks worthless to me. What do you think, Nora?"

"I think you may be right. It may turn out to be nothing, or at least nothing identifiable."

"Can't you tell *anything* about it?"

"Not yet. It's still too wet, and too dirty. We need to let it dry a bit before we can poke around some more."

This time it was Peg who balked.

"Seems Doug spent a lot of time on something that can't even be identified."

Nora grinned to hear someone more impatient than she was herself.

"I didn't say we wouldn't be able to identify it, Peg. Just not yet. It could be a treasure, you know; a one-of-a-kind something, though at the moment I can't think what. And Doug had to spend all that time because destroying the only-known-something is seriously frowned upon in archeology. But I'll tell you what. I'll take a look at it this evening after it's had a chance to dry a bit; see if I can tell anything more about it so you won't be kept in suspense any longer. Okay?"

There were mutters of reluctant agreement. Even Peg recognized that there wasn't much to be gotten from the lump in its present state. Doug was charged with delivering it safely across the road to the lab and the others returned to their squares, hoping their own next finds would be more rewarding than his had been.

"So is it a treasure?"

Peg's brisk voice was startling. Nora peered into the shadows at the far end of the lab and saw the older woman standing by the door.

"Almost. I didn't expect to see you here tonight."

"Well, I got to thinking about the lump, and knew you'd be looking at it, and decided I'd just poke my head in. You don't mind?"

Nora pushed back from the table and set down a magnifying glass.

"Of course not. But I'm afraid there's not much to see. Come take a look."

Peg pulled a pair of reading glasses out of her canvas jacket as she crossed toward Doug's lump. It was centered in a pool of intense light under a halogen desk lamp. Little piles of dirt surrounded it, and she noticed an array of dentist's tools and cotton swabs, tweezers and a Swiss army knife nearby. She studied the lump, significantly drier now, in frowning silence.

"I still don't know what I'm looking at. What do you mean by 'almost' a treasure?"

"It's the remains of a notebook. You're looking at the cover, opened out. The thing must have landed facedown when it was tossed into the cellar. See?" Nora used the tweezers as a pointer. "This is some kind of coarse paper, or cardboard maybe. I'm guessing the damp and the plaster lime in the pit worked together to preserve what's left. Unfortunately, that wasn't enough."

Nora gently grasped one edge of the cover with the tweezers and lifted it just slightly, for Peg to see what was there. Under the once-sturdy cover, the thinner pages had melted together over time, forming a congealed mass of sodden paper.

"What a mess. What would you guess it was?"

"Oh, I don't know. A daybook, maybe. They were common enough."

Miss Wentworth's face brightened as she made the connection to her own interests. "Of course! I've run across a number of those in the archives. Business records, right? Lists of credits and debits?"

"Probably. I had a brief nightmare that this could have been a record from Chapman's mill, but that's not very likely, I guess."

"Gracious, no. You know a lot of those little books are positively useless. I've seen one that was just comments on the weather. And a journal over in Dedham that was nothing but quotations – inspiring thoughts some lady had copied in her spare time. It's much more likely your book was something like that. Still, can't we save it, Nora? Isn't there somebody who can fix things like this?"

"Oh, sure, in the best of all possible worlds. One of the best document conservation centers in the U.S. is right here in Massachusetts. If the Board wanted to spend hundreds, or more likely thousands of dollars, we could get the covers stabilized, probably most of the pages unstuck, maybe even have each one separately mounted so they wouldn't disintegrate when they dry completely. All of which might make sense if this were some rare and valuable document…"

Miss Wentworth was shaking her head.

"I can't imagine the Board spending that kind of money. Unless we knew for certain it was important. Have you been able to separate any pages at all, Nora, to see what's written inside?"

"That's the other problem."

Miss Wentworth watched Nora lift the cover again, gently holding it up as she turned a scrap of the page beneath. There was something peculiar about the girl's expression. It was flat somehow, missing the intensity that always lit up her face when she was working. Peg shifted her attention to what Nora was doing, but a seed of personal concern started to grow.

"Nothing's written inside anymore."

"It's just a blank book?"

"No. It was used. For something." Even her voice was flat. "See these brownish smears?" Nora lifted another corner. "Those are ink stains. I don't know what kind of ink, but it sure wasn't waterproof." She eased the ruined pages back down and met the other woman's eyes. "Whatever somebody recorded in that book melted from the wetness in the cellar. It's gone, just as completely as if we'd never dug it up. We'll be able to say we found a home-made book, but we'll never know what it was used for. Even why it was tossed into the trash."

She gave an uncharacteristic shrug and Peg frowned to herself. For a space of time, the two women contemplated the useless pages in silence. Eventually Peg stirred, her voice cutting briskly through the gloom that had descended.

"Here's a backward thought to cheer you up."

"What's that?"

"Daybooks are definitely *not* seventeenth century. Seventeen-fifties, maybe. Common after 1800, but not seventeenth century. So at least you haven't lost that one definitive piece of evidence George Majors has been badgering you for."

One of Nora's eyebrows rose at Peg's twisted logic. She noticed a conspiratorial gleam in the other woman's eye. It was good to have a friend when so much was going wrong. A corner of Nora's mouth quirked up and she switched off the high-intensity light.

"You're right. It could have been worse, couldn't it? Given what we're aiming for. Let's get out of here and try again tomorrow."

Between the barn and Peg's station wagon they purposefully talked of other things. Nora waved goodbye and headed toward her apartment, thankful for the lift that came from Peg's encouragement, arguing to herself that the next day would be better. It was probably just as well, she reflected, that they were still dealing with late colonial artifacts, considering the book's useless condition. It could have been worse. As things stood, they just had to keep digging, and eventually they were bound to find...

You don't want to go there, a tremulous voice warned.

She frowned as she reached for the door and wondered where on earth that thought had come from. What had she been thinking that set off such an internal alarm? Late colonial ... could be worse ... just keep digging ...

And suddenly Nora knew what could be worse. Eventually they would bottom out. Only it wasn't 'eventually' at all. That's what the soil change in Doug's pit had meant, and the slanting bedrock wall Andrew had found. Doug was about to hit bottom. Right in the middle of the cellar, a foot sooner than she had expected. And once they bottomed out, there was nothing more to find in the granite cellarhole.

But where is the seventeenth century? the voice whimpered.

An Archeologist's Handbook
Part Three: Bottoming Out

At some point in every test pit and excavation square, there is an end to cultural deposits. Sterile subsoil is exposed, in a process casually known as 'bottoming out.' The investigator has removed all the evidence of human activity in that particular location. She has brought all her skills to bear on the small patch of dirt, sifting it cautiously for every speck of evidence and even appraising the soil itself for information it may carry. Much work remains to be done to thoroughly analyze the data collected, but field work is over.

Bottoming out is a value-laden cultural event in itself. In the best instances it brings closure to a satisfying investigation. As the archeologist backfills the pit, she has the satisfaction of knowing that her skill has combined with earlier people's evidence to form a bridge between past and present. She has an understanding of who occupied and what transpired on that site. A process of relearning has occurred that, while it may not restore the past to life, at least restores an immediacy, a vividness to it that had been lost

In other instances bottoming out is less fulfilling. The investigator may find vital evidence destroyed, due to time or weather or the acts of man. Or the initial research design itself may prove to have been faulty. The investigator's expectations may have been too high. They may not have been *adjusted in the course of research, to those field conditions actually encountered. When this occurs, it is essential for the archeologist to reevaluate her position, examining closely the body of data that <u>has</u> been accumulated for clues on how to proceed differently in the future. In such situations, bottoming out is not a process of relearning past behavior at all. Rather, it is a whole new learning experience and, as such, may be at least as disturbing as it is satisfying.*

After the discovery of Doug's 'almost' treasure, work at the site proceeded with what was to Nora depressing predictability. She derived little satisfaction from seeing that her archeological instincts were right. Doug's square bottomed out the next day. A day later Ralph's did as well, next to the stone staircase. Nora found herself dreading the walk to work each morning, the moment when she topped the rise and had to face the increasingly empty cellar. By Saturday even Marilyn, working on the far side of the cellar next to the outer wall, had exposed a drill-marked corner of bedrock.

The others still took pleasure in their finds. They were ecstatic when Peg Wentworth turned up a single rim shard showing the unmistakable blue dashes of a seventeenth century delft charger. Nora was staring at it, unmoved, when Peg surprised her by taking the devil's advocate role on herself.

"Come on now, boys and girls. Chargers were decorative pieces. You've all read that. Chances are just as likely this rim was chipped a hundred years after it was made as when it was new. More likely, matter of fact."

They looked to Nora to protest, but she just nodded and went back to the motions of finishing up. Occasionally she rallied. The crew still looked to her for direction, after all. And it was not as if finishing here meant work was over. Three more weeks remained of the season, and they'd have to see how much broad area survey they could complete before the summer ended. Especially since, with every empty square, it was clearer that there'd be no chance of work again next summer.

Nora caught herself thinking in finalities. Final plan drawn of Doug's square. Final afternoon chat with Ralph Whiting, leaving for vacation. The finalities carried over after hours as well, draining pleasure from the habits of a summer. At night Nora pored over records, looking for the clue she'd overlooked. *One last time. Let's just check the field notes one last time and see if there's something I missed.* She reread every deed and inventory, stared at Hank's deep-rooted family tree, willing the documents to disclose the secret that the cellarhole would not.

By Sunday afternoon she still had not found the missing key to the seventeenth century. Artie's complaints finally roused her from her desk to let him out and she stood at the screen door watching him stalk away. Why was she bothering? What on earth made her think one more look at the same old stuff would turn up something new? It was about time she started remembering what she'd told the Board in the first place. There just might not be a seventeenth-century component to this site. That wasn't her fault. About time she stopped flagellating herself for something that wasn't there and stopped feeling morose about something she couldn't change. She drew a deep breath and decided she needed a good, brisk walk.

Following Artie's determined route, she strode out through the stone-walled barnyard to the road beyond, turning north past the Big House door. Her memory winced at the suffocating attic heat. It followed Hank again down back stairs to the kitchen she'd immediately loved.

Past the Big House, Nabby's Arbor sat cool and serene in afternoon shade. Nora didn't want to remember being there. She hurried past internal photos of Hank by a reconstructed mill wheel and the heart pain incongruously linked with lemonade dripping down her leg. It was safer to stay in the present, to study the sequence of stones neatly fitted along the top of the wall. Little ones and big ones, angular and round, tucked together symbiotically, holding and being held the whole length and height of the centuries-old structure. A chipmunk scolded, diving into one of its dozen holes. Through the trees, the mill pond glittered with afternoon reflections. Nora cut across the road and looked for a break in the wall. Finding one, she rested a hand on the top stone and stepped through. She and Hank had cut through here, the evening they'd eaten triple-deckers. That was before they'd known anything about each other, when things had been so simple he'd even kissed her goodnight. She carefully concentrated on her feet, avoiding the squishy drops under each apple tree, less successfully avoiding remembered fantasies of seasons yet to come in this place.

Nora walked out of the trees onto a late summer low-water shoreline. Ten feet away, the family of geese grazed on young weeds. They were indignant at her intrusion and protested with much neck-craning and nasal muttering. One gander flapped his wings in threatened attack but had second thoughts, and the gaggle lumbered into the water, turning instantly graceful as they glided away.

Nora watched them re-emerge at the bottom of Hank's lawn. They settled back to grazing with a nonchalant disregard of their surroundings. *As if it's their own lawn*, she thought. *Just as if they lived there.* It occurred to her that they did, in a way, that they were as much permanent residents of Mill Farm as the Chapmans. The ache that brought made her turn on her heel and head the other way. What a stupid fantasy that had been. Why did she have such a penchant for fantasy and then – stupider yet – manage to be surprised when it didn't come true? It was about time she came to terms with real life. Pity it had taken her over thirty years to do it.

So what was real life? Nora walked along the water's edge. First they would finish the cellar-that-came-too-late. She stepped over a rotting branch, automatically scanning its length for signs of woodworking. Then they would do some testing between the cellarhole and the mills. An interesting stone drew her up the sloping shore to check it out, but one kick disenchanted. After that, they would monitor the first stages of reconstruction to make sure Hank didn't throw out useful information with rotting sills. A shiny object beckoned in the midst of drying muck. Nora pulled it out, only to recognize a fractured piece of soda bottle. The plastic hit the water with a splash, and she wiped her slippery fingers on her denim shorts. And that would be it. The season would be over. She would pack up and store the last artifacts, write her final report, give her last lecture. Then there would be no more reason left to stay.

The shoreline turned rocky near the dam and Nora scrambled up the granite outcrop, emerging by the old sycamore on the bluff. She stopped to catch her breath and contemplate the times she'd sought the comfort of this tree. This was where she'd first encountered Hank and his unlikely ambulance. Savored the pleasure of being at Mill

Farm. Sat on peaceful evenings and fooled herself with fantasies about a past for which there was no proof.

She turned her back on the tree and fisted her hands on her hips in frustration. For an instant she caught a glimpse of herself, feet apart, glaring out over the pond. Superwoman. That was it. If she were only Superwoman she could train an x-ray glance downslope and find the missing treasure. Strip away the grasses and bramble, delve beneath the windblown leaves, push back duckweed on the shore – all with one penetrating look. There to see at last, all at once, just where the missing midden bulged up from the ground. Spot the line of postholes marking some early enclosure. Outline the scant foundation where the very first Chapmans hunkered down against the cold and threat of Indians.

Deep down she knew it wasn't going to happen. The cellar was bare and she wasn't Superwoman after all.

"Nora. I wondered if I'd find you here."

She turned so quickly at Hank's words she had not yet composed her face. There were hurt and disillusionment in her expression, and an unaccustomed pain that left Hank fumbling for words.

"I, uh … I went by your place just now."

"Not for long."

"Hmm?"

"Not my place for long." What did it matter if a little bitterness showed? It wouldn't make any difference. "Another month or so, you'll have The Shed back again."

"Well … There isn't any hurry, you know."

He drew in a breath as if he intended to say something else, but let it out again instead. Both of them winced at how badly they were handling the situation.

"Look, I'm sorry." Nora backed off. "I didn't mean to bark at you. Fall thoughts, I guess, same as most archeologists. We do that every year, you know, about the time the geese start flocking. Maybe it's our migratory instinct."

"You couldn't prove that by me. Most of the geese on this pond never seem to go away."

"You must be undermining their instincts. Feeding them. Heating the pond, maybe?"

Hank chuckled and shook his head. "No. I think they just want to stay." Then he was serious again, studying her.

"Do you ever feel that way, Nora?"

She answered very carefully, with a cool smile to suggest she knew his was just a theoretical question.

"I didn't when I first started out in archeology. New projects and new places were part of what made the job exciting. Of course, not many places were quite so nice as this one." The smile faded. "You have a very special place to call home, you know."

"You made sure I knew, a number of times this summer. Even against my will sometimes. You are very convincing."

"No. *The place* is very convincing. And I'm afraid some of the glamor of moving is wearing off. It has been a rare treat to stay in one place this long, working with likable people." The words hung between them as Nora reached for something else to say. Something that would not reveal too much regret at losing a game she had barely known she was playing. She settled for a shrug.

"Oh, well. I can stay put somewhere when it's time for a desk job. But I bet you weren't looking for me to discuss life choices, were you?"

Hank rearranged himself as if he were putting aside one set of thoughts for another.

"No... Though I'm glad you've been comfortable here. Sort of like the geese ..." His tone changed as if he, too, needed to get back to business. "I was looking for you to tell you about my latest meeting with Crosswell, our engineer. He agrees we have to work on a couple of posts before we let a whole crew tromp around in the mill. Wouldn't do to have the floor collapse under the volunteers. Anyway, the corner post comes first – you remember the one I showed you? The base and sill are all eaten away. It's amazing, actually, the thing's still standing at all, but I think it's a case of the building holding the post up, instead of the other way around. You want to be there when we start?"

Nora consciously shifted to professional mindset.

"Are you disturbing any ground surface when you work?"

"Nah. The whole thing's set on a single course of boulders. We'll just sister another post in temporarily, take out the rotten base and sill section, splice in new pieces and put it all back together. Closest we'll come to 'ground surface' is the punk wood coming out of the post. It's pretty good compost about now."

"You don't need any official blessing then. Though I wouldn't mind seeing how this splicing works. Could I watch from the sidelines?"

"Sure. The lumber's due on Monday and we'll be ready to go, end of this week sometime. Want me to send someone up to get you?"

Nora was caught up in an image of Spokeshave's men unloading tree-trunk thick timbers. Every one unloaded sounded another note in the archeological death knell.

"I'll be there," she replied absently.

"Good. I like having you around."

He was chagrinned to notice she didn't even seem to hear his confession. She was staring at the mill. Behind her eyelids, through the walls, a smock-shirted miller stood in a cloud of fine white dust. The counterpoint of waterwheel and millstones filled the building with sound as a silent rush of flour poured down into swollen bags.

COIN OF THE REALM

February 1676

Benevolent Lord, protect us from the wildness all about. Bring us through the terror of this very night. Shelter us a few short hours more for Thomas must rest. Thou knowest I willingly watch over him, but my vigil is naught without Thy strength. Love us, Lord, I beg Thee, that we may live.

Comfort drew herself deeper into the featherbed, curling herself close to the slow-breathing form of her husband. They were of a height, she and he, and she fit snugly back against his broad chest. Her tired mind clung to an image that came as she prayed. Somewhere she stood in sunlight, brown hair falling loose behind, warm in only her shift. Her arms rested, relaxed, at her sides, with hands held out, palms turned upward to receive...what? Some transparent golden treasure flowing toward her from a shadow of benediction across the sky.

An owl hooted out in the woods, snatching Comfort's thoughts away from the peace they sought. Night still, hunting time. Some timid, twitching vole would soon be dead. Snatched from an open space between the trees where he feared to move, but was forced to scrabble for food. Broken and destroyed by the omniscient savagery of a great-eyed owl. Comfort pressed her chapped hands tight together and retreated to her inner thoughts.

It was always thus, Thou sayest. Hunter and hunted, weak and strong. It was for this that Thou didst send Thy Son our Lord Christ, that we might put away fears of the here and now, dwell instead on radiant thoughts of the hereafter.

But how is a frail and sinful soul to proceed in the toils and turmoils of our days and nights? Especially our nights, o Lord? What wouldst have us do when, day by day, each hour, it would seem, the threats about us grow more fierce? We are not made of martyr's stuff, to put aside the howls and arrows of savage beasts and men.

Surely Thou knowest how we try. Thou seest my husband each day, and other brave souls with him, work till they fall exhausted, building Thine own vision of a more perfect world. Thou hast seen us come together in faith and humility, hast heard our fervent prayers. If the Governor himself sends troops to guard us as we go about Thy business, Thou canst not be far behind. Surely now, as winter drags on to desperation, and the savages daily draw closer and grow more bold, surely now, Lord, Thou must intervene on our behalf?

She strained to listen in the silence, the word "surely" echoing insistently in her ear. A shifting ember on the hearth. Her husband's slow, deep breathing. But no answers.

Comfort could not remember how long she had held these conversations with God. She had begun, perhaps, aboard the Arabella, the night of the great storm, when the hatches were battened tight and the shipload of terrified landsmen clung to their bunks and prayed to their Lord. They all prayed that night, and Comfort remembered knowing, for the first time in her ten years, that God was truly all that stood between them and horrible death.

When the pastor had ended his exhortation, the only sounds in the terror-filled between-decks were sobs of fear and moans of seasickness. Comfort, clutching her younger brother with one arm and the bunk's edge with the other, began her own pleading with the Lord. She squinched her eyes shut and searched for words to convince the Lord to make the terror stop. It was, she knew, a brazen thing for her to do, probably sinful, but she asked as humbly as she knew how. When He did not immediately accede to her plea she tried a different tack, talking to Him the way she talked to her earthly father, using her most convincing arguments to bring Him around to her side. She fell asleep in the midst of her appeal, despite the pitching bed and the roaring noise beyond the ship's hull.

Much later, when she woke again, the erratic waves had slowed to regular deep swells and drafts of fresh air and gray light from hatch openings pierced the fetid room. Comfort was never sure that her own discussion with the Lord had added greatly to the heartfelt prayers offered by the company of saints with whom she traveled, but she knew she had done what she could, and resolved to continue doing so in their new life.

In the middle of a cold and wakeful Medfield night, there was respite in memories. One of God's gentle miracles, Comfort thought, how present-day trials and fears smoothed themselves out in the backward-looking tunnel of her mind.

Long ago she had seen that smoothing happen in real life, when they still lived in England. She had been a little girl, sitting backwards on the tail of her father's cart, staring at the rutted track that rolled out underneath her swinging legs. Then her eyes followed the ruts as they stretched out behind. Receding track and jumbled hedgerows on each side magically smoothed themselves out, drew together to a neat line in the distance.

Memory was like that track, she reflected. Smoothing itself out in the distance of time to a pleasant reminiscence of past moments. The storm at sea was only ten years since, yet all she remembered now was a glimpse of fear and the determined devotion it created. Comfort purposefully turned her mind again to memories.

A week after the great storm, the Arabella sailed into Boston harbor. Comfort's parents, holding tight to her and little Jonathan, joined the dozens of pale passengers who intently lined the rails, fear and excitement warring on their faces as they caught a first glimpse of the New World which was to be theirs.

Boston by 1660 was a well-established port. Seen from the harbor, the town was dominated by a watchtower on the Trimount, with a great brush heap nearby, ready to set ablaze as warning to inland communities of attack from the sea. In the distance the watchers saw more ranks of hills, and could make out on nearer ones the same, dome-shaped piles of wood. A sobering first view, to people who'd come from the stable towns and quiet villages of England.

Yet, as the eye scanned this new horizon, there were more surprising things to see. Boston itself was brown and black, a seemingly colorless place, until the new arrivals drew close enough to see that every building of this closely built community was made of wood. None of the red brick or gray stone of England. Few, even, of the striking white-and-black half-timbered houses which filled the East Anglian villages they had known. There was green here, though. Patches showing between the dwellings, where kitchen gardens and young apple trees grew. On a broad expanse of green below the beacon hill, grazing cattle identified the town's common land.

At the base of the hills which defined Boston, a dozen or more wharves were clustered, some half built, others with factors' sheds already running the length of them. At the head of the wharves, the waterfront was crowded with warehouses and shops, taverns and chandleries. No one could doubt that this town looked to the sea. Small fishing boats and heavy, broad-beamed cargo vessels lined the wharves and tacked about the islands which dotted the harbor.

A great road stretched west from the city along the narrow neck of land that was Boston's only link with the mainland. Small industrial sites dotted the low flats beside the road. One, identified by the line of rectangular pits beside it, was a tannery stuck out at the downwind edge of town to save inhabitants' noses from the stench. Another, a long and flimsy building, covered the first of many ropewalks that would serve the growing port's demands.

Soon the Welles family traveled the great road west to Watertown. Comfort's first impressions faded in the cozy familiarity of life there, growing up listening to the thump of the mill wheel, hearing the harsh commands of farmers to their oxen, as carts backed up to the open mill doors. The house where she and Jack continued their growing up was not so different from the one they left behind in England, though there was not so much window to peer out of and it was, she guessed, smaller than the other.

But there were other differences. The grown-ups of Watertown were more absorbed in the business of salvation than Comfort remembered parishioners being in their home village of Pakenham. Sunday meetings were, if possible, even longer and more serious than back home. One of their first Sabbaths in the New World, as families came up to greet the newcomers and talked on interminably, Comfort had left her parents' side in restless search of her brother. Spotting him across the way, she called to him and ran to where he was making his own friends. Barely had she joined him, than her mother followed after and, drawing her aside, quietly chided her on the unseemly loudness of her voice. And Jack was made to stand forever by a tree, in punishment for running too far and free.

Later, as the children stood at their own table taking the evening meal, their father had raised his head from prayer and spoken of the day's events. His voice was severe, and the measured way in which he spoke signaled that his words were very important. He looked directly at Comfort as he began.

"I would have you remember, children, that we are, indeed, come to a new world. The Lord has blessed us with a new life here. A life of immeasurable opportunity and, within reason, immeasurable freedom. But," he frowned sternly, "I would have you understand that God does not grant freedom without limits."

He glanced at his wife, seated quietly on a bench opposite him. Mrs. Welles nodded in agreement. Comfort was distracted by the nodding wisps of brown hair like her own, which had escaped her mother's cap.

"We must make the acquaintance of new people here," her father continued, "and if my business is to prosper, we must be sure that our lives and our manners in all public forms accord with those expectations set by the elders and selectmen of this town."

He studied Comfort and Jack for a moment.

"For your part, you must do your utmost to behave in a manner which does not draw censorious attention."

Then his voice softened, and Comfort heard more of the understanding and warmth which normally characterized her father.

"Some of our life here will be strange at first. There will be none of the old festivities whose observance in Pakenham bordered on pagan rites. No harvest suppers, no wild May Day prancing."

A small sound of protest escaped Jack, whose favorite yearly event was the children's games around the village May pole. A sympathetic spark came into his father's eye, but he went on.

"I would have you remember that many who came here gave up all they had in this world to worship the Lord soberly and with

347

devotion. While this family may not be as rigorous in religious observance as some are here, we will not intentionally offend our neighbors or the authorities by going against their ways. You will remember that we need them at least as much as they need a miller."

That closed the subject. Mr. Welles turned to his meal, and the rest of the family ate in respectful silence.

Jonathan Welles had not brought his family across a fearsome ocean so they could tout their Puritan tendencies. He came to take on the job of miller for the village of Watertown. In return for plying the trade he'd known his whole life, he received a grant of more land than he could ever hope to see back in England, with promise of yet more when the commons were split. And with the land came a ranking in this astonishingly level social order which set him nearly at par with the wealthiest husbandmen in town. On his part, the only requirements were to carry out his job well, manage his holdings with care, and see that his family walked decorously in the ways of the Lord. There could be no question concerning the benefits to any of them.

Comfort did raise her own questions later that evening, however, as she lay waiting for sleep.

Dear Lord, surely the Scripture must be right in saying Thou dost walk in mysterious ways. Thou must know how deeply our family loves Thee. How could we not? Thou didst save us from an awful death by drowning. I do believe Thou snatched up our poor boat and, even as we slept, held it safe above the waves. Thou art our best and only guardian, and for that we will always give Thee thanks and adoration.

She considered the tone of her communication and gave a small nod. She hoped she had made it clear that there was no disrespect intended by what she was about to ask.

But here Thou hast made a mystery. Why is it Thou dost not permit here such simple pastimes as adorned the year in Pakenham? Why in this new place must we give up our dances and sport? Did not the people in old times honor Thy blessings in celebration and song? Not that I would ever doubt my father's word. But Lord, when we offer thanks to Thee, are we never to laugh and rejoice in Thy mercies? Teach me to understand, I pray.

Comfort held very still for a long time, waiting for clarification from above. Then she remembered the Lord had only rescued the Arabella after she had fallen asleep. She settled herself more comfortably under the sheet and abandoned her vigil for the night. A small wrinkle of determination creased her forehead.

The next morning, she was disappointed to realize her understanding of God's ways was just as unclear as it had been when she went to sleep. But there was a new sense of reassurance inside her, that somehow things would work themselves out. And slowly, over those first months, the children learned that their father's (and thus, Comfort assumed, God's) restrictions would bend from time to time. It was Mr. Welles' hand that appeared from nowhere to tickle Jack as the boy sat glumly reading on a Sabbath afternoon. It was his order from England that contained a superfine shift for his wife to wear, bordered by lace indiscreet in its ostentation, were it not hidden beneath her tightly buttoned jacket.

Another of Mr. Welles' decisions was to take them on a country ride toward the western settlements on a May Day a few years later. He excused their lapse from work by finding it politick to visit the mills in Dedham and Medfield. He also reminded his wife that the Arnold family, old neighbors from home, had recently homesteaded in Medfield. Then he lifted Comfort and Jack onto the broad back of one horse and his wife onto his own mount behind him. Saddlebags laden with cold lunch for the family and with city supplies for the Arnolds, they set out to ride the ten miles that separated stable coastal towns from the western edge of New World settlement.

They stopped in Dedham first, meeting the Whiting family and viewing the corn and saw mills on Mother Brook. Afterward they found a spot along the riverbank to eat their luncheon. Comfort was surprised at how overgrown the land was. Not at all like the carefully cultivated fields around their old mill in England, or even the Watertown mill. When she said something about it, Mr. Welles explained that much of the riverfront was left as wild meadow, free hay for the taking, as it were. It bothered her that things were so wild and untended.

Looking back on the trip later, Comfort would remember little of the village of Medfield or the people she met there. She had, she thought, enjoyed visiting with Elizabeth Arnold. She and Lizbeth were both seventeen and had much to whisper about as they tied up a steam pudding and later, sat together in the loft. Jack, as usual, played the pest, and the girls were frequently interrupted by him and a troop of younger Arnolds swarming up the stairway and bursting in on them. The men were out in the barn comparing notes and tending to the livestock. Mistresses Arnold and Welles finished preparing the supper they would share.

Young Thomas Chapman joined the families for supper. Chapman was a journeyman miller recently come from Devon to work for Henry Adams, owner of the town's grist mill. Comfort remembered thinking Mr. Chapman had a strong body and a stubborn jaw, but little to say until the talk turned to mills and milling. Then there was an eagerness about his speech, and excitement in his face that made him seem more approachable, and younger than his weighty twenty-six years. She even dared to whisper a self-conscious answer to him when he thoughtfully asked how the morning's journey had been. Lizbeth giggled uncontrollably when he vainly tried to engage her, too, in conversation. The exchange was brief, but Lizbeth exchanged speaking glances with Comfort when she could do so without being noticed.

Later, across the dish pail, she teased Comfort in conspiratorial undertones. Did not Master Chapman's politeness border on excess when he insisted on standing as Comfort rose from the table? And was she not the least bit taken with the long considering look that followed her out the door?

Comfort was surprised at the other girl's suggestion that the miller might have singled her out for notice. She had not thought much of men in that way and, in retrospect, decided Lizbeth's fancies stemmed from the girl's own wishful thinking. Lizbeth clearly thought the miller immensely admirable. Comfort lost no sleep over the matter, however, and passed a dreamless night despite the crowding in the Arnolds' sleeping loft.

Yet here she was, only three years later, lying in a high bed, crowded only by choice snug against the warmth of her husband. *But sleep is no longer dreamless,* Comfort thought with regret. *And too many hours are sleepless, to boot.* She shifted impatiently. Where had she left off, along that soothing track of memory?

*   *   *   *   *

From that first trip to Medfield, Comfort remembered the narrow dirt road that passed for a highway through the town and the huddle of houses and barns, all squeezed between the road and a brook or clustered about the meetinghouse. Next morning, on their return trip to Watertown, they followed a different cart path south from town, past a broad field where men and oxen worked to open up long strips of rich soil for planting to rye and barley, flax and corn. Beyond the field, at the very edge of cleared land, the path dipped down and ended at a roughly made building by a brook. From the rhythmic thumping she heard, Comfort knew this must be Mr. Adams' mill. There was a house too, where the family lived, Mistress Adams and their six grown sons who were off working in the fields. Mistress Adams offered cakes and cider while the men talked. Comfort sat on the doorstep and kept her brother out of the way. It seemed strange that the mill sat so far from the center of town. Just at the edge of the thick woodland. Heavy oaks and dark pines across the brook lowered over the building. The high water of spring rushing through the sluice gate seemingly threatened to carry the puny wheel right away downstream.

This place was nothing like her father's comfortable, orderly mill. There was nothing placid or benevolent about this brook, so different from the slow, winding river in Watertown or the gentle streams of East Anglia. Even more than the mill they'd visited in Dedham, this place made her uncomfortable. It must be strange for a family to live way off by themselves, in such a foreign wilderness. The dark trees, the rush of sound and the wild wet smell closed in around her.

Benevolent Lord, protect me from the wildness that crowds me about.

Comfort was thankful when they left the place. She was thankful that their quiet mare was content to follow her father's horse. She spent long stretches of the journey with eyes closed, shutting out the miles of dark, wretched trees that crowded the way.

351

From time to time the group would emerge onto cleared land. She knew that much, even with her eyes closed. The world lightened beyond her lids. A silence settled over them as the rustling leaves and creaking branches receded. She would open her eyes and see sheep wander across a rocky pasture. Or men stride purposefully behind ox and plow. At one place, a group of children fished on the shore of a pond. She relaxed as they rode through the clearings.

Then the woods would close in again. First the berry bushes vying for space among sharp-thorned briars. Then skinny saplings and tufts of young pine crowded against a massive rock. Each plodding step pulled them deeper into shadows. The horses made their way between tumbled granite boulders bare of even ferns and moss. Only the stubborn oaks survived here, and soaring pines that blocked the light and threatened silent magic in the gloom.

Jack whispered, taunting, that this was a giant's trash heap. Any moment he'd stomp back with more. Comfort hushed her brother and sat straighter, proving her maturity by forcing herself to look, all the while wondering how her parents could be oblivious to the dangers on every hand. They were the ones who'd told the stories, after all. Stories about great forests and the wild men who lived in them. About evil happenings and children lost forever. No giants, of course not. But every crevice in the rocks might be a wolf's den. Every thicket twitched by sparrow's wing was the movement of a watching Indian.

Her father was watchful as they rode through the woods but he didn't seem overly concerned. Indeed he and Mother carried on a murmured conversation much of the way home. Her little brother was too knuckleheaded to be scared, she decided. Jack seemed to think wolves and Indians were all good fun. But Comfort knew better. Forests were bad. And they were riding directly through a forest.

Only the steady sound of horses' hooves was familiar. That and the presence of this track they rode on. Comfort's thoughts seized on the track as reassurance. The track was made by good English men, who had dragged away the boulders and had scooped great loads of dirt from the verge to fill the worst of its dips and depressions. In places there were even rudimentary bits of stone wall to mark the road and draw a line between the world of men and wilderness.

Benevolent Lord, protect me from the wildness...

Later, she acknowledged to herself that the portion of their trip that went through *ye Rocks*, as the place was called, probably took no more than half an hour, all told. But in the months to come, when their May Day expedition came to mind, Comfort was hard-pressed to remember pleasure in their visit to Medfield, except a stray thought of Mr. Chapman. The woods intervened, looming dark and threatening over other memories.

When this happened, she forced herself to push the wilderness away by occupying body and mind with useful activity. Frequently, she turned to the kitchen garden her mother had planted between their house and the mill. There she would turn back her sleeves and, seizing a hoe, root out the weeds that dared to vie for space with turnips and salad greens. When she rose early, startled awake by a dark forest dream, she would improve her time by cutting lavender stalks to dry, or filling her apron with marigold heads which would find their way to the dye pot.

Then she would carry on her private conversation with the Lord, striving to assure in Him an ally. Or perhaps a guide through the confusion of growth and learning and the struggles of new life in a new world?

The image she came to have of Him did not exactly accord with that she heard at meeting every week, but she prayed it would not offend, especially if she kept it between themselves. The God to whom she addressed her thoughts bore great resemblance to the grandfather she remembered from England. He was ever to be considered with the utmost respect, but without trepidation, for everything that came from Him came from the good, and could lead to no harm.

The true puzzle in this complicated life was to be sure what *did* come from the Lord, and this was the source of much of Comfort's internal discussion, for surely on this new continent, with its strange people and unfamiliar ways, they were set about by evil in many forms. Comfort knew that her fear was brought on by evil. When dreams came, or dark memories, she knew they were temptations to her faith, casting doubt on the goodness of the Lord. So she renewed her faith as one renewed an old acquaintance, by picking up the thread of conversation left from the last meeting. Every time she did so, she smiled at the reassurance she felt within.

353

A deep-pitched creak brought Comfort back to the February night. She startled, and shifted in the curtained bed that filled one corner of their small room. Torn between hiding deeper under the heavy bed rug or pulling back the hangings to locate the sound, she wondered should she rouse Thomas from his heavy sleep?

Finally, heartbeats loud in her ears, she slipped a hand silently out of the covers and fumbled for the curtain's edge, invisible in the darkness. Two fingers drew back the heavy wool, barely enough to let in a flicker of light from the small fire that burned all night during deepest winter. Her eyes flitted up and down the opening, straining to see around the edges, into the dark corners of a room filled with shadows cast by chests and barrels, chairs and cooking pots, innocent furnishings of daily life which took on an evil aspect in the shifting firelight.

What was it she expected to see? Her sensible side did battle with her fears. A savage, who by some dark magic had made his way right through the bolted door or barred shutter into their home? The fearful side saw him even now raising a musket just out of sight behind the curtains, ready to shoot a gaping hole in the last line of her heart's defense, the wool-wrapped cocoon of their bed.

Some framing timber groaned, her sensible side argued. It was only wood shrinking upon itself in the cold. Comfort let the curtain close on her imaginings and sighed. These winter nights stretched endlessly through hours of dark wakefulness when even her earnest prayers were not enough to lull the fear to sleep.

Perhaps they might have found room for a soldier in their home? A man with proper military training would go a long way toward securing the house. Not that Thomas wasn't strong and quick and brave. But he was, after all, a miller, not a soldier of the Crown. Other houses in town had taken them in, the trained soldiers sent from Boston to reinforce Medfield's own militia.

But then, she reminded herself, Mr. Wheelock's house and the Reverend Mr. Wilson's, and Joseph Allen's house up the Natick road were all a good bit more commodious than theirs, four or five full rooms at least with attic above. Their own two-room cottage with its storage under the eaves was sizable enough for them, but hardly left bunk space for strangers.

Besides, Thomas would keep them safe, she reassured herself. Had he not managed admirably so far? Just then he reached out and curled his arm across her chest, holding her close as he returned to sleep. She smiled softly at his unconscious embrace and reveled in the warm weight of his arm over her woolen shift.

Thomas Chapman is a good man. I thank the Lord on bended knee who gave this man to be my husband... And I also pray that he may see the light, and put away his fancy of moving farther into the wilderness.

A wrinkle of worry drew her brows together as she composed herself again to try to sleep.

When Comfort turned nineteen Mr. Chapman had come courting. The first Comfort knew of it was her father's announcement at supper one evening.

"Thomas Chapman came by today when you women were marketing."

"Indeed? And what was he about?" Mrs. Welles prompted.

"On his way down river after a new mill stone, he said." Mr. Welles looked at Comfort. "He asked after you, daughter, as well."

Comfort's eyes widened in surprise.

"He did?"

It had not occurred to her that the handsome young miller whom Lizbeth and she had giggled over would remember her existence.

"Aye. In fact once he'd hemmed and hawed a bit, he came right out and asked were you betrothed."

Mr. Welles and his wife exchanged a significant look while he let his comment sink in. A quick catch of Comfort's breath cued him to proceed.

"I said you were not so." He paused. "I also assured him it was due to no flaw or lack on your part."

Then he went back to his supper as much as to say the topic was closed. Color rose in Comfort's cheeks as she watched her father bite off a chunk of his bread. Her impatience grew as he followed that with a spoonful of stew. Finally she had to ask.

"Father, did Mr. Chapman say no more than that?"

She could see his close-trimmed whiskers twitch in amusement as he deliberately finished his mouthful. When he at last answered, however, his voice was serious.

"He did. He asked if I had objection to his proffering his suit to you."

Comfort gasped. Mrs. Welles' hand went to her breast.

Mr. Welles continued in a puzzled tone.

"And then when I said I did not, he asked did I think you would find his address to you distasteful? Though I confess I cannot imagine why you might do so. He would appear to be a thoroughly suitable husband."

Comfort just stared at her father, as if expecting him to make sense of this extraordinary announcement. Her face by this time was completely flushed. The words "proffer his suit" repeated over and over in her head, "… his suit…his suit," blocking entrance to coherent thought. A mental glimpse of the miller leaning over the Allens' table, intent in discussion with the men. A movement frozen in memory: Mr. Chapman at the mill, shifting a full grain bag aside with effortless strength. The sound of his voice addressing her and even Jack with such respect as most people reserved for proper adults only. The way he'd studied her with deepset eyes when others would not notice, that made her feel a proper adult indeed.

"Well, child?" Mrs. Welles' question was gentle but her voice betrayed a mother's excitement at the news and recalled Comfort from her trance. "Think you Mr. Chapman's suit would be unwelcome?"

Suddenly shy, Comfort studied her bowl and answered in a low voice,

"No, mother, I think it would not."

Then she looked up and smiled. A look of tentative delight spread across her face as she contemplated life as a married woman.

Five months of anticipation passed remarkably slowly. Not that there was lack of work to occupy the time. Food must be put up for winter and the Watertown house secured against the cold. There was the constant round of chores to keep a family fed and clothed, the house swept and animals tended. But sometimes, especially in the short days of thin winter light, Comfort and her mother would draw their seats close to the south-facing windows where bright sunlight almost made up for the drafty cold sneaking in around the window frame. There Comfort would work on hemming the last sheets and pillowbiers to fill her dower chest. The fine linen which covered her lap had been brought from England by her mother all those years ago, against this occasion when Comfort would be wed. As Comfort's needle moved in and out of the crisp cloth, she lost herself in memory of gently rolling fields of startling blue, acres of flax in bloom which every June transformed the East Anglian landscape of her childhood. It was from fields such as those that this linen had come. There was nothing like them in New England. What flax did grow near Boston was in kerchief-sized plots and, come blossom time, there were near as many field weeds as blue flowers to be seen. Some things, Comfort admitted to herself, she still missed from her first home.

As Comfort hemmed, Mrs. Welles squinted close at an ornate design of scrolling leaves and flowers on the quilted petticoat that was her marriage gift to her daughter.

"There is naught unseemly in dressing yourself, as well as your house, to make your husband proud," she had advised one day as they studied the contents of the dower chest. "As mistress you need bring to your new home such linens as will adorn its best rooms and reflect well on its master. But as wife, you need bring to your marriage such garments as will adorn your own self – oh, in seemly fashion certainly – but with a thought to what will put a gleam of pleasure in your husband's eye."

She nodded definitively, as one who spoke from experience, and Comfort could not help blushing at the intimacy suggested by her mother's words. After that, she found that her visions of blue flax fields were frequently interrupted by thoughts she was ashamed to acknowledge and questions she was embarrassed to ask. The commitment to marriage was more complicated than had occurred to her that night she impulsively agreed to Mr. Chapman's courtship.

No one in the Welles family, Comfort included, found fault with Mr. Chapman as a suitable husband. A journeyman miller in the New World was assured of his own mill privilege in short space, what with the spread of new communities across the Commonwealth. Then Chapman would rank among a town's finest citizens, his status only a bit below minister and rich proprietors. Beyond that consideration, and equally important to Mr. Welles' mind, the young man shared his calling. The older miller approved young Chapman's gift of the "miller's thumb," that instinctive judgment of flour quality which came late to many and to some, not at all. A father need ask no more for his daughter.

Comfort's mother did not dream of questioning her husband's judgment of Mr. Chapman's prospects. But as she contemplated her daughter's life with this man, she added silent thanks that he was young. Not too young, mind you. Twenty-eight was old enough for him to know his mind, to guide and support her daughter as she learned the ways of married life. But his nearness in age to hers, less than a decade separating them, augured well for a long life together. And – Mrs. Welles dimpled at the thought – a lusty life as well, God willing. The daughter would be blessed indeed if she were given a marriage and a husband such as was granted to the mother. All else counted for little next to that.

Comfort herself was not sure what to think. She listened intently as her parents discussed Mr. Chapman's prospects. She attended with a new sense of urgency to her mother's advice on household management, though she had learned much of it long before. She observed Mr. Chapman himself whenever possible, and drew up a mental list of his merits. Mr. Chapman came to call as frequently as work and distance allowed, often staying for supper where he sat close beside her at the table. His clean scent went on her list. There were a few moments together without the elders' supervision, and Mr. Chapman's behavior towards Comfort at those times conveyed his attraction to her as well as his respect. His not-quite-chaste kisses which lingered on her cheek and gave her hot shivers also went on her list. There were many aspects of this man which she found pleasing and which led her to believe they were well-matched. But how would they proceed together when they were wed? The strictures of time and courtship gave little hint of married life, so Comfort had to make do with vague imaginings. She felt a growing impatience for the marriage to begin.

She tried to imagine living in Medfield, too, on the outskirts of that little village all set about with wilderness. About this she was not so eager. But she cheered herself with the thought that, after all, she had visited Medfield only once and perhaps had not conceived a true picture of the place. Then too, Lizbeth lived there and would companion her. Reassuring, as well, was the knowledge that the house Mr. Chapman was building for them was right in the village, by order of the Selectmen, not away in the dark woods like the gristmill she had seen. At times Comfort's thoughts would drift toward creeping rattlesnakes and wolves, fearsome savages and untold devils infesting the unregenerate wilderness. But she would close her eyes tight against the visions and conjure instead a solid field of gentle blue.

Benevolent Lord, protect us from the wildness... she would whisper, and purposefully go about her business.

One concern shared by Mr. and Mrs. Welles was not discussed. That was the growing discord between the Commonwealth's planters and the Indians on whose lands the English had settled. Over the past months there had been increasing reports of savages, individually or in roaming bands, harassing outlying English settlements. Incidents ranged from crop stealing, an outrage to hardworking farmers, to true atrocities like the slaughter of a defenseless Englishman in Hadley last month. Those savages who were caught paid the full penalty exacted by English law, but too many escaped capture, sneaking away into forests and swamps, to threaten Christian lives again another day.

The growing danger concerned everyone, though it posed no immediate threat to the Welleses and their neighbors in the colony's well-established coastal towns. But their daughter would not be going to a coastal town. Medfield lay out on the frontier, with no strong English presence west of it until one reached the tiny settlements lining the distant Connecticut River.

Comfort's own experience of natives was limited to glimpses of dark-skinned men in strange garb, passing through the marketplace. Or black-eyed women with intricate woven baskets for sale. They did not seem so fearsome, she thought, but she was aware of her innocence.

Each Sabbath at meeting, ministers from Salem to Plymouth preached that the natives' discontent was a trial sent by the Lord. Comfort listened, and tried to understand. The heathen savagery like a plague was being visited upon the faithful as a test and as a punishment for their sins and their complacency. She bowed her head and prayed that she not be judged complacent.

Mr. and Mrs. Welles felt little complacency. They could not shelter Comfort from God's terrible word, they agreed, nor should they do so, for her prayers might afford her more protection than anything of this world. But they worried and prayed for her safety and her peace of mind, as she was to take up married life at the edge of the English world. By common consent they avoided discussion of the preacher's words. Savages or not, Comfort would remove to Medfield, leaving her mother and her father and cleaving only to her husband. Little would be gained by frightening the child with talk of dangers about which she could do naught. This threat to lives and faith would pass, God willing. Mr. and Mrs. Welles heard the minister's exhortations to repent and they trembled, bowing their heads in fervent prayer that the Lord would see fit to spare Comfort's life from the devils in this world as well as the next.

The February wedding day was cold and glittering with frost. Comfort remembered little of the brief ceremony except the surprising warm assurance of Thomas Chapman's hand holding her own. The Reverend Mr. Sherman offered solemn prayers to the Lord while Comfort's earthbound thoughts strayed back to England and the wedding of her cousin Joan. Comfort had been the youngest witness of Joan and Arthur's vows. The cluster of relatives, small though it was, spilled out of the church's ancient entrance porch onto the path outside. The vicar, standing at the door, droned on and Comfort, mindful that she must be still, had studied the grotesque oak faces overhead, which served as anchors between the arched roof vaulting and the wall. They must be faces of the saints, she decided. Very old saints keeping watch over what transpires below. Then Joan and her husband signed a paper, and the vicar entered their names in the parish register. Joan's husband kissed her right out in public while wedding guests cheered and the oak faces stared unblinking from the ceiling above.

Now her own wedding day had come. Despite years of familiarity with New World ways, Comfort regretted not standing in Pakenham's ancient vaulted porch. Speaking their vows in Watertown's four-square meetinghouse was not the same. The strict geometry of a carved pulpit was no substitute for a band of silent watchers overhead who testified to the vows of a thousand souls who had come before.

Despite the group of relatives and friends surrounding her, Comfort felt surprisingly alone.

Thomas's grip on her hand tightened and Mr. Sherman intoned "Amen."

Then came the walk together back to her parents' house and food aplenty. Mrs. Welles outdid herself on a collation to refresh their friends. Later, giggling girls and young wives with a knowing gleam in their eyes escorted Comfort upstairs to the chamber where she and Thomas would spend their first night together. They combed out her long brown hair and arranged her new nightclothes around her as they teased about the mysteries to come. They sprinkled the room with lavender and rosemary and threw open the door to the men who, boisterous with posset and ale, grandly ushered the bridegroom into his chamber. Comfort, propped against a mound of bolsters, was too embarrassed to respond to the good-humored joking. She was actually grateful when Thomas, grinning self-consciously, shooed the guests from the room. Comfort's last glimpse as the door closed was of her mother smiling encouragement and reassurance.

And, of course, her mother had been right, Comfort thought a year later, drawing closer to Thomas in the night. Mr. Chapman was a most admirable man and his prowess, she reflected with satisfaction, was not confined to his work at the mill. First-night fears had given way to many nights' pleasure as her husband and she grew to know each other in the flesh and cherish each other in spirit. His solicitude for her comfort and her welfare came close to making up for his man's inability to fathom her fears. And she had been afraid, more often than she wished to remember, since leaving her parents' home. Wishes or not, her memories continued to unroll in the dark night.

When, after the wedding night, they left Watertown for Medfield, Comfort could tell that her husband was as nervous and impatient as a boy to show her their new home. Perhaps that was just as well, she thought at the time. It would not do for him to see her trepidation. The route they traveled was the same as that the Welleses had ridden that long ago spring day. Now, in midwinter, the trees did not crowd quite so close, but the bare-branched oaks and chestnut, drooping hemlock and crow-laden pines still overhung the way. And, Comfort added uneasily to herself, they were headed for a place she did not know at all. *How did I allow this to happen?* she thought in sudden panic. *Why did I ever agree to being taken away from everything familiar, everything that is safe and known?*

Just then Thomas turned to her and asked after her well-being. Were the skins and blankets tucked in warm enough against the cold? Was the tumbril seat too hard for her to bear? He leaned close to her ear and whispered unseemly thoughts about her own seat as his free hand rested warmly on her knee. Comfort blushed under the stern stare of the crows perched overhead, but smiled as well in shocked delight at her husband's intimate attentions.

My husband and my Lord shall be my strength. Through them this wilderness shall be overcome; likewise the unruly and senseless fears of my heart. Through them and in their care I shall prevail.

She buried her chin deeper in her heavy cape and watched the oxen's horns nod up and down as they plodded imperturbably ahead.

Comfort's welcome to Medfield began before she even climbed off the cart. Lizbeth Arnold was waiting at the Chapman house to greet her on arrival – though how she knew to be there was a mystery to Comfort. Lizbeth flung her arms around her old friend and whispered, as Mr. Chapman unloaded the cart, that Comfort had made the marriage catch of Medfield. Although, Lizbeth asserted, Mr. Morse, to whom she would be wed come summer, would not stand far behind.

The little house was warm, a spendthrift fire blazing on the hearth to greet them. As they stood close to the welcome heat, there was a knock. Thomas opened the door and ushered in a man whose words of congratulations overlapped his own of welcome. The gentleman must be her father's age, Comfort guessed, his white hair flowing as he removed his hat. He had to stoop to enter the low-ceilinged room. His eyes shone with humor and intelligence as he bowed to her and introduced himself as Timothy Dwight, one of Medfield's governing Selectmen. A thin little boy followed silent and wide-eyed and his father introduced young Timothy. Then Master Dwight carefully assisted a woman over the threshold, who held a cloth-draped basket on one arm. This was Dorcas Dwight, and Comfort could see despite her voluminous cloak that Mistress Dwight was well along with child.

The Dwights had walked up from their place by the meetinghouse to welcome the newlyweds and 'bring them a bit to tide them over,' Mistress Dwight explained modestly as she uncovered a basket filled with meat pasties, hard cheese, and baked apples. Young Timothy handed over a loaf of fresh bread, and Master Dwight presented a jug of cider to Thomas, joking about this being the last time he'd have to depend on others for his daily bread. Comfort was surprised and immensely grateful for the Dwights' generosity, since she had been wondering how to put food on the table these first few days in a new home. Dorcas assured her there would be more coming, as soon as word of their arrival got around.

"You should have seen our larder when Mr. Dwight brought me to town as his new wife," she laughed. "'Twas not so long since his first wife had died, God rest her soul. Everyone was so concerned to inspect his new young bride," Dorcas and Timothy exchanged a speaking glance as she emphasized *young*, "that I had no need to cook for a week!"

Comfort imagined Mrs. Dwight was putting a generous face on what had surely been an awkward situation. She was old enough to know how small town gossip worked. What would Medfield have to say about her?

Thomas insisted the cider be uncorked immediately and shared around, so Comfort sent the men to bring in her chests, in order that her first guests might drink from something more fitting than the few random vessels found in Chapman's house. As Lizbeth and the Dwights shared cider and conversation with her husband, Comfort sat quietly absorbing her new surroundings. The handful of guests filled the room, which seemed cozy against the cold gray outside, but Comfort saw how little space there was. There was a storeroom, Comfort had seen, in back of the chimney, with a ladder in one corner that must give access to storage under the eaves. *The house is very small*, she thought. *I cannot even tell where what I've brought might go.* Taking up a large corner of the main room was a bed, unseemly in its nakedness. *Though not for long,* Comfort reassured herself. *By tomorrow Mr. Chapman will have the hangings up. The tall chest where they're stored might look well across the room.*

The whole place smelled of fresh-cut wood, the sweet smell of pine planks mixed with sharper tang of oak. It was so new, she noticed, the wide floor boards were unworn. Even the ceiling above the hearth was not yet darkened with smoke.

This is my house now, she thought. She took pride in its neat aspect, and the notion of being mistress in her own home. *My husband has brought me to this place to make a home. May the Lord guide me in making this house, so raw in its newness, as warm and welcoming a place as that my mother made in Watertown. Make me a good wife, Lord, and a good house wife as well, that I may show the working of Thy grace in the actions of my every day, as well as in my surroundings.*

Comfort's meditation was interrupted by high-pitched coughing. The harsh sound came from young Timothy, who had been sitting close by Thomas as the adults talked. Immediately the Dwights moved to him, and Thomas made way for Dorcas, who fed him sips of cider between coughing spasms. Timothy patted the boy's shoulder in frowning silence until the coughing subsided. Then Dorcas awkwardly rose from her kneeling position and indicated they had overstayed their time.

"The cold is hard on such as suffer from the ague," Comfort commented sympathetically.

Dorcas shook her head and drew the boy close.

"Our Timothy has coughed so since he was only a babe. Not so badly in the summer months, it's true, but he never loses it completely."

She exchanged a worried look with her husband.

Master Dwight read her thought. "We were not wise, perhaps, to bring him out on such a bitter day, but our young man was as anxious to welcome you as we ourselves." Dwight's frown disappeared and he nodded toward Thomas. "Your husband holds a special place in our hearts."

"As shall you, I am sure, Mistress Chapman," Dorcas finished.

Comfort returned her smile and was heartened by what she saw. It did not take long in the company of the Dwights, Comfort thought, with their shared thoughts and concerted actions, to recognize that the parents were wed by love as well as children. God grant that she and Thomas might be so blessed.

Just then Timothy, recovered from his coughing spell, brightened and finally spoke. "I'm to apprentice at Master Chapman's mill some day," he explained to Comfort. "He promised me so my last birthday. But he won't let me start yet." The five-year-old's impatience was clear.

Thomas nodded seriously at him but shook a warning finger.

"Now, Timothy, be in no such rush to tie yourself to a millstone. Milling's a hard taskmaster and it won't let up because you've a mind to go fishing. Besides," Thomas lowered his voice and went on confidentially, "if you hold on a year or two, I'm going to build us a bigger and a better mill than the county's ever seen."

He nodded assurance at the boy and Comfort wondered briefly what on earth her husband meant, but the Dwights were putting on their cloaks, bundling their son in as many layers as his shoulders could carry, and Comfort dismissed Thomas's comment as exaggerated foolishness meant only to spellbind a child. It was good to see her husband had a taste for fun.

Over the next week Comfort found that Dorcas's prediction was right. A steady stream of visitors came to congratulate the new couple and, for every discreetly measuring glance at Comfort or her belongings, there was also a chain of sausage or a brace of pigeons, a pot of soft soap or a new broom for the hearth.

Mistress Adams came up from the mill with her youngest boy as escort. She brought a small straw basket woven with brightly colored stripes. Comfort was immediately struck by the fineness of the work.

"Truly, Mistress, I cannot feel it right to accept such a valuable gift."

Elizabeth Adams waved off Comfort's protests. "In faith, the baskets are easily come by. You need look no farther than the south end of the planting field."

At Comfort's obvious bewilderment, she went on.

"Lucy lives there, one of the natives from hereabouts. She and her man watch the corn fields in the summer months. Scare off the crows, watch for raccoons and such. Come winter Lucy works at basket weaving. In fact, you would be well-advised, Mistress Chapman, to seek her out for any needlework needs doing. The squaw may be old but her eyes are sharper than my own and her fingers are still delicate. She takes instruction well, too – more than can be said of her husband."

"They live not far from your own house then, do they?" Comfort asked hesitantly.

"Aye, just down the way."

"Are you not concerned, with savages so nearby?"

Mrs. Adams laughed shortly and dismissed Comfort's fears. "Not likely! With seven strapping men nearby to guard me and mine. Besides, there's naught much to fear from those two. Why, Lucy's nearly one of us. And Mapshet, he's useless for much beyond waving at crows. Nay, Mistress Chapman, the two of them are Medfield Indians. They belong here as much as we, and they need us for simple survival. I've no concern."

Comfort remembered the women she'd seen at Watertown market, and wondered again at the savagery attributed to these people.

February melted into March and then April as Comfort accustomed herself to life as Mistress Chapman. The bare raw house she had entered that first cold afternoon began to fill with color and texture as bed curtains were hung and Comfort's prized Turkey carpet was spread lovingly over the high chest. She set a pair of pewter tankards on top, flanking her grandmother's big round charger, and in the evening light her eye cherished the pewter's soft glow in the shadowed corner.

It was a rare day that saw Thomas at home. More often he was out at first light, tramping out through the snow with others from the town, to the timber land in Rocky Woods where they felled trees and dragged them out on sledges over the frozen trails. Then spring thawed the stream that ran the mill. Thomas set off alone in the opposite direction, a musket in one hand and luncheon in the other. He took the Dedham road through the woods crowning the hill called Mount Nebo. Then he cut southward to the mill. His days were spent with Miller Adams, grinding the measures of grain brought by folks from Medfield or Walpole, or from the few isolated homesteads on the border with Dedham. Adams' own sons looked to have the makings of husbandmen, working the broad acres granted to the miller by the town.

Comfort's thoughts followed her husband, worrying over his solitary trip through the wilderness. Unconsciously she would breathe deep, in time with his every imagined step, as if her company could see him safe past dangers in his way. Then unexpectedly, in the middle of the day, reassuring images would come of her husband tipping a bag of grain into the hopper, rubbing the meal between thumb and forefinger, lightly adjusting the delicate rub of stone against stone, or the pressure of water pushing the clumsy tub wheel around. When she knew he'd be heading home, the worry would return and she'd work distracted until his solid footsteps sounded outside the door.

Some days he left before light and returned when she could no longer see outdoors. One night he did not come home at all. It had rained hard the two days preceding, and occasional showers still kept the hen yard muddy and the eaves dripping. Thomas had left hurriedly that morning, concerned about the dam. As night fell and Comfort's worry approached desperation, there was an abrupt knock on the door.

"Evening, Mistress."

Comfort's half-cry of shock faded to fearful silence as she took in the specter who'd appeared out of nowhere on her doorstep. Thin to the point of gaunt, his high cheekbones hinted of some alien ancestry. His hair straggled out from under a misshapen hat whose felt had long since faded from black to dingy brown. He was tall and lean and wild looking, yet unmistakably English. His eyes narrowed to slits as he took in her fear.

"Jack Peters," he mumbled, grabbing off his hat. The rain streamed down his taut face. "I'm come from the mill."

Comfort's panic shifted focus.

"My husband? Has anything happened? Is he all right?"

"Well enough. He asked would I stop on my way, tell you he'd not be home tonight."

The narrow slits of eyes watched her. Was he telling truth? Was he sent indeed by Thomas? His appearance was so sinister, so uncivilized as to make her fear for her own safety. Then something unexpected happened. Jack Peters smiled. Just a crack of a smile, as if his face found the act a challenge. But when he did, his eyes opened from cold, inhuman slits to brown eyes full of concern and sympathy.

"Water's high, you know." His explanation came with a nod of his head in the direction of the mill.

Comfort, the miller's daughter, nodded in understanding. In time of flood, a miller's place was by his dam, keeping watch on the sluice boards and the rising water, lowering the boards to control the flow and doing what he could to protect the building from washing away. This was not easy at Adams' Mill. The first miller in town, George Barber, had sited the mill on a level stretch of brook which made construction easy but protection hard. If the storm water, filled with tumbling trees and rocks, did not damage the sluice or wipe out the dam as it rushed downstream, then the water which inexorably rose in the valley would flood the mill and clog the tailrace with branches and silt.

Henry Adams, who bought the mill from Barber, seemed to think the situation did well enough. Thomas, on the other hand, had grumbled more than once at Barber's shortsightedness.

"Mark my words, wife, when it comes my turn to build a mill, it won't be in the middle of an infernal swamp. We Devon men know better how to site a wheel. Down from the swamp, on a short fall, lifted well out of its own backwater."

Comfort had reminded him of the Selectmen's recent edict that all new houses in Medfield be located within a mile of the meetinghouse. He grumbled at that too. It made oversight of a mill next to impossible, and would never be supported back in England.

Comfort listened to her husband's grumbling in sympathetic silence, but thanked the Lord for the Selectmen's adamant insistence. It was, after all, an order made out of consideration for the whole community's welfare. It was far better, in this time of troubles, to live near to one's neighbor for mutual support and protection. She shuddered at the idea of having to dwell a mile outside of town, away from open fields, away from the sociable gossip of neighbors, buried in the woods with only the howl of wolves and the rush of water to listen to. How could Mistress Adams stand it? When Comfort imagined living by the mill Thomas would build one day, she seemed to forget her husband would be there beside her, just as Master Adams was by his wife. What came to Comfort's mind was fearful isolation.

Now, during the spring floods, she was safe in the village, at home. But she realized, for all her proximity to others, she was alone. She spent a restless night thinking how sodden and chilled Thomas must be, praying for his safety and his speedy return, with no one to share her qualms until the morning. She lay awake, deep in her own bed, wrapped in fearful isolation.

By the coming of May the river meadows were sprouted with fresh green grass, the well-drained soil of the upland fields had dried, and the men shut down the mill for a spell in order to join in spring planting. Cool weather crops were already in, peas and beets and the tiny seeds of salad greens and radishes, set in kitchen gardens by the April full moon. But May was the time for field crops, grain for man and beast sowed in the long parallel strips that each man owned at the planting field south of town.

The Reverend Mr. Wilson offered a special prayer on the sabbath before they began.

"Benevolent Lord, whose goodness towards us surpasseth the farthest reach of man's understanding, we beseech Thee now to watch over this company of farmers who go forth to cultivate the wilderness and make it fruitful in Thy name."

Comfort bowed her head and silently added a private thanksgiving to his prayer.

And I offer Thee particular thanks that Thou seest fit to remove Thomas from the dangers that encompass him about each day he walks alone over Mount Nebo. I offer Thee thanks that Thou hast placed him in the company of brave and godly men whose presence will protect him as Thou dost Thyself.

The minister's voice intoned, "Amen."

The following day was sunny and warm, reflecting the lightness of Comfort's heart as she opened the shutters to the morning air. She had not realized until that moment how worry had weighed her down all those days Thomas had set off alone with one old musket and her prayers as his only protection. It was truly said that there is safety in numbers, she nodded to herself. And today neither he nor she need worry about his safety. Naught could happen, after all, in company with another dozen men. The only savage they were likely to see was old Lucy, or perhaps her husband Mapshet. And Lucy, at least, was Christian like themselves.

Comfort studied Thomas as he rushed through the morning meal. He was distracted, head bent over his porringer, and she could look her fill, caressing him with a smile of love and amusement, tinged by envy. He was clearly looking forward to the day, despite the

369

backbreaking work of tilling for long hours until dusk. What he really looked forward to, she was sure, was the companionship that went with planting just as it did with harvest time. How was it, she wondered, that the longer they labored – till their joints ached and their muscles trembled – the more these taciturn men would draw together? The somber elder who never cracked a smile would quip as lightly as a joker. The loner who neither lent a hand nor took one, would step forth unbidden to help a neighbor. And when it was all over, they came home satisfied. Faces lined with dirt or hair dressed with straw, they bid each other goodbye with a tired nod and a smile of solidarity. A job well done.

It seemed there was nothing quite like it in women's work. Besides, she reminded herself wryly, woman's work, though it might be well done, was never all done. One task just melded into the next in great loops from day to day, and only over years could one look back to judge a task completed.

Thomas kissed her on the cheek as he settled his hat on his head. His grin was boyish with anticipation of the day to come.

"You'll not forget me while I'm gone, wife?" he asked, mock serious, as he nonchalantly reached above the door for his musket.

Comfort was amused by this sign of his obvious distraction and chaffed him in return.

"Come now, Master Chapman, has your head gone on before your feet? Or do you intend hoeing with your musket today?"

"Nay, mistress, the hoe's behind in the shed where it ought to be. I but obey the Selectmen's recent caution to go about armed."

Comfort stared at him a moment in disbelief.

"I do not mean to doubt your understanding, husband. But surely they mean for you to carry a weapon only on such occasions as warrant extra care? When you are hunting in the woods, perhaps?" She waved her hand toward an imaginary trail. "Or travelling deserted paths from town to town?"

Thomas shook his head uncomfortably.

"Nay. They declared we are to walk so at all times."

Comfort's tone became indignant.

"You are but going to South Plain, for heaven's sake! What untoward disaster do they fancy might befall you between here and there?!"

Thomas set his gun down next to an abandoned porringer and gently took her by the elbows.

"Comfort, you know 'tis but for our own protection. Each week the savages grow more threatening. Why, only last week there was rumor of a great band coming together to the southward. We know not what they are about, but it is sure their leader, Philip, is no friend to Englishmen."

Comfort had stiffened as her husband spoke. Thomas smoothed his hand up her arm in reassurance.

"But there's little to fear here, wife. Do you but stay along the village paths you're apt to travel anyway, you are bound to be safe. Those who might be enemies dare not come so close to Christian settlements."

He read the mix of anger and trepidation on her face and tried another tack.

"Come now, my love, you're overwrought. Did you not say Lizbeth Arnold was coming shortly with her dower linens? And Mistress Dwight? Her young ones will keep you occupied till the cows and I come home. And then I do believe I might find some way to do likewise — unless the children will have worn you out by then?"

She knew his lascivious suggestion was but an attempt to relieve her mind. Raising her chin in determination and her eyebrow in suggestion, she put a good face on the matter and bid her husband a fond Godspeed. But as he strode off past the neighboring Morse house, catching up with other men headed toward South Plain, she remained still in the doorway, stunned by the implications of what Thomas had said.

He looks so confident. So certain in his strength and his fellowship. But muskets in the fields? In case of attack? No one ever spoke of such near danger when I contemplated coming here. Why did they not forewarn me? Why did they not tell me that this must be supported as well as all the other exigencies of the edge of wilderness?

Indignation became stronger than fear.

I came here to be a miller's wife. Helpmate to a simple hardworking man. Not to a militiaman! And this place. Does Medfield even warrant the name of town? This place is naught but an armed

371

camp! Soon it will house cannons instead of bells, soldiers instead of farmers. And we, the wives and mothers, must needs start each day beseeching, rather than thanking the Almighty for what He has in store! It is not right!

She brushed away the angry tears that pressed against her eyelids. Impatient with her weakness, frustrated by her helplessness to make the danger go away, she rushed about the small room, looking for distraction in daily chores. But there were few dishes, the bed was quickly straightened, and she could not start a longer task with Lizbeth and Dorcas coming soon.

Comfort replaced a wooden bowl on top of her dower chest, then paused and frowned consideringly. Setting the bowl aside, she knelt in front of the carved oak box and raised the lid. Lavender filled the room with whispers of sky-blue summer days. She lifted out Thomas's and her heavy winter cloaks. Underneath was the white chemise she'd worn their wedding night, and she contemplated it, conjuring the lace-trimmed linen to evoke such memories as would smooth away her frustration. The memories would not stay within reach, so she laid the chemise carefully on top of the cloaks. Other garments followed, and she studied each one. Some were used as padding for the handsome silver cup which Thomas had from his family. Others were wrapped lovingly around Comfort's few ornaments, brought out to wear on holidays.

The feel of their possessions was almost soothing, like an anchor holding Comfort to the familiar. They were almost enough to calm her immediate worries. Thomas was safe today. He would come home to her tonight and their lives would proceed on a steady course in the weeks to come. But the comfortable familiarity of the objects she studied was not enough to rid her of the helplessness that underlay her fears.

Near the bottom of the deep chest, Comfort found the quilted petticoat her mother had made, the color of goldenrod. She drew it out and stroked the dense fabric, the rounded shapes of padded leaves and petals. Her fingers moved up toward the gathers at the waist. There, hidden among the folds, she searched out five round shapes evenly spaced around the skirt. Five gold sovereigns, worked into the design and stitched into the padding for safekeeping. A deathbed gift from her Grandmother Welles, long ago in England. Because *a female should have more to call her own than a cupboardful of linens*, the still-decisive voice had said. Comfort remembered the smooth, chill forehead she had kissed as she said goodbye to that extraordinary lady.

It was her mother's idea to stitch the coins into her petticoat. They'd be worth a pretty penny now, she had observed, what with the dearth of coinage in New England. Enough for a few good sheep – or a milk cow, she nodded significantly, when the first child is weaned.

Comfort thought of her own ideas for what that money could buy. The sovereigns were enough to pay for a barn set apart from the house, not like the lean-to shed they bore with for the present. They'd not have to smell the byre quite so close, nor battle the flies which plagued them, eating or sleeping. Enough to pay for a new millstone, were Thomas to need one. That was an unfortunate thought, which brought her full circle to the horrible situation she was trying to ignore.

Need one! More like to need sword and helm to shield himself from savages! And me? What will shield me?

For a guilty moment the learned response to that question – that her husband and her community, her faith and her Lord would guard and comfort her – the response would not come. Comfort knelt frozen in place. Slowly she became aware of the weight and shape of the sovereigns in her hands.

The sovereigns would shield me if all else failed. With one sovereign alone I could flee the madness of this place. I could buy transport – a guard even – back to Watertown. Back home. Back, if need be, all the way to Pakenham where people have never heard of savages. Where the most fearsome weapon to be found is an old dress sword. Just a decoration, more often than not, like the one used to hang above the hearth in my parents' chamber.

She clutched the coins tight in their hiding place and glowered belligerently at the chest as she contrasted innocent memory to her present state. Then she nodded decisively and set down the garment. Reaching beneath her skirt she untied the strings of her workday petticoat and stepped out of it. She slipped the quilted garment on in its place.

Comfort tied it tight and called on God to be her witness. *This shall I wear always on my person, no matter what the season or occasion. Until such time as Medfield warrants the name of home,* she vowed in defiance of her fears. *And no,* she continued her silent dialogue with the Almighty. *I do not hold myself disloyal to my husband by this act. Is it not written in Scripture that Thou helpest him who helps himself? Surely I must do no less.*

Comfort returned the other contents to the chest and greeted her friends with stronger determination and lighter heart than she had felt for a long time.

In the long twilight that marked the year's turning to languid summer Thomas returned from the fields. He raised a hand in weary salute to neighbors Morse and Clark, then turned toward Comfort with a face whose glow of satisfaction was strong enough to shine right through the caked-on dust. He ate like a horse and fell into bed so tired his intended attentions to his wife took place in dream only. Comfort understood and did not mind. There would be time for attentions. Tonight they were safely together again, and that was all she asked.

Late spring sprouted into summer. The rush of planting slowed to steady growth. The August weather stretched hot and dry and Mill Brook dwindled to a trickle which had Thomas muttering in frustration to anyone who would listen. One midday Comfort was working her way down an endless succession of rows to hoe in the kitchen garden when a sudden hand clasping her waist made her squeak in surprise. She whirled around to find Thomas grinning behind her. Sweat had soaked through the front of his smock and showed dark around the crown of his hat but there was a sparkle in his eye which told of something better on his mind than the heat.

Comfort smeared the damp hairs off her forehead and looked him askance. She never knew what he was scheming when that one dimple appeared in his cheek, but she almost always enjoyed the outcome.

"What are you about, husband?" She laughed and scolded at the same time. "You near scared me to death, and me with the carrots yet to hoe!"

"Well, Mistress Chapman…" Thomas drew out his words. "Would you walk out with me this afternoon? I know a place with shade aplenty. Soft moss to sit on. Cool water to soothe your toes..." His voice had dropped to a murmur.

"Why, Master Chapman! What would you have me do with the carrots? And you, are you flirting with the sin of idleness this summer's day?"

Thomas shrugged. "The carrots will hoe much faster in the cool of evening. And I flirt with naught but my own true love." He kissed her lightly on the cheek, then went on in all apparent seriousness. "So do not suspect me of idleness. The place I'd take you bears directly on our future. I am all business, madam, and have only Comfort's comfort at heart when I offer to take you with me."

Her husband was hard to resist when he was lighthearted. And Comfort had no love of labor in the noonday sun. So with only a token show of reluctance she gave in to his proposal. They walked hand in hand back to the house where she hung up her hoe and, at Thomas's suggestion, gathered a packet of bread and cold meat to eat along the way.

As ever, Thomas shouldered his musket on the way out the door. Comfort could not resist a sigh. Her husband suddenly stopped and fixed her with a hard stare, as if daring her to voice complaint at his action. Her breath caught in shock at his glimpsed disapproval. Then the moment passed and Thomas drew a stout walking stick out of the corner, offering it to his wife.

"Goodness! Where are we headed then?" she asked. Her voice quavered. But he shook his head, refusing to say more than that she'd see in due course.

They set out on the east road, the one that led eventually to Dedham village. Comfort watched Thomas disappear this direction every day he went to the mill. As always when she left the open farmyards of Medfield, a tingle of unease began to tighten her shoulders. But she and Thomas were of a stride, and the companionable rhythm of their steps together kept the tension at bay, while the cool shade of the trees bordering the path was welcome relief from the heavy heated fields they left behind.

Mindful of Thomas's reluctance to name their destination, Comfort made small talk as they went, relaying to her husband the minor occurrences which set one day apart from the one before: the rooster's latest outrageous behavior, Goody Morse's news from

Boston. Thomas nodded and briefly responded, but she noticed that the farther they walked, the less attentive he was to her chatter.

As talk died down, the path they followed crested Mount Nebo, then angled down the other side. The terrain was rocky and unsuited to much more than summer pasture. Clumps of high-bush blueberry interrupted Comfort's restless scanning of the shadowed forest. She spotted bits of cranberry bog, damp even in midsummer and wished that her wayward imagining did not turn every granite outcrop and briar thicket into a hiding place for crawling or walking beast.

How could Thomas so confidently travel through these woods? Surely he was wise enough to see the ever-present danger. Did he have some knowledge she did not, protecting him from harm and the fear that went with it? If so, she wished he would share it with her. But she didn't know how to ask.

Thomas turned abruptly to the right, and Comfort found herself on a narrow footpath veering south from the main road.

"This is the shortcut to the mill." Thomas helped her over a rough patch. "You see 'tis no good for carts, though. Jack Peters says it's an old Indian track down past the Great Plain."

"Jack Peters?"

"The woodsman. You remember him spooking you the night of high water?"

"Oh, yes." Comfort reddened and hurried to change the subject. "You come this way alone, do you, Thomas?"

"Sure I do. It cuts a good bit off the distance."

"Think you 'tis safe, husband?" The look she gave him held all the worry she kept out of her voice.

Thomas's glance was tolerant. He shrugged.

"No less safe than anywhere around these parts. Peters says the savages have pretty much all gone the other side of the river. I'd guess they're avoiding us as much as we are them. Good idea, too," he added in a frowning afterthought.

"Still I cannot help worrying, husband."

"Well, love, that's one reason we're off on this expedition. I've something in mind to allay your fears as well as serve other purposes. Not much farther now. You'll see."

The path skirted a long swampy patch of ground. Somewhere, Comfort knew, in the middle of the swamp was the brook that eventually flowed past Adams' mill, though a body would be hard put to guess where swamp left off and brook began in all the undergrowth.

As she picked her way along the narrow track, a long branch of catbriar hooking itself in her skirt brought Comfort up short. She bent to untangle the persistent thorns, irritation temporarily replacing her fear. She muttered under her breath at her husband's idea of a summer outing. Once the linen skirt was free, Comfort tucked its sides up into her waistband, work-fashion, to keep it out of harm's way. She caught a glimpse of one of the sovereign rounds stitched into the yellow underskirt. Her jaw set with determination. *I can leave this unholy place whenever I choose. I need not spend my life wading through briars.*

Thomas interrupted her silent defiance by taking her arm.

"We'll step off here," he said, drawing her off the path. "A bit beyond, the track crosses the brook and heads off downstream. But here, wife, this is what I want to show you."

The quiet excitement in Thomas's voice, his hand at her elbow, both drew Comfort out of her annoyance. She looked around to discover what Thomas's surprise might be, but saw nothing to warrant great enthusiasm.

True, they had climbed a short rise up away from the exasperating briars. The trees thinned out, leaving the top of the rise almost clear, for which, despite her earlier perspiration, she was grateful. A sound of burbling water told her the brook must emerge from the swamp nearby and trip down to a lower rocky streambed. But still she didn't know why Thomas had brought her to this place. She looked at him in puzzlement.

"Here is the place for Chapman's Mill." He imbued the name with special pride.

Comfort raised her eyebrows in question.

"Is this what you've talked about since I came? The bigger and better mill?"

Thomas nodded eagerly.

"This is where the mill should have been, right along." He gestured out beyond the rise, where the brook could be heard.

"A short fall there." His arm swept upstream. "Acres of swampland upstream to hold the flow." He took her hand and drew her to the water side of the hill, which dropped off abruptly in rough granite ledge. "And here's the anchor for a good, solid dam: high enough for a tidy millpond, but small enough to manage easily. There's ledge on the other side of the stream, too. And right out there," he swung both arms up to gesture toward the invisible dam, "is a tidy little mill with an overshot wheel and power enough, spring and fall, to run two course of stones. None of those flatland mills like you East Anglians build."

Thomas turned to Comfort with such conviction on his face that he almost had her believing it wasn't all imagining.

"There're springs enough upstream to keep the water flowing year round. We'd have a mill could show a profit. Not the on-again, off-again operation Adams has."

Touched by her husband's use of *we* when he spoke of the mill, Comfort sought to be encouraging.

"Can you build here, then? Speak to Master Adams? The town would benefit from a second mill, would it not?"

Thomas shook his head.

"Looking ahead it would, aye. But 'tis nowise so simple as you conceive, Comfort. An earlier time, perhaps, the Selectmen might have listened. But think what I'd be asking. This is town land we're standing on, so I'd need a grant of land, and water rights much broader than Adams has."

Comfort started to speak but was cut off by Thomas's continuing thoughts.

"And then there's the labor needed. Back when Barber put up his mill, the townsfolk turned out to help with the digging and building. But it won't happen that way again."

"Why ever not? Think you they will not work to their own advantage?

"Don't you see? To their minds Adams' mill is enough. They see the grain they grow being ground and that's all they care about."

Thomas hunkered down on his heels and became silent. He soberly stared at the drop before him as if it might offer some answer to his dilemma. Comfort, guessing they might linger some time, settled herself next to him, on a patch of the soft moss that she remembered he'd promised as one of the afternoon's delights. She wryly contemplated the difference between her expectations and

Thomas's purpose for walking out. Her husband's voice broke the silence.

"No," he shook his head, "if there's ever going to be a new mill here it'll have to be built and paid for with gold and silver. Sure, I could probably talk the Selectmen around – there's vacant land aplenty on the stream – and I could find the men to help. Jack Peters comes out of the blue whenever he needs a few coins to rub together, and there're others. And plenty of men would delight to sell me boards and shingles and nails. But I've neither the gold nor the silver to pay for it all." He shrugged helplessly. "And country credit will not pay this piper."

Thomas looked at Comfort almost as if he expected her to offer a solution.

She could, of course. At least a partial one. The sovereigns in her petticoat weighed against her. *Is this then, the occasion they were saved for? Should I not offer them now?*

Her hand moved unobtrusively as she tried to decide whether her impulse to surrender the coins to her husband was loving or foolish. He glanced away again, following still the track of his thoughts.

"Then too, there's the house to be thought of...," he mused aloud.

"House?" Comfort was surprised by Thomas's consideration of her wants in the middle of his own concerns. "Truly, husband, enlarging the house will wait. I know we've spoken of it, but we've small need for more room yet. Certainly not while there's a mill to concern you."

Thomas's brows drew down in confusion, then raised as he realized Comfort's misunderstanding of his words.

"Ah! Nay, wife, 'tis not more room I think of, but *different* room. You know as well as I that a mill with a decent fall requires full-time tending. There's no way we could remain in the village any longer. We'd build a house here, of course, close by the mill."

"By the mill?" Comfort was stunned. "Out here? You cannot think of doing that, Thomas!"

"Come, sweeting, you know the way of milling. You know we cannot live so far from the stream."

"But the Selectmen have said it is necessary! 'Tis not safe so far off from settlement! What do you propose we do, should the savages attack, and us way off here? Where do we hide? How do we defend ourselves in the middle of the wilderness? This idea is daft, husband!"

"It is not so, mistress!" he snapped back. "You and your wilderness. What is daft is living near a half-hour from the mill. We're far more likely to lose the whole works in a good freshet, being in town, than we are to lose our lives to some passing Indian here. You are being womanly and unreasonable about this whole affair!"

His words struck Comfort like a slap on the face.

"Unreasonable?!" Her voice rose higher as she went on. "I am unreasonable? What do you call yourself? Here the entire colony is on alert. Even you go about armed day and night. Innocent people are being cut down in cold blood, scalped, abducted – and *you* propose to build in the heart of nowhere! Now who, I ask, is the more unreasonable?"

Thomas's voice was bitter as he answered back.

"What would you have us do then, Mistress Chapman? Would you have us sit in the village, and bide our time for God knows how long, doing nothing? Making no move to improve our lot? All because of some threat which may never be realized? We cannot guess how long the discord will last. We cannot wish the Indians away, much as we would. I tell you, I, for one, did not come all the way across the ocean to waste my life away in fear and trembling of a danger which may never go away! If it's not to be here, then Chapman's Mill will be built in some other town. Even farther out, like as not."

Comfort jumped to her feet and set hands on hips, as if superior height would give her words more weight.

"Well I, for one, did not leave the safety of Watertown and come out here to be massacred!"

"Oh! So now you wish to return to your parents?" Thomas surged upward as well, and flung the words at her.

"No, I do not! I didn't say as much!"

As Comfort paused for breath she suddenly heard the hatefulness in their voices. A few words more and something truly awful might occur. Could she win her husband back if she pushed him away now? And whatever would she be without him? She struggled to curb her panic-sparked anger.

"I do well enough here, husband. I would not depart from Medfield."

"Or from you," she added softly. "But please, I beg you. Do not make me live outside the village, all alone."

The pleading in Comfort's last words cut through Thomas's defiant indignation. His whole body sagged and a scowl of mixed defeat and self-reproach seamed his face.

The brook sounded loud in the stillness.

A sigh finally broke the silence as Thomas moved toward Comfort who stood, frozen, hands gripped together and head bowed. She had never raised her voice in anger toward her husband, and was horrified at what would happen next.

Thomas gently raised her chin, forcing her to meet his eyes.

"I had not known, wife, till now, your distaste for outliving was so strong. I will not force you ever, to do what you find to be abhorrent."

She read sadness in his eyes as well as love.

"But I would beg you consider well what is to become of us, if we must always be constrained within the village bounds. Our own fortunes and our children's fortunes will be just so tightly circumscribed as is this little village."

He searched Comfort's face for any sign of agreement. Instead, she dropped her eyes to study the stitching on his collar. Her chin was set.

"You are precious to me, Comfort Chapman. I would not have you unhappy with your fate. What we do, we must do together, agree upon, for I'll not drag you into something to be regretted later. This business of the mill is naught but whimsy anyway, until we save a sight more than we have now. Meantime, I would ask only that you reconsider your feelings. Will you do that for me, wife?"

Comfort's eyes remained downcast as she nodded her agreement and whispered, "I will. And Thomas, I beg your forgiveness for my behavior. I know not how I lost my temper so."

Thomas placed a careful kiss on her forehead.

"There is no more forgiving to be done on your part than on mine own. I am likewise ashamed."

Comfort briefly nodded and shrugged at the same time. She could not bring herself to look at Thomas again. Silence stretched out painfully between them.

"Well." The word sounded final. "We might as well start back."

Thomas turned abruptly and led the way back down the hill. Comfort followed his broad shoulders in silence, overwhelmed by their falling out. For once, she was unconscious of the forest's sounds and shadows. But the coins weighed heavily on her.

Across the Commonwealth and south into Rhode Island, few people could ignore the forest's sights and sounds that summer. Stories from six months back of the Indian sachem King Philip rallying other leaders for war against the English, had turned into the real thing. Towns in Plymouth Colony, not far to the southward, had been attacked or burned. On July 14 the town of Mendon, next settlement west of Medfield, was abandoned after five men were slain and the houses torched. Medfield was suddenly the frontier, with little but wilderness between it and the Connecticut River.

By September the Connecticut River valley was under attack. Deerfield evacuated and solitary homesteaders fell back on towns and settlements farther east. Medfield bought a cannon for protection and wary townspeople drew together to wait out a dismal winter.

But the colony moved to end the savage threat once and for all. In December a government force invaded a large tract of swampland near Kingstown, Rhode Island, on the information that Philip and his men were hiding there. They destroyed everything they found, including the women and children whose winter camp this had been. It was enough to harden the Indians' resolve to leave no English village standing.

February brought gruesome tales of isolated farms attacked, settlers killed or captured. Lancaster, to the northwest, lay in ruins, with over fifty killed.

A regional militia is formed and a mounted troop is sent out from Boston to patrol the frontier. Eighty government soldiers are quartered in Medfield, as rumor comes that Indians are moving east from Lancaster to Sudbury, from thence toward Medfield itself. What work is done, is done with weapons at hand. Even Sunday meeting sees muskets laid on the floor in every pew. Be vigilant, the Reverend Wilson warns. There's word of savages seen as close as Mount Nebo. Be vigilant as well, he urges the congregation, to do battle with evil and put away sin, that the Lord may see his flock repentant and remove this scourge from among us.

Amen.

February 21, 1676

Comfort sighed, and resigned herself to leaving the warmth of the heavy bedcovers. Her nose was colder than usual, and the room's darkness was deeper, both signs that the fire demanded another log. Besides, it could not be too long to dawn. Well enough, to have this endless night be over. Thomas's ability to sleep through times like these – when cold and fear warred with each other to chill the soul – was a gift of God and a mystery to Comfort. *Will it ever be thus for me?* She wondered. *Grant me, o Lord, the strength of my husband's faith, that I might sleep sound in the knowledge of Thy eternal protection, as does he this night.*

Gathering up a shawl that lay next to the bed, she pulled it tight around her and slid chilled feet into the rundown shoes that served as slippers. She fumbled in near blackness for a log, and laid it over the charred bits still smoldering on the hearth. There was a hint of warmth here and she lingered, relishing the flickering heat that reached up from the new flames.

After a moment she moved to a window, heavily shuttered against the night and the cold, and lifted the cross bar with care so as not to rouse Thomas. Was it truly near dawn? Or was her sense of time misled by nightlong ramblings? She swung a shutter open to see the eastern sky.

And screamed. A noise of uncomprehending panic, bringing Thomas up out of bed before the sound had died. Looming close to the small wavy panes was a face distorted by fear: eyes wide, nostrils flaring. Even in the near darkness, Comfort could see the apparition gesturing wildly at her, mouth open in soundless speech.

"'Tis Goodman Morse."

Thomas recognized the distraught figure and rushed to open the casement. Urgent whispers hissed in with the cold.

"Savages! Saw one hid in my barn not ten minutes since! Get ye out soonest, afore they know they're discovered! Sound the alarm at Fisher's house; soldiers there. I'm for Thurston's; then the garrison."

And he was gone, swallowed in the icy dark, only a quick crunch of bootsteps tracing his direction. Thomas clamped window and shutter closed in one sweep, dropped the bar across with his other hand. He swung toward Comfort, caught her wide-eyed stare and, for one suspended second, husband and wife stored up all they cherished in each other for what lay ahead. No words, but inside Comfort's head the frantic prayer began that would echo throughout what lay ahead.

Most powerful Lord, stay by us now in our direst need...

They had rehearsed this so often, awake and in nightmares, that response was without thought. Top boots on; musket grabbed down from the wall. One arm in a jacket sleeve, no time for lacings. Thomas turned to check on Comfort. She had clothes, of sorts. Small blessing, the night's cold kept her in all her petticoats. Short jacket gaping over her chemise and the dawn's slippers on her feet. Could she run? She'd have to. He was shocked to see her clutching a knife.

They nodded to each other and were out, door gaping wide behind. Are they here? Will they shoot as we stand? Run now, slipping, frantic looking everywhere at once. Two short lots, a few trees more to nearest safe house. Noise there, down the street. Sam Morse at Thurstons, pounding now upon the door, no more whispered warnings. Nearer, only the hurried crunch of running feet on hoarfrost. Are the heathens right behind? Necks taut anticipating bullets in the back, arrows piercing flesh and halting flight. But surely they must not die! Comfort's slipper caught. She stumbled. Thomas grabbed at her and dragged her on. The road was sharp with stones and ice beneath her stockinged foot. People now, ahead. Morse's family at the house. Soldiers gaping out the door, trying to sight the enemy. Every panting breath brings safety closer. A soldier's hand reaches out, hustling Comfort inside.

She threw herself into the room, gasping her relief, and turned. Thomas was not behind.

"Thomas!" Comfort screamed, and started back out, fighting against hands that held her. The strength of panic dragged her to the doorway. Only then, as she spotted him yelling to a soldier, did she remember he was to rouse troops quartered at Joshua Fisher's.

"Inside, now!" An irate voice forced her attention and Comfort was hustled out of the way. A dozen men, some bumbling with sleep, some with swords already drawn, forced their way out of the heavy-beamed garrison house as other half-dressed neighbors pushed inside. Dorret Clark and Elizabeth Morse struggled to control a dozen children. Others elbowed past, desperate to find room before this final refuge was shut up.

Not that this house was much of a fort. Its walls were thicker, perhaps, than their own homes, its shingled roof less quick to burn than thatch; windows and doors had shutters and bolts and the two rooms inside were stocked with water and wood. Three of these garrison houses stood in Medfield, shields against the bullets and arrows of the enemy. But those crowding inside knew that, if fire once took hold, the walls would be a flaming coffin for them all.

Comfort kept a vigil at the door, watching for Thomas. Praying.

Most powerful Lord ...

Suddenly a shout went up among the massing soldiers.

"Fire! Look!"

"The heathens have fired Morse's barn!"

"After them!"

"Stop!"

One soldier, with more authority than the rest, halted the men long enough to form up and get their arms in order. New figures loomed out of the predawn shadows, two tall men in the field across the way, pulling a gasping woman between them: Sam Bullen's sons dragging their mother. The aged Bullen stumbled close behind, helping as best he could two girls running, screaming in pure terror. Benjamin Clark was shouting as he ran up.

"They're in the swamp back of my house! The Morse house is afire! Head 'em off before they burn us all out!"

Clark was the Chapmans' nearest neighbor, his house a few yards east of theirs. A shiver of horror ran through Comfort as she pictured their own house in flames.

"Medfield men, to me!" The troop leader issued brief orders to the handful of local militia who had gathered, detailing married men to defend the garrison house and its growing clutch of refugees. Troops and militia set off at a run toward the fiery east while Clark, Morse and the other family men turned grimly toward their last defense. They moved to close the heavy oak door. Comfort shrieked and grabbed at it.

"No! Thomas! You cannot close him out!"

Strong hands seized her shoulders and dragged her back. Samuel Morse's curt words cut through her desperation.

"He'll not be left to die, mistress! *We* need him here a sight more than you do, so move out of the way!"

Morse was hoisting one of two huge beams to bar the iron-studded door when it suddenly burst inward. Bellowing an alarm, he swung the beam around, aiming to sideswipe the invader. Thomas ducked just in time and threw himself into the room as the beam made resounding contact with the door. Comfort's heart stopped suddenly, then speeded up as she realized her husband was safe. *Blessed Lord, I will praise Thee forever.* She leaned faintly against the wall and stared at Thomas until his eyes found hers across the room.

"What were you about?" Morse's voice grumbled at Thomas.

"Did you see aught?" another voice called.

"Where are the other troops?"

Thomas's look was grim as he passed on sketchy information. Troops from Fisher's house had come east. 'Twas a band of Nipmuck attacking, they'd been told. Savages were skulking by the brook, in the swamps, seeming all about. The night watch from the meetinghouse had gone west toward Sherborn. Shots sounding that way, by the Great Bridge. Plumes of smoke to the south now, too, by Thurston's house. No count of the enemy, no telling where they'd strike next.

The questions began before he finished.

"What of the other troops?"

"How did the bloody heathens get so close?"

"They're on all sides at once!"

"Any sign of Chenerys? The Wights?"

Goodwife Clark's voice caught as she called across the room.

"What of our house then, Thomas? Does it stand?"

Thomas ducked his head helplessly, then glanced toward the Clarks, drawn together near the hearth. Comfort held her breath awaiting his answer.

"In a fashion, mistress, but there were flames atop your roof."

He turned even more reluctantly toward Samuel Morse, who stood rigidly gripping the barrel of his musket.

"And Samuel, your barn's nigh gone."

A groan escaped Morse at Thomas's words. Then there was silence in the face of woes too enormous to take in. Men shook their heads and exchanged glances. Some drew near their families, others moved toward the shuttered and barred windows to guard against dangers they could not see. Thomas took up a post at the door.

Comfort shuddered, chilled in the aftershock of their frantic escape to the garrison, and in her dread of where the day would end. She wedged herself into a corner, hugging her jacket round her tightly and pressing her shoulders against walls whose cold solidity was the only thing that made sense in the room. The words came unbidden, no longer a discussion with the Almighty, but a profound plea.

... stay by us now in our direst need ...

Shots sounded near at hand. Ruthey Morse started screaming, a high-pitched, endless, child's scream which echoed around the closed room. Her mother, hampered by the baby she held, vaguely hushed her daughter.

Comfort stared at the little girl who voiced the scream inside them all. Ruthey would not be comforted, and the shrill cry went on and on. Other children, too scared before to make noise, began crying and grabbed for their mothers.

"Hush them up now!" one of the men ordered. "We must hear what goes on without!"

A husband snapped at his wife; a mother shook her wailing son and ordered silence. Ruthey's screams went on.

The pulsing sound shocked Comfort out of her trance. She pushed through the rising din to Goody Morse and held out her hands.

"Give Joseph to me."

The mother, too distraught to understand, stared at her blankly. Comfort pried the whimpering bundle from her arms and roughly turned the woman toward her screaming daughter.

"See to the child who needs you!"

Elizabeth Morse roused and, loudly calling Ruthey's name, slapped her hard. The sound of her slap shocked the whole company. Sobs turned to whimpers elsewhere in the room as Ruthey let out one last rising wail and buried her face against her mother's bosom.

Comfort looked down at the baby she was holding and instinctively drew him closer. His face was drawn into a wrinkled frown, and his mouth searched impatiently for food. *Soon, baby, soon, please God, you'll feed. Just hold tight now. A little longer. Please, dear Lord, let that be true. Only a little longer.*

More scattered shots sounded loud in the restored silence.

"Where do they come from, can y'tell?" The question came in a quick undertone.

"Back of us then, by the brook?"

Shouting English voices became muffled behind the house.

"The troops are giving chase."

"They're heading 'em off, back toward the swamps."

"Don't be so sure! Indians are sneaky as wolves. Who's to say there aren't some right outside?"

Another silence as they strained to hear the inaudible. Comfort eased herself down silently near the hearth and peered around the darkened room. How long had they been shut up inside? Pale light coming down the chimney told of a gray morning come. Quick sizzles on the coals were snowflakes melting. But what else was left, familiar, in this place? In this house? In all of Medfield? Women and children cowering and men helpless to defend, within. Flames and cries and death and devastation out of doors. Surely it must be thus, at the end of the world. What had man done, to so incur God's wrath? What had she done, and Thomas? And the little baby cradled in her arms?

For long minutes Comfort stared down at the infant's swaddled form, straining to understand. There was no comfort in her contemplation of the Lord. There were certainly no answers.

A heavy pounding at the door startled the listeners.

"Name yourselves!" Morse bellowed at the door.

More pounding.

"Name yourselves or stay without! We open for none who are nameless!"

"Whately, Governor's troops," came a strained answer. "I've Sergeant Kerns with me and a bullet in him. Boyden, too, from across the way. For God's sake, let us in!"

Thomas and others unbarred the heavy door and hurried the three men inside. Whately half-dragged, half-carried the sergeant whose white knuckles, clutched around his gun, testified to the agony of a blood-smeared hole in his side. Dorcas Clark took in the state of the wound and pointed the men to the other room, away from the children. She was ordering Mary Bullen to bring water when Tom Boyden, gray hair flying, backed into the house, gun pointing still at invisible enemies. Blindly, he pivoted and glared into the dark room. Mary gasped and Boyden swung the barrel in her direction. There was madness in his eyes and suddenly Comfort saw death breaching their last defense.

In a blur she saw Thomas step toward Boyden, arm outstretched. He grasped the musket barrel, wrestling it downward as he called out.

"Boyden!"

Comfort held her breath. The men struggled, one against all the demons who had chased him to the door, the other against the devil within who would steal a soul. The musket swung crazily. Any moment, Comfort knew, it would go off and shatter the semblance of safety to which they clung.

Boyden roared, a tortured sound of warring sides within him.

"Tom Boyden!"

The command in her husband's voice – or was it the sound of a Christian name? Comfort wondered – pierced the battle haze that had Boyden in its grip. He stopped struggling suddenly, and let the gun be lowered to the floor, turning anguished eyes toward the others as he did.

"Come, sir. You are safe." Thomas's voice was remarkably calm. "Friends only here, see? Here's Samuel Morse and Benjamin Clark. Their families, too. My goodwife by the fire. Good English folk only are in this room. Come now, sit."

Thomas helped Boyden to a bench. The two women crossed into the other room to tend Sergeant Kerns, though Comfort wondered what help they might be, with little but water for doctoring. The tall young soldier, Whately, came in to warm by the fire. He awkwardly accepted water from Comfort, with hands that were stiff from the cold. His gloves were long gone, she noticed, fingers turning blue.

Whately sketched the news as he chafed his hands together. When he left, headed back to the troop with hands wrapped in makeshift flannel mitts, Boyden picked up the story, and the gleam of wide-staring eyes in the dark room reflected the horrible fascination of the tale.

The nearest soldiers, they reported, were indeed chasing Indians back from the settlement's east end. Fearsome work, though. The savages would vanish, silently most times, only to send a bullet flying from some unexpected place, whooping their elation when it hit its mark. 'Twas thus the sergeant had been wounded. *Cowards, all of them*, Whately bravely insisted. *Like wild deer more than humankind, never standing to maintain an honest fight.* Yet Comfort watched, with pity, as the young man found a dozen small excuses to put off going back outside.

The devils had been turned back before this end of town was wholly wasted, Boyden added, though Clarks and Morses had a sorry sight waiting. Could be Chapman's place was spared, though he couldn't say for certain. The worry now was what they'd do downstream, by the meetinghouse. Old John Frairy's place was there, below the thickest piece of swamp cover. Master Dwight's, next door, was even closer.

Dorcas! Comfort's heart cried out. *And what of your babe and Timothy?* She leaned her cheek against Joseph's fine hair.

Thoughts swung to other thicket places where the enemy could hide. Farther up the north street by Allens' or Wights'. All along the river's edge, where swamp bushes and sprout land nudged close to Bridge Street and the dozen houses there. Thomas had spied smoke from that direction hours before. What of the Bowers and Lovells, the Sheppards and all the Rockwood clan? Where had they run to? Were they alive?

Tom Boyden had to be pressed to tell his own tale. Reluctantly he described running outdoors at the sound of gunfire. At first he saw nothing. Then a gloating cry heard down the way, a glimpse of some poor woman running frantically, young child clutched to her, tripping, Indians appearing from nowhere about her.

"They tore the babe away, threw him down. I heard his head strike the ground, even from where I was standing."

"But the woman, what of her?"

He lowered his head.

"I know not," Boyden muttered. "One, I saw, grabbed her hair. Stopped her running thus. Jerked her head back by her hair. Others grabbed at her clothes. I dare not even think what went forward after that."

"Dare not!" Samuel Morse exploded. "You know not then? How could you not go help her?"

Boyden's head swung up.

"Do not act the heroic defender with me, Master Morse! My gun was still within doors. I had no weapon other. By the time I'd fetched it one of the devils had spied me. He cried out to his fellows and headed straight for me. I fired my one shot in his direction and God must have been with me, for he fell in his tracks. But more were coming, shouting so as the earth seemed to tremble. I fled for my life. I'd be no help to that poor woman, dead now, would I?"

Boyden glared at Morse defiantly.

"You were no help to any but yourself, it seems!" Morse snapped back.

"And what of you then, so high and mighty? I do not see you out there tracking down the villains!"

Morse stepped threateningly toward the seated man, shouting his reply.

"I do what I am told! I keep to my post to defend the innocents you see here. And when I am no longer needed you may be sure I'll be among the first giving chase!"

"Good then. You see how well you fare between the bullets and the flames. Then dare to call me coward when you've saved us all!"

Thomas stepped in before the two came to blows.

"Peace, sirrahs! There's war enough in Medfield this day without you bringing it indoors. Goodman Morse, save your ire for the enemy. If Whately spoke true, our arms will be needed elsewhere in this town, as soon as there's an inkling of safety hereabouts."

Thomas turned to Boyden and laid a hand on his shoulder.

"And none, I think, question your intentions. If I hear right, you have no ball or powder in that gun?"

"Nay." He shook his head despondently. "They're hanging on the wall at home. If there is a wall still standing."

Comfort had listened, stunned, as the catalogue of evils unfolded. Not that the images were too fearsome to bear. It was simply too much to take in all at once. She absently rocked the baby back and forth until Boyden's last words sank in. Then a strange bark of laughter came out, startling herself as well as the baby.

The others around her turned horrified looks in her direction. Thomas moved quickly beside her, incredulous.

"Wife! What are you about?"

"Do you not see?" Comfort giggled helplessly. "Master Boyden has no powder and ball!"

Thomas hesitated, then spoke slowly, as to a child.

"Aye, Comfort, 'tis true. But that is little cause for merriment."

"Then you *don't* see, husband. 'Tis the only merriment of this whole day: Master Boyden could harm no one when he came inside our door! All our terror and your valiant struggle to control him, when there *was no armament to be taken away!*"

Comfort's laughter evaporated and she gazed up at Thomas, willing her husband to comprehend, to feel the same relief she felt in knowing that just one single thing was not so dire as they had feared.

After a moment he nodded, but his voice was heavy when he spoke.

"Aye, you're right. Would God the day's other woes might be so easily banished."

He reached down and pushed the hair back from her face, then slowly placed a kiss on her temple. The rest of the room looked away.

Clearly, no one else saw reason for levity. Comfort wondered if her wits were weakened, but she could not find it in herself to feel abashed. On the contrary, a weight began lifting off her soul. Here, in the heart of doom, where every sound and movement and every piece of news or lack of it was cause for infinite terror, one small event had transpired that held no cause for fear. Perhaps it was a sign.

Before she could explore her strange sensations, a deep roar sounded in the distance and reverberated inside the thick walls. The crowded listeners froze as they frantically tried to identify the sound.

Suddenly young Sam Morse shouted.

"The gun! 'Tis the great gun!"

Cheers and exclamations filled the room. The cannon at the meetinghouse had been purchased just last summer, chosen for its deep voice, loud enough to warn surrounding villages of danger. Excited speculation replaced the gloom brought on by Boyden's story.

"The militia must hold the center of town!"

"Perhaps more troops have ridden in!"

"Could be they've routed the Indians even now."

A young child "boomed" explosively and more than one head bowed in thanksgiving. The solid declaration of the cannon stirred the men to action.

"They must need help." Thomas raised his voice to be heard over the excitement. "We need to know what's going on out there. What of the south of town? The mill and Henry Adams? There's no word yet from there. I'm willing to scout it out, help if I can. Will any go with me?" Thomas carefully avoided looking at his wife, unwilling to risk seeing her reaction.

Her gasp was lost in a new flurry of exclamations.

"'Tis nowise safe yet!"

"Who'll stay with us?"

"I'll go." Sam Morse's voice was loud among the protests.

Boyden's expression was haunted as he frowned in indecision.

"Some must stay; some only go," Thomas directed. "You women need see to defenses here as well, should any savage think to circle back."

"Not likely!" Morse cut in. "From what the boy said, they're on the run already, down towards the river. I'll lay odds they won't stop, now the gun's been fired, until they're on the other side."

"I'd not risk my wife's survival on your betting, Goodman." Thomas's reply was sharp. "Nor should any of you," he cautioned the others. "Hold tight to the weapons you brought and bar the door well until such time as someone sounds the all-clear."

Comfort found herself watching her husband in surprise. When had he become a leader of men? Yet the voice of authority came naturally to him, and he was accepted. No one in the room thought to argue with his words.

She did not even think of it herself, until the bar was lifted and Thomas was already at the door.

He must not leave! A silent voice protested. *He must not seek out danger when the others stay within! He'll be killed!*

She started toward him but her way was blocked by Benjamin Clark, who fell in behind Thomas. With him were the Bullens, young men armed with cleaver and pitchfork and ignoring their mother's pleas. A handful of others stepped up as well, men and stripling boys, their expressions grim and weapons at the ready.

Something held Comfort back, restraining the silent protests that screamed in her head, until even those were silent.

Then a still, small voice inside her whispered, *He must go. Pray rather for his safe return than hinder his departure.*

She watched Thomas's broad, familiar shoulders disappear outside the door, watched the others go and the salutes of those men staying behind. Heard the quiet sobs and prayers of resignation muffled by the door's closing thud. A waft of cold air pressed into the room, carrying consciousness of frost and smoke, and a dreadful smell of something burning. Comfort waited for loneliness to overwhelm her. Instead, Baby Joseph let out a cry of simple indignation. His morning meal was long past due.

The cry drew Elizabeth Morse's attention at last. Letting go of the other children she was hugging tight, she stood and reached for Joseph, nodding thanks to Comfort.

"You've seen to my babe overlong, Mistress Chapman. You'll join us closer by the fire?"

Comfort acknowledged the awkward invitation by finding a place among the Morse children crouched on the hearth. They quickly drew near another warm body. The youngest snuggled silent against her while ten-year-old Samuel, too old for such display, whispered a drawn-out stream of excited comments as his own talisman against the waiting.

Endless minutes or hours went by. There was little way to judge how long. From time to time those guarding the door opened the peephole shutter and peered outside, but there was nothing to report. Comfort took her turn watching at the other room's window. A futile exercise, she knew, since the shutter there was closed just like the others, and there was no way to see out.

It was colder in the other room with only one log burning. Sergeant Kerns lay on the floor. His breathing was heavy. Sometimes – Comfort guessed he was hit by a wave of pain – every breath out was a moan. Inhale – pause – moan. Inhale – pause – moan. Every moan conjured images she did not want to see. Indians crouching in wait as Thomas and the other men marched by. War cries and attack. Thomas spinning, crying out. Falling to the ground in unimaginable pain. Moan. Inhale. Pause. Comfort begged God to render the man

394

unconscious, for his sake and, she admitted, for her own. Then she remembered the small voice.

Pray for his safe return.

With all my heart and with all my soul, she promised. So in the cold, dark endless waiting she put aside Sergeant Kerns' moans and carefully rebuilt her imaginings. Indians, crouched in terror of being discovered. Thomas and the men draw close. One savage yells and brandishes his weapon, then swiftly runs away. The others vanish in the swamp. Medfielders begin pursuit but Thomas recalls them to their task. They proceed, safely through one encounter.

I can do nothing here but wish and pray. Relief came with the realization. *'Tis not an unworthy combination. But when my time is come to act, dear Lord, grant me the strength to help Thy will be done.*

Mary Bullen came to spell her at the window and Comfort started to leave the room. Instinctively she stepped a broad detour around the soldier's prostrate form until sudden impulse made her pause and, crouching down, she took the sergeant's frigid hand in hers. He squeezed her fingers in wordless thanks. Comfort nodded at some private decision and settled herself by his side to wait.

The all-clear, when it came, startled everyone. Heavy pounding on the door set them grabbing for their weapons, but the welcome sound of an English voice soon had the bars down and the door swung wide. Venerable Ralph Wheelock stood on the doorstep, bringing word it was safe to venture out.

The brittle light of midday surprised them all. They crowded around Wheelock, calling for news, glancing nervously about for unseen dangers. No one quite believed it could be safe to stand outdoors. Few wanted to leave the refuge that had sheltered them or witness firsthand the devastation. Instead, they looked to Wheelock for the news, instinctively trusting the schoolmaster to bring order and reason to the dreadful tale he had to tell. But the deep sorrow in his voice told them, sooner than words, that the day's grief had not ended.

The savages were gone. Hundreds of them, fled across the bridges to the west to wreak God only knew what havoc on the isolated homes over the way. Closer by, they'd caused such damage, a body'd be hard put to recognize the village that, just yesterday, had stood so prosperous an outpost of civilization. Houses and outbuildings burned on all sides – some still burning. Cattle perished in their stalls. Grain stores up in smoke inside the corn barns.

All the news was not yet in. Parties scouting south and east of town had not reported back, though smoke in that direction warned of more destruction near Henry Adams' house and mill.

Wheelock paused for a moment and the group whispered. Comfort sent up a brief plea that God not forget Thomas and the others who still stayed away. The schoolmaster took a deep breath, as if sucking in the strength to go on with his litany. Bridge Street was wiped out. There was no final count, but so far not one house was known to be undamaged. The Indians, it seemed, had risen right up out of the river meadow and attacked along the road's whole length at once. And there'd been no time there to sound a warning as Goodman Morse had done, this part of town.

"The men?" A timid voice dared to ask the question they all dreaded.

Wheelock bowed his head, strands of gray hair slipping limp into his face. When he raised his eyes, his look was haunted.

"John Bowers is dead. His son as well, killed as their families escaped. Word's in from the garrison north of town that most of the women and children are safe but no one knows yet what's become of the Masons. And there's no word at all across the river. The damned savages set the bridges both afire. Troops are stopped this side, the water high and nowhere ice enough to cross. There's no going over the way to aid the Sherborn folk, or our own. They're all cut off. God have mercy on them."

Comfort's prayers flew to Lizbeth and her husband, so proud of their new house across the river. Murmured "Amens" underscored her thought.

The sound seemed to drag Wheelock back to awareness of his listeners, and their need for any hint of good to be found in the tragedy unfolding.

"In truth, the ways of God this dreadful day are wondrous. The minister's house, a short while past, opened its door to a wild woman shrieking in the road. No clothes but a blanket thrown about her, gory face half hid by hair and blood. 'Twas passing strange they let her in at all but, God be praised, 'twas Goodwife Thurston pleading! Caught by savages a hundred rods from thence, her babe torn from her bosom, herself sure for cruel death. Only a miracle drew the hellhounds away before more evil was done. She dragged herself to Wilson's door, and so they found her thus, screaming for her dead boy and her own salvation."

Wheelock shook his head at the mystery. Suddenly Tom Boyden shouted.

"Sarah Thurston! 'Twas she I saw, caught by the hair! She lives!"

Boyden abruptly dropped to his knees and grasped his hands in prayer.

"Mighty art Thou, o Lord and the power of Thy redemption! I give thanks for Thy great mercy, succoring a needy soul when I, poor wretch, was helpless."

Gratitude and relief mixed in Boyden's voice. Goody Clark glared at him as she hugged a child more tightly.

"And may He have as much mercy on the soul of young Samuel Thurston, who was left to die so horribly this day."

Comfort offered a shuddering Amen.

Then it was time to discover what was left of their lives in Medfield. Fading wishes of "Godspeed" followed the Clarks and Morses as they headed back with Comfort toward their houses at the east end.

The distance was surprisingly short, that had stretched so far just hours ago. Near the garrison, the houses were untouched, sitting solid and reassuring along the way. Comfort's thoughts reached out to other villagers. What of the Dwights and their children? The dozen families with no homes left, by the bridge? And Lizbeth and her husband? What had happened as she sat immured in that dark hole? Her silent prayer returned, keeping pace with their hurried steps, *when my time is come to act, dear Lord, grant me strength...*

They emerged from a clump of trees to their homelots and stopped as one, paralyzed by what they saw. Boyden had been right: the Chapmans' house was there, still standing and whole. But from that point east was total ruin. Wattle fence lay trampled in a kitchen garden. The Clark house was a skeleton of blackened beams. Across the way, dying flames still licked at the Morses' house. Their cattle barn was reduced to a right-angled corner of stonework that held the charred and smoking frame. The little granary was a heap on the ground.

Samuel Morse walked heavily toward all that was left of twenty-five years' work. Dorret Clark moved the other direction with aimless steps. She wandered through a dooryard strewn with shattered delft and torn bed curtains. One wide board on top of a smoking pile caught her eye and suddenly she exploded in a cry of pain and anger. Grabbing the board, she dropped to the ground, desperately beating at it with her skirt to damp the smoldering end.

Benjamin Clark dragged her away.

"Wife! Leave off! You'll burn yourself."

Dorret's eyes were wild.

"It's the baby's cradle, Benjamin. Put it out!"

He looked at it sadly.

"Not much left to save, Dorret."

His eyes swept the wreckage of their house. "Not much at all."

Dorret's sobs were uncontrollable. Clark grasped his wife's arms and turned her away from the pile of rubble that had been a home. He moved stiffly, like an old man, but his voice was steady when he spoke.

"But God has chosen to save us and ours this day. In the midst of this ruination we must not lose sight of His greater mercies."

Dorret tearfully stared at her husband for a moment as she tried to control her sobs. Then she drew their four young children together, bidding them remember the Lord's goodness in preserving them.

Comfort watched the children. Too young to fathom the words, they looked from one parent to the other, finding solace in their reassuring closeness.

They prop each other up, Lord, as Thou dost all of them together. 'Tis therefore Thou didst ordain families, is it not? To be helpmeets in times of sore trouble? They are blessed, then, if only in this. May Thomas and I one day be so blessed.

The Morses came back from their sorrowful examination across the way. They quietly joined the Clarks in prayer, though Comfort thought the bitter scowl on Goodman Morse's face reflected other thoughts than thanksgiving. She continued her own silent meditation.

Neighbors, as well. They are one of Thy mercies. Thou hast brought us together, side by side to stand by each other. These good people watch over me when Thomas is away from home...

The prayer done, Dorret Clark asked the question worrying them all.

"Benjamin, what are we to do?"

Clark had no answer. The Lord who had saved his family had shown no such mercy toward their belongings. The Clarks owned little in this world save house and livestock, and the land they had been granted by the town. But land afforded them no shelter, nor the money to replace what they had lost.

"Benjamin? Where must we go? We need a place of safety!"

His stricken look took in the ruin around them. "We thought there was safety here, in Medfield."

They watch over me, and I must do as much for them.

"You must stop at our house," she heard herself saying, "till you find yourselves a proper place to stay." She was surprised at the matter-of-factness in her voice but wished that Thomas would return. He would know what to do, where they would be safe. Wouldn't he? Goodman Clark sounded so hopeless. Small wonder. The Clarks, the Morses too, were without food or shelter. All of them had been standing too long, half-dressed in the cold, with nothing to warm their bellies.

The little group did not stand on ceremony. Parents accepted gratefully as they hugged shivering children. Clark and Morse saw their families into Comfort's small house and bid the women keep a sharp watch out of doors. Then the men turned back outside, to join up with others who patrolled the village.

Inside the Chapman house, the business that needed attending to was wonderfully mundane. Comfort built up a fire and opened every shutter in the house, as much to let in light as to afford a clear look outside. She wanted no reminder of the dark and airless garrison house where they had trembled together. She even set a candle in the small back room. The few hours left in the day were filled with porridge pots and mulling cider, extra shirts and shawls and blankets. Toddlers cried, mothers summoned children to eat, the houseful of people set about trying, each in her own way, to retrieve some semblance of everyday life.

For minutes at a time Comfort did not think of Thomas or the other men who still stayed away. Then her mind's eye would catch a glimpse of him and a sharp pang of worry would stop her in mid-action. She searched for strength in her memory of the wordless looks they had earlier exchanged, filled with love and trust. *The eyes are the windows of the soul, they say.* But Thomas had avoided her eyes when he left with the scouting party. *My fear. He was avoiding my fear. It would weaken him just when he needed sustenance. Come back, Thomas. Feed on my soul. Surely you may find strength in me as I do always in you.*

She recalled herself to the task at hand.

Thomas and the other men came in at dusk, stiff with cold. Their presence cheered the entire household, bringing reassurance that the raiding parties were well and truly gone from town.

"Though not half far enough for safety," Thomas cautioned.

"Just beyond firing range, damn them all." Samuel Morse's face reddened as he described what they had seen. "You'd not believe the gall of those savages! A handful of 'em still hang about on the hill, far side of the bridge they burned. There they are, whooping and prancing round a great bonfire. In plain sight of all the wretched folk whose houses they destroyed! Taunting us, that's what they are. Minions of the devil himself!"

He glared about the room as if challenging his listeners to contradict.

"It's a mystery indeed why God did not just strike 'em all dead, then and there," he muttered in disgust.

"Perhaps, husband, the good Lord felt there'd been bloodshed enough for one day." Elizabeth Morse was not known for gainsaying her husband, but the others silently agreed with her as he snorted his disapproval.

The full effect of the morning raid on the town was just beginning to be understood. Thomas told the women of the hurried landowners meeting they'd attended. Near half the folks in Medfield were burned out, many with no place nearby to stay. They would put up for the night at houses in town but many families were leaving, come morning, to board with relatives elsewhere. Others had chosen the safety of bigger towns to the east. The list of those killed had grown longer and the wounded were still being tallied.

"Master Dwight's among them, wife." Thomas warned her. "Word is, the Nipmuck teased him to his door, throwing stones and such at the house." He shook his head. "Shot him in the shoulder before he even ventured outside."

Comfort gasped. "Dorcas? And the boys? Are they hurt?"

"Nay, they're well enough, and Dwight got back inside. 'Twas just bad luck he was hit at all. The savages were on the run down the brook, and must have thought to work one final bit of evil near the meetinghouse. God alone chose Dwights' house instead of Frairys' as their mark."

More government troops had arrived, Thomas added. The troops and a large militia band were due to set off at first light, vowing to search out and destroy every last Indian in the New England, if need be, to put an end to this terror and destruction.

Thomas was one of those remaining behind, to guard against another sneak attack and begin the long process of putting things back to rights. The town was a shambles, much more than its buildings destroyed. Livestock wandered unfenced and unprotected from the wolves who'd follow their noses into town. There were burials to see to, of humans, and animals as well. The raiders had taken cruel delight in savaging the cattle that meant so much to English farmers.

"What of Master Adams, husband? And the mill?"

There was a moment's silence.

"Dead. Died on his own doorstep, shot through the neck. His sons escaped harm and just the night before he'd sent his wife to board here in town, thank the Lord. But you know Adams. He'd never leave his mill." Thomas shook his head in grief and respect.

"Oh, Thomas!" Comfort grasped his arm. She knew how close he'd been to Henry Adams. The man had dealt with him as one of his own sons. "And the mill?"

Thomas looked at her with a strange expression and shook his head in answer.

Comfort sucked in a breath. The mill gone too? What was their future to be then? What would Thomas do, now that there was no mill?

"Nothing left at all?"

"Not enough to repair," he answered shortly. But he refused to say more and Comfort remained silent, not knowing how to ask the questions that were foremost in her mind. Would they, too, be leaving Medfield now? And if they did, would they be coming back? She realized she was fingering the coins in her petticoat.

There was a haunted look in Thomas's eyes which neither hot food nor strong beer erased. That night, Comfort curled up with him under a blanket on the floor. Their bed was given over to four of the Clarks; two more slept near the fire while the Morses crowded into the back room. Comfort lay quietly listening to the sounds of tired people trying to rest. A cough, finally stilled, from the next room. A child's whimpering memory of the day's terror, gently hushed in the bed nearby.

Thomas muttered incoherently beside her. She rested a hand on his arm in reassurance, concerned that the man who slept through anything was troubled by dreams. *Benevolent Lord*...She began the prayer which had become ingrained over the past months...*protect us from the wildness all about.*

Comfort stopped in surprised recognition.

Nay, dear Lord, protect us <u>still</u> from the wildness about us, as Thou hast so miraculously done this day. Protect us as well from the turmoil within our own souls. Grant my husband peaceful sleep. Show our neighbors the path they must follow. Turn the Indian Philip's wrath away from us that we may learn to live in peace, to build Thy kingdom in this promised land.

A soft blue blanket of sleep drifted down behind her eyelids. She noticed with drowsy surprise the absence of fear at the end of this fear-ridden day. Comfort sighed, and slept.

Pallets had not yet been cleared off the floor two mornings later, when a boy appeared at the door. Sent by Mistress Wilson, he said, the minister's wife. Would the women come, she asked, to help lay out Elizabeth Adams and Lucy, the Indian woman?

Heads bowed as the neighbors contemplated the passing strange ways of the Lord. Mistress Adams had been one of the fortunate ones when the attack came, thanks to her husband's premonition. Safe and sound at the minister's house through the attack.

"But the grief on her face, when they brought her husband's body in, was painful to see," Dorret Clark sighed. "Who could have imagined, how quickly she'd be joined with him again?"

There were nods of agreement as the women found washing cloth and comb, soap and a spare coif, and headed down the way, leaving the older children tending young ones. Each woman silently marveled as she walked.

The night after the attack, the men had brought in Henry Adams for burial. His was by no means the only body and the meetinghouse, they'd heard, was filled with sounds of mourning and fervent prayer as the dead were hastily assembled. Eventually all but the dead and a guard of soldiers had dragged themselves to rest, Elizabeth Adams with the others. She'd been made to lie down at last in the chamber over the entry hall at Wilsons'. What transpired next could not have been imagined. A soldier entering the minister's house, so they were told, was careless with his gun. It went off, the ball penetrating right upward through the ceiling and into the helpless form of Widow Adams. By the next night she was dead.

So she would be buried with her husband after all, the Lord knowing better than Mr. Adams, how best to help his wife.

"But what of Lucy?" Comfort finally asked aloud. "What do you suppose happened there?"

"Better you ask why we are bidden to lay out a savage." Elizabeth Morse's tone was as grim as her husband's when she spoke of Indians. "They should have found some of her own kind."

"She is a Christian," Comfort reminded. "And I cannot think there are many Indians left hereabout to do the service. None I know of in our own town. And what with Natick and Ponkapoag being shipped out to the harbor…" She was not sure, even after what had just transpired, that the internment of all 'praying Indians' from the Christian Indian villages was a wise act. Comfort was not one to doubt the Governor and his council, but it did seem to her just possible that natives who had seen the light of Christian faith and English ways might be more help that harm in the vicinity.

"Good riddance, I say, to them!" Mrs. Morse pronounced. "Would that all the heathens had been thrown into the sea ere they had worked their evil on us and ours."

Silent tears rolled down Dorret Clark's cheeks and Comfort squeezed her arm in sympathy. She saw Elizabeth's Morse's lip curl up as she spat out her final word.

"I, for one, will dance with the devil before I touch that old squaw. She can go in the ground as filthy as she lived, for all of me."

The three had reached the Wilson's door and were let in by the minister's wife. Sarah Wilson was more than a little distracted, finding herself in demand for the living and dead alike. She apologized for the confusion and pointed them in the direction of the two bodies, telling them where to find hot water and what garments could be spared, to make the dead women decent to meet their Maker.

"Mistress Fisher has agreed to see to Old Lucy, though 'tis certain she could use support, for the odor there is truly rank. Poor Mrs. Adams lies above, as peaceful as one might hope for such a sorry end. Indeed, I cannot say whether I am more bowed down, being in some way Death's unwitting accomplice, or thankful that the Lord saw fit to bring her to Himself for solace." She shook her head knowingly. "Upward of thirty years' marriage, the Adamses had. Truly the Lord is marvelous in His ways."

Dorret and Elizabeth exchanged glances and moved toward the stairs.

"You will get on well enough with Mistress Fisher, Comfort?" Dorret Clark's look mixed dread and shame.

Comfort nodded shortly, having guessed it would fall out so, and headed toward the kitchen, looking for Mistress Fisher and the other body. She caught up with the older woman at the back door. Anne Fisher smiled a brief greeting and passed Comfort a pan of steaming water that she had been trying to juggle along with an armful of cloth.

"In faith, I'm grateful for your aid to get this over quickly. I bear no ill will to poor Lucy, mind you, but even in the cold the smell's a mite hard to stomach."

"She's been dead long, then?" Comfort asked, following Mrs. Fisher into the lean-to shed that stood off the back of the house.

"Not so's anyone can say, but circumstances were not the best."

As they entered the drafty room, Comfort saw a blanket-wrapped bundle lying on a storage chest. The blanket was old and not of the cleanest, but its appearance did not warrant the ghastly smell that hit her as she came near. Sickness, she thought at first. Vomit. But spirits too. Fumes of gin. And already the slight smell of death.

"They found her yesterday," Anne Fisher went on, taking shallow breaths and talking through the smell. "Alone in her wigwam, dead. Drank herself to death, so it's been said."

"What? Surely 'tis a tale, Mistress Fisher! Why Poor Elizabeth Adams told me Lucy never touched spirits. Indeed she said 'twas one of the virtues she liked her for."

"I know, I know." The blanket was off and they cut away filthy clothes, holding their breaths and touching as little as they could. "'Tis rumored the spirits were meant for Mapshet. But he's off and gone. Took what weapons he had with him, too."

"Is not Mapshet an ancient man?"

"Aye. Though I've heard it said he was a warrior once, before we ever came to Medfield. Some say he left with the savages. Sam Sheppard swears he saw him dancing over the way, when the Indians fired the bridge."

"But I thought Mapshet and Lucy were friends to civilized men?" Comfort's confusion distracted her through the worst of the washing down. How wrinkled the squaw's skin was though. Her joints were swollen.

"Lucy, mayhap. I never had aught but civil encounters with her. Not Mapshet, though. Sure, he stayed here and the townsfolk let him. Too old to do damage, after all. But I, for one, never felt comfortable with that look he had. Like some devilish spirit glared out of his eyes, hating us all. Gave me shivers when he ever came about."

Mistress Fisher untangled the snarls of Lucy's thin white hair and braided it back into place. She retied it with a beaded thong. Comfort thought the long wrinkles on the dead woman's cheeks made her face seem drawn. She tried to conceive of what had transpired there, at the south edge of town, as the Adams houses and mill burned to ash and an ancient warrior sought out one more fight. There was nothing left in Medfield for an Indian. Lucy knew that. Yet it was her home. Her church. A lifetime of worsening changes. So she turned to the gin as a poison to finish the disgrace and mourning. Another life lost in building the new Jerusalem.

Mistress Fisher was holding out a clean shift for Comfort to help slip over Lucy's head. It was jarring to put such an English garment

405

on someone who'd chosen to remain in tribal dress throughout her life.

"Are there no garments of her own we might dress her in?"

Anne Fisher snorted. Her voice was scornful.

"Mayhap there could have been. But some brave soul thought it wise to put a torch to the wigwam, rather than seek such out. I cannot help but wonder how poor Lucy herself might have fared, had they found her alive inside it." She shook her head as she eased the well-worn linen past the white braid. "As it was, they could afford the semblance of Christian charity that brought her corpse here."

Comfort reached out in silence and took the dead woman's hands, arranging them carefully on top of one another. Lucy was prepared now to go into her unmarked grave.

In the days following the attack, the same question was on everyone's lips: what to do next? Stay or leave? Comfort's father rode out from Watertown to urge the couple to return with him. Or, if Thomas felt duty called him to stay in Medfield, Mr. Welles went on, at least let Comfort escape to more secure surroundings. Thomas had no right to put her life at risk when the Lord alone knew how soon another attack might come.

Comfort and Thomas listened respectfully to the older man. His loving concern for them both was apparent. Thomas was further swayed by his argument for Comfort's safety. But when the couple went aside to consider together, they talked of how many hands were needed to restore order to the town. Neither of them doubted it could be done.

"And I, for one, cannot believe the raiders will return," Comfort declared bravely.

"In truth, there's little left to be destroyed."

Thomas's practicality reinforced Comfort's faith.

"I do confess, husband, that I would be lonely, even in the bosom of my family, were you not nearby."

His intense kiss was thanks and agreement combined.

So they decided between themselves to remain for a few weeks, until the business of the mill was settled, until their neighbors could get on as well without them, until the town was back on its feet. It was not a permanent decision, they reassured each other, but unless immediate danger threatened again, their hands were needed here.

Comfort felt a momentary clutch of doubt as Mr. Welles rode away. For an instant she was a girl again, riding away from this village on the edge of nowhere. Riding toward the safe embrace of her mother and their house in Watertown. Then a whiff of boiling beef recalled her to her own doorway. With a lingering shadow of regret she turned back to the kettle of food that required attention, supper for a dozen people whose own kitchens had been destroyed.

It took a fortnight for the Chapman's house to empty out and some semblance of order to be restored in Medfield. The Morses and Clarks left to stay with family. The garrison force had been strengthened. The Indians were in full retreat, past Marlboro, all the way to Petersham, to the northwest. The dead had been buried and prayed for and the town tended its wounds as it mourned its losses. No word came of other villages attacked, but not a soul in Medfield believed the danger was past. Everywhere the question still hung: stay or leave?

The frozen ground of February had melted in a series of hard rains which, by early March, mired the roads and seeped into every unprotected corner. Comfort carefully picked her way through town to the Dwights' house, a space of barely half a mile. Even so, by the time she arrived, her shoes were mud-caked and her cloak soaked through despite its heavy felting. She had not paid it much mind, as she was worrying over Thomas's continued sleeplessness. The night just past, she'd woken to find him lying wide-eyed in the dark beside her. Yet when she asked what made him wakeful, he'd turned her concern aside with foolish muttering about her perfect face in moonlight. Other than the fact the shutters obscured any hint of moon, Comfort knew Thomas had been wakeful more nights than not and doubted loveliness to be the cause. She repeated a heartfelt prayer to the Lord, to ease whatever troubled him.

As she lifted a hand to knock at the Dwights' door, Comfort carefully sheltered a loaf of bread under her other arm. She was surprised that no one answered right away, given the weather and Master Dwight's wound. She frowned and drew off her mitt, knocking a second time more loudly.

As soon as Dorcas opened the door, Comfort knew something was very wrong. The woman's face was haggard. Untended wisps of hair escaped her cap. Her pristine entrance hall was tracked with more than one day's mud. Even her voice was unfamiliar.

"Comfort." The word was flat, with none of the pleasure and warmth that Comfort had come to expect and that always made her feel so welcome.

"Good day, Dorcas. I've come with a bit of bread and time to lend a hand, if you could use it?" She hesitated, not sure if she should stay.

A flicker of appreciation lit Dorcas's eyes. She seemed to rally, and reached out both hands to draw Comfort in from the rain.

"Well! Come in out of it, then. You're welcome to stay a bit..." She hesitated, glancing toward the doorway to the best room. Her voice faded. "But I know not what kind of company I'll be..."

Comfort touched her arm in reassurance.

"I'm not here to chatter, Dorcas. You've enough to do with two young ones and an ailing husband. How is he faring, Master Dwight? The wound mends at last?"

Her concern was not mere politeness. Dwight had had trouble with his wound; the bullet had lodged against the bone and could not be extracted. He'd never have full use of his arm again, they said, and that his right arm, too. Comfort wondered more than once how Dorcas would make do, her two sons just babes and her husband unable to tend the farm. But then, she thought, there was no saying they'd try to manage out here anyway, now that half the town was gone.

Dorcas frowned at the question and her face set. She drew Comfort into the old part of the house, away from the best room and its big bed, where Timothy Dwight lay. Her voice was so low that Comfort had to bend near to catch the words but the unaccustomed harshness in them was unmistakable.

"Nay. It mends scarce at all. Some of it festers. My husband is not ever free of pain, though he'd keep it from me. But he's hot with fever and I know." She paused, staring off across the room, a small wrinkle on her forehead. Then her look swung back and she forced herself to go on. "Comfort, just now he said 'tis time to write his will. He has sent for the Reverend Mr. Wilson."

She searched her friend's face and Comfort caught a glimpse of the fear the woman held so tightly checked as she asked the next question.

"Can that bode anything but ill?"

"Oh, Dorcas, I'm so sorry."

Comfort was hard put to find words to temper the dread. Timothy Dwight was a man in his sixties, though certainly hale enough till now. In fact he'd sworn his young second wife had added years to the ones the Lord gave him. Still, everyone knew that a body was worn down by living, and advanced years made healing a much more doubtful process. Had God chosen a heathen bullet to be Dwight's summons to his eternal home? Comfort kept such thoughts to herself. She gave a small shrug.

"I've heard tell of many who settled their worldly affairs, the better to draw near to God, only to find the very act of drawing nigh worked miracles. Master Dwight would not be the first to rise up thus healed from his bed of pain, would he?"

She tried to sound heartening, but her throat ached. She doubted Dorcas believed her, but the woman grimaced in a weak attempt to smile.

"'Tis a good thought. Much better for my husband than my gloom." Her lip trembled. "But I cannot seem to hold long to any cheer. If it is not my husband, it's Tim and his coughing."

She pressed her lips together.

"And the baby!"

Dorcas hugged herself tightly, her voice rising in pitch and urgency.

"I keep asking, what have we done, bringing a baby into this purgatory? This hell? There's nothing can protect him here save God's will. Nay! God's *whim!* There's naught but an almighty whim to keep my child alive until tomorrow. What has God done, Comfort? Why does He punish us so?!"

Comfort held the woman's shoulders to still their trembling and silently shook her head.

After a moment Dorcas's tight hold on herself relaxed, as if Comfort's touch had conveyed some silent reassurance. She motioned her friend into the kitchen.

Tim and baby John were both there, the baby napping in his cradle by the fire. Tim sat on a stool alongside, rocking the cradle slowly with one foot while his hands were busy shaping and reshaping a string game. His greeting was animated, for he was always delighted to see anyone connected with the admirable Master Chapman. But he watched his mother carefully as he talked to Comfort, and the anxious wrinkles on his forehead didn't go away. After a few words he lapsed back into silence and the ever-changing webs of string.

"Dorcas," Comfort kept her voice low, "might I go speak with your husband? I would offer him our sympathy."

"I think he sleeps. Though it becomes more and more difficult to tell. Times I think he feigns sleep when I go to him, just so I will go away again… Oh, I don't know … Your kindness cannot do him any harm."

Dorcas led the way into the dark parlor. A smoky candle in one corner and the flickering fire were the only light, the windows being closed against bad vapors. In the shadowy interior of the massive bed, Comfort made out Timothy Dwight. He was propped up with pillows and bolsters, a heavy comforter drawn up under his chin. As her eyes adjusted to the gloom, she saw a nightcap crumpled by his head, as if he'd worked it off in sweaty thrashing. An extra bolster guarded his right side, where the wound was.

Comfort hung back in the doorway as Dorcas tiptoed to his side. She passed a gentle hand across his forehead, unconsciously smoothing lank strands of hair as she went. Her voice, so bitter moments ago, held nothing now but love and reassurance.

"Husband?"

Dwight's head moved from side to side restlessly, eyes shut.

"Timothy?" Dorcas's hand smoothed again. "You've a visitor to cheer your day."

The bushy brows drew down in a frown. Dwight's inner struggle with consciousness was almost palpable. His eyes flew open.

"The minister's here? Wilson?" There was urgency in his strained voice.

"Nay, husband, Mr. Wilson's not yet come. But Mistress Chapman is by, bringing greeting from her spouse."

410

"Well enough." His voice became clearer, as if his will had won another round with mortality. "But wife, the minister must come as well."

"I know, Timothy. Jack Adams has gone to search him out. I've no doubt he'll come soon."

Dorcas gestured Comfort closer to the bed and stepped aside, cautioning Comfort to mind she avoid the wounded shoulder. A smell which, from a distance, had been masked by other smells was sharp as she approached the bed. It was heavy, acrid. Rot. It seeped from under the carefully tended bandage and out of the gently washed wound. She had smelled it before, but never so unexpectedly. Her grandfather's death; a family friend. Long ill and needing surcease. But here the stink was an obscenity. Her nostrils dilated and she blew out a huff of air. She felt a panicked urge to flee the room. *Dear Lord, grant me the strength!* Other words slipped into her mind.

Taking careful shallow breaths, she collected herself and leaned over the dying man.

"Master Dwight, it is a sorrow to see you abed and unwell."

"No more for you than for me. Your husband?"

"Well, thank the Lord. He labors with the others to set the town to rights again."

"Would that he could do as much for me."

Comfort desperately searched for words of encouragement. "Come now, sooner than you know, you'll be up and about, I warrant."

Dorcas had left the room to fetch water and a damp cloth for her husband. Dwight's honest gray eyes held Comfort's as he slowly answered.

"I am past such expectation, Mistress Chapman. I think you know 'tis so." Comfort returned his intent gaze. "But I would beg you befriend my wife in her need." He turned his head toward the doorway. "She's forfeited much being tied to an old man. Never said so but I've known it all along. I've tried to make it up to her."

His gaze shifted to a dark corner of the bed curtains, as if he addressed an invisible listener in the shadows.

"But never did I think I'd leave her in such desperate times. Never would I leave her alone not knowing if the sun should rise on the morrow."

411

His words were at once protest and appeal, and Comfort felt her throat tighten again, hearing the pain in this strong man's soul.

"I swear, Master Dwight, as God is my witness, that Dorcas is my true friend, and I will help her any way I might."

Dwight searched Comfort's face, then briefly nodded.

"Your strength is the consolation she needs most."

Strength? She knew of no strength in herself that might help Dorcas, or anyone else, for that matter. What did he see that she did not? Or was his weakening mind simply misled?

Dwight moved restlessly, wincing at an incautious shift, and turned his thoughts to his other abiding concern.

"Where is Wilson?" he muttered. "I've need to make my peace with the world." He reconsidered. "Peace, indeed. Where is peace when the world itself's imperiled? What keeps the man so long?"

Dorcas reentered the room to hear his querulous words. She raised his head to give him a sip of water, then answered as she lay a cool cloth on his forehead.

"If it would ease you, Timothy, Mistress Chapman might be willing to be your scribe. She knows her letters as I do not, and might begin what you would have Master Wilson finish when he comes."

Comfort was startled at the suggestion. She had had little use, since coming to Medfield, for the writing her father had taught her long ago, joking as he did so about keeping a close eye on her husband's books. Dwight gave her a questioning look and she nodded reluctantly.

"I'd be obliged. Time runs short. The Lord demands my attention. But my sons need their inheritance. And my wife must have assurance of her keeping in the years to come."

Dorcas froze in the act of turning the damp cloth. She glared indignantly at her husband.

"Timothy, no!"

"Hush now, wife. It must be written."

"You'll not leave us, Timothy! You'll not go off and leave us here alone! God won't let that happen after all the senseless cruel pain He's caused already!"

Dwight frowned at his wife's words. Comfort felt as helpless as when she was in the garrison house, watching her friend attempt to beat back death through sheer will. Meanwhile, Dwight's frown changed to pleading.

"Dorcas. Sweet Dorcas."

His voice begged her to understand. Or was it forgive, Comfort wondered? No matter. It broke the horrible spell that paralyzed them.

"Will you fetch the writing tools then, for Mistress Chapman to begin?"

Dorcas gave one last furious look at her husband, then frantically tugged a small trestle table over to the bed. Comfort roused herself from her painful fascination and found a stool. Dwight's writing box was set on the tabletop, ink bottle searched out from its warming cupboard, paper and quill readied. As Comfort sat down, she wondered if she could manage to sound out the words that Dwight would have her write. The baby had awakened and Dorcas left to nurse him. Her tight-lipped instruction to call if aught were needed hung in the tense silence. Comfort looked to Timothy to begin.

Dwight sighed deeply and closed his eyes. A silence followed, long enough for Comfort to wonder if Dwight were dozing. Then he cleared his throat and began to dictate, words coming slowly.

In the name of God Amen.

Then date and name, age and dwelling place, acknowledgment of his mortality. Comfort knew the form, had heard wills read and even signed as witness once herself. She thanked God for the calm familiarity. But Dwight's next words stretched the familiar form.

Especially being sorely wounded & not knowing how the Lord will deale with mee in lengthening out my days or calling me home suddenly unto himselfe I doe therefore think it meet to set my house in order ...

Her heart ached for the young family who could not be so simply set in order, his *most beloved wife Dorcas Dwight,* his elder and younger sons. The voice went on, apportioning the estate in time-honored thirds.

... my will and testament is that my Son Timothy shall have the house and barn ...

She thought he paused to let her pen catch up. But Dwight's next words brought home to Comfort, more than any of the past weeks' horrors, how fragile their place on earth had just become.

... if it shall please God that they stand.

413

There was a silence then, as Dwight struggled to force order onto his ultimately disordered existence. Comfort's hand shook as she wrote. How could a dying man set his house in order when its very existence was in question? How could he make provision for his family when, as they had all witnessed, it could in an instant vanish in flames? *What is a man to do, Lord? Where does he look for answers when all his props are struck down? When nothing solid remains?*

Dwight recovered an equanimity that Comfort could not share. He went on to distribute his land and his cattle, furnishings and farming tools. Then one more worry crowded in on him, and his voice caught as he turned his thoughts to his first-born.

...if my Son Timothy live and grow up to change his condition ...

Not "when." He had said "if." Such little phrases to mark the natural order gone awry.

Comfort had to ask Dwight to stop while she scratched through the word she'd just blurred with an escaping tear. *This cannot be right, Lord! Canst Thou not see fit to ease his suffering? Some sign, at least, of Thy forgiving mercy?* The tightness in her throat had reached her chest and she felt it constricting as she waited desperately for Him to answer.

There were voices at the front door, and Dorcas ushered in the minister, John Wilson, followed by Edward Adams, who came as witness to the will. Comfort curtsied and stepped aside. The minister bent over Dwight and gave him prayerful greeting. Then he turned to Comfort, his eyes full of sympathy for the painful work she was about.

"Goodwife Dwight tells us you do valiant service recording her husband's will, Mistress Chapman. Would you continue at it, or shall we rather finish the task?"

Comfort struggled with the inbred duty that dictated she stay. But as she stood away from the sickbed, the sorrow and the smell, the pain and pity threatened to overwhelm her. She felt the same urge to bolt from the room that she had fought against on first entering.

"I would do as Master Dwight thinks best," she managed to answer.

Dwight's own words were a reprieve.

"You've done enough. Spend your time with Dorcas, not with me."

He reached his left arm out to her, and clasped her hand intently.

"My thanks, Goodwife Chapman." The words were quiet, between the two of them. "For the affection you bear my wife. Now leave me to these good men and to God."

Comfort squeezed his hand in return and whispered, "God be with you, Master Dwight."

She turned away quickly and went out the door, her head bowed to hide her face from the others. The fevered tightness followed her out to the kitchen and she strode to a back window, pressing her head against the glass to stop its throbbing. Her eyes searched the orchard as if answers to her questions might miraculously emerge from behind the black-branched apple trees.

When Dorcas's steps sounded behind her Comfort swung around and said the first words in her mind.

"Dorcas, what will you do … after? Has your husband advised you?"

Dorcas shook her head. "He never mentioned death until today. As if by not thinking it, he'd ward it off." She looked at Comfort in hurt confusion. "And I believed in his belief. I trusted him! I believed he'd live to raise his sons and guide me well toward my own old age. Not end this way, with us all in need and everything to be done and no one to see to it. I trusted him," she repeated plaintively as if Dwight's dying were a personal affront. Then her face set and her words were vehement.

"But I know one thing for certain. We'll not stay in this wilderness. I'll not put my babies in danger another moment longer than need be. We'd have gone a week ago, but he could not be moved. Morning, noon and night, nearly my every prayer is that the Lord withhold His wrath for just the little time we need to get to safety."

"Dorcas, this is your home!" Comfort protested. "Where else can you go?"

"His nephew has place enough, in Dedham. My parents, perhaps…though there's little room there for three extra souls with my brother and wife in the house…"

Suddenly she glared at Comfort with angry determination.

"Comfort, I swear to you, I'd rather sleep in a stranger's stable, safe away from here, than stay in this town longer! This place is godforsaken. It has killed my husband. It has ruined my life. I will not have it destroy my sons!"

Her voice rose. "I will not stay here and let my children suffer punishment because of an unfeeling God's misdirected wrath!"

Comfort gaped. She had never seen Dorcas bitter. This sweet, loving woman whose mere presence made people smile was trembling with the strength of her emotion. She was ready to turn her back on everything she'd worked for and come to know. She was so filled with bitterness – or fury, was it? The thought stopped Comfort in her tracks. That was the word, wasn't it? It wasn't fear that drove her but an anger so strong, at the Lord and His unfathomable ways, that it obliterated faith.

Comfort trembled at the turmoil in Dorcas's soul. Faith was the latch that closed the soul's door against chaos. She thought of Dwight's plea to befriend his wife in need. What greater need could there be than loss of faith? But what could Comfort do? Her prayers were little help against the force of Dorcas's anger. How could she offer any hope to this woman whose life appeared so hopeless?

Suddenly, Dorcas's harsh features crumpled and Comfort's agonized self-questioning was cut short by a wordless groan of misery. Unthinking, she reached out and drew Dorcas close. The woman buried her face against the thick wool of Comfort's jacket, muffling a sob she could not hold in any longer. Arms close around each other, they huddled together while sorrow and anger mixed in tears and wracking sobs.

Finally Dorcas broke away with an impatient swipe at her face that dismissed tears, and a self-conscious word about tending to chores and her children. The rest of Comfort's stay was awkward. Dorcas was embarrassed by her outburst. Comfort was upset. Tears had eased the tightness in her chest but she still felt driven to quit the house. She struggled against what was clearly a weakness, this urge to escape the pervasive sense of doom. Or to escape her own inability to help? She knew of no medicine, to heal the other woman's pain.

So the two worked in near silence about the kitchen. When Comfort finally lifted her cloak off the peg to leave, she thought it some small consolation that, if nothing had been resolved, at least the next meal was ready. Dorcas placed a quick kiss on her cheek.

"Thank you for your patience with me, Comfort. I have faith in your goodness, if not in much else these days. You are more help than you know."

Comfort was embarrassed by a trust she felt was undeserved. She wished Dorcas a quick Godspeed and stepped out into the rain with guilty relief.

The relief evaporated as Comfort strode up the slope past the meetinghouse. All the questions besieging her at Dwights' had followed out the door. The imminent question of where to call home – should they flee like Dorcas, away from the scene of such suffering? Perhaps they were meant to stay here and wait out God's will. But Dwight's despondency, Dorcas's anger, young Tim's worried confusion, all raised a far greater question of doubt and faith. Where would they find an anchor in the middle of the whirlwind?

Comfort hurried to outpace the fear and doubt that chased after her. But through the rain she felt as well a mysterious pull dragging her up the slope with inexplicable urgency. She forced herself to stop where the path met the main road, breath coming fast as she searched the crossroads for some explanation of her hurry.

A high-pitched keening echoed in her head and she startled, shocked at first into thinking it might have come from her. But tilting her head up into the rain, she spotted a white-bellied hawk glide through the gray. Another cry, he tipped a wing and curved around in slow, unhurried spirals, searching for dinner in the empty fields below. She stood in the middle of the muddy track and watched, spellbound. Was this a portent she had been drawn to see, God's warning that predators would strike again? Should she take heed and rush headlong home? Her eyes fell to the ruts that marked the way and she felt a moment's panic.

Where was home? A dozen houses down the street? Or Watertown perhaps. If she searched as far as the sky-blue flax fields of England was she any more likely to find God's answers? Comfort intently scanned the crossroads as if answers could be wrung from the landscape.

Houses in this part of town stood close to the road, facing across narrow dooryards to home fields over the way. The fields ran south in ordered strips, some fenced, some neatly edged with stone walls laid between. The fields were empty this time of year, with a patch of hardy clover and a foraging pair of crows, the only signs of life against the dark wet earth.

In this part of town things looked surprisingly as they always had. Comfort had to search for sign of war and read it only in a smokeless chimney here, a shuttered building there. That and the road stretching empty at midday. An empty place. It did not seem so fearsome a place to her, whatever Dorcas felt. But it was lonely. Would Watertown be any less so? Or even Pakenham, for that matter?

Through the questions racing inside her, came a glimpse of Thomas and his quiet faith. Thomas was not an overly religious man. He put his faith in the shared community of which they were part. He trusted its members to support each other through whatever might come. As he had done since the time of troubles began. Comfort knew if she went searching, she would not find Thomas or his faith in England or even in Watertown. Thomas believed in Medfield's survival and he would stay. The notion of living apart from him was chilling and she shivered at the emptiness around her and within.

A distant noise intruded on her musing. A growing sound of talk, men's voices, and the heavy squelching noise of feet in mud. Comfort glanced over her shoulder to see a yoke of oxen emerge from the curtain of rain, dragging a sledge piled high with wood. Despite the drooping hats and bowed heads of two figures walking beside them, she could tell that Thomas was one of the men coaxing the oxen along. Three or four others followed with muskets and axes sheltered in their cloaks. Their desultory conversation echoed deep and mellow in the damp air.

Suddenly it was the most important thing in the world for Comfort to be with Thomas. She stood very still until he came abreast. He peered out from under his dripping hat brim and contemplated his wife.

"Good day, mistress. One finds comfort in most unexpected places."

She stuttered a passing explanation. The near ox tossed his head at being forced to stop. Comfort stared back and forth between the men, desperately wanting to prolong the human contact.

"You went for firewood?" She heard herself asking the obvious.

"Aye. And never a savage did we see, either. The woods about Noon Hill seem safe enough, for the nonce."

The men muttered in agreement.

They seemed so sure, these men. Not foolhardy; they were too serious for that. Determined, she thought. Confident that what they were doing needed to be done, and determined to see the task through. Suddenly, overhead the hawk wheeled as he gave up the hunt, his keening call fading as he glided out of sight.

Comfort marveled at the Lord who gave His answers in mysterious ways. The bird's flight was no portent of evil after all. Rather it was a heavenly sign that He would stay His hand. That these men – perhaps that all the town – should continue as they were. Thomas's voice calmly interrupted her reflection.

"Wife, do you choose to stay here in the rain, or might you come along with us instead? I, for one, relish the thought of a dry shirt and a full belly."

Thomas's question was so very simple, she thought. Not complicated at all. And the answer was so simple, too, not so far away. She silently offered her first thanksgiving of the day. Aloud, she answered him.

"Aye, husband, I'll come home with you."

They moved companionably down the muddy road.

Comfort's newfound confidence carried her through the burial, a few days later, of Timothy Dwight, and the sad farewell she bid Dorcas and the boys within the month. It steadied her through endless reports of other settlements attacked and burned as spring progressed. Groton, Northampton and Sudbury to the northwest; Warwick, Seekonk and Rehoboth to the south. Marlboro had been scourged not once but twice within the space of three weeks. As if the ever-present threat surrounding them was not enough, Comfort knew that, tucked away in the back of her mind carefully unexamined, was one more question that could not be avoided forever.

She should have seen it coming. Thomas was the one who led the younger men in opposition to the Selectmen, when they tried to forbid work at the south planting field. It was too far from town, the Selectmen said, too exposed, inviting attack. Comfort agreed with them. But the younger men prevailed at town meeting, and in April they set out to till the soil. They worked in groups, with an armed watch, but the south plain was planted.

She should have seen it coming when Thomas volunteered to drive a load of grain to Dedham for grinding. Medfield still had no mill, and hand grinding in a household quern demanded more time than the women had to spend, with planting season upon them.

The night he returned from Whiting's Mill he was more distracted than ever. She knew he must be chafing at spring mill time slipping away, and him without a pair of stones to run. Comfort watched him staring at the fire as she ladled stew into a bowl and handed it to him. She could see he was tired, but there was a tension too, which had never completely gone since the day of the attack. Finally she could not stand his brooding any longer.

"Your silence is too loud, husband. Do you mourn Master Adams still?"

Chapman started out of his reverie and looked up. Comfort had always welcomed his looks. She loved the play of expressions on his open face. But this night she found it disconcerting. Instead of the sadness she had expected, Thomas's look was uneasy, his eyes sliding away from hers. Before they did, she glimpsed another emotion there: a glitter of what she could only think was excitement. It was very confusing. Thomas cleared his throat and nodded, as if building his courage to begin.

"Aye. He was a good man."

"Indeed."

"I passed by the mill today. What's left of it."

"It must be a sorry sight. Does aught remain to speak of?"

"Nah. Adams' house is most gone; his son's, across the brook, burned to the ground. The mill too." He stopped, silently contemplating something that he was not telling. He shrugged.

"Well, there're scraps left of that sorry tub wheel, lying all black in the stream, but the building's gone, and most of the gearing. I'm guessing the stones could be salvaged."

Finally Thomas shifted on the bench and looked up at Comfort.

"I'faith, wife, though I'd not say it loud, the savages have brought us a great blessing in burning the mill."

Comfort's confusion was easily read in her face. He went on.

"You know it should never have been there to begin. It needs to be upstream, where I showed you that day. You remember? Where the water flows faster, and the wetlands above will keep us in power after others have to shut down?"

Comfort had not missed the use of *us* in Thomas's question, or the growing eagerness in his voice. And she remembered the rupture in their marriage occasioned by that long-ago afternoon by the brook. Her response was wary.

"I know it's a shame the town has lost its grist mill."

"We could rebuild, Comfort." He almost whispered it, staring at her intently.

"But did you not say that building would cost too dear? And the Selectmen would not grant you water rights? And what of Adams' sons? Do they not inherit their father's privilege?"

"Adams' sons don't wish to rebuild."

"Still, what of the money?" She pressed her palms against the yellow petticoat and unconsciously set her jaw.

"Comfort, don't you see?" Thomas laid out his reasoning. "Now, right now is our chance. The mill has to be rebuilt by someone. The town can't do without it. If Adams' family don't want the right, there's no cause for the Selectmen to turn me down. They know I can do it. And there's talk in town of petitioning the Governor for funds. If Medfield gets help from the Colony to rebuild, I want to be on that list."

There was a silence as Comfort held back.

The determination in Thomas's voice grew more urgent. "Don't you see, wife? This is the moment when God's plan for this new world and His plan for us draw into conjunction. This is the moment when what we do can benefit everyone around us and build us a future at the same time. The things of this earth may be as nothing in the sight of the Almighty, but what we do with them means everything. We *must* move now. If I have learned nothing more from the terrible storms of wrath visited upon us these past months, it is that we cannot sit and wait for any more tomorrows. There may be no more tomorrows. We must do what we can today or be forever left behind, in this world and the next."

He stopped suddenly.

"Does any of this make sense to you, Comfort?"

She held very still for a moment, palms pressed against her skirts. Then she answered reluctantly.

"I had not thought to see any good come of this winter's evil. God knows, what you speak of is little enough against all the suffering. But I believe you, husband. For a host of heavenly and earthly reasons it would seem right to go forward now with building your mill."

"You know what this means?"

"About a house?"

He nodded, his eyes begging her to understand.

"You know a faster flow means keeping a close watch." The corner of his mouth quirked up half-heartedly. "Not for nothing the old saying about a miller and his pond only sleeping together when they've bare bottoms or frozen ones…"

As Comfort remained silent and solemn, Thomas grimaced, and tried again.

"I have not forgotten my pledge to you, nor will I change it. I will never force you to leave the village if you cannot find it in you to do so. These past weeks we've seen the worst calamities that can befall those living apart from near neighbors. Comfort, I believe in my heart that the direst risk is over for us. For Medfield. But I'd be worse than a fool to pretend there won't be always some risk."

She nodded silently and thought about life on the edge: the edge between the village and the wilderness, between the safety of numbers and the dangers of solitude. Then she thought about the daily pleasures of dropping in on nearby friends and gossip over the dooryard fence, and how silent her days would be away by the mill. Her thoughts brought more sorrow than fear.

As if he read her thoughts, Thomas's next words worked at being cheerful.

"On the other hand, I've thought about your saying 'twas too distant from society. You could bid your women friends to visit while their grain is ground. We'd be barely a mile out of town, plenty close enough for you to stop over to Mistress Clark's when you've a mind. We'd stay for nooning on the sabbath day. You know yourself a mill's a natural gathering place for folks from miles around. We could make our place as sociable as any in the village. Don't you think?"

His last question was nearly a plea. Comfort's face softened at the gentle cajoling in her husband's voice. She was touched that he counted her happiness so dear. She wished she could simply say yes to him, wholeheartedly subscribe to his energetic optimism. But an inner reluctance made her hold back, resist the words and the vision behind them.

She rubbed her hands against the coins under her skirt in an unconscious gesture become habit.

"I do not want to be a burden, Thomas. I do not doubt a word that you have said. Or that the mill will benefit us all. I want your success, the success of Chapman's Mill, as much as you. But try as I might, I cannot see my way to living out of town."

Thomas made as if to interrupt but Comfort shook her head and went on.

"I know not why this one step seems so hard. I had no wish to return to the city. I agreed to stay in Medfield with you. Please believe I do not wish to balk your will in this, husband. Perhaps if I had a bit more time to think on it? To accustom myself to the notion?"

Thomas's reply was heavy with regret.

"I have no more time, Comfort. If I don't offer to build, the town will find another miller. There's already muttering about being too long without. And if there's to be a mill by next season, we must ready the site by midsummer to dam up the stream. There's much work to be done ahead, the Selectmen to see, workmen to arrange ..."

He scowled in concentration as his mind listed and tried to order the hundred tasks that accompanied building. Finally he sighed and shrugged his shoulders tiredly.

"I guess we might begin on the mill alone. And if you'll not be swayed, I'll look for a watchman to live by the dam. We'll lose our profit to wages though, I fear. And I confess I'll have trouble trusting another to do well, what I ought to be doing myself ..."

His voice trailed off. Comfort felt a flare of resentment at Thomas for deepening the guilt she felt already. She did not think her request was unreasonable. Had he but warned her well beforehand, instead of wanting an immediate response, perhaps she might be able to agree.

"Why did you not bring this up before it was urgent, husband?" she snapped. "Given me some warning of it?" She felt a briefly comforting indignation as she spit out the words.

"I tried to," he said helplessly. "I started to tell you half a dozen times. But every time I stopped. I could not think of any words to sway you or any way to make you change your mind. I told myself perhaps you'd come around when the woods were safer and planting begun nearby. But when you kept silence I knew it hadn't made a difference. I couldn't bring it up, Comfort, because I couldn't bear your saying flat-out *no*."

He broke off abruptly and moved toward the door. A small part of Comfort's mind recognized he was headed out to the evening chores. Thomas stopped in the doorway and shook his head as he looked back at her.

"I'll not live without you, wife, but your stubborn refusing to live by the mill makes living together harder than might be."

Comfort felt as if the door Thomas quietly pulled shut had closed on their lives, instead of the room. She hated the disappointment hardening his voice. She hated setting herself in opposition to him. She hated the old fear that crept back inside with the thought of dark woods and isolation. Senseless. Hurtful. Somehow she had to make it go away.

Angrily she turned back to the hearth and reached to swing the trammel away from the fire. The hot iron burned her unprotected hand and she snatched it away in shock and indignation. The cry she uttered was as much fury at herself as pain.

The passing weeks of summer gave Comfort more than enough time to reconsider. She was often alone, or at least without Thomas.

He had been right about the Selectmen's welcoming his proposal, and the men of the town were subscribed to help ready the mill site for construction. They cleared Thomas's chosen spot of debris. Cartloads of boulders and ballast stone were moved into place where the dam would eventually be. As stream flow decreased to a trickle in the dry summer months, they defined a channel. It curved from upstream over an exposed fall of rocks and on down far enough so the mill wheel would not sit in its own backwater.

Thomas talked Comfort into visiting the work in progress. She was surprised at how much had already been accomplished. At the same time, she was distressed by the nearness of its completion. Thomas did not raise the question of outliving again, but Comfort felt pressed from within, to put an end to the silent difference holding them apart. As she sat on the ledge that overlooked the mill foundation, she watched Thomas at work with the others.

He is so right here, she thought, *so content in what he does.* She wanted the same feeling. Then her eyes strayed up to the dark pines towering across the stream and a chill of old fear rushed down the slope and settled around her. She was grateful when Thomas found a boy who returned with her to town.

Back in the familiar surroundings of the village, she often caught herself staring at nothing, seemingly thinking of nothing, in the middle of a task. Standing at a window with a half-dried bowl in her hand. Leaning on her hoe in the middle of a row, contemplating beet greens. When she roused from these spells it was to visions of Thomas fading farther and farther away as she stood rooted in place, helpless to recall him. Eventually she would rally, force her arms to pick up the towel or the hoe and go about their business. It was harder than usual to get through a day's chores. Nightfall brought the relief of Thomas coming home but it was clouded by his unspoken question of their future. She could feel them losing the simple joy of being together.

In late July Comfort accompanied Thomas again to the mill. This time, she vowed to set her thoughts to finding what was *good* about the place. She would try to think as Thomas did, see as he did, in hope that his good might outweigh her lingering doubts. As they came out of the woods, the heat baking the stream banks hit them. It had not seemed so hot on her last visit.

She climbed to the ledge above the dam, where there was a fine view of the goings-on. It was too hot though, and she looked for someplace cooler. Seated again beneath a nearby sycamore, she suddenly understood the newly glaring heat. There were almost no trees left around the swamp that would soon be a mill pond. The trees lay stacked, some for use in the crib dam taking shape across the brook, some for framing timbers. There was another major change as well. Instead of the rocky track that she and Thomas had clambered over a year ago, the makings of a broad cart path now led to the mill. The effect was astonishing. In place of crowding trunks and overarching branches, the landscape opened upward to the sky. Comfort watched the puffy clouds of summer slowly ease across clear blue and sighed with relief. Her gaze moved to her husband and followed him as he worked.

He is content. And without doubts. My husband trusts himself and his decisions, trusts the others to know their work. And underneath it all, dear Lord, is Thomas's unshakable faith that Thou dost guide him to further Thy purpose as well as his own. Benevolent Lord, protect him... And show me the way, that I may be content to follow him.

On August 12, 1676, King Philip and what remained of his army were tracked down in a swamp in Rhode Island. Most were killed. King Philip's head was put on public display to signal the end of fighting. Within days, word of the English victory had spread throughout the Commonwealth, and settlers in Medfield as elsewhere breathed their first thorough sigh of relief since hostilities had started twelve months before.

Soon after, Thomas worked late at the mill, coming home when it was already dark. He was grinning, and his voice was boyish in its excitement.

"'Tis done, wife! The frame is cut and pegged. Ready for raising on the morrow. Wilt come to see the operation?"

Comfort felt a stab of something close to panic but she covered it with housewifely concern.

"Thomas! I am proud for you indeed. And certainly I'll be there but you're giving me scant warning. Surely this calls for something special. Food, drink. Have we a keg to spare? The makings of punch?"

"Come now, wife, you're not alone in this. The other wives'll come along, children and all, to cheer us on. I've no doubt, between the lot of you, there'll be food and drink aplenty."

He paused a moment, as if hesitant to bring up an awkward subject.

"And though I need be there at crack of dawn, you needn't do so. There'll be a cozy group to walk over with, later in the day. You needn't fear going alone."

He watched Comfort for a reaction, but she only nodded, apparently absorbed already with plans for the next day.

Later that evening, as Thomas lay asleep, Comfort watched him in the dim light. He was sprawled out next to her, half-smiling even in sleep, totally relaxed. She noticed the dreams that had had him tossing during the spring were gone. Thinking back, she realized they had been gone since he'd begun the mill. She envied him the peace of an undivided mind.

Curling up against him, she tried to draw some of his assurance, his energy into herself, but his words kept repeating in her head. "You needn't be afraid of going alone," he had said. She was, of course. Wasn't everyone? She thought and answered herself. *He's not. He's not afraid of anything. His faith and his trust are so strong as to uphold him, when mine falter.* The elusive inner voice took exception again. *Not just faith and trust. There's one element more, binds those two together in unseverable strands.* Comfort frowned in effort to remember. *You knew it once. You found it at the crossroads as the hawk's cry died away.*

She could picture the crossroads. The day Timothy Dwight had written his will and Dorcas had lost her faith. The day she had escaped into the rain and chosen to call Medfield home. But she was forgetting something.

Comfort sighed and rolled onto her back. Tomorrow she would cross over Mount Nebo to watch the mill building rise. And very soon, if not tomorrow, she must also cross over the quagmire of her own indecision. She must, once and for all, affirm her commitment to Thomas or risk losing the abiding love that made life on the edge of wilderness worthwhile.

An idea began to take shape as she contemplated risks. It seemed very fitting, but it made her shiver in its irrevocability. The night dragged on as the idea became a plan and she wrestled with memory. What was the third strand? Faith and trust and – what? – for strength to put her plan in action. It kept eluding her and she finally closed her eyes in surrender. It was not going to come tonight, despite her need.

Next morning she woke to a hum of wellbeing in her head. Thomas's own excitement was infectious and spilled over into the great hug he gave her before he rushed out the door at dawn. Comfort wiped out the porringers from their early meal and set them on the chest. Wooden mugs were rinsed of their cider dregs; pewter spoons laid in the drawer. She carried a dish of crumbs and food scraps to the door and, swinging it back on its heavy hinges, stepped outside. The chickens set up an immediate squawking at the sight of food, and raced towards her for their breakfast. Absently, she scattered the crumbs, adding a handful of cracked corn from the grain box in the entry.

The air was soft on her face, the breeze slightly cool as it brushed away early ground fog. Leaves and grass glistened with drops from a late night shower and sunlight picked them out like diamonds. Mockingbirds and robins called across the yard. It was a day for celebrating, Comfort thought, a day when the soul should shout thanksgiving to the heavens, for God's goodness. She leaned against the doorframe in the sun and stared at the narrow dooryard before her. If she looked only here, it was difficult to bring to mind the past year's fears and losses. For just a moment, she withdrew into prayer, searching there for the element of strength that still eluded her.

Benevolent Lord, show mercy still to thy children who suffer so greatly from the winter's scourge. Watch over Dorcas and her sons. Guide my husband in his work, that it may be to Thy greater glory. Forgive me my countless sins and doubts.

She paused a moment, hoping for a sign of absolution. Not finding one, she continued. She was hesitant that she might ask too much and incur God's displeasure in place of aid, but, she argued with herself, surely He, if anyone, should be compassionate of a wife's need to be by her husband.

And, Lord, if it be Thy will, grant me the courage to persevere. Grant me the wisdom to meld trust with faith, and the grace to see Thy intention in whatever transpires.

A frazzled brown chicken plucked at the hem of Comfort's gown, rousing her from her meditation. It was attracted by the yellow of her underskirt and kept coming back. She admired its stubbornness even as she flicked her skirt to shoo it farther away.

"Oh no, silly bird, you're not going to get the best of me, you're not! Off you go. Find someone your own size to peck at!"

His persistence reminded her of her own resolution, made while she lay awake in the night. She had decided to head out to the mill early, on her own. The half-hour walk on a well-traveled path was something she must become used to, wherever the house might be.

There could not be anything so fearsome between the village and the mill, such as would require an escort along the way. She would surprise Thomas. And he would be pleased.

Comfort collected a basketful of food for the men and tied down a shade hat over her cap. She set her jaw against the familiar inklings of fear, and walked out the door, shooing away the brown chicken one last time as she passed the snug wattle fencing of her kitchen garden.

Turning eastward, Comfort was on the edge of the winter's destruction. Thomas Clark's house remained uninhabitable, a charred shell. He and a dozen others had just petitioned the General Court for aid and must wait on their generosity to rebuild. Morse's barn was broken beams and rafters, where the hens pecked among the foundation stones. Samuel Morse had started over, though. The frame of a new house lay in pieces on the ground like a child's game waiting to be assembled. Morse would have been there now, Comfort reflected, swinging his adze in strong even strokes, but that he was helping Thomas with the mill. Morse would have help in return, she nodded to herself, when time came to raise his house frame.

She passed the last of the home fields and turned southeast where the path entered the woods. Her blood beat steadily, in rhythm with her feet. Chickadees kept pace with her, playing aerial leapfrog from tree to tree. She heard a flicker shrilly scolding in the distance.

This is not so bad a journey after all, she encouraged herself. *I may regret the load in this basket before I'm through, but there's little other cause to doubt the wisdom of going alone.*

It was cooler here, and damp, still, from last night's shower. Comfort rolled down the sleeves she had turned back during the morning's chores. It was not really chilly, she reasoned. 'Twas mid-August, after all, and the same shade in her own yard would be a welcome relief from the sun.

Her footsteps were almost silent on the damp leaves and pine needles. An occasional crunch of gravel sounded loud underfoot. Comfort tried to distract herself by picturing what lay ahead, at the mill. The voices, the clamor, the open sky. But the contrast only made her surroundings more silent and herself more completely alone. She felt her optimism weakening. *This is a place of doubts and trepidation. A place of wildness where a Christian's faith is tested.*

The path climbed up Mount Nebo, and the way became more rocky. It was shrouded here by the dark mystery of close-set hemlocks and the rustle of tall oaks. An acorn dropped in the leafmold beside her, inordinately loud. Comfort startled and glanced aside at a ledge with overhang deep enough to harbor Indians. Then she studiously watched the path before her feet. One rock. Another. *No savages here, no wolves even, this time of day,* she tried to convince herself. *A few stray rattlers perhaps. Though even they'd be dozing, like as not, high on a rock in the filtered sun.*

Eyes to the ground, step by step, heart beating faster as the path grew steep, she urgently repeated a snatch of prayer. *Benevolent Lord, guide my way.* Comfort struggled to convince herself this fear would pass, the Lord was but testing the strength of the decision she had made.

"Morning, mistress."

Her head jerked up to find a wild man right beside her. Come out of nowhere. Deep-brimmed hat that hid his face. Hid perhaps a faceless wraith in service of the devil. But just as she turned to run her calmer self remembered.

Jack Peters. The woodsman. He worked for Thomas sometimes, when it suited him. Comfort thought it must have been his charcoal-burning pits she had smelled off to the eastward. She remembered his scaring her before, the night he'd appeared out of the dark, bringing word that Thomas would stay at the mill.

Then he pulled off his hat and she remembered what had calmed the fear before, and did so now. The brown eyes full of concern and interest that glowed with a secret wisdom drawn from deep in the woods.

"Dinna mean t' discomfit ye, mum."

Comfort dropped the hand she had pressed to her heart, and breathed again.

"Mr. Peters."

"Goin' for the mill." His laconic words were more comment than question.

"I am. My husband is raising the frame today." She tried a tentative smile and took a step on her way again.

"Aye. Been there. Busy place." Peters turned and fell in beside her, his loose-limbed form a respectful distance away. Comfort wondered what he was about. After a moment's silence, Peters uttered another burst of speech.

"Not much goin' on twixt here and there, though."

"Indeed?" she asked stiffly. There was another space of silence that made Comfort uneasy, although she doubted Peters felt that way. He was used to silence, as much time as he spent alone in the woods. No one knew much about him. She wasn't sure it was a good idea to encourage familiarity by talking to him, no matter how much relief she felt at having company.

"Not a wildcat for miles."

Pause.

"Nearest den of rattlers is south side the hill."

She nodded. And waited.

"There's many a wild thing closer in to town, though, if you know where it be." This time he nodded, confirming to himself the merit of unaccustomed talk. Then, as if a long-closed floodgate had been opened, he launched into what was for him a lengthy speech.

"Why, one time, on Boston Common itself, I heard tell, a pack of wolves driven by winter made off with two young lambs before the watch could stop them. Providence alone kept the shepherd from harm. That and a good stout stick, I wager."

He nodded again to himself as his eyes roamed the landscape ahead of them. Comfort's resolution to keep her distance broke under this strange man's flood of words, and she looked at him in puzzlement. Where did all that come from? Was there a point to his story?

"It must have been dreadful."

Peters frowned in brief consideration. Then his brow cleared.

"Likely so. But there's naught to dread in these parts. Real comfortable feel to the woods these days."

A smile skimmed across Comfort's face at the timeliness of this strange man's assurance. Almost as if he'd read the wild imaginings in her mind. They walked a bit farther in silence, over the crest of the hill. From under the brim of her hat she caught a glimpse of gentle brown eyes studying her. For some reason, his silent study didn't make her nervous. Suddenly he clamped the dilapidated hat back on his head.

"Heading north here, I am. Good hunting still up past Rocky Woods."

Hand to his brim in salute, he stepped off the path into the trees and disappeared. Comfort stared after him, marveling at how solid flesh and blood could vanish so completely and so silently, leaving nothing but words of reassurance behind. Perhaps he was sent, she mused. *Didst Thou send him, Lord? He and his strange tale of wolves in the city and peace in the wilds? What is Thy meaning?* Comfort searched her recollection of Peters' words for a heavenly message.

Even though Thou guided our steps here, yet is this new world not an elysium. Even the settled places on the land. Thou didst bring us here for greater purpose than easy delight. This is our earthly trial, is it not? Our test of faith? And if we succeed it is only through Thy grace and our own determination.

A stillness draped itself around her as she echoed the word *determination.* And with it a conviction that her fear could be overcome. The elements had come together in her soul, and even now were twisting, one around the other, into unbreakable bonds. Faith, trust and determination together were pulling her forward to the mill. Old words echoed joyful in her head.

When my time is come to act, dear Lord, grant me the strength to help Thy will be done.

The time in company and prayer had brought Comfort near the upper end of Thomas's new mill pond. Here, the path opened out and was sunlit as it skirted the water. At the inlet, green and blue headed mallards paddled through the muck. Their muttered quacking blended with the gurgle of water trickling through the rocky narrows.

Although late-summer drought had kept the pond level low, the beginnings of a sheet of water spread out smooth downstream. It was a rich blue, reflecting the cloudless sky overhead. *Sky-blue,* Comfort thought with delighted recognition. *Just like the flax fields of Pakenham.* From the pond's lower end came the harsh rhythmic echoes of a two-man pit saw carving its way through planking for the mill. *But not quite so peaceful,* she amended without regret.

There were other sounds of building. An ox-driver confidently commanded the team hauling gravel to finish the road. Sledge hammers drove posts into the stream bed to frame the sluice gate.

Men whose houses Thomas had helped rebuild earlier in the year had turned out to help him in the last weeks before harvest, knowing that the new mill would benefit them all, come fall.

Comfort stared at the vibrant scene with a sense of wonder. *I can feel the new life here, Lord. The determination and perseverance, the shaping of wilderness to better humankind. This is a wonderful thing.* She picked out Thomas among the crowd of men working on the frame of the mill building.

I am sorry, Lord, for my earlier doubts. I thank Thee heartily for bringing me to this place. This mill may be a small and unsure haven in the wilderness. But one must begin somewhere. Each one of us must begin somewhere, or be found wanting at the throne of judgment. And if one's duty may be lightened by love and trust, as mine is by Thomas, then surely that must be the easiest of pilgrim's paths to follow.

Comfort closed the gap that separated her from Thomas, her steps in time to a silent incantation. *Faith and trust and determination.* She amended the final word. *Stubbornness.* Then she smiled at herself. It was time.

"Goody Chapman! Ye're early with a nuncheon."

Stout Ralph Whiting rubbed his hands in anticipation of food. Thomas glanced up from what he was doing with a smile of pleased surprise.

"Mistress. You couldn't bear to poke along with the others?"

"Nay, husband." Comfort's voice was light. She did not want the other men to know how tremulous she felt inside.

"I thought to have a word with you before the raising starts."

Impatience briefly wrinkled Thomas's forehead and he glanced at the work around him.

"It cannot wait?"

"'Twould be better not, I think." Comfort was quietly insistent.

"But wife ..."

"Ah, see to your wife, Master Chapman," Whiting chaffed him. "She's that look about her, women get when they won't be gainsayed."

Comfort threw the man a grateful glance as Thomas shrugged and laid down his mallet. She led him a bit away from the inquisitive group.

"So, mistress. What is it brings you here in such haste? That won't wait till nooning?"

Comfort gave him a silent smile and set herself down on a large rock. She undid the bottom button of her jacket and loosened the ties of her green overskirt. Thomas looked befuddled, but amused.

"Wife, I must believe you're not intending what you seem to be, as this is surely neither time nor place for merrymaking."

Silent still, Comfort reached into her pocket and drew out the small eating knife she always carried. Thomas watched in growing confusion as his wife took hold of a pleat in her yellow underskirt and began to cut a small rip in the fabric. A senseless act, as far as he could tell, for he knew how much she favored the garment. He could not bring to mind a time in recent months when she did not have it on.

He watched her lay the knife aside and stand up, shaking her skirts down as she did so. She looked at him then with unexpected solemnity and extended her hand.

"This is for you."

The gold coin shone, heavy and valuable, in her palm.

"A sovereign? In your skirt?"

"From Grandmother Welles. To use as I see fit. I confess to hoarding it as my escape, these past months."

Thomas still could not grasp what was going on.

"But Comfort, you know I cannot leave. Not now."

He hurt at the thought of losing her.

"I know, husband. This is for you, for the mill. 'Twould be tempting fate and any forest folk remaining hereabouts," the corner of her mouth turned upward, "to raise a structure without an offering beneath. Surely you've not been gone so long from England as to forget tradition?"

She held his gaze, silently asking him to understand the greater meaning of her gift.

"An offering buried beneath? From you? You'd place your treasure in my mill?"

"Aye. And my trust in you."

He studied her for a long moment, almost not daring to believe.

"You're determined then?"

Comfort's smile broadened. "Not just determined. Stubborn. You said so months ago."

Thomas took the hand with its coin and slowly kissed the palm. A silent understanding flowed between them. Comfort sighed, and knew the treasure had found a home.

Noise from the workmen broke in on their private communion and the moment passed. When Thomas raised his head from kissing her, it was clear he was already eager to seal their new bargain. He put an arm around Comfort's shoulder and turned her away from the mill. Free hand sketching an arc along the edge of the pond, he looked at her.

"And where then, wife, is our new home to be?"

Comfort's eyes came to rest on the granite ledge above them and its broad-branched sycamore tree.

LAYER IV: ANOMALIES

*"Anomalies. Every archeological site has its anomalies.
You know, the single item that doesn't belong? That has no
logical explanation? Like the nineteenth-century deposit that
has one broken arrow head in it."*
— *from a conversation with Dr. Nora Tunney*

August 18, 1995

The Skil saw's whine was piercing as Nora approached the mill.
She felt a tug of excitement stronger than the knot in her stomach, at
the scene that met her. Hank was operating the saw, leaning over a
huge squared-off timber and maneuvering the whining blade as
delicately as a carving knife. He abruptly shut it down and another
man moved in, lifting off a hefty chunk of wood to expose a perfect
scarfed end. The acrid smell of fresh-cut oak assailed her. Hank
glanced up.

"There you are. Good timing."

She almost hadn't come at all. With only two weeks left to finish
any archeology that would be accomplished at Mill Farm, almost
everything she was doing seemed more important than watching the
replacement of rotten beams. Besides, she had worked very hard the
past week to develop what she thought of as a 'sensible resignation'
about the whole situation. Never mind that it involved carefully
ignoring unpredictable sharp pangs of loss. Watching the removal of a

436

piece of Mill Farm's history would strain her hard-won resignation, but there was a lure to construction that Nora found irresistible. And there was a certain lure to watching Hank on the job, as well, seeing what made him tick.

He was giving directions to a skinny kid in jeans and a dirty tee shirt. "Tony, why don't you handle the peg hole this time. You have any questions, ask Jake *before* you bore, not when it's too late. Jake, check the length again on that tenon. I don't want any gaps around the mortises when we're done." Jake nodded noncommittally in reply and gestured to Tony to grab the tools. Tony had the wide-eyed, intent look of an apprentice whose future depended on wresting approval from the weather-worn face beside him. Nora guessed that Jake had been around old buildings long enough to parcel out approval sparingly. A good working pair, she thought, energy and experience.

"You want to come see what we're doing?" Hank cut into her musing. He turned at her quick nod, and led the way around the grist mill. The room they entered took her by surprise. Shutters always closed were now open. The wide ground-level doors swung wide, letting in breeze and fresh air. A patch of sunlight came down from the loft and she guessed the second-story grain door was open as well. Nora felt brief regret for the building's loss of mystery, mixed with surprise at how far a little fresh air could go to transmute history into every-day space. It was unexpectedly welcoming. Hank was already talking again. He stood by the wall at the upstream end of the mill and she realized part of the light came from a large hole there. The exterior sheathing had been removed on both sides of the corner post.

"Here's the join we're replacing." His gesture sketched a horizontal line where a gap in the flooring exposed the ground sill of the building. His arm then swung upward along a rough-hewn timber that disappeared into the grain loft above. "You remember the old post I've been talking about?"

Nora nodded, remembering the way Hank had patted the huge beam affectionately when they had first toured Mill Farm together.

"This section of sill and the post are only held together by inertia. We've decided the damage extends about up to here." He pointed to a spot chest-high, where yellow chalk lines stood out against the dark wood. "So this brace…" A garish new four-by-four stood next to the sill and hugged the post, nailed in place at ceiling height. "…will prop everything up while we take out the rotten wood and splice in new. That's what I was working on when you arrived, cutting a scarf for the sill."

"Are you going to have to do this around the whole building?"

"Oh no. Just a bit here and there. This was the only spot that really suffered. It's the north side, and the sill is only resting on a single run of stone here. So the wood kept alternately soaking up water from below, and drying out. That brought the termites, then dry rot. It's a miracle there's anything left to save." He was shaking his head, then brightened as he went on. "But, today we'll fix it for another two or three hundred years. Come on outside. Let's see if the guys are ready."

Tony and Jake had been joined by a third workman who flashed Nora a wide appreciative smile when Hank introduced him as Harley. He was too busy to be more sociable, however, the pumped-up muscles in his arms straining as he held two beams together while Jake tested the fit of the joint. Hank bent to help them and Nora knew enough to stay out of the way.

She wandered around to the north end of the mill, where shingles and weatherboarding had been removed to expose the rotten timbers. There was hardly more than a pathway between the building and the edge of the dam. The pond was nearly empty after a long dry summer. The cloudbursts of two weeks ago, when Nora had realized they were bottoming out at the site, had been the only substantial rain in over a month, leaving Mill Brook a lazy trickle snaking its way across the cracked pond bottom.

Barren was the word that came to mind. As empty of life as the cellar had turned out to be. Nora was shaking her head in disgust when a splash came from one of the few puddles that marked low spots along the stream. One of the little catfish, she guessed, that appeared out of nowhere and made the pond a fishing hole in more prosperous times. She wondered if he and his puddle would survive until the next rain came.

"Nora? You're going to have to move over a bit."

Hank was talking over his shoulder as he backed toward the corner, carrying one end of the massive sill patch. He and Harley set it down by the skeletal wall, while Nora scrambled to a safer observation post. She sat on the edge of the sluice abutment, twenty feet from the workmen and as far as she could go without ending up in the pond. Jake and Tony rounded the corner with another beam end, laying it near the first before they turned back for more. Harley came back, effortlessly carrying an oversized Sawzall, crowbar and sledgehammer. As if they were just Pooh-sticks, Nora couldn't help thinking, with one of her unpredictable pangs. A whisk broom dangled incongruously from his other hand. Hank started issuing directions.

"Okay. Jake? We'll cut out the dead wood and Harley, Tony, I want you ready to lay in the new pieces as soon as we get all the punk cleaned off the foundation."

"Nothing's going to happen, is it, if we leave a hole for a few minutes?" Tony, new on the job, couldn't keep a small hint of worry out of his question.

Hank's smile showed a memory of understanding. "Not too likely. But this building's going to get a good shaking in the next few minutes, and I don't want to take any more chances than we have to. Jake, you ready? Nora, look out for flying debris."

"There isn't anything I can do, is there?" Nora offered weakly. It was pretty clear they had a team here, and could manage what they were doing just fine.

Hank hesitated. "Well, actually there is, although I'm afraid it sounds like housework. You want to help clear off the foundation stones? All the sawdust and frass and rotten bits should be cleaned up before we lay in the new sills. You know, ounce of prevention and all, to make sure the new sills won't rot because of the old ones." He looked at her uncertainly as if she would any moment accuse him of chauvinism.

"I was trained in Whisk Broom, you know. It's part of my job."

"Oh, yeah. Well, stay where you are for the moment. Then move in when things settle down."

Harley grabbed the whisk broom along with the sledgehammer, and made a show of presenting it to her along with a look that managed to combine invitation and admiration in one disconcerting grin.

"Harley, you ready?" Hank snapped.

Harley sauntered back to the others and work began.

In the next few minutes Nora discovered there was less need for concern about flying debris than dust. As the Sawzall carved along the yellow-chalked lines, and then as sledgehammer and crowbar went to work jarring the rotten wood out of place, a cloud of powdery dust grew and thickened. It billowed from the old building out over the pond. Nora was spellbound by an image of Chapman's Mill running amok, puffing runaway bursts of flour out into the Medfield air. Beneath the dust came the pounding of sledgehammer meeting wood, resonating across the pond, and the nasty squeal of the crowbar meeting resistance. A pause finally, and then a flat thud that sent tremors as far as the stone wall where Nora sat. Dust began to settle and she could see a gap where the post had been. Harley gave one last underhand swing of the sledge and a section of sill disintegrated onto the ground. Tony, nervously mindful of Hank's admonition, rushed forward to begin clearing the area. Nora took that as her cue to get to work.

It didn't take much thinking to understand Hank's concern for clearing off the line of flat-topped stones that supported the sills. The rotten wood had disintegrated as it was cut away. Spongy slivers of it lay all around the stones, damp and riddled with old insect tunnels. Heaps of soggy sawdust – what Hank had called 'frass', further evidence of insect damage – had sifted down between the stones. A variety of unappealing bugs squiggled and slithered away from unexpected exposure to fresh air.

Nora raised an eyebrow and wished she'd brought her work gloves along, though why she would have thought to do that was beyond her. Then she crouched next to the wall and set to work. Hank and Tony had already cleared the bigger pieces off one end and were working their way down the line. Nora followed behind them with her broom, sweeping hard, sometimes using it almost like a scoop, to dig out frass deposits the men had missed.

It was small-scale work, almost like archeology, so when she paused for a breather she was surprised to find she'd cleared as far as the missing corner post. The others had moved on to begin assembling the replacement pieces, all except Harley, she noticed, who was still comfortably leaning on his sledgehammer. He was, if she was not mistaken, ogling her. She turned back to her work, studiously ignoring him.

The stone positioned under the corner post was larger than the others, almost a boulder. It had been sunk into the ground to level it with the smaller stones on each side. Nora's broom whisked back and forth across the top as she thought about the contrast between Harley's stare – a leer, really – and the intense look she caught on Hank's face, watching her when he thought she wouldn't notice. No question but Hank won hands down for stare appeal. She could get lost in those stares that made her feel shy and important, cared for and wanted all at the same time.

A gleam of something caught her eye as she pushed the last dirt off the stone. She almost missed it in her contemplation of Hank and his eyes. Then she caught herself and gently pushed a finger through the little pile she'd just swept off. Ever the archeologist, she thought. Can't even leave the bugs' trash alone.

Her fingers found the object she had spotted and she raised it for a closer look. It was round and flat, metal of some sort, the size of a dime. A token, maybe, or a long-lost button? But the edges were surprisingly thin. And there was no sign of the rust that ate away iron, nor the blue-green tinge of copper. She scraped the caked-on dirt and mud with her fingernail, entertaining a delightful thought. It looked like she'd found a coin.

"Whatcha got?"

Nora looked up, startled at the question right above her, confused for an instant that the voice might be Harley moving in. Instead, she found Hank's face a foot from hers as he leaned over in friendly interest to see what she was doing.

"It's a coin," she said, holding it up for his inspection. "It was sitting right here, on top of this stone. I love finding coins on a site. They're so rare. You must have a lucky mill here."

Hank had been frowning at the object as she spoke. He drew a small jackknife out of his pants pocket and opened it. Then he hesitated and glanced down at Nora.

"Mind if I take a scrape?"

The archeologist winced but curiosity won out. "Be careful?"

"I will."

He gently drew the blade toward his thumb, across the face of the coin. The accretions on the surface resisted. He scraped again, then scowled and eased the tip of his knife under a fleck. He let out a low whistle.

"What?" Nora, unable to take the suspense, stood up beside him for a better look.

"Looks like gold to me. Sure isn't very well made, though. Look how uneven the edges are, like it was homemade or something."

Nora took the coin back and examined it more closely. She found her fingernail could do as well as the knife tip removing flakes of dirt. With the added benefit, she thought silently, of not harming the surface. The other men had gathered by then, joking about pieces of eight and pirate hordes. Their scoffing tones only partially hid young boy excitement at the mention of gold. But Nora was only vaguely listening. She was frantically trying to recall everything she knew about coins. It was pitifully little, especially about gold ones. They just didn't show up on New England colonial sites. She'd had no need to know. But as she exposed more and more of the coin, she began to feel an excitement that topped anything the men were hiding. Finally she looked up at Hank.

"Are you ready for this?" A smile spread so wide across her face she almost started laughing. Hank nodded patiently.

"I think, I *think*, mind you, that we just found the seventeenth century."

"Are you serious?"

"Um-hum. Look. Here's some probably royal coat of arms. Hard to tell what, but there're books for that…"

"But coats of arms were used for centuries." Hank's interruption was skeptical.

"Um. But that's not the important part. Look at the edges. They're skinny. Uneven. This coin was hand-hammered." She looked up at Hank with triumph in her eyes. "And one of the few things I happen to know about old coins is that pretty much all of them were machine-struck after 1700. You know – flat edges, regular shape? Not like this crooked little thing at all.

They bowed their heads together over the coin, turning it this way and that to study its shape. Eventually they gave it up to the crew who carefully passed it from hand to hand amid expletives of awe and disbelief. Meanwhile reaction began to set in and Nora found herself devil's advocate again.

"Look, Hank, I'm no expert on coins. We need to get this to somebody who knows what they're talking about. I mean, suppose it's really just some homemade substitute – bootleg coinage from the Civil War or something? I don't want to get any hopes up just to find we're two centuries off. After all, what's the likelihood of finding a seventeenth century coin anyway?

Hank had been staring at the gap in the corner of the building, as if answers hung magically in the air.

"Exactly where did you say you found this?" His voice was distant.

"Right here." Nora pointed to the top of the corner stone. "I almost missed it. Come to think of it, why on earth would a coin end up *under* the sill? If we find them at all, they're in the builder's trench outside. You know," she glanced up at Hank, "fell out of somebody's pocket or something."

But Hank was shaking his head as a smile broadened across his face.

"Wrong. You're thinking like an archeologist."

Nora's eyebrow rose. Hank went on.

"You have to think like a seventeenth century builder. Then there's all the likelihood in the world that a coin would be under a building."

"And just why would that be so?"

"It's like topping off. You know, that pine tree builders stick on the top of a new house frame? Only it's bottoming off, sort of. I don't know the old term for it but it goes way back. Offerings to the earth mother, sacrifice to the forest gods. The whole idea must have seemed pretty pagan to Puritan thinking. I wonder what that says about my ancestors..."

"An ancient builder's ritual?" Nora was trying to resist the obvious conclusion. "Why didn't I know about this?"

"Would it have made any difference if you had?"

"Apparently not. Even if I'd tested more around here, I never would have found the coin, hidden the way it was."

"Wrong, Nora. *You* did find it. It's a safe bet none of us would have noticed it in the dirt."

Nora was drowning in the deluge of new information. Every instinct she had was on the alert, her thoughts wildly chasing in different directions. The coin was a key to so many doors at once, she didn't know which to open first. She needed space to sort everything out – history, Thomas Chapman, the Mill Commission, Hank, her place in all of it. Ignoring Hank's reassurance, she withdrew.

"I…ah…There are some articles back at my place about coins. I want to go see if I can find this one. We really need to identify it before we get all excited."

"It's too late, you know. We're all excited anyway. But it sounds like a good idea."

Nora carefully tucked the coin in her pocket.

"I'll be back as soon as I can," she yelled back over her shoulder, already halfway to the road.

Nora's search was a failure. She had taken the little coin out as soon as she got to her study and placed it on the windowsill by her desk. It lay there softly gleaming in the light, tantalizing in its anonymity. She had spent an hour frantically searching her shelves of reference material. The books and articles she did find never mentioned gold coins. They were too rare, too unlikely to be found on New World sites.

For a moment she sank onto her desk chair and just stared, willing some magic connection to take place, brain to coin, clarifying its significance. When no burst of inspiration occurred she picked up the phone and called a well-known coin dealer who had helped her in the past. He was attending a show in New Orleans, his voice-mail said, and would be out of his office for a week. Nora left him a half-hearted message, knowing he took his time returning calls.

She picked up the coin and laid it in her hand. Cool at first, it warmed against her skin until it radiated heat back into her palm. This could have been Thomas Chapman's coin. Rested in his own hand centuries ago. Placed by him upon a stone as neighbors stood by, waiting to raise the mill frame into position, waiting to haul up the huge posts and tip the sill slowly, slowly, until it thumped with certainty into place above the gold. There it had sat, year upon year, as water seeped around it and little bugs crawled by, radiating its timeless magic through the building as countless Chapmans came and went. Somehow it was proper – 'meet' was the old fashioned word that came to mind – somehow it was meet that Hank be the cause of its discovery. He was a builder, whatever she thought about his approach to preservation, and he was a Chapman. Someone who understood wood the way his ancestor must have done, able to make a structure that stood the test of time, like the family itself had stood it.

Hank and his men would be working now at the corner, maneuvering the splice into position. Behind them was another group, men invisibly dressed in smocks and jerkins, offering silent advice as the four live men worked. Hovering to the side a woman watched, whose hands rested flat against her skirt. A hint of the color of goldenrod peeked out from the quilted underskirt beneath.

Suddenly Nora squeezed the coin tight. A quiet sound of distress came from her throat and she frowned in urgent concentration. Setting the gold back on her windowsill, she ran upstairs. When she emerged a few moments later, she pushed open the screen door, nearly tripping over Artie in her hurry, running back toward the mill.

There were none of the sounds of construction she'd expected as she neared the building and when she swung around the corner, she thought the place was deserted. The big black Harley-Davidson was gone, along with Jake's battered old pick-up. She couldn't imagine why they'd quit in mid-afternoon. Unless, she thought in panic, they finished the repair. But the gap still remained at the corner of the building, although she noticed extra stabilizing timbers bracketing the amputated post. Crouched at the corner, contemplating the stones, was Hank.

"I'm not too late!"

"Hmm? No, I guess not. We couldn't finish until I conferred with you, so I sent the boys home."

Nora was momentarily distracted from her mission. "Conferred with me? What do you mean?"

"About the coin."

She interrupted before he could elaborate.

"The coin …I haven't found anything yet. I looked at everything I had, tried to call a guy I know, no luck."

"That complicates matters."

"I know. But I think I have a solution."

"Maybe I'd better explain what I mean. It's about replacing the corner." He gestured toward the stones and the new wood still lying on the ground nearby. "I got this weird feeling that we shouldn't rebuild it without putting back the coin." He snorted in self-derision.

"I know. I really do."

"You do?"

"And I told you, I have a solution."

Nora reached into her pocket while Hank studied her doubtfully.

"It would be a mistake to put that coin back. We need to identify it, we need it as evidence, and it would be an anachronism: a seventeenth century coin under twentieth century wood. Everything I hate about bad restoration."

She smiled at him in a mollifying way and held out her hand.

"How about this instead?"

"A silver dollar?"

"Um-hum. A real one. The kind they stopped making in 1980. I know it's not as valuable as a gold coin but it's special to me. My gramma used to give one to each of us at Christmas. She'd tie them up with a bow and hang them on the tree after we were asleep. I think she'd like one ending up here. That is, if you want?"

Hank had been studying her again in that way he had that made her self-conscious.

"Why do you want to do this?"

"Oh…I don't know…I guess it's a stupid idea…"

"No, I don't mean that. I want to know why this mill is so important to you, that you're willing to give up a family treasure?"

He took the dollar out of her hand as he spoke. Her skin tingled.

"Well … This is kind of a family treasure too, isn't it? Of course it's your family… But, um, I have some others at home." She shifted uncomfortably under his gaze and realized what she'd just said. "I mean, back at The Shed."

"Nora, would you stop avoiding my questions? I'm asking why you think this is so important? Why have you thrown yourself into everything here since you came? Caught us all up in it and made us think this is the most important thing on earth to be doing?"

"I don't know. I guess I wanted to. Mill Farm just seemed to open great old arms and draw me in and with me, all the Chapmans for generations back. I've never felt that way before." She paused, suddenly embarrassed. "And I'm sure this isn't making a lot of sense…"

She desperately wanted Hank to disagree, to tell her he understood, that he felt the same things she did, cared about the same things she did.

"It's making some sense," he started out, but then he seemed to falter. "I wish I knew how to do this. I don't have much experience talking about what's important. What do you want, Nora, anyway? I don't want to rush in with the fools if I'm going the wrong direction."

"Oh ..." Nora's voice trailed off. Hank waited patiently through the silence.

If somebody's got to do it, it might as well be me. I'll only have three more weeks to stay here in utter humiliation if what I say is off the wall.

Nora gave a great sigh and addressed her words to the catfish in the pond.

"No one ever asked me that before. What I want. So here goes. At this moment there are really only three important things in my life. This place, Mill Farm, is one of them. Finishing the research I started is another."

Was she crazy enough to keep going? She drew a deep breath.

"And the third is getting to know you better. If you happen to feel the same way..."

She finally dared to meet Hank's eyes and shrugged self-consciously. His reply took forever to come out.

"I've been meaning to ask if you wanted to stay on at the farm over the winter. The Shed would just go empty otherwise."

"I just got a publishing contract for the *Archeologist's Handbook* I'm writing. It would be a great place to write."

"While you're at it, maybe we could spend some more time together. We might be able to work something out, you know, between restoration and preservation?"

"I need to spend some time drumming up business for next season."

"Not on my account, you don't. That *Smithsonian* article brought in so much new work I'm already booked through the summer. After we finish stabilizing, it'll be a while before we do any more on the mill."

Both voices had dropped to an intimate murmur belying the everyday words. Nora studied Hank's cheekbones as he stared at her lips. She stirred at last, as if the time hadn't come yet for total absorption.

"Maybe by the end of next season," Hank's voice continued, low and considered, near her ear, "we'll both know more clearly how much of the draw is Mill Farm and how much is you."

The catfish stirred in the shallows. Nora caught a glimpse of sky-blue in the ripples. *Flax fields in June*, the thought came. She wondered why.

HISTORICAL AFTERWORD

Old Wives Tales is a work of fiction and it is populated by contemporary characters whose resemblance to persons living is purely coincidental. On the other hand, many of the earlier characters, places and events are as historically accurate as extensive documentary and archeological research can make them. The following is offered in an attempt to keep some distance between 'truth' and 'falsehood,' and in case readers wish to learn more about the history of Medfield, the region, and the people who made it happen.

The Chapmans and Mill Farm

There is no evidence of a Chapman family having lived in Medfield in the past, although Chapman was a common name in England, as well as in the New World after 1634. A number of branches still exist. Mill Farm is also fictitious, but many of its elements resemble buildings and landscapes familiar throughout the small towns lying outside Boston, and other communities in southeastern New England.

The use of small stream waterpower, especially to run sawmills, continued well into the twentieth century in northern New England, where the only remaining stands of substantial timber were located. Local gristmilling, on the other hand, was slowly phased out of business during the 1800s, due to the growth of the midwestern "corn belt" and development of more sophisticated milling machinery. A surprising number of mill buildings still exist; however, most date from the nineteenth century. An earlier example is the Kingsbury Gristmill in Medfield, open to the public on an occasional basis.

The Ancient Cellarhole that Nora and her crew excavated during the summer of 1995 is based on a real, eighteenth-century site in a neighboring town, excavated in the late 1970s. Some liberties were taken with the artifactual record, to adapt it to the present story. The real site was an early victim of the "mansionization" craze that has since swept this region. What remained in the stone-lined cellarhole and the surrounding soil layers was removed in a rapid and private backhoe operation so the site could be relandscaped as a hilltop terrace. The cellarhole was to serve as aesthetic focal point, transformed into a reflecting pool.

Sarah's Story: Medfield and Dedham in the Great War

While Sarah, like Abby and Comfort, is a fictional character, Will Robertson definitely is not. Robertson's life and occupation were as represented in *The Blue Bunny* and *Dragon's Blood*, despite lack of evidence that he ever spent time with a woman named Sarah.

What is known of Robertson's personality, opinions and thoughts comes from an extraordinary documentary survival: a group of forty-two letters written between 1914 and 1925 to Mrs. William Nicholson, in Washington state. Robertson had made friends with Jenny Nicholson and her husband during several stays in a Washington mining camp and kept up the friendship through a twice-yearly correspondence until he became too ill to do so.

The Robertson letters are now at the Dedham Historical Society. They provide a unique perspective on Robertson, Dedham Pottery, Charles and Maude Davenport, and the exigencies of life and work in wartime New England.

A second rich source of regional information for the period are the files of the *Dedham Transcript*, also at the Dedham Historical Society. An early wartime entry in the "Stroller's Notebook" column (July 7, 1917) summarizes a situation familiar to Sarah Chapman and countless other women between the summer of 1917 and the end of 1918.

> *All the womenfolk are being urged to do their bit these days... make gardens, ...conserve the food supplies...preserve fruits and vegetables, ...help on the good work of the Red Cross... [all] in addition to their usual household and social duties. Do their bit! ...When peace is declared none will be more pleased than the women. They will then have a chance to rest.*

The year and a half of direct American involvement in the Great War did not have the visible impact on domestic life that World War II did. In some ways, however, I suspect that the impact was actually more profound, at least in agrarian New England. The demand for war industry workers in urban areas drained rural towns of the unskilled labor on whom agricultural production still depended. At the same time, local small industry could not compete with the relatively high wages offered by munitions plants like the Watertown Arsenal. Will Robertson's complaints about finding dependable help arose from the same dilemma that Sarah faced when she and Hub were confronted by harvest time without harvesters.

The war, coming after a seemingly endless period of prosperity, positive thinking and, most of all, stability, upset much that had been taken for granted. It destabilized the social order and the economy, offering unimagined opportunities and freedoms to the rural populace. At the same time it interrupted the functioning of traditional support systems that had existed, substantially unchanged in New England, for nearly a century.

One of a relative handful of books to survey the changing texture of American life during this period is Allen Churchill's *Over Here; an Informal Re-Creation of the Home Front in World War I* (NY: Dodd, Mead & Co., 1968). Readers may also find a useful overview in Edward Robb Ellis, *Echoes of Distant Thunder: Life in the United States 1914-1918* (NY: Coward, McCann & Geoghegan, 1972).

Abby's Story: Dover and the Move Toward Industry

Old Deacon Fisher's sawmill in Dover, which the Chapman family fictitiously bought in *Encre de Chine*, had stood by the Charles River since at least the early 1700s. The peninsula on which it was located came to be known as Charles River Village during the nineteenth century, due largely to the investments of Josiah Newell who developed the land as a commercial site. Thus 'Fisher's Bridge', over the Charles from Dover to Needham, became 'Newell's Bridge.' By the 1830s, a cluster of factories stood on both banks of the river including a rolling and slitting mill, a nail factory, a paper mill, and assorted ancillary shops.

The iron-working operation was the earliest of these concerns and it was, in fact, a tourist attraction during its early years. According to a 1795 census of manufactures, there were only eleven "iron works" in Massachusetts. Dover, neighboring Dedham, and Stoughton each had one, but Dover's claim to fame was its location directly on a river, rather than a stream. Ebenezer Chapman was not the only contemporary to think that trying to span large waterways was tempting fate. While the Charles River might only be middling-sized by national standards, even the significantly smaller Quinabaug River in Sturbridge, Massachusetts, was not spanned until the 1790s. The Connecticut River, which splits New England north to south, was not dammed until 1798.

The Dover Iron Works, also known as the Dover Nail Company, was one of dozens of industrial experiments in Norfolk County. The problems that infuriated Colburn Whiting were common to many of these early enterprises. Insufficient capital, inconsistent supply and demand, inexperienced management, and the psychological difficulties inherent in running an industrial enterprise in a largely agrarian environment all contributed to a high rate of failure among the proto-industries. As Nora pointed out to Hank, the golden age of Norfolk County industry waned as Waltham and Springfield, Lowell and Lawrence grew.

At Charles River Village, the iron works were absorbed by the more successful paper mill, which in turn became a cloth factory. Today the site is idyllic, the Dover side consisting of private property with a single house located on it; the Needham side still preserving a few of its mill houses, with municipal park land marking the site of the last industrial building.

The Dover Iron Company's first group of proprietors included both local and Boston investors. While Theodore Lyman was not among them, his inclusion would not have been surprising, as he invested in numerous other early industries, most notably in The Boston Company whose founders went on to build a brave new world in Lowell.

Lyman was also known for his interest in horticulture. The Vale, his country estate in Waltham, included a year-round, heated greenhouse. It became famous for its collection of rare American and imported plants and trees. Today the Vale belongs to the Society for the Preservation of New England Antiquities. Its house, grounds and greenhouse are open to visitors.

Both Chickering and Whiting are venerable Dedham/Dover names. The Whiting family exercised a virtual monopoly on the waterpower of Dedham's mill creek, Mother Brook, during the colonial period. Ellises also lived in the vicinity, although they tended to live south of Dedham in the vicinity of present-day Westwood and Walpole.

The development of American industry and its impact on the nation is a subject of unending interest to scholars and a source of local pride to almost every community in eastern Massachusetts. The years during which Abby's story takes place are largely neglected among industrial historians, however, their investigations of the period seeming to focus on debate over obscure machine parts and a definitive meaning of the term "industrial." Readers interested in learning more about some of the driving human forces behind the industrial wave are encouraged to look at Robert F. Dalzell Jr.'s *Enterprising Elite: The Boston Associates and the World They Made* (Cambridge MA: Harvard University Press, 1987). A basic understanding of the traditional and developing uses of waterpower must begin with Louis C. Hunter's classic *Waterpower: A History of Industrial Power in the United States* (Charlottesville: University Press of Virginia, 1979). Lyman and his circle of friends, as well as their vision of recreating English country life in New England, are well-described in Tamara Plakins Thornton's *Cultivating Gentlemen* (New Haven: Yale University Press).

For the more local scene, the newspaper files at the Dedham Historical Society provide erratic insights. The *Columbian Minerva* and the competing *Norfolk Repository* were both published bi-weekly in Dedham beginning in 1797. Most of the actual articles address issues and events of national or international import. As much as half of each paper, however, is made up of obituaries and auction notices, personals, help wanted and commercial advertisements. Together these offer glimpses of what was available and desired, who was in trouble and who was succeeding in the new shire town of Norfolk County.

Another, even rarer documentary source is a diary kept by Sally Haynes Mann in Dedham from shortly after her marriage to Herman Mann (newspaper editor, printer, inventor and erratic provider) until 1824. It is a very personal document, full of reflections on her children, her husband – including one that echoes Abigail's attempts at decorating with field flowers – and, in later years, Sally's increasing absorption with salvation. The diary is among the Mann Papers at the Dedham Historical Society. Sally Mann's first entry, dated 1794, captures the earnest intent shared by Abigail Chapman.

> *Monday. this is the first day of the Fall, which justly reminds me of the swiftness of time recolecting how short has been the Summer season, how quickly it is past! one season moves on after another and leaves me still I fear without improveing in any things that woud be most necessary for my greatest happiness, that that woud be everlasting.*

Comfort's Story and Frontier Medfield

Any research on Medfield must begin with William S. Tilden, *History of the Town of Medfield...1650-1886* (Boston: Geo. H. Ellis, 1887). Tilden's summary of town affairs is the only extant version of the town's early records, which burned with its town hall. His extensive genealogical notes are largely accurate.

To the best of my knowledge there was no Welles family in Watertown nor were there solitary Peters men living, seventeenth or twentieth century, in the woods of Medfield. Numerous branches of the Adams family did settle in the town including Henry Adams, the miller, and Peter Adams, whose son John married widow Dorcas Dwight in 1677.

Old Wives Tales strays from the historical record at Henry Adams' death, allowing Thomas Chapman to rebuild the town's gristmill and found a new dynasty of Medfield millers. In fact, Henry Adams' son, called "John Adams, miller," seems to have continued the family tradition after King Philip's War, but John died unmarried and the mill privilege passed out of the family in the early 1700s.

The Dwights were substantial residents of the community from 1651 until the family's fourth generation sold the last of Timothy Dwight's land grants. Those portions of *Coin of the Realm* that concern the Dwight family are substantially accurate, including the circumstances of Timothy's death and the wording of his will. Young Timothy, their son, did not live past childhood, leaving baby John to inherit his father's entire estate when he grew up.

Much has been written about King Philip's War and the destruction of frontier communities in the course of that vituperative and bloody conflict. It is not my intention to recapitulate what has already been written, or to participate in the recent spate of revisionist discussion about the events or their causes. It was a defining event of colonial New England history.

For those who wish to be better informed about the first war that changed America, two interesting recent additions to the historiographic debate are Jill Lepore's *The Name of War* (NY: Alfred A. Knopf, 1998) and Schultz and Tougias, *King Philip's War: The History and Legacy of America's Forgotten Conflict* (Woodstock VT: Countryman Press, 1999). A broader introduction to the people who first occupied New England will be found in Esther K. and David P. Braun, *First Peoples of the Northeast* (Lincoln MA: Lincoln Historical Society, 1994).

The coins that Comfort guarded in her skirt could have been any one of a number of different issues. Coinage was anything but standardized in the seventeenth century, and coins, especially the more valuable ones, apparently remained in circulation for a long time. One of the reference books that Nora did not have at her disposal because it was not yet published, *Coins of Colonial America* (Lasser, Greve, Pittman, Caramia. Williamsburg VA: Colonial Williamsburg Foundation, 1997), identifies half a dozen coins that might have found their way to Comfort's underskirt. These include English guineas, French *Louis d'or*, Turkish chequins, Italian, Spanish and Dutch ducats – all standard trade coinage at the time. I chose to have Nora discover a Spanish *dos escudos* dating from about 1588, early enough to have belonged to Comfort's aunt and to have made the transatlantic crossing to the New World. I have no doubt Nora will eventually track down the coin's identity.

It is a quirk of New England historical research that more is known about some aspects of the first generations than about any later period of history. Antiquarians, genealogists and historians alike have been so eager to document "the beginnings" that we can name every compact signer, every original grantor, every early tract of land. Births, marriages and deaths are surprisingly thoroughly recorded and the level of detail in legal documentation for the period has never been improved upon.

On the other hand, it is extremely difficult to find information about the silent ones: about those who moved or owned no land; about the vast majority who, although they may have read and been able to write a bit, were not 'writers' by nature or profession; about women almost without exception; about Native American and all other minorities whose presence is known but whose actions were almost always invisible until they ran afoul of English law.

Researchers have been attempting to reduce this information gap by working with materials long considered to be beyond the purview of History (with a capital "H"). Nora's exploration of what remains under ground, and Hank's investigation of what remains above ground are only two instances of the increasing use of tangible remains as evidence of the material culture that furnished the past.

But going from furnishings to human beings is still, and will always be, more than a little, a leap of faith. That is why *Old Wives Tales* is a work of fiction.

E.K.T.
Medfield, Massachusetts
May, 2002

ABOUT THE AUTHOR

Electa Kane Tritsch has been a practicing archeologist and historian for twenty-five years. With degrees in American Literature and New England Studies, she has worked as teacher, archeological survey director, historical society guru, and research historian. Most recently, she has been documenting a 350-year-old house in Medfield, Massachusetts.

Her essays have appeared in a wide range of publications; she has edited books on ceramics and architectural history, and is author of numerous studies on the history and archeology of New England communities.

She lives in the town she writes about, with her husband Geoff and sons John and Ben.